D1327432

NEW HARVEST

*Jesse and Naomi Deane Stuart at their home in
W-Hollow, Greenup County, Kentucky — circa 1943.*

NEW HARVEST
Forgotten Stories of Kentucky's
Jesse Stuart

Selected and Edited by
David R. Palmore

Jesse Stuart Foundation
Ashland, Kentucky
2003

Dedication

New Harvest is dedicated in memory of world-renowned lecturer, poet, author, educator, and bardic chronicler of Appalachia, Jesse Hilton Stuart. He lives on in print through his monumental literary legacy. Like the "immortal teacher," he "lives on and on through his students." He lives on and on as the dreams and aspirations of the poets, authors, historians, readers, educators, and students of Appalachia are fulfilled through the efforts of the organization that bears his name, the Jesse Stuart Foundation.

Library of Congress Cataloging-in-Publication Data
Stuart, Jesse. 1906-1984.
    New harvest : by Jesse Stuart ; selected and edited by David R. Palmore.
       p. cm.
    ISBN 1-931672-17-2
    1. Kentucky--Social life and customs--Fiction. I. Palmore, David R., 1957- II. Title.
PS3537.T92516N49 2003
813'.52--dc21   2003042824

Published By:
Jesse Stuart Foundation
P.O. Box 669 • Ashland, KY 41105
(606) 326-1667 • JSFBOOKS.com

Contents

Author, poet, educator, lecturer, Jesse Hilton Stuart, — circa 1938

Foreword

Few American authors attained the popular success and captivated the reading public like Appalachia's Jesse Hilton Stuart. Born on August 8, 1906, in a one-room log cabin in Greenup County, Kentucky, Jesse was the second oldest of Mitchell and Martha Stuart's seven children.

The Stuarts were a family of limited means. Mitchell, a tenant farmer and coalminer, could neither read nor write. Martha had attended school only through the second grade. These parents, however, instilled in their children the virtues of hard work and honesty, and encouraged them to value education.

Jesse's teachers fired his early ambitions and dreams as he attended the nearby one-room school at Plum Grove and later Greenup High School. As a high school student, he wrote some of the stories that would later bring him widespread recognition, and he taught for a term in a local school two years before his graduation in 1926.

In the fall of 1926 Jesse began his college studies at Lincoln Memorial University in Harrogate, Tennessee, and he completed his degree there in 1929. In 1931 he enrolled in the graduate program at Vanderbilt University in Nashville and studied there for a year. Several of Jesse's college teachers fueled his writing aspirations, professors who, themselves, were developing national reputations as writers: Harry Harrison Kroll at Lincoln Memorial University and Donald Davidson, Robert Penn Warren, John Donald Wade, and Edwin Mims at Vanderbilt.

Stuart funded his intermittent graduate studies at Vanderbilt and Peabody College (where he took summer classes in Education) with his emerging career in education back home. He served as principal and teacher during the 1929-1930 school year at Warnock High School and as principal of Greenup High School (his alma mater) during the following academic year. After his year at Vanderbilt, he returned to

Greenup County in 1932 to become Kentucky's youngest school district superintendent. Jesse continued his career in education intermittently as a teacher or administrator for the following twelve years, resigning in 1944 in order to direct his full attention to his growing reputation as a writer.

Man with a Bull-tongue Plow, the first of Jesse's books to attract national acclaim, was published by E. P. Dutton in 1934. This collection of autobiographical sonnets prompted some reviewers to call Stuart "an American Robert Burns." By 1935, Stuart's short stories were beginning to appear in national periodicals. *Head o'W-Hollow*, a collection of these stories, was published by E.P. Dutton in 1936, prompting the following observation in a *Time* magazine review:

> When homespun Kentucky Poet Jesse Stuart sat down and wrote a big stack of sonnets...a few critics sat up, called him a modern Bobbie Burns. Others just laughed at his unconscious, bull-tongued humor. Last week Poet Stuart made the scoffers scratch their heads over a book of stories that were partly funny, partly serious, in the main tantalizingly good. These tales of Kentucky farmers were written in racy Kentucky dialect, with a wild-eyed, straightforward outrageousness.... Some of his yarns were well worth inclusion in any anthology-of-the-year.

Jesse Stuart, an energetic young American writer was emerging as the voice of Appalachia. Gradually he became Kentucky's most popular author. His career spanned five decades, and he published over 60 volumes of poetry, novels, short stories, autobiographical accounts, textbooks, and children's books. Bibliographer Hensley C. Woodbridge, in his *Jesse and Jane Stuart: A Bibliography* (1979), attributed over 500 published short stories and a nearly equal number of articles to Stuart—a total of over 1000 publications appearing in magazines, journals, and newspapers throughout the United States and the world between the early 1930s and the late 1970s. This figure does not include the publication of myriad poems in hundreds of periodicals.

Although literary critics often ignored Stuart during his lifetime (and during the years that have followed), his books, short stories, articles, and poems were highly popular with the reading public, appearing in the important literary journals as well as the popular magazines of his day. A diverse sampling of the periodicals which published his work includes *Scribner's, American Mercury, Atlantic Monthly, Harpers, Collier's, Esquire, Story, Saturday Evening Post, Household Magazine, Saturday Review, Ladies' Home Journal, Nature Magazine, Country Gentleman, Farm Journal, New York Quarterly, Christian Living, Country Beautiful, Progressive Farmer, Reader's Digest, North American Review, The Land, Prairie Schooner, Better Homes and Gardens, New Republic, The Yale Review, Today's Education*, and *Today's Health*.

Unlike literary critics, the reading public refused to ignore Stuart. Publishers were eager to use his publications because they helped sell magazines. So important were his short stories to *Esquire* magazine, for example, that they (along with a few poems) appeared in more than sixty different issues during four early decades of the magazine's publication. Moreover, through such magazines as *Esquire, Progressive Farmer, Household Magazine, Country Gentleman, Saturday Evening Post, and Ladies' Home Journal*, especially, Stuart captured a wide reading audience in America's rural heartland, and even today, his best stories remain a staple in secondary school American literature anthologies.

While Stuart was achieving literary recognition, he was also becoming widely known as a lecturer and proponent of educational reform, with an expertise grounded in his extensive experience as a teacher, principal, and superintendent working in poor rural school systems. He lectured at various U.S. colleges, and served for a year at the American University in Cairo, Egypt as a visiting Professor. He was also appointed by the U.S. Information Service to tour the Near, Middle, and Far East as a good-will ambassador from 1962 to 1963. This lecture tour earned him an international status and enhanced his reputation as a farmer, conservationist, educator, and civil servant on the lecture circuit at home. His poems, stories, and articles, meanwhile, kept pace with his lecturing; they were published in a dozen different languages around the world.

Stuart's early fame brought him recognition as a guest on national radio—and later television—programs. In 1936 New York socialite Amy Vanderbilt, traveling to Greenup to interview Stuart and discovering that his home was inaccessible by automobile, was forced to hike to W-Hollow for her interview. While serving as a Guggenheim Fellow in Europe in 1938, Jesse accepted an invitation from Lady Astor to spend a couple of weeks with the Astor family in London. Thanks to his early fame, he also shared podiums with such notables as Eleanor Roosevelt.

Not surprisingly, Stuart's growing national stature also brought him a legion of offers from admirers: college presidencies, appearances in British movies, and the directorship of two radio programs, one funded by the BBC. Alluding to one 1930s offer, he noted, "I was offered a thousand dollars a week to be a script writer in Hollywood." Jesse turned them all down.

Nor did such opportunities decrease as Stuart grew older. His strong republican political leanings and his conservative thinking, expressed indirectly in such works as *Taps for Private Tussie* and *The Land Beyond the River*, prompted numerous pleas for him to run for public office. He declined to do so. The Nixon Administration offered him a position with the Department of Health, Education, and Welfare. He turned this offer down, too. While Stuart's lectures, travels, and periodic teaching stints around the world drew him away from east Kentucky, his heart remained close to his beloved farm in W-Hollow, the source of his writing inspiration. "This land is as close to me as my skin," he insisted in 1971.

As an American public figure, Stuart was featured in major newsmagazines such as *Time, Newsweek*, and *Life*. Time magazine, for example, covered Jesse over a dozen times with book reviews or with stories on major events in his life.

Now, a quarter of a century since Jesse Stuart's writing hand was stilled by a stroke which left him partially paralyzed and bedfast in 1978, and twenty years since his passing from his Kentucky, the region he insisted was "the heart" of the United States, his literary legacy lives on. As Kentucky's most prolific and popular writer, he established an enduring national reputation as the endearing and beloved voice of Appalachia.

Stuart's death is survived not only by a remarkable literary legacy; it has prompted his admirers to erect numerous monuments to his memory: his tombstone in Greenup County, Kentucky's Plum Grove Cemetery; his nine-foot Georgia Granite monolith on the Greenup County Courthouse grounds, the Jesse Stuart Lodge at Greenbo State Park, and the 730-acre Jesse Stuart Nature Preserve, occupying a portion of Stuart's W-Hollow farm. Perhaps his most significant memorial, however, is the Jesse Stuart Foundation in Ashland, Kentucky. Founded in 1979, the Foundation publishes a variety of books related to Kentucky and Southern Appalachia, but the organization's central focus is the preservation of Stuart's literary legacy. From its beginning, the JSF has been engaged in the republication of Stuart's out-of-print works, and it has periodically published some of his never-before-released pieces.

New Harvest represents a collection of 22 of Stuart's short stories that have never appeared in his 17 previously published collections. These stories have been selected from 19 periodicals and two anthologies. Some of the stories appeared in obscure journals, others in nationally recognized magazines. One story, abstracted from an unpublished manuscript, appears in *New Harvest* for the first time. These stories cover the entire span of Stuart's writing career. They offer a representative sample of his writing ability—of the characteristics which attracted so many readers during the course of his life.

These 22 pieces are the Stuart stories that perhaps even the most dedicated fans have never read; they are the *forgotten* stories. *New Harvest* represents the first new collection of Stuart's stories since McGraw-Hill published *The Best Loved Short Stories of Jesse Stuart* in 1982.

In these stories, readers familiar with Stuart will recognize anew

Stuart's alter egos, Shan Powderjay and Jason Stringer, his familiar use of the Appalachian world around him in his settings, his characters, his use of dialect, and his written record of a time now past. While Stuart was generally recognized as a wholesome writer with a positive outlook on life, his stories were often filled with crude, lusty, and cruel people, whose behavior finally catches up with them. The *New Harvest* stories are cut from this same cloth, and they bear all the hallmarks of Stuart's writing style. As the reader will learn from the bibliographical notes which follow the stories, a number of them received notable recognition upon publication. "The Accident," for example, appearing in the November 19, 1966 issue of the *Saturday Evening Post*, was later selected by Foley and Burnett for inclusion in their B*est American Short Stories of 1967*. While the piece was later anthologized and published in other countries, it has never been included in a Stuart story collection.

Stuart readers may be surprised to learn that his avenues of publication included even the premier edition of *Playgirl* magazine in January, 1973. This early issue, which hardly resembles those of the current *Playgirl*, featured Stuart's "The Guests in King Author's Court," another *New Harvest* selection.

Even Stuart's own introduction to *New Harvest* has been taken from an article originally appearing in a 1975 literary magazine. The essay not only reveals his source for the first story in the collection; it also discusses the source of many of the ideas and characters in his stories and the thought process he generally followed in shaping his short fiction.

Throughout his adult life, Stuart had a burning desire to leave a lasting literary legacy. This dream prompted him to form the Jesse Stuart Foundation in 1979 and to entrust the organization with his literary estate. Much earlier in his career, when he was a Guggenheim Fellow living in Ireland in 1938, he celebrated the publication of *Beyond Dark Hills*, his third major book, by writing a letter, dated May 6th, to Lena Wells Voiers, a former influential high school teacher. In it he observed, "My dust, my body, shall be as nothing in the end. The earth gave it. But what shall my books be? Weaklings that will not survive? Or shall they live and grow? Time will settle this question."

August 2006 will mark the centennial of the birth of Jesse Hilton Stuart. The Jesse Stuart Foundation, acutely aware of the question Jesse posed in 1938, is determined to use every means at its disposal to help this remarkable writer's books live and grow. It is, consequently, with great pride that the Foundation presents *New Harvest*—the *forgotten* stories of Jesse Stuart.

David R. Palmore
Villa Hills, Kentucky
August 2003

Jesse Hilton Stuart — circa 1978

Author's Introduction

"A Story of a Story" by Jesse Stuart

In the summer of 1940, less than a year after Naomi Norris and I were married, we were invited to go to Vanceburg, Kentucky and spend the night with Mr. and Mrs. William Augustus (Gus) Voiers. Before her marriage she was Miss Lena Wells Lykins. And she had been, as a very young woman, Superintendent of Greenup County Schools. In those days city superintendents and high school principals in small town school systems taught classes. Miss Lykins, as we called her then, taught us Algebra.

Our being invited to spend a Saturday night and take a Sunday drive with our former teacher and her husband was quite an event. Her husband was one of the best, if not the best businessman in Vanceburg, county seat of Lewis County, Kentucky. With a population of approximately 2,500 people, Vanceburg was the largest town in Lewis County. Rural people over Lewis County will tell you all roads lead to Vanceburg. Lewis County is a real rural county. Its principal money crop is and has been tobacco. If I may speculate, let me put it this way. South Dakota was or is the most rural state in the United States. Mississippi is second and Kentucky is third. And let me proffer this speculation, of Kentucky's one hundred twenty counties, Lewis County is most rural and is most likely to remain so. Changing with the times in Lewis County will be slow. But the surprise is how friendly the people are and how much wealth has been amassed by so many people. Also, the scenic beauty in this county along the Kinnikonick River is breath-taking. Now, before I continue farther, my reason for all this explanatory writing is for a purpose.

After Mr. and Mrs. W.A. Vioers' marriage, she quit teaching school.

Marrying a little late in life, this couple never had children. But they had each other. And "Lena Wells" and "Gus," we of her students later called them by their first names, was one of the most delightful couples we have ever known in our lifetime. After this first friendly visit of going and spending the night in their home, we traveled with them over the United States, Mexico, and Canada. Later we traveled all over Europe with them. But in earlier years we couldn't keep pace with their traveling due to money. They made it a point to travel, sleep at least one night, eat food, visit the capitol cities of every state in the Continental United States and the Provinces of Canada. Their hobby was travel. He ran a men's clothing store with a large shoe department which supplied the young and old, farmers and their sons, and city men and their sons with their types of wearing apparel and shoes. He had the clothes and shoes for everybody. He had "the trade" of Lewis County. "Gus Voiers" was a household word in Lewis County. People came into his store from the vast rural areas and bought summer, winter and spring supplies. They came in when they didn't buy and just sat in the store. They liked "Gus." And so did Naomi and I. We liked him and his teacher wife. They were younger than springtime. Time never changed them. They never stopped dancing and traveling. How many all-night dances we attended with them.

Gus, not having any posterity to carry on his name and his being the last of his family, continuously kept a distant cousin's son in his store to help him. Often he had more than one working for him. And sometimes he used unrelated help. And he helped send a few of these through college. When he and Lena Wells were away traveling, he'd turn the store over to the young distant relative or the unrelated young man he had employed and let them run the business.

"They're honest and good and will never learn any younger," he'd say with a laugh. "What I make or what I lose I won't be taking it with me when I leave this world."

Lena Wells would say: "That's right, Poppie! Let's make every day count. Let's live each day to the fullest. We won't be here forever!"

Their love for one another and their attitude toward love, living, dancing, and life naturally intrigued all the young people. And my Naomi and I became their closest friends.

And now I have given you this background, which to me is a fertile one for creativity. I will tell you what happened to us after we had spent the first night with them in their home. We went for this Sunday drive along the Kinnikonick River to enjoy the scenic breath-taking views of river and land. Along the highway a man came from nowhere in front of the car and was struck and knocked upon the side of a tree. Gus slammed on the brakes. We were not going too fast. Had Gus been driving fast, the man would have been killed. But the four of us, in Gus and Lena Wells Voiers' large car, almost had heart attacks.

I remember how elated all of us were, especially Gus, that the man came to his senses. We took him to a doctor in Vanceburg to have him examined and X-rayed. And then Gus took him to his home.

"He will recover," Gus said. "This is the doctor's report. But I will be sued. I am positive I will be sued."

When we left Lena Wells and Gus' nice home, a couple that had so much fun, lived real well, made money and spent it, our over joyous friends were not laughing. They were depressed. Our visit with its happy beginnings had ended in contemplation and depressive moods.

As Naomi drove our small car toward our home in W-Hollow, forty miles from Vanceburg over a dirt road in 1940, I took from my pocket my little notebook. It was about four by three inches, nice size to slide into my hip pocket, with the front two-thirds an orange-color and the lower third black, with large white letters on the orange, "AGRICO" and beneath the word in smaller white letters "The Nation's Leading Fertilizer." And now below in the third black, large print letters in yellow, "MEMO BOOK." And in this book I made my twenty-ninth notation: "GUS VOIERS KNOCKED MAN VS. TREE—WENT TO STORE. MAN COMES IN. HE WAS AFRAID OF SUIT. RESULTS." Since this time the number of ideas has climbed in this little notebook to eighty-seven. I record the germ of the story. The way I record, only I can unravel. And at any time later, no matter how many years have passed, I can turn to my little book, read the notation, and give my mind time enough to go back through the threads of the story as I remember them, so I can write the story in my mind. Then I put it on paper in my typewriter. I never write a story in longhand unless I'm out on a plane or ship and am compelled to write this way. Once crossing the English channel by boat in 1937, I wrote a short story, "Storm," which was published and many times reprinted in textbooks. It's still being reprinted after 33 years.

But now to shorten this story about a story. Of course, we never stopped visiting our good friends Lena Wells and "Poppie" Gus Voiers and from time to time we picked up developments. The man "Poppie" Gus hit with the car (I shall not use his real name), his father and brothers later came into Voiers' Men's Store in Vanceburg. Gus was afraid of them. He sent his young distant cousin to wait on them. Gus was positive they were looking things over in regards to increase the amount of the suit they contemplated. His distant cousin's son, sold father and sons some merchandise. Weeks, months went by until autumn and tobacco selling time came to Lewis County. When father and sons, one of whom Gus had hit with his car, got paid for their tobacco, they came to Gus' store. Their clothing and shoe orders were tremendous for a country family. They asked young Mr. Voiers to see Mr. William Augustus Voiers. He came out of his office, where he had hidden, shaking and trembling. "Poppie" Gus Voiers was no fighting man. He was a happy fun-loving man filled with good jokes and laughter.

"Mr. Voiers," said the father, "we will trade with you all we can. You are the finest man we have ever known. Mort, my son, has a fault. He has a fault running in front of automobiles and getting hit. He was born with it I guess. You know we are born with certain faults. And his is a bad one. Of all the times he's been hit by cars, you're the only man who took him to the doctor. You had them X-ray pictures made to see if any of his bones were broken. And you even took him home. What a man you are, Mr. Voiers!"

When I heard this, I knew it was a story. But I left it recorded it my Agriculture Notebook. Once I went back to this notebook and I wrote eight stories in eight days. I was on a writing binge. Again, I wrote twelve stories in fourteen days. Again, I wrote six stories in six days. All from ideas recorded here. But I never got around to writing the Voiers' story. Not until Naomi and I, and our niece, Naomi Vivian Keeney (named for my wife) were spending the summer in Athens, Greece where our daughter, Jane Stuart, was a student in the Greek-American School. Jane was compelled to stay, during this summer of 1966, in a Greek home where Greek, and perhaps French, were spoken. She couldn't stay in a home where the Greeks knew English. My wife, our niece, and I stayed in the Galaxy Hotel. It was advertised as an air-conditioned hotel. Knowing that Athens could get very warm during the summer months we chose this hotel since we would be spending the summer here while Jane was in school.

The three of us did a lot of traveling over Greece. The Greek Island Cruise in the Mediterranean was the second one for us. And we went many other places, Delphia, Thebes, Corinth, down to the Epidarus Country to see Greek plays. Yet, we had time in Athens. And I had my little Agriculture Notebook with me. Jane had brought over with her a small typewriter which had come apart. When I borrowed this little typewriter from her, I borrowed it in three pieces. Not being mechanical or a typewriter repairman, I did manage to put this typewriter back in one piece. And I could use it. For this achievement I was delighted with myself for I felt the urge to do some stories.

Each morning my wife and niece slept late. I got up early. This was for a reason. I would go to the dining room and eat alone. And I could eat what I was not supposed to have. I could have fried eggs and Danish bacon. Such food had long been off my diet list. Being a cardiac I shouldn't have such foods, but the tastes of food a cardiac isn't supposed to have, are beyond descriptive words. It was bacon and eggs for me each morning. Now, after breakfast, I would take my little typewriter to the mezzanine floor where there was a table and chairs. Here I would sit and type, never bothered, and look down at the activity on the lobby floor. And there was another reason I came here. There was a display of Greek painters' paintings hanging around this wall. Beneath each one was a sheet describing the painting, name of the artist, and price of the painting. On one side all this information was written and published in Greek, while the other side was plain paper. And this was the only size paper that would fit into my typewriter. I couldn't buy any paper in Greece that would. So each morning I went around and picked up this paper while hotel management was wondering where their artists' advertisements were going. They went into my stories. Again, I wrote eight stories in eight days. And when we left Greece and returned on the Greek Liner Olympia, I revised these stories. In the meantime, I kept a journal, did articles on Greece and a few poems about Greek subjects.

One of the eight ideas I selected from the Agriculture Notebook was the "Poppie" Gus and Lena Wells Voiers story. Now I had recorded this idea in 1940. This was the summer of 1966.

When we got back to the United States I had my stories typed. I don't know what made me do it. *Saturday Evening Post* had never purchased a story from me. I believe my stories were too much on the literary side. But I sent "The Accident" to the *Saturday Evening Post*. Later, a garbled telegram came to me which I couldn't make out. The way I read the telegram, *The Post* had accepted the story and was willing to pay me either seventy or seven hundred dollars.

"Either fee is all right," I said. "I'm happy to say I've made the *Saturday Evening Post*. I've had three hundred stories published in good quality literary magazines but never the *Post*. I doubt the fee is $700 for the *Saturday Evening Post* is having a hard time staying alive. It's more like seventy. I've heard the *Saturday Evening Post* used to pay well."

"Get on the phone and call Western Union in Ashland," Naomi

said. "See if there's not some mistake."

What had happened was when the telegram came they had tried to phone me. Naomi and I were away at the time. They had posted the telegram to our post office.

When I called and asked what the real message was from the *Saturday Evening Post,* a man read the telegram back to me. When he read it, I didn't tell him what the one I got had read. I could hardly speak. The telegram asked me if $1,750 would be pay enough for the story. If so to let them know.

"Seventeen hundred and fifty, Naomi," I said.

"I can't believe it," she said. "Mighty good for a day's work."

"My highest fee to date," I said. "My only story in *The Post.*"

Before this story was published William Augustus Voiers (good old Poppie Gus) had gone suddenly in a heart attack. He never got to read it. Due to the sorrowing for her husband, I didn't tell Lena Wells about the published story. But when it was published in *The Post*, Lena Wells found the story.

"The greatest story you ever wrote," she said over the phone. "You described even the movements of Gus's hands and arms. You really got us. Not anything left out. That story is as if you had painted our portraits and told the story."

The artist who illustrated the story almost got their portraits. Lena Wells was so happy over this story, she ordered one hundred copies of the *Saturday Evening Post* and gave them to their many friends. Then, the story was reprinted in Holland. And it made *The Best American Short Stories* edited by Martha Foley and David Burnett. And just a few days ago, I called Lena Wells, our beloved teacher and friend, now in her middle seventies for I had more good news about this story.

"Lena Wells you and 'Poppie' Gus are going to be in a Secondary English textbook, by a big and good company," I said. Being a former teacher she was overjoyous. This time she wept over the phone.

"Oh, if Gus could see it," she said.

Had "Poppie" Gus lived one more year he would have seen it in print. I had recorded the idea twenty-six years before I wrote it. The story was published the year after I had written it. Today all the other seven stories have been accepted and published. I gave three away and sold five. I had lacked five hundred dollars paying Naomi's and my way over Europe and for a summer in Greece with these five stories. One of the three I gave away was purchased for eight hundred dollars. I was promised this. But the editor left the magazine and was succeeded by an editor who returned this story. If the first editor had remained and I had received this $800 fee, I would have paid for our entire trip and had three hundred dollars left. I did this in eight days. To earn more than five thousand dollars from my Agriculture Notebook, on Jane's little typewriter had surprised me. I had no thought of doing this. The other four stories I sold were for good fees, good fees for me, two eight hundred dollar stories, and two one thousand dollar stories, and three giveaways to excellent literary magazines.

Naomi and I had not spent all of our money on ourselves. We looked after our daughter Jane who was now married, as if she were our little girl again. And we looked after my oldest sister's second daughter, Naomi Vivian as if she were our daughter too. She was unmarried, living alone in her own home and teaching school. Each morning Jane came from the Greek home where she lived and ate breakfast with her mother and cousin in the Galaxy Hotel. And we took Jane on the Mediterranean Cruise with us. Although a lover of Greece, Greek people, and the heritage the Greeks have given to the world, on this beautiful Greek Island Cruise, Jane often sat with a book of Greek in her hand reading native Greek since she was getting a Master's Degree in Greek and Latin.

This is not a short story. This is the story of a story, "The Accident," of how I got the idea and how long I was writing the story. This is the story of how many of my stories have been written. I have always had fun doing them. And I have got them from the people, my friends and neighbors. I've got several more notations of stories in my AGRICO,

The Nation's Leading Fertilizer, to write. Many have been written; but hardly any of the ideas recorded before No. 29, which was the Voiers' story, have been written. I must take time and do more of these, for no one on earth can read my notes and my mind on the many threads running through these story-ideas created by the people I have known and I have been told about by others.

Jesse Stuart
W-Hollow, Kentucky
1974

"Author's Introduction – The Story Of A Story" was first published as "The Story Of A Story" in *The New South,* Vol. 6, No. 3 (January-February, 1975), pp. 18-21. It has never been reprinted.

Left to Right: Lena Wells Voiers, Gus Voiers, Naomi Deane Stuart, and Jesse Stuart aboard the "Queen Elizabeth" on their voyage to Europe in August of 1949. "The Accident" was based on an incident in the Voiers' life.
(Photograph courtesy of Mary M. Hampton and Helen L. Smith, Vanceburg, Kentucky)

The Accident

"How would you like to go for a ride with your Aunt Effie and me?" Uncle Jad said. "It's a nice Sunday afternoon and we won't have many more such days before snow falls."

Uncle Jad Higgins ran the Ranceburg Men's Clothing Store in Ranceburg. He had inherited this store from his father, and there was a sign above the door which read: SEVENTY-SEVEN YEARS IN BUSINESS. The Higginses were without posterity, and I was Uncle Jad's sister's son; it was understood that I would take over the store someday after Uncle Jad retired or was deceased. Since my father was a farmer, Uncle Jad had invited me to live with him and Aunt Effie while learning the business from A to Z, and of course I couldn't let an opportunity like that pass. Naturally, if Uncle Jad asked me to do something, I did it. If he wanted me to take a drive with him and Aunt Effie on a sunny fall afternoon, I went along. I'd seen enough of the Lantern County hills to do me a lifetime, but if they wanted me with them, then that was all right with me.

"It's a nice idea to take a drive, Uncle Jad," I said. "You are so right. We won't have many more afternoons as pretty and as sunny as this one."

"Yes, and your Aunt Effie and I have seen more seasons—winters, springs, summers, autumns - than we will ever see again," he said. "The years take their toll. But it's always nice just to get out and drive around."

"You want me to drive so you and Aunt Effie can relax and look at the countryside?" I asked.

"No, Tom, I'd rather have my own hands on the steering wheel," he said. "You know I have faith in you. But this is just my nature. I've never had a wreck in my life. And I've been driving since I was sixteen."

Aunt Effie came into the room dressed like she was going to church.

Aunt Effie was a big woman, with twinkling blue eyes. She was always smiling and she always had something to say. She dressed in the latest style, wearing big hats and dresses with frills and laces. No wonder Uncle Jad and Aunt Effie were considered the best-dressed couple in Lantern County. They spent a lot of money for clothes, and took plenty of time getting properly dressed for an occasion. Uncle Jad warned me about wearing the right clothes when I took over his store after he was gone. He said I'd be selling men's clothes, and young men would be watching what I wore, so I'd have to be a living example of the well-dressed man. Uncle Jad himself was a living example of the well-dressed man in Lantern County.

Uncle Jad was not tall, and he was big around the middle and little on each end, which made him hard to fit, but he wore the kind of clothes that made him look good. He wore small hats with broad brims, and pinstripe suits to give him height. On this particular fall Sunday afternoon he wore a pair of gloves, not because he'd need them in the car, but just to accent the positive. He never missed a trick when it came to wearing clothes or selling them. He wouldn't wear a pair of shoes out of his own house onto the porch unless they were shined.

"Effie, you look real well," Uncle Jad said. "You look real nice in that blue suit and that white blouse with the lace collar. It's most appropriate for early winter wear."

"Well, Poppie, you look wonderful," she complimented him. "Yes, I've got the most handsome man in Lantern County." She pulled him over to her and kissed him. She was always very affectionate with Uncle Jad.

Well, they were telling each other the truth with their compliments. I thought as they walked toward the garage. I got ahead of them and raised the garage door. Then Uncle Jad opened the car door for Aunt Effie and, after she got in, pushed the door shut gently behind her. Then he walked around to the other side, got in, started the engine, and backed the car out. He waited for me to pull the garage door back down and get in the back seat. This was our regular routine.

"Well, which way shall we go, Mother?" he asked Aunt Effie.

"Let's drive up Kinney Creek Valley and over to Taysville," she replied quickly. Aunt Effie always knew where she wanted to go. All Uncle Jad had to do, if he was undecided, was to ask. She could soon make a decision.

"Then up Kinney Valley and over to Taysville we will go," Uncle Jad said.

"The valley will be beautiful this time of year," I said. "I am glad, Aunt Effie, that you have chosen this route. There'll still be autumn leaves on many of the oaks."

"You are so right," Aunt Effie said.

Uncle Jad drove slowly and carefully down the street. When he came to the railway crossing at the edge of Ranceburg, he stopped and looked carefully this way and that, though he could see for a mile either up or down the tracks.

"It always pays to be careful," he said. "Never had a wreck or hit a person. I can certainly boast of my record."

"I've not been driving very long, Uncle Jad," I said. "But I've never hit a person or had a wreck either."

"You're a careful young man, Tom," he said. "That is why I'm turning everything over to you someday. You're a lot like my father and me. By looks and by nature you could well have been my son!"

"Thank you, Uncle Jad," I said.

"I've got security in life," he said. "Mother and I could live to the end of our days without my working anymore. Mother and I have had a good life. We go to our church, vote for our party, belong to a few organizations. We are somebody in Ranceburg now, and remember, Tom, it pays in this life to be somebody. So be a somebody when your Aunt Effie and I are no longer around. Marry a nice woman. Drive a nice car and wear good clothes. Make your life a safe adventure."

We were in Kinney Valley now. There had been a few killing frosts, and the grass on the pasture fields was brown, but the oaks in the wooded areas were still filled with multicolored leaves. As we passed farmhouse after farmhouse, Uncle Jad called out the name of the man who lived there, and told how many sons he had and if they traded at the store. Uncle Jad also mentioned which men he had to ask for cash, and which could be trusted to buy now and pay later.

There were green areas on the Kinney Valley bottoms where winter wheat had been sown. When the wind swept through the valley, the wheat bent and rose up again after the wind had passed. The sun was bright, and when a crow flew over, though we didn't always see the crow, we could tell where he was flying by his shadow on the brown grass of the fields.

"Life is just so wonderful, Poppie," Aunt Effie said with enthusiasm. And she put her arm around Uncle Jad's neck, pulled him over, and kissed his cheek.

"Do be careful, Mother," Uncle Jad said. "You could cause me to have my first wreck." Actually, he liked for her to do him this way. He was just pretending that it could be dangerous.

"Yes, I have a fine automobile, fine store, fine home, prettiest wife in Ranceburg," Uncle Jad said. "When a man gets old enough to have security and enjoy life, the tragedy is he's about old enough to die and leave this world. Not a very pleasant thought, but how true it is!"

If life could shape up for me, I thought, like it had shaped up for Uncle Jad and Aunt Effie, then I'd be a happy man. They had everything they wanted. They had security. And they would go to the end of their days like this!

"Look, out, Poppie!" Aunt Effie screamed, and covered her face with her hands. Uncle Jad slammed on the brakes. The car skidded, tires squealed, and there was a thud. I saw a man fly up and hit a tree.

"Where did he come from?" Uncle Jad said. "I didn't see him until he was in front of the car."

"I saw just as you hit him!" I shouted.

"I wonder if I killed him," Uncle Jad said. His face was extremely white. He had lost that redness of color that made his cheeks pink. He sat with his hands on the steering wheel, looking out of the car at the man who lay at the foot of a large oak close to the highway.

"Oh, Poppie!" Aunt Effie wailed. She kept her hands over her face. "We bragged too soon! Life has been too good. We couldn't go until the end with all this good fortune we have been having."

"He's not dead," Uncle Jad said. "He's trying to raise his head up to see what has happened. He's looking at the car. The poor fellow is looking at me! He's looking at me and trying to smile."

When Uncle Jad got out of the car, I got out with him.

"I never saw you," Uncle Jad told the man. "I'm sorry. How bad are you hurt?"

"I don't know," he answered softly. "Lift me upon my feet."

Uncle Jad got on one side and I got on the other, and we lifted him up. The man put his arms around our shoulders.

"See if you can bear your weight," Uncle Jad said.

The man tried one foot and then the other, and took two steps.

"Thank God," Uncle Jad said. "No broken legs."

"It knocked the wind from me," the man said. "It jarred me to my foundations!"

Well, I knew that the big car had done that much and more too. The Man had hit the side of the tree about six feet up and then fallen to the ground in a crumpled mass of humanity. Such a lick should have killed him outright.

"What is your name?" Uncle Jad asked.

"Mort Simmons." He sighed softly. "I'm John Simmon's boy."

He was a less-than-average-sized man who looked like he weighed about one hundred and thirty pounds. He was wearing a work shirt and jeans and brush scarred brogan shoes without socks. His face was unshaven, with a growth of stubbly black beard.

"And where do you live?" Uncle Jad asked.

"On Shelf's Fork of Kinney."

"I thought I knew about everybody in Lantern County," Uncle Jad said, "but I'm sorry to say I don't know you or your father. Have you ever traded in my store in Ranceburg?"

"No, but I will in the future," the man replied.

"Poppie, let's take him to Doctor Raike and have him checked," Aunt Effie said.

"Not a bad idea, Mother," Uncle Jad said, and sighed.

We helped Mort Simmons to the car. When we took his arms from around our shoulders, he stood up all right, and although we helped him to get on the rear seat, I think he could have done it by himself.

"I feel much better," he said.

"What about going back to Ranceburg with us and letting Doctor Raike see you before we take you home?" Uncle Jad asked him.

"That will be all right," he said. "Yes, I'd like to go see how bad I'm hurt."

"You watch over him now, Tom," Uncle Jad told me. "If he gets dizzy he might just pitch over! Watch him!"

"I will, Uncle Jad," I said as I got in the car. "Don't you worry!"

"No, I've got a lot to worry about now," he said.

Aunt Effie, who couldn't stand much excitement, was trembling like a leaf on a November oak. Uncle Jad was still pale, and his hands shook so on the steering wheel that the car swerved back and forth. But there was still very little traffic on the country roads this time of year, and we made it safely back to Dr. Raike's office in Ranceburg.

"I'm glad you are here, Doctor Raike," Uncle Jad said. "I hit this man and knocked him upon the side of an oak tree. I never saw him until my car hit him. Seems like he just came up out of the ground. Mort Simmons. You ever have him for a patient before?"

"Can't say that I have," Dr. Raike said. "No, I don't know that name Simmons in Lantern County."

Dr. Raike, who was almost as old as my Uncle Jad, was a little man with blue eyes and a kind face. He had once had golden blond hair, but time had turned it white.

"I'm John Simmon's boy, and we live on Shelf's Fork of Kinney Valley," Mort Simmons said.

"Well, I wouldn't know all the people who live on Kinney Valley anymore," Dr. Raike said. "Now, let me see about you."

Dr. Raike went over Mort Simmons's head and arms and legs. Then he had Mort slip off his shirt so that his back could be examined.

"You've been shaken up," Dr. Raike said, "and you've got a lot of minor bruises. But you don't have any broken bones. I can release you, all right."

"Doc, how much do I owe you?" Uncle Jad asked.

"Not anything, Jad," Dr. Raike said. "Glad to do it. I hope everything will be all right for you."

"Thank you, Doc," Uncle Jad said, with a worried look.

Mort Simmons walked out of the office under his own power, though he limped and moved his legs very stiffly, and Uncle Jad wasn't as nervous on the drive back to Kinney Valley as he had been when he drove Mort in to Ranceburg. He had more self-composure.

"Let me out here," Mort Simmons said at last. "You can't drive up Shelf's Fork. The road is too bad. I don't want you to hurt your fine car."

"Sure you can make it all right?" Uncle Jad asked. "I'll try to take you on. I don't mind hurting my car."

"I can make it," Mort Simmons said. "Thank you for taking me to the doctor, and thank you for bringing me back."

"I'm so sorry this happened," Uncle Jad said. "I truly am."

Mort Simmons smiled and walked up a narrow little slit of a road alongside a small stream. Uncle Jad drove back toward Ranceburg.

"Well, Mother, our pleasant Sunday afternoon didn't turn out too well," he said. "It seems like I've dreamed what has happened! But when I wake up in the morning I'll know it did happen. We might be sued for everything we have. We might not have any more security in this life."

"See John as soon as we get back," Aunt Effie said.

"John Lovell is a good lawyer," Uncle Jad said. "I'm glad we have him."

He asked Aunt Effie and me if either of us had seen where Mort Simmons came from at the time of the accident, and we said we never saw him until he was in front of the car and it was making contact with his body.

"I'd just climbed a rise," Uncle Jad said. "I wasn't going fast. If I had been going fast, he wouldn't have known what struck him. I am a lucky man."

"It's worked out for the best," Aunt Effie said. "I believe what is to be will be."

That evening Uncle Jad told John Lovell what had happened and how it had happened. John Lovell said that one bit of luck Uncle Jad would have if he were sued was that he would have two witnesses while Mort Simmons would only have himself. Uncle Jad told John Lovell how pleasant the man was and about his good manners. He told how Mort Simmons had been thankful for being taken to Dr. Raike and examined, and for being brought back to the Shelf's Fork road that led to his home. But John Lovell admonished Uncle Jad that Mort Simmons might nevertheless be thinking he had a good chance to sue, for everybody in Lantern Valley was pretty sure Uncle Jad had plenty of money.

When Uncle Jad came back from the lawyer's house, he told Aunt Effie about how he had been warned, and that night he was so worried he had to take medicine to put himself to sleep. The next morning he said to Aunt Effie, "Mother, yesterday is still a bad dream."

"I can't believe it either," she said. "But all three of us know that it did happen."

After breakfast Uncle Jad and I walked to the store, only two blocks away. We always opened at seven to catch the early-morning trade of men on their way to work. It didn't seem like anything special was going to happen that day, but that afternoon I looked out of the office at the back of the store and saw Mort Simmons looking at some shirts. "See what he wants," Uncle Jad said when I told him. "I'll stay out of the way. I think I know what he wants. He wants to know more about this business before he sues me."

I went out to Mort Simmons and said with a smile, "Good afternoon."

He smiled and said "Howdy." Then he said, "I've come for some work shirts. We've been working in tobacco, and I've got glue from the tobacco on all my shirts. I want a couple of clean shirts to go against my body. But I can't pay you until tomorrow. Our tobacco sells today in Taysville, and Pa will fetch the money home. So I'll pay you tomorrow, if that will be all right?"

"It will be all right," I said.

I knew Uncle Jad was in the back listening, and I knew he wouldn't want me to contrary Mort Simmons. I hoped I was doing things the right way, and I decided that I would make the debt good if it didn't get paid.

I showed Mort Simmons all the work shirts we had, and he ended up buying two, size fifteen with a thirty-two-inch sleeve length. He smiled when he left, and I smiled and thanked him for purchasing in this store. When Mort Simmons was gone, Uncle Jad came out of the little office where he had kept himself hidden.

"You played it just right," he said. "You are a good diplomat, Tom! I feel sure he's going to sue, but it doesn't hurt to soften him up. We've let him know how friendly we are. We have built our business here because the people know we are friendly and reliable. We serve the public! And this will be the first time a Higgins has ever been sued. My father before me, Abraham Higgins, was never sued. And I have never been sued."

"I can't figure that man out," I said.

"Well, I can't either," Uncle Jad said. "But I don't think he will be back to pay for the shirts. I think this is the last time we will see him before he sues me. The friendly man that looks at you and smiles and asks some little favor, this is the man who will sue you quicker than you can bat your eye."

At home that evening we told Aunt Effie what had happened, and Aunt Effie, who had always been good at judging people, said she didn't know what to think. She said she was puzzled.

The next day went along very quickly until the early afternoon. I was restacking some shirts when I turned around, and there stood Mort Simmons again. I looked back and saw Uncle Jad scurrying into his office.

"Pa is here with me," Mort Simmons said. "And four of my brothers have come too."

I thought I was going to sink through the floor! His father and his brothers! They had come for Uncle Jad and me! It ran through my mind that this was the way with the people who lived among the high hills and in the deep hollows. Do something to one, even if it is an accident, and his blood kin will never stop harassing you as long as you live. Uncle Jad and I were in a lot of trouble!

"We've come to get some orders filled," Mort Simmons said. "It's shoe and clothes time before real winter sets in."

"All right," I said.

"Come and meet Mr. John Simmons, my pa, and my four brothers," he said.

I said hello to the five big men standing over by the door. And then I filled the biggest order I have ever filled for one family since I came to work in Uncle Jad's store. They took two pairs of shoes each; they took socks, underwear, handkerchiefs, work pants, work shirts and Sunday shirts. And all five brothers picked out suits. I handed out almost five hundred dollars' worth of clothes and shoes, and I was sure there would be no mention of paying 'till Mort Simmons got through suing Uncle Jad.

After they had everything, John Simmons said to me, "Where is your uncle? I would like to see him."

Here it comes, I thought, I knew that Uncle Jad couldn't run from trouble. He would have to meet this Simmons family and tell them he had an attorney to represent him. They would have to consult his attorney. Or his attorney could talk to them.

I went back to the office and told Uncle Jad that John Simmons and his sons were asking for him, and that they had ordered almost five hundred dollars' worth of merchandise. Uncle Jad's face lost its color just like it had when his car hit Mort Simmons and flung him upon the side of the big oak.

"Guess I'll have to go and face them," he said. "You with me, Tom?"

"Of course," I said.

We went back to where the Simmonses were standing with bundles of merchandise in their arms, and more bundles around them on the floor. Uncle Jad was shaking. His lips were twitching nervously, and he kept jerking his head.

"Mr. Higgins, I wanted to meet you," John Simmons said. "You are a fine man. That's the reason my son Mort was in here yesterday. And that's why I brought my other sons here today to get new Sunday suits and winter clothes and shoes."

"Thank you, Mr. Simmons," Uncle Jad stammered. He couldn't understand why he was being called a fine man.

"We've got our tobacco money now," John Simmons said. "No charging anything. Here is what we owe you, including the cost of those shirts Mort bought yesterday."

Uncle Jad and I stood there, so surprised we couldn't speak, and John Simmons handed over the money, every cent. "As I have said, Mr. Higgins," he said, "we know from what happened last Sunday that you are a fine man."

"Last Sunday? You mean the accident?" Uncle Jad was still stammering.

"It was not the kind of accident you mean," John Simmons corrected him. "You see, my son Mort has a fault. He's as absent-minded as can be, never thinks what he's doing or looks where he is going. I have warned him many times about that fault, but he keeps walking out in front of cars, and he tells me he just can't think why it's so hard for him to remember not to do it. He will be marked by a car one of these days."

Uncle Jad was beginning to recover himself. Color was beginning to come back into his face.

"You see, Mr. Higgins," John Simmons said, "My son Mort has been struck by cars half a dozen times, and you're the only man who ever picked him up, took him to the doctor, and was even nice enough to fetch him back toward his home. I just want you to know that his mother and I appreciate what you did. And buying from you is a good way to thank you. We will be back to your store and trade with you from now on. Thank you."

Uncle Jad and I shook hands with all the Simmonses, and they smiled and we smiled. I have known my Uncle Jad since I was a little boy big enough to remember anything. And I never saw him so happy as he was right then, though he still had a puzzled look on his face.

"The Accident" was first published in *Saturday Evening Post,* Vol. 239, No. 24 (November 19, 1966), pp. 54-62. It has been reprinted in Martha Foley and David Burnett, editors, *The Best American Short Stories Of 1967* (Boston, Houghton, Mifflin, 1967), pp. 279-289, and in *Saturday Evening Post,* editors, *The Automobile Book* (Indianapolis, Curtis Publishing, 1977), pp. 66-75. It was also reprinted as a Dutch translation, "De Aanrijding," in *Cri,* No. 16 (April 22, 1967), pp. 12-14 and 16-17. Stuart included this story in his unpublished manuscript, *These Are My Best—Twenty-five Short Stories Selected From Five Hundred Published Stories And MSS*—edited and typed January 1975 (The Jesse Stuart Foundation Collection, Ashland, Kentucky). "The Accident" is featured in Jesse Stuart's "Author's Introduction—The Story Of A Story."

Big Charlie Had a Party

If you've ever been in love you'll know how I felt. My heart beat fast as I pulled my blue-serge pants from the clothesline pole upstairs. I got a white shirt from the dresser-drawer. I pulled my black low-cut slippers from under the bed. I put my clothes on my body and my shoes on my feet. I was in a hurry.

I pulled my black bowtie from a nail on the wall. I hurried over to the lookin' glass above the dresser. "This tie's nearly too short to go around my neck and make a bow," I thought. I looked at my big bull-neck. I didn't know it was so big before.

"It's a funny thing, how a girl as purty as Tessie Honeywell can love me," I thought. "She's a purty little angel—curly hair, blue eyes, and white teeth. Her soft lily-white hand feels like a baby mouse's paw when I hold it in my big fireshovel hand."

I started over the hill to see Tessie. I'd plowed terbacker all day in the new ground and I was tired then. I wasn't tired now. I could feel the muscles in the calves of my legs pushin' the crease out'n my pant legs that Ma'd ironed fer me to wear on sparkin' nights. But my leg muscles had two hundred and twenty pounds of man to lift up a mountain path so steep that I had to hold to the trees and sprouts to keep from goin' backwards.

The moonlight was purty on the dewy sourwood leaves. The stars winked at me from the sky-roof. The whippoorwills sang love songs to one another from the mountain tops—and the night birds chirruped lovin' words to one another. The whole world was in love—because I was in love.

"Whooie," I sighed when I reached the ridge path on the mountain top. This was the dividin' line betwixt Pa's and Tessie's Pappie's farm. I stood on the mountain top and let the cool night wind dry the sweat on my face. I wanted my shirt to be white and dry so Tessie could lean against me. I cooled a minute and started down the mountain to Tessie's shack.

I saw the lamplight in the winder of Tessie's shack. But I didn't see Tessie's face against the winder pane watchin' fer me as I'd seen before on Wednesday nights. Tessie didn't come out and throw her arms around me and kiss me as she'd allus done. I thought somethin' was wrong. I knocked on the door. Tessie came to the door.

"Sweetheart," I said. "You look like an angel sent from Heaven with Peach blossoms in your brown curly hair! You didn't meet me. I didn't see your face at the winder tonight."

"No, Worldly, I didn't watch fer you at the winder tonight."

"Is there somethin' wrong?"

"Oh, no, not exactly."

"There's another mule in my fair pasture of love."

"Not exactly."

We walked back on the porch. We sat down in the swing. I put my big arm around her. I started to draw her close to me.

"Don't Worldly," she said. "Let's just be friends tonight. Let's watch the moon up in the sky."

She took her little lily-white hand and moved my big fence-post arm from around her shoulders.

"Honey, I know somethin' is wrong now," I said. "You ain't the same. Has your Pappie got after you fer sparkin' me?"

"No, Worldly, it ain't that."

It broke my heart to look at Tessie's purty face in the moonlight. Her curly locks fell down over her shoulders. Her purty soft eyes just gazed at the moon. They wouldn't turn toward me.

"Is that Worldly and Tessie out there on the porch?" I heard Tessie's Pappie, Big-Charlie Honeywell ast.

"Yes, you know it's Wednesday night, Charlie," Tessie's Mammie answered. "Why ast that? Worldly's been comin' here on Wednesday nights for the past five years."

"I want to tell 'im about the celebration I'm havin' Saturday night," Big-Charlie said.

I heard Big-Charlie lumber from the kitchen to the front room. He sounded like an elephant walkin' across the floor. He slammed the doors behind him hard enough to tear 'em off the hinges.

"Howdy, Worldly," Big-Charlie said. He had to stoop to walk under the front door to the porch.

"Howdy, Big-Charlie," I said.

I thought I was a big man but I was a boy beside of Tessie's Pappie. His head was almost up to the porch loft. His big fence-post arms dropped nearly to his knees. His long beard fell nearly to his waist.

"Has Tessie told you about the celebration I'm havin' Saturday night?"

"No she ain't."

"Well, I'm getting' my new teeth Saturday," he said. "We're goin' to have a big supper and atter the supper we're goin' to have a shin-dig."

"That's great."

"I tell you I was a strong man before I got my teeth knocked out with a rock," Big Charlie said. "My mouth was in sucha shape atter Bud Pennix hit me in the mouth with a rock I had to have the few jaw teeth pulled he didn't knock out with that rock. If the WORD hadn't plainly said, 'Thou shalt not kill,' I would a pulled my gun right there and filled Bud Pennix with hot lead. I hadn't lost a tooth until I had that fight with Bud. It's caused me a heap of worry. I ain't been able to eat meat. Have you got all your teeth, Worldly?"

"Yes, I got 'em all but one," I said. "I broke out one crackin' hickory-nuts."

"Hold to your teeth long as you can," Big Charlie said. "You just try once to gum the shoulder of a mutton and see how hard it is—'r try to eat three stewed hens without teeth. It tires me out. When I had my teeth, a shoulder of mutton just made good pickin' fer me. I've had to eat so much soft grub that I don't weigh but two hundred eighty-eight pounds. I've fell off over seventy pounds. I just look big. I ain't heavy."

I looked at little Tessie and then I looked at Big-Charlie. I didn't see how a man big as Big-Charlie could be the Pappie of a girl so little and purty as Tessie.

"I hope I'll like my new-cooked grub Saturday night," Big-Charlie said. "I've never et grub cooked by a man before."

"Who's the cook?"

Tessie figited beside me.

"Dennie Whitt."

"Oh," I said. I didn't say anymore.

"Yes, he left here when he was a fairly young sprout," Big-Charlie said. "He's made good cookin' in a big hotel in Ohio. He's back here now larnin' the wimmen in Tanyard Hollow to cook. The wimmen says he's wonderful."

"Can he make dresses?" I ast.

"Can he make dresses?" Big-Charlie repeated. "It does sound funny to see the wimmen in Tanyard Hollow flockin' atter a man just because he can cook." Big-Charlie went in the house stretchin' his long beard and laughin'. "Be shore and be to the big supper Saturday night and the shin-dig," Big-Charlie said as he slammed the door behind 'im.

"Okey-dough, I'll be there."

Tessie kept her head turned from me. She kept watchin' the moon on the June sky. Tessie didn't speak a word. I didn't say a word to her. Dennie Whitt was the mule in my pasture. He had tried to spark Tessie when we went to school together. Now he'd gone to Ohio and learned to cook in a hotel and he'd come back and was somebody.

"Where are you goin', Worldly?"

"Home," I said. "I've got to be gettin' over the mountain. This place ain't the same."

I didn't try to kiss Tessie good night. I just walked off'n the porch. I was on my way home.

"Ain't you comin' to Pa's celebration Saturday night?"

"Big-Charlie ast me to come and I'm comin'."

I didn't keer how wet my shirt got with sweat. I climbed the mountain path in a hurry. I jerked sourwood sprouts out by the roots pullin' up the mountain side. Sweat streamed from my face into my eyes. When I reached the ridge path on the mountain top, I didn't stop to cool. I thought about Tessie. I thought about Dennie Whitt. When I got off'n the mountain to my home, I slipped upstairs and lit the lamp. I stood before the lookin' glass. I looked at myself. "What kind of cook would I make," I said. I looked at my big hands.

When I worked in the terbacker patch on Thursday, I was mean to my mule. We just couldn't get along.

Friday, June the thirteenth, and that was a day for bad luck. The plow hit a stump. The plow handle stove against the left panel of my ribs and broke a couple. The hame-string broke. The mule slipped out'n the harness and took through the terbacker patch fer the barn. I limped to the house. My ribs hurt me so I couldn't draw a long breath. I was laid up all day Saturday.

"Where are you goin' Worldly?" Ma ast when she saw me shaving.

"Goin' over to Honeywells."

"You're gettin' sorty sweet on Big-Charlie's gal to cross that mountain path with your ribs broke."

"Big-Charlie's gettin' his new teeth today and we're goin' to celebrate tonight."

"Yes, I heered about Eif Whitt's boy, Dennie, comin' back to Tanyard Hollow and larnin' the old wimmen and the gals how to cook," Ma laughed. "Maud Stapleton told me he wouldn't be cookin' and wastin' his time at Honeywells but he's sweet on Tessie."

I got my blue-serge pants from over the hickory-pole clothesline. I jerked 'em on and pulled a white shirt from the dresser drawer. My side was sore but I couldn't tell I had a couple of ribs broke now. I tied my black bowtie before the lookin' glass. I put my black low-cut slippers on and I hurried downstairs and up the mountain path.

I didn't keer if I was a little short of breath. I climbed the mountain faster than ever before. I jerked sprouts out by the roots as I ketched hold of 'em pullin' myself up the mountain. I didn't stop to cool on the mountaintop. I hurried down the other side. I worked the soreness out'n my ribs but I couldn't work it out'n my heart.

"Come in Worldly," said Big-Charlie. His voice was different. Somethin' rattled in his mouth. He stood before me in his Sunday clothes. His long beard was neatly combed. When he opened his mouth to speak I could see somethin' eggshell white betwixt the beard on his chin and the mustache on his upper lip.

"You look good, Big-Charlie, with your new teeth," I said. "I come nigh as a pea not knowin' you."

"I'm goin' to be the old Big-Charlie Honeywell again," he said, "soon as I get a shoulder of mutton under my belt. I'll feel like goin' out and turnin' a mountain over to see what is under it."

"I'm glad to hear it."

"Supper is ready," Big-Charlie said. "Let's get our feet under the table. I don't know about this cookin'. I've just been wonderin'."

I followed Big-Charlie into the dining room. I never saw sicha table of grub in my life. There was a mutton on the table, taters, soup-beans, turnips, poke-greens, fried apples, apple struddles, blackberry cobbler, goosberry pie, wild strawberry short-cake, basket of fried chicken, six stewed hens, strawberries, blackberries, coffee, milk, ci-der, applejack, dandelion wine, molasses, and soup with noodles. This table was filled with grub until there's hardly room for our plates. We didn't have elbowroom to eat.

"You sit at the end of the table with Big-Charlie," Tessie's Ma said.

"Okey-dough," I told her.

Tessie sat down and there was an empty plate beside her. I didn't see Dennie Whitt. I guessed he was in the kitchen workin' with the grub. I think all the fathers and mothers and most of their oldest youngins in Tanyard Hollow had come to celebrate Big-Charlie's gettin' his new teeth. I never saw sicha crowd gathered around one table. Everybody was so quiet around the table.

"Why don't you say somthin' Pappie?" Tessie ast.

"My little gal, Solomon was a wise man," he said. "If you had been in his presence you wouldn't a-heered 'im blabbin' his head off."

Big-Charlie started to reach fer a shoulder of mutton.

"Just a minute Poppie," Ma Honeywell said. "Dennie's got a new way of doin' things."

"I've had the patience of Job," Big-Charlie said.

I looked at the kitchen door. There stood Dennie Whitt. I wanted to get my hands on that smart-alec. He stood there with a white hat on his head, a high white-collar and a black bowtie around his bird-neck. He wore a long white apron. He had the palm of his hand turned toward the newspapered ceilin'. On the palm of his hand rested a big platter and on that platter were some little things that looked like biscuits.

"Better read the plate, Poppie," Ma Honeywell said. Dennie stood in his tracks at the kitchen door. The men and wimmen, boys and girls bowed their head while Big-Charlie looked at his plate, stroked his beard with his big hand and blessed the grub.

"Now this is the horsdouvre folks," Dennie said. "It's just to whet your appetites."

"What did you say it was?" Big-Charlie ast.

"Horsdouvre," Dennie repeated.

"I never heard of sicha grub," Big-Charlie said.

"I never either," Mort Higgins said.

"It's a new one on me," Big-Charlie said. "I don't need my appetite whetted anymore fer it's already whetted."

"Horsdouvre, Pappie, is what Dennie serves before a meal at the Skylark Hotel," Tessie said.

The men and women looked at one another. The boys and girls looked over the big table o' grub. I looked at Dennie. Tessie looked at me. Blood rushed to my face. I know my face was red as a sliced beet. I kept my hands in my pocket. I was afraid to take 'em out. I was afraid I might flatten Dennie on the floor when he got around to me.

"Take one," Dennie smiled as he helt the platter down so Murt Hix could reach it. Murt was slow about it. She'd never done this before. None of us had. After Murt took one off'n the platter then the others took one as Dennie walked beside the table. But he didn't leave one of his horsdouvres at the empty chair beside Tessie. He didn't leave a horsdouvre for himself.

I was thinkin' fast. I was feelin' for somethin' in my pocket. Everybody was lookin' across the table at one another and laughin' now. No one was lookin' when Dennie got to me. A thought flashed in my mind.

I pulled my hand from my pocket with a dum-dum cartridge between my fingers. As I picked up my horsdouvre, I shoved the dum-dum down in the one beside it. Dennie wasn't lookin'. He was castin' sheep-eyes at Tessie. He wouldn't look at me, the man he'd jilted in love. Big-Charlie looked at the horsdouvre. I just prayed he'd pick up the right one.

"Funny little thing to have sich a funny name," Big-Charlie said.

I took my horsdouvre at one bite. Big-Charlie looked at his. He rolled it on the palm of his big hand and laughed.

"I have the longest beard in Tanyard Hollow and the best appetite," Big-Charlie said. "And I take this little biscuit to whet my appetite. It's the first bite for my new teeth."

Dennie was nearly around the table passin' the horsdouvre when Big-Charlie clamped down with his big jaws on the horsdouvre.

"Whow"—something popped.

I saw something bigger than a white soup-bean fly across the table. It fell in Burt Hailey's plate. It was one of Big-Charlie's teeth. Big-Charlie emptied his mouth in his hand and held the dum-dum cartridge.

"I'll kill you," Big-Charlie roared like a lion. He jumped up from his chair. He yanked his .38 Special from his hip holster.

"Oh, Poppie, thou shalt not kill," Ma Honeywell screamed. "Don't do anything rash!"

Dennie stood with the tray on the palm of his hand. He didn't know what was the matter. He looked at Big-Charlie. He looked at Tessie and smiled.

"This is a new-fangled way of doin' things," Big-Charlie shouted as he put the .38 Special back into his hip holster. "I don't like it!"

"Samson with the jawbone of an ass smote one thousand Philistines," Big-Charlie yelled, "and with this shoulder of mutton, I'll smote a quack-cook."

Big-Charlie grabbed a shoulder of mutton from the table. He raised it above his shoulder—"I'm just too weak," he panted. "I'm weak as a cat. Young David, take this shoulder of mutton and kill that cook!" He reached the shoulder of mutton to me and dropped back in his chair.

Tessie looked at me. Her face was red as a wind-blown ember.

"I don't need a shoulder of mutton 'r a slingshot," I said. "Just let me to 'im with these fire-shovel hands. I'll break his damn neck. I'll dirty his white clothes fer 'im."

"It's a dum-dum bullet," Big-Charlie shouted, "that I come down with my new teeth. If it had exploded I'd a-been blown into eternity! Life is too sweet to live even without my teeth."

I was tryin' to get to Dennie. But Bert Hailey was a-holt of my arm. Lum Didway was holdin' me around the waist—Tessie was in front of me beggin' me not to do anything. "I can't do anything," I said, as I looked out the winder. I saw a man dressed in white a-runnin' like a ghost across Big-Charlie's terbacker patch. A foxhound couldn't a-ketched 'im.

"Honey, I'll take my old place back," I said.

"Love me, Honey?" Tessie ast.

"Love you," I said. "If I wasn't afraid of hurtin' you, I'd bear-hug you. But I'm afraid of breakin' your ribs."

"That's the neartest I've come to meetin' my doom," Big-Charlie said. "I wouldn't a-lost that tooth fer nothin' in this world. Brought that fool thing here to cook! Horsdouvre, who ever heard of sicha damned grub? I'll never ferget the first one I tasted."

Everybody looked at Big-Charlie and laughed. "Let's start eatin' at the table like we've allus et," Big Charlie said. "Let's ferget about this appetite whettin'. I'm hungry as a lion."

Everybody was too busy eatin' to watch Tessie and me. Big-Charlie was gummin' a shoulder of mutton. I put my arm around the back of Tessie's chair.

"Big Charlie Had A Party" was first published in *American Book Collector,* Vol. 16, No. 3 (February 1966), pp. 30-33. It has never been reprinted. Stuart included this story in his unpublished manuscript, *Twenty-five Tall Stories Selected From 461 Published Stories And Fifty Manuscripts,* circa 1975 (The Jesse Stuart Foundation Collection, Ashland, Kentucky).

Jesse Stuart in Plum Grove Cemetery, Greenup County Kentucky. Plum Grove Church is visible in the left background — circa 1942. Those buried here are the basis for many of Stuart's fictional characters.

Brother-in-law, Eif Tongs

"Get every speck of dirt swept up from the floor," says Ma. "Sweep every spider web from the ceiling. Have everything spick and span. It's about time for your sister Effie to bring her beau home. She's goin' to bring him home today. It looks like serious business to me!"

"Do you mean she's goin' to get married, Ma?" I says.

"It looks that way to me," says Ma.

Ma lifted a cap on the stove and set a teakettle of water over the bright flames in the firebox. She took a cherry pie from the oven of the stove, let the big door of the stove down, and set the pie on the stove door for the crust to brown.

"Havin' cherry pie, I see," I says. "We're sorty puttin' on the dog for this new brother-in-law of mine."

"He ain't your brother-in-law yet," says Ma, "but I'm sure he will be. He's the second man your Sis ever brought to the house. You know what happened to th' other man?"

"Oh yes," I says, "he left the Free-Will Baptist Church and Sis dropped him like she would a hot coal of fire."

"That's right," says Ma, "and I don't blame her. I didn't want Lester Trent for a son-in-law after he turned against his religion!"

"What's Eif Tongs' religion?" I asked.

"He's a Free-Will Baptist, of course," says Ma.

Ma jumped around like a moth around a lamp. Sister Belle helped Ma. She was running this way and that. They were gettin' a good dinner for Sister Effie and Eif Tongs. They were comin' up the hill to the house bouncin' like a rabbit over the last year's corn furrows.

"W'y he's got a car," I says to Ma.

"Yes," says Ma, "he's somebody. That Tongs family is a fine family. I've heard a lot about 'em!"

"Tongs family," I says, "seems like that name sticks in my mind! Ma is this the set of Tongses that live on Hog Branch?"

"Yes," says Ma.

I never said anything more but I thought a lot. I'd met with them before! I was at the Free-Will Baptist Church on Hog Branch one night and a Tongs stepped out'n the dark and broke a two-gallon glass whiskey jug over my head. Ma ought to a-remembered this when she picked glass out'n my head for a month. It ain't all out yet. A sliver works out every once in a while. Ma'd forgot all of this. But I hadn't forgot. When a man hits me I never forget 'im. I never forgot his name either. It lodges in my head to stay.

"They're out there in the yard," I says to Ma. "You'd better get out to meet them."

Ma run out'n the house. Pa run out from the barn. I saw them shaking hands with Eif and Effie under the big pine tree in our yard. I didn't go out. Just seemed like a frog come up in my throat and I could hardly speak a word. I get that way when I've been mistreated and find it out. I just wondered if he's the Tongs that hit me with that bottle. I looked out the winder and watched Pa and Ma. They were talkin' to Eif and Effie. I heard them laughin'. I saw steam goin' up from the hood of Eif's car like steam from a sawmill biler. It had got hot climbin' the hill to our house. I saw them start into the house.

Sister Belle came out'n the kitchen to meet Sister Effie's beau. Little Whirly, Susie, Murt and Jim looked on. They walked to the front door. Pa opened the door. They walked in. Lord, I looked at Eif Tongs. He was a big tall redheaded and freckled-faced devil. I just didn't like his looks. I'd seen him before. I'd seen him on Hog Branch.

"Brother Laff," says Sister Effie, "this is Eif."

"I think we've met before," I says. "Maybe Eif don't remember but I do."

"No. I've never met you before," says Eif.

"Oh, we didn't exactly meet," I says, "I saw you one night at the Free-Will Baptist Association on Hog Branch!"

"I met so many over there," says Eif, " I can't remember you. I'm sorry that you've slipped my mind."

"I have a good memory," I says. "I never forget a face."

Eif looked funny like I was makin' fun of the freckles on his face. His face got red. He patted my little sisters on the head and said he was glad to meet them. Then he met Sister Belle and shook the hands of my little brothers. I just didn't like Eif. I didn't like his looks. I didn't like what he had done to me. He was dressed fit to kill.

"Is that a good car you got?" says Pa. "I saw you come boundin' over them old last year's corn furrows! You come up the hill like a rabbit and that engine was just singin'!"

"It's a wonderful car, Mr. Spradling," says Eif. "I got that car in 1918. It can pull more than a mule team. I take it over mud holes and rocks in the road big as bushel baskets. I haul my terbacker crop away in that car. I've hardly been out'n it the eight years I've had it. It runs like greased lightenin' yet!"

"Wonderful," says Pa. "I never thought a car could get up this road over the rocks, stumps, and the last year's corn furrows!"

"They didn't bother us did they, Honey?" says Eif.

"No," says Sister Effie. "We come right over 'em. Sometimes I could hardly stick to the seat, but we never stopped comin'!"

"Great," I says.

"I'll be lettin' you drive that car Laff," says Eif. "I'll be lettin' you take it to town one of these days!'

"Dinner is ready," says Mom. "Come on all of you."

"Yes," says Pa, "it's time to feed our face for awhile."

We walked in the kitchen to the table. I never saw so much grub on one table. It hurt me to think Ma would work and slave like this to cook grub for a man that beat her boy over the head with a jug. Every time I took a bite I thought about the way I whopped and hollered when Ma picked glass out'n my head with a darning needle. I thought about the way Pa had to clip all the hair off my head. I thought about the scars on my head. I looked at Sister Effie. She was so purty. She was settin' by a big ugly devil. Why couldn't she a picked a man from a family we hadn't had any trouble with when she wanted to get married?

"Well, Ma," says Sister Effie, "I just want to tell you I ain't goin' to get married, I'm already married. Eif is my husband!"

"Well, I'm so glad," says Ma. "He belongs to my church. He belongs to my party. That makes everything just right!"

"Are you a good terbacker raiser, Eif?" says Pa.

"Ain't no better in the county, Mr. Spradling," says Eif. "I've raised terbacker ever since I've been knee-high to a katydid!"

"Fine," says Pa. "I've got a house for you on the fur end of this place. You and Effie don't haf to be a hired gal and a lackey-boy no longer. Come right here and live. There's land here for all of us."

"Plenty of trouble," I thought. I was afraid to say anything. If I could a-seen Effie before she met Eif I'd a put a plenty in her ear. I know the Spradling blood well enough to know when a body does a member of their family a harm the Spradlings hang together to right the wrong. That's not in Ma's blood. She was a Jacobs. It's in Pa's blood. It's in the Spradlings.

"I'll take my car home," says Eif, "and get all the furniture Ma promised me. I'll have a load of house plunder."

"I'll give you a young heifer and a feather bed," says Ma. "That's what I've promised my girls when they get married!"

When Ma said that, Eif dropped a big piece of cherry pie on the table. He acted like his hand was stiff. He acted like he was scared.

"Excuse me," says Eif. "My hands are a little cold and stiff from drivin' the car this cold March day."

Eif was looking at me when he dropped the pie. I was lookin' at Eif. He must have just remembered the night on Hog Branch at the Baptist Association when he hit me over the head with the big two-gallon glass whiskey jug. He thought he'd killed me. He went away and left me for dead. My second cousin, Jones Spradling, come along and found me. He carried water from the creek in his cap and poured it on my face. He wiped the blood from my eyes with his handkerchief. He got his mule and rode me home on the mule behind me. I was so weak he had to sit me up behind him and rope me to him to hold me on the mule. I hadn't forgot. Brother-in-law Eif's hands were not cold and stiff. He'd just recognized me.

That afternoon when the sun was out purty and bright and the cold wind was blowin' high among the bare March trees, Sister Effie and Eif got in the car and bounced away over the hill toward Eif's home. They had to go to Leather Creek and get the furniture Eif's mother had promised them. Pa went across the hill to the fur end of our place to fix the two-roomed log house upon the hill. Pa would take clapboards from the stacks and patch the roof. He would put the winder sashes back in the house since Effie was going to move there. Pa took them out because the boys in the district was so bad they'd break them out with rocks just to hear the glass crack. Ma went with Pa to build a fire in the house and dry the dampness. She took some newspapers to paste over the cracks. Ma took a broom to sweep the floors and get the house ready.

I hardly knowed what to do. I would haf to do something. I couldn't go through life with a brother-in-law like Eif. He would wreck our family. He would divide us and get us to fightin' one another. Ma already leaned a little toward Eif. I could see it because he belonged to Ma's church. Ma couldn't see, no matter what church he was in, he was a sinful man. It takes a sinful man to hit you over the head with a two-gallon jug and just go off and leave you for dead.

I guess Pa must a-norrated it around the district. He must a-wanted Sister Effie and Eif belled. When the car came back in the holler with the load of furniture, it was dark. The stars were in the cold blue March sky. A million stars looked down on the old house Ma and Pa had sorty fixed up so Eif and Effie could move in. The whole hillside was lined with people from the district. They had come to bell Eif and Effie. They brought shotguns, plow-pints, washtubs to beat on and cowbells and sheep bells to jingle. I never heard sicha racket in my life. I didn't take any part in it. I stood back in the dark among the oak trees near the house and looked on.

Pa furnished Eif a mule. "I want to see Eif and Effie get along," says Pa. "Poor Effie had to hire out to the rich farmers over in the bottoms. She done housework to make a few dollars and send home. Eif had to work hard to pay for his car. Rented land from his Pap just like he was a stranger to him. And after he was twenty-one his Pap hired him to work by the year for him for $75 and his keeps. I want to see 'im make good."

I never said anything. I didn't go about Sister Effie's house unless I nearly burned up for water when I's hoein' terbacker on the hill just opposite their house. I went over to the spring and got me a drink of water. Then I got away. I knowed the water any place on Pa's farm was free. I knowed the wind I breathed was free. But I was not free of my thoughts about Eif. I had to do something about it. I didn't like the name of Tongs.

During the summer of 1928, I'd look at Eif's terbacker field. It looked so fine and purty and smelled so good when the wind blowed from his side of the hill across the holler to my hill. I could see the green blades of his terbacker flap in the wind. I never hollered across the holler and talked to him like I did John Watts. Yet, Eif was my brother-in-law. I just didn't like Eif. There was a mountain that stood between us. We couldn't get across that mountain. It couldn't be moved. I had to do something about it.

Eif raised his crop of corn and terbacker. I never told Ma why I didn't like Eif. I think Ma smelt a mouse. She knowed I didn't like him. She knowed Eif never fooled around me. Sister Effie noticed we didn't have anything to do with one another. When Eif and Effie visited Ma and Pa, I always got out and went some place. I couldn't stand to be around where he was. Effie told Ma she thought I didn't like Eif because he married her and took her away from home. She said we'd had sicha good time together when we's children building playhouses with moss and broken dishes under the pine tree in our yard. It wasn't that. God knows I wanted Sister Effie to marry and have a home of her own. I just wanted her to marry a good man from a family we hadn't had trouble with. I didn't want to see Spradling blood in a man-child bearing the name of Tongs.

We's cuttin terbacker. It was fall time and the leaves had started to turn. One day I went to the spring to get a drink of water. I was hot and dry. After I got a drink, I saw Sister Effie in the yard. She was raking off the dead leaves. I'd noticed she hadn't been out in the fields helping Eif lately. I could see now while she was in the yard why she hadn't. She was going to have a baby. I couldn't do anything to Eif now. If I shot Eif it might make Sis have a marked baby. I'd wait until she had her baby.

Eif sold his terbacker in January 1929. Eif and Pa hauled their terbacker off in Eif's car. "It takes it to the market faster than mules," says Pa. "Darned if it don't. People are growin' weaker and wiser fast. The world is goin' to come to an end one of these days!"

Pa liked the car. He would sit up beside of Eif and ride. Both of them had long beards on their faces. I couldn't tell which looked the oldest—Eif or Pa. I wondered why they didn't get their beards on fire the way they smoked cigars and burned the wind in Eif's car.

"I can take 'er Dad," says Eif, "anyplace you can take your mules-only my car can go faster. It has better wind. I can go over rocks, stumps, chug-holes and ditches. I can cross creeks and go over frozen ground. Just when the mud barrels up in front of the engine, and the wheels spin, it's nasty to haf to get out and take a pole and prize the dirt away."

Sister Effie had her baby in February. It was a girl, thank God! It wasn't a man-child to bear the name of Tongs with Spradling blood in him. The same month Eif sowed his terbacker beds. He was goin' to raise terbacker again. He'd made $512 out'n his last year's crop. Terbacker was a good price. Eif had good terbacker, better'n mine except where the "spot" had hit the late terbacker.

"Your brother-in-law, Eif," says Pa, "can make money like dirt. It's a shame you don't like him no better than what you do! I like Eif like he was a son of my own!"

I just couldn't come out and tell Pa why I didn't like Eif. I thought someday I might be able to. I just let things drift along. I thought the time would come when I could get everything settled with Eif.

I'd look over on Eif's end of the place when the leaves started to come back to the oaks. Eif had his sprouts cut and his ground plowed. It looked good to me. Eif was a worker. There was no doubt about it. He was beatin' Pa and me put together. I wanted to tell Ma what I was goin' to do to Eif. I went down to the milk gap one evening. When I started to tell her, just seemed like a frog came up in my throat. I couldn't speak for five minutes. Then I thought it was better to hold my thoughts and not tell them to anybody.

Eif had the purtiest terbacker a body ever looked at durin' the summer of 1930. It shot out of the hot loamy earth like green racer snakes. I just couldn't understand how he could grow sucha fine lookin' terbacker. We had the same kind of land. My terbacker never looked as good as Eif's terbacker. Sister Effie was out in the field workin' with him again. She put the baby on a pallet in the shade on one end of the terbacker patch. She'd take a hoe and help Eif hoe the terbacker in the hot sun. She worked as hard as Eif.

It was terbacker cuttin' time. The corn was ripe and the leaves of terbacker had started to run. I went over to the spring by their house to get a drink. I was hot and my throat was dry. I saw Sister Effie in the yard again. She was rakin' the dead oak leaves from around the spring. I saw the reason why she hadn't been out in the fields helpin' Eif. She was goin' to have another baby. It made my blood bile. I thought maybe she might have a boy. It would be part Spradling and he would bear the name of Tongs. It hurt me because I'd let Eif get back and I hadn't done anything. I would have to do something soon after her second baby was born.

Eif wore a long red beard during the winter. "My beard keeps me warm in the winter," he would say. "When spring comes I want my beard cut so my face will keep cool when I sweat."

That was the way Pa always done. He would wear a long beard durin' the winter to keep his face warm. In the spring when the warm sun shined and when he started plowin', I had to cut his beard off with the scissors and then shave 'em. I always cut Pa's hair and shaved him. Just seemed like I had a knack for cuttin' hair. I liked to cut hair and shave people.

Eif sold his terbacker in January 1931. He got $597 for his terbacker. Pa got $456 for our crop. The price of terbacker held up. It was a lot of money. But Eif would need his money. Sis was goin' to have another baby. Eif smoked big cigars and went over the farm with Pa just like he owned the land. They went places in Eif's car together and smoked their cigars. I had hoped Eif's beard would get on fire and burn him up. Evertime I thought about Hog Branch and the Baptist Association over there that time, I wanted to walk over and tell Eif about it. But he never told me when he hit me over the head with a two-gallon glass whiskey jug! He hit me without saying a word. I couldn't get over it! Then to think of all the boys in the country, Effie would marry Eif Tongs! I just couldn't understand how it happened.

Sister Effie had her second baby in February. Thank God it was another girl! Eif wanted a boy. "I need boys to help me raise terbacker," he says. "What am I goin' to do with a whole slew of girls! They ain't as good to work in the fields!"

Eif laughed and puffed his homemade cigar. Pa laughed with Eif. Pa puffed his cigar. They pinted to the dark hills they would have in terbacker another year!

"You won't plant any more terbacker if I can help it," I thought. "You've planted your last unless time slips upon me again. I have had to wait for my chance."

Eif had just got his terbacker beds sowed. I could see the white streaks of canvas runnin' up and down the hill. It looked like a patch of snow that the spring sun hadn't melted. Eif was getting' ready for a bigger terbacker crop than he had ever planted. Sister Effie had two children now. It looked like they were gettin' along fine. Pa thought I liked Eif better than I did. Ma thought we'd about buried the hatchet. It wasn't a hatchet we had to bury. It was a mountain. We couldn't bury a mountain in a lifetime. One of us just had to get rid of the other. Eif wouldn't try to get rid of me. He had done the harm to me. He pretended like he didn't remember it. But from the time he dropped that piece of cherry pie at our table I knowed he remembered.

It was on Sunday. It was in March. The sun was warm. It covered the dark earth and made the black woods glisten. It seemed like life was comin' back to the dark hills. Greenbriars had started to put out leaves. Oak buds were swellin'. Eif walked over home. He was carryin' the big baby. Sister Effie was carrying the little baby. They walked up the bank to our house.

"Good mornin' Laff," Eif said to me.

"Good mornin', Eif," I says. "Looks like you and Sister Effie are getting' a right smart family started to be just married two years!"

"Yep," Eif says, "but I need a boy. I need boys."

"I'm satisfied with girls," says Sister Effie.

Eif laughed and puffed his cigar. He was so friendly. He thought I'd forgot everything he'd done to me. I was polite to him because he was in our family and because he was at our house.

"They tell us you're a real barber, Laff," says Eif. "Dad said you cut his hair every spring and shaved his beard. Is that right?"

"Yep," I says, "that's right. I do all the hair cuttin' that's done in this district."

"What do you charge?" says Eif.

"I don't charge my kinsfolks nothing," I says. "The neighbors pay me in a roundabout way. When they butcher in the fall they send me a mess of backbones, 'r spare-ribs. Sometimes they send me sausage when they get it ground. Sometimes they send me a mess o' quails or a fat possum when they hunt. Sometimes around Christmas they send me a horse-quart of good moonshine!"

"You give me a real haircut and shave," says Eif, "and I'll do more than that for you. I'll find you the purtiest woman you ever laid your two peepers on. She's my first cousin. She lives on Uling Branch, just a little piece from Hog Branch!"

"I'll fix you up," I says. "I've got to cut Pa's hair and shave him this morning. I spect I'll be busy about all day. A lot of men in the district will be in today to get their haircut and their beard shaved. It's gettin' warmer weather, you know. Winter is over. Croppin' time is here again."

I took the clippers and clipped Pa's hair. Eif stood and watched me. Sis took one baby in the house. Then Sis came back and got the baby Eif was holdin'. Then I took the scissors and trimmed Pa's hair. It was awfully long.

"Pa, why don't you let your hair grow a little longer, plait it up and put a ribbon on it?" I says. "You'd look good."

Pa laughed until he rocked the mowin' machine. I had Pa up on the seat of the mowin' machine. It was under the apple tree down below the house. Pa puffed his cigar until I had to wait for the clouds of smoke to thin and float away before I could see to use the clippers on his beard. After I clipped his beard, I put gobs of lather from the mug on the beard stubble, took the big black-handled razor and shaved Pa. He really looked like a new man.

"Dad, Mom won't know you," says Eif. Eif laughed and smoked his cigar.

"Effie won't know you either," I says, "when I get through with you. You won't be the same man. You'll be a spirit in another world."

Eif laughed and laughed. He dug his boot heels into the ground and laughed. He puffed big clouds of smoke into the air. He clapped his hands and laughed.

"I'm ready for you now, Eif," I says, "before a big crowd of men come in here for me to work on today."

Pa stepped down from the mowin' machine. Eif climbed up and took the seat. I started cuttin' his red hair. It fell in great wisps in front of my clippers. I trimmed his hair with the scissors.

"Eif you have a well-shaped head," I says. "I've cut the hair off many a head and shaved many a face but I don't believe in all of my work I ever come across a finer shaped head. It is shaped like a bird egg. I've cut the hair off a lot of heads shaped like mushrooms and a lot of heads shaped like bullets. But your head reminds me of a purty speckled bird egg."

"Thank you," says Eif. "I'm glad you see something about me that looks good."

Eif laughed and puffed the smoke from his cigar. I waited for the smoke to clear away so I could clip his beard and then shave him. I clipped his beard. Then I put on big gobs of lather from the mug. I pulled the big black-handled razor Grandpa give to Pa. I whetted it a few times on my britches' leg.

"Be careful with that razor," says Eif. "My face is tender. I ain't shaved since last fall sometime, October I believe."

"I'll be careful," I says. "Never worry about my razor. I ain't cut a man yet in all the faces I've shaved, enough to make him bleed. I've shaved people when I's so drunk I could hardly see their faces, with dull razors too. I managed somehow to get their beard scraped off."

Eif laughed and I laughed. Then he talked to me about the purty girl over on Uling Branch. I ast him about her and shaved away.

"Now Eif," I says, "let me put a little powder on your face to keep it from chapping!"

"Fine," says Eif, "it will make me smell good too."

I took Sister Belle's powder puff from my pocket. I dusted Eif's face and smoothed the powder down the puff.

"You look fine," I says.

"I feel fine too," says Eif.

"Let me stand off and look at you," I says. "I want to give you the last once-over before you leave the mowin' machine."

"Oakay, Laff old boy," says Eif. "You've shore done a good job. I feel like a new man."

I stepped back about two steps. I looked around. Pa had gone to the house. I didn't see anybody. Eif looked at his feet while I was lookin' at his head. I pulled my 38. I plugged Eif in the temple. He fell from the mowin' machine chair. Ma, Pa, Sister Eiffie, Sister Belle come runnin' out'n the house when they heard the gun.

"What have you done to Eif?" Sister Effie screamed.

"All that should a-been done before you married 'im," I says.

"Oh my Lord," says Ma, "what made you cut his hair, shave his face and then powder it before you killed 'im?"

"So he'd make a purty corpse," I says.

"Why did you kill 'im?" says Pa.

I couldn't talk for Sister Effie screamin'. Then Pa got her quiet so I could talk.

"Pa, you remember the time I got hit over the head with that two-gallon glass jug?" I says. "Remember how I was left by the side of the road for dead and Cousin Jones found me and tied me on the mule behind him and brought me home? Well, right there is the feller that hit me!"

Ma was sheddin' tears. She was holdin' to Sister Effie. My little brothers and sisters were cryin'.

"Ma," I says, "you remember pickin' the glass out'n my head and how you and Pa said you could kill the person that hit me free as you ever et a bite of grub! I've been waitin' for the past two years to get 'im. I would've killed 'im before but Sister Effie was goin' to have a baby. I was afraid it might mark the baby. I just waited because of Sister Effie. I waited too long. I saw she was goin' to have another one and I waited again, prayin' it would be a girl-child and not a man-child to have Spradling blood in its veins and bear the name of Tongs! Now before the terbacker season starts again or Sister Effie has time to have another baby, I thought this would be a good time to get Eif."

"We might have a tussel with the Law over this," says Pa.

"I don't know how," I says. "How can you get a jury that will convict me when he hit me over the head with a two-gallon glass whiskey jug and filled my head with glass—left me bleedin' and dyin' beside of the road on a cold night in March! He never could be my brother-in-law!"

"What will I do with my children?" says Effie.

"We'll take care of 'em," says Ma.

"I'll hep," I says. "I'll hep you Sister Effie!"

"I didn't know he was the man that hit you with that jug," says Ma. "If I had, he'd never lived on this place. He couldn't have darkened a door of mine or et a bite of the grub I cooked."

"I'd a-never married 'im either," says Sister Effie, "and had my children with 'im."

"It's just too bad," says Pa, "I didn't know he was that sort. I'd begin to like old Eif. "Peared to me like my own son. I liked to go places with 'im in the car. Just to think he's the fellar that hit you! I didn't know it! I wouldn't a-rid any place with 'im!"

Effie sorty stopped cryin'. Ma dried up her tears.

"The best thing," says Ma, "is to get him back to his people!"

"Then forget about 'im," says Pa. "Guess we'll haf to spend the rest of our days watchin' his people."

"We'll never be able to go to Hog Branch Church again," says Ma.

"No, we'll not," I says.

"I made a mistake by marryin' him," says Sister Effie, cryin' like her heart would break.

"Take it easy Effie," says Pa. "You didn't know the kind of feller he was. A body's children is liable to make mistakes."

"Brother-In-Law, Eif Tongs" was first published in *Story*, Vol. 15 (September-October 1939), pp. 73-81. It has never been reprinted. Stuart included this story in his unpublished manuscript, *Twenty-five Tall Stories Selected From 461 Published Stories And Fifty Manuscripts*, circa 1975 (Jesse Stuart Foundation Collection, Ashland, Kentucky).

Catalogue Girl

"It would do my heart good," I thought, "to beat Millie Spens at her own game. Not a girl on Lost Creek has a chance of getting a beau with Millie Spens around."

I sat in the Lost Creek Church House by the window. I sat there every Sunday morning now to watch Millie Spens ride her fine horse into the church house yard with Larry Currie riding his horse beside her. I used to ride in a rubber-tired buggy beside Larry with a big red-checked lap robe over our laps. But that was before Millie Spens came along. That was before she took a notion to take my beau. While I was going with Larry, she was taking other Lost Creek girls' beaux. She waited until I got in love with Larry; then she took him.

"Why do they always ride to church late every Sunday morning?" I thought as I watched them dismount from their panting horses whose sides were dark with sweat and with foamy flakes gathered around the corners of their bridle bits. "I know why they get here late. They take a ride up Lost Creek and back together before church begins."

It hurt me to see Larry tie her riding skirt to her new brown saddle with a red plush seat . I saw him tie it to her saddle carefully while she pressed the wrinkles from her skirt with her white-gloved hands. I know our preacher, Brother Sizemore, looked at me when he preached. He saw me getting fidgety in my seat. He saw how nervous I was as I looked out the window. He was preaching the love of God and I was pining for the love of Larry Currie. But Millie Spens had his love.

When they walked into the church house together, everybody looked at them; then they looked at me. I don't think they could hear my heart pounding. I think everybody understood. Everybody knew that my father, Ezekial Doore, rented a house to live in and land to farm from Millie's father, Archie Spens. Everybody knew that Archie Spens was the richest man on Lost Creek; that he owned five hundred acres of land; that he had sheep, cattle, fine horses, big apple orchards, and fields of strawberries. Everybody knew that his tenants farmed tobacco, corn, wheat, and potatoes for him and that his share of the crops was half. Everybody knew that he had money in the bank, that he bought anything his daughter wanted. They knew that he had the brown leather saddle with the red plush seat made especially for Millie. It was the only saddle of its kind on Lost Creek. I think everybody felt sorry for me. That's the way they looked when Larry Currie walked into the church house holding Millie's hand.

When Larry and Millie sat down on the seat in front of me, Millie put her arm on the back of the long seat around Larry's back. She didn't have her white glove on this hand. It was off, so I could see her move her fingers. She wanted me to see her new diamond ring. It was bright enough to hurt my eyes if I'd looked at it long enough. But I didn't. I wouldn't please Millie that well. I pretended I didn't notice her engagement ring. Other girls from Lost Creek noticed it. They were glad. If Millie got married she wouldn't be stealing their beaux any longer, they thought. But they didn't think about what she had done to me. My heart kept pounding as I thought about it. I don't remember to this day what Brother Sizemore preached about the morning I saw Millie's engagement ring.

Soon as church was over, I hurried out the door. I walked up the path slowly. I stood upon the hill where I could watch people shaking hands at the church house door. I could see them, but they couldn't see me. I watched Larry untie Millie's skirt from the saddle; and while she stepped into it and drew it around her, Larry untied the bridle reins of her horse from an oak branch. I saw Millie mount her horse gracefully while everybody in the churchyard watched her. I heard them saying to one another how beautiful and graceful Millie Spens was. That hurt me so much I could hardly stand it. But what hurt me most was when Larry untied his horse's bridle reins from a low-hanging oak branch, leaped into the saddle, and rode down Lost Creek beside Millie. I watched them ride away—their saddle horses pacing side by side down the winding Lost Creek road.

"I can't stand it," I screamed where no would hear me, wiping tears from my eyes. "Why can't my father be rich and own five hundred acres of land and raise cattle and sheep and fine horses? Why can't my father have tenants to raise his tobacco, corn, potatoes, and wheat? Then he could buy me the latest riding skirts from Ohio. And he could have bought me a brown leather saddle with a red plush seat!"

"What's the matter, Maudie?" Mom asked me soon as I reached our shack.

"There's nothing wrong with me," I said, rushing upstairs.

"I thought you'd been crying," Mom said.

I didn't answer her. I looked into the mirror in my room upstairs. My eyes were red. My face looked broken. From my upstairs window I looked down Lost Creek valley—down the winding road that wound under the sycamore trees, the water birches, and elms that grew along the creek banks. There I saw two horses racing side by side—down the sun-dried yellow road where the thin spring leaves rustled on the trees. The riders were Larry and Millie.

"I won't cry," I said to myself, getting mad all of a sudden. "It will please Millie too well. I'll never shed another tear for her. I'll whip her at her own game. I'll beat her yet. Never will I run up these stairs again to cry like a calf. Mom will never ask me again if I've been crying; she'll be asking me why I come home from church laughing."

"I'll have new clothes," I said, smiling, as I picked up a catalogue. "I'll never buy any more clothes from Larry Currie's store. He'll not know where I get my clothes. I'll dress better than Millie Spens, though I don't have a fine horse to ride and a beautiful saddle to sit on. I'll make all the young men on Lost Creek look at me twice."

I had an idea as I fondled the catalogue. I'd order me some clothes. I'd find a girl in the catalogue that I wanted to look like; then I'd order the clothes that she was wearing. "I'll hunt a pretty girl in the catalogue," I said to myself. Then I laughed as I turned the pages looking for the girl that I wanted to look like. I turned over many pages before I found the right one. She was beautiful—just the girl I wanted to look like—and she was the girl that I would look like.

"Larry Currie, when you see me looking like this girl, you'll turn your head to look at me twice," I said. "Larry Currie, she's wearing prettier clothes than you keep in your store. Millie Spens won't be wearing that diamond long."

But I stopped smiling when I thought about the money. How would I get the money? Pa couldn't let me have it. He had seven mouths to feed and seven bodies to clothe. He had to give Archie Spens half of everything we raised. I couldn't sell things at Larry Currie's store. He'd know if I sold him young fryers, eggs, and butter that I was doing it for a purpose! But it came to me. I could trade these things to Huckster Charlie Hunt. He came every Friday so he could gather his produce and sell it in Ashland on Saturday. He came to our house. I knew that he would help me. I'd ridden so many times with him from school in years past in the huckster wagon.

Friday morning I'd gathered a basket of eggs for him. I met him down the road a mile from our house. And then I told him my secret.

"I'll hep ya, Maudie," he said. "I'll hep ye to look jist like that gal in the catalogue. I can git ye that fine dress, that very hat, and them slippers that she has on."

"You'll certainly be doing me a favor," I told him as he put my eggs into a crate on his wagon. "I'll pay you along as I can," I told him. "Some of our produce will go to you instead of Larry Currie's General Merchandise Store."

Huckster Charlie Hunt was pleased when I told him he'd get part of our produce. He knew that Pa had been trading our produce at Larry Currie's Store for groceries and spices. He took the page that I'd torn from the catalogue—the picture of the girl that would take Larry Currie from Millie Spens. He laughed as he folded it up and put it in his watch pocket.

"I'll fetch ye a purty spring outfit," he said, slapping his horses with the lines, driving up the winding, yellow clay road.

I could barely wait for next Friday to come. I hunted more eggs and heard Pa grumbling about our hens being on a strike. I managed to hide a few pounds of butter for Huckster Charlie. Everything I managed to get didn't go to Larry Currie's General Merchandise Store to help Larry buy diamond rings for Millie. And it pleased me to slip out every egg and every pound of butter I could for Huckster Charlie.

When Charlie came that Friday, he brought me a dress, slippers, and a hat. I didn't unwrap them. I gave him twelve dozens of eggs and five pounds of butter on my account. My outfit came to sixteen dollars. It would take me a long time to pay him, but he knew that I would. So he gave me a receipt for all I had paid him. And he gave me the page I'd torn from the catalogue.

"Now if ye don't look blank like this girl, only a lot purtier," he said, "ye fetch this stuff back and I'll get ye another outfit."

"All right, Huckster Charlie," I said as I ran up the path to the house with my bundle under my arm. I could hardly wait until I got to my room upstairs. I heard Huckster Charlie's huckster-wagon bell tinkling at the next Lost Creek farmhouse when I slipped through the front room and upstairs to my room.

I put on my silk stockings first. And they felt like butterflies' wings against my brown sun-tanned legs. Then I put on my new slippers. They felt tight on my feet, but they made my feet look so much smaller—just like the girl's feet in the catalogue. Then I tried to put on my skirt. But it wouldn't fit over my petticoats. So I had to take one off. Then my skirt fit. I put on my light green taffeta blouse. And I tied my yellow and green plaid sash around me in different ways. I tied it with a big bow in the back, for I still thought the skirt was a little tight. But I thought it looked fine.

I stood before the mirror and worked on my hair until my arms and back ached, but I couldn't make it look like the girl's in the catalogue. Then I got another idea. I stooped over and brushed all my hair over my face; then I tied a ribbon around my head. I combed the front part of my hair back over the ribbon; it had a pompadour effect. It was easy then to twist the back of my hair into a knot. Now, when I put my hat on, I looked like the girl in the catalogue, for my hat, like hers, was not bigger than a saucer and had a bunch of red roses on it and two velvet streamers that tied under my chin.

Saturday, every time I could slip away from my mother and sisters,

I ran upstairs and practiced putting my clothes on. Then I would look at the girl in the catalogue. I wondered how she would walk and talk. I wanted to be like her. I practiced walking across my room in my new shoes. I talked to myself in the mirror. I looked like a different person. I talked to myself in the mirror so I would know just how I looked when I talked to the Lost Creek people at church.

I worked so hard at all this that on Sunday morning, when I dressed, I felt at ease in my new clothes. I felt they were a part of me, that I had always worn this kind of clothes. Before I left the shack, I took a last look at the girl in the catalogue, then I looked at myself in the mirror.

I hurried down the patch to the Lost Creek road. I was alone, but behind me I heard voices speaking about the girl ahead. They were wondering who I was. I hurried to the Lost Creek Church House, and crossed the churchyard, where many young men were standing. I didn't know whether they knew me or not. They just stood and looked at me and I heard them saying soon as I entered the church house that I was "beautiful." I took my seat by the window while everybody, even Brother Sizemore, stared at me.

Before church services had begun, I saw two sweat-damp, foam-flecked horses dash into the churchyard. Larry dismounted his horse and helped Millie from hers. While Larry tied the horses to the low-hanging branches of an oak tree, the same branches where they had tied them last Sunday, Millie stepped from her riding skirt.

Not knowing who I was, they sat down on the seat in front of me. Larry glanced around and saw me—his eyes were slow to leave. He turned his head slowly, and then Millie looked around to see why Larry looked so long. Millie looked at me quickly and then she looked away. Larry turned to look at me again—I don't believe he knew me. Larry looked at the young men over the church house who were looking at me. Then he would look around to see if I was looking at them. Millie would look at Larry—her face was a little stern as she watched Larry move nervously in his seat. He would rub his face with his hands and then he would twirl his hat around and around. He would pull his watch out and look at it all the time church was going on. He even pulled his fountain pen from his pocket and screwed the top off and on again until I thought he would wear it out.

When church was over, I started walking slowly toward the door. Larry followed me out of the house as other young men stood along the aisles looking at me. I felt as I had never felt before. I wondered why Larry was following me before the whole church crowd. I wondered if Millie knew what he was doing—Millie, whose face must have been getting red as she talked to her mother's first cousin. Maybe she didn't want to see what was going on. And I wondered if she put the white glove on again.

"Maudie Doore, is that you?" I heard Larry ask as he followed me into the churchyard.

"It is," I said as I kept walking like I thought the girl in the catalogue would walk.

"You're beautiful, Maudie," he said. "I didn't know you were so pretty!"

I didn't answer.

"Today will be a great day at Upper Lost Creek," he said. "I wonder if you would like to go with me to the baptizing there?"

"Why, yes, I think I would," I said softly.

"Wait here, until I get my horse," he said quickly.

Soon we were walking up the Lost Creek road side by side. Larry was leading his horse.

"Would you like for me to bring along a horse for you to ride next Sunday?" Larry asked.

"Well, no, I'd rather walk," I said shyly, remembering the girl in the catalogue and my tight skirt.

"Catalogue Girl" was first published in *Commonweal,* Vol. 40 (May 5, 1944), pp. 57-60. It has been reprinted in J.M. Ross and Blanche J. Thompson, editors, *Adventures In Reading* (New York, Harcourt, Brace, 1947), pp. 50-54.

Jesse Stuart revisits a schoolhouse where he once taught and finds it being used as a barn — circa 1950. (Photo by Thomas V. Miller, Jr. — the Louisville Courier-Journal)

Clothes Make the Man

"I'm gettin' tired of this quiet life," Eif Stone said and sank his ax into the hickory. "I'm tired playin' stud poker and strip poker, too. Burgis, I'm nearly goin' crazy here. We've worked here since last September and it's March now and nothin' excitin' has happened."

While Eif talked to me he left his double-bitted ax stuck in the tree with his big hand on the handle. Sweat ran down his face and his long beard was wet as August cornsilks after rain. His hair came down to the middle of his red neck. His boots were scarred by greenbriar scratches.

"I'd like to have a little fun myself, Eif," I said. I looked down the mountain at the highway that followed the Sandy River. "People down there in those cars must be having a good time."

Eif looked over the side of the mountain at the cars. He wiped the sweat from his beard with his big hand and slung it off on the dead brown leaves while he grinned at me with devilment in his steel-blue eyes.

"They're havin' a good time down there, shore enough," he said. "Wonder if they've ever seen a wild man in these parts?"

"Only the pictures of 'em in story books," I said.

"They're a-goin' to see a real live one in a few minutes," he said.

Eif began pulling off his checkered shirt. He threw it on a sawlog we'd just cut. Then he pulled his undershirt over his head.

"What are you doin' Eif?"

"I'm goin' to start something," he said.

Eif pulled off his scarred boots while the cold March wind whistled around us, drying the sweat on my face. Eif didn't mind this wintry wind for he was as wooly over the back and arms as a rabbit and his chest was woollier than a billy goat's chin whiskers.

"Are you goin' to take all your clothes off?"

"You happy tootin'," he replied. "If I'm goin' to be a wild man, I aim to be a real one."

"You're not goin' barefooted, are you?"

"You know a wild man wouldn't have shoes on his feet!"

Eif pulled off his drawers and his socks and stood on the mountaintop and beat his chest with his big fireshovel hands. He let out a yell that echoed from the distant mountain rocks across the valley. He looked like a wild man.

"Aren't you cold?"

"A wild man never gets cold."

"Won't your feet be too tender to walk over them briars and rocks?"

"The bottoms of my feet air too thick for a thorn to puncture!"

Eif practiced beating his chest and letting out his wild screams until I thought the sawmill crew would hear us. They were working in the valley below. Eif's screams sounded like a lonesome wildcat among the mountain cliffs. And he really looked wild. The calves of his muscular legs were like gnarled tree roots, his long feet were like sled runners, and his ankles and big toes were wooly. I had seen many lumberjacks stripped, but I'd never seen one as wooly as Eif.

"Wait right here for me, Burgis," he said. "I aim to go out yander where we found that dead animal and pick up one of his bleached bones that's got a hoof on it. I'll put the bone across my shoulder and take off over the mountain close enough to the highway to be seen but not close enough to be shot with a pistol. I aim to let out a half dozen screams, thump my chest and wave this bone with the cloven hoof. Then, I'll take back up the mountain. I'll skeer the wits outten 'em."

Then, Eif took off with the bone across his shoulder. The long hair on his head floated on the wind as he went over the brush and briars like a scared red fox. I climbed up on a cliff, for I wanted to see Eif when he got close to the highway. Everything was leafless now but the pines and cedars, and a few tough-butted white oaks.

Eif was a scary sight as he leaped down the mountain toward the highway. I watched him as he got closer to the road. He held the legbone across his shoulder with one hand and parted the brush and briars with the other. He had gone so far down the mountain now he looked like a two-legged varmint. Then he stopped, dropped his bone and beat his chest. I heard him give his hellacious wildcat squalls. After the squalls, he picked up the bone and ran along above the highway.

I watched the cars down there pick up speed. One was making 90 miles an hour in the direction of Greenwood. Then one stopped and a man jumped out and emptied his pistol. I was worried about Eif for he fired so fast I couldn't count the times. More cars raced on at full speed, and another stopped and a man jumped from it and fired a pistol. Eif was a safe distance from them now, climbing the mountain with the white bone across the shoulder. They reloaded and kept shooting, and then a lot of other guns went off. There were so many I wondered how many men in these parts didn't tote firearms. Two cars raced back toward Greenwood.

While they kept on shooting from the highway, Eif let out more wildcat squalls from the top of a cliff halfway up the mountain. Then he jumped down, with his bone over his shoulder, and climbed the mountain faster than a possum.

When he reached me, each nostril was letting out a white cloud bigger than you'd see escaping from the pistons of our overworked sawmill engine. Sweat was dripping from his billy-goat beard and his crab-grass eyebrows. His long hair was wet and flat on his head. His tongue hung out over his beardy lips and a little blood was oozing from briar scratches on his ankles.

"It's a wonder to me you didn't get plugged," I said. "You have started something."

"I hope so," he grunted.

"While you put your clothes on, I'll bury this bone under the leaves," I said. "Somebody might snoop around here."

"But I'll need it again," he said.

Soon we were pulling our sharp-toothed saw through a shellbarked hickory. We had just got the tree down when we heard the noises of men coming up the side of the mountain in our direction.

"You're shore you got that bone kivered in the leaves?"

"Yes, I am."

We started trimming the big tree. Eif was going up one side and I was going up the other with our double-bitted axes. We hadn't reached the top, when Sheriff Bradley topped the mountain with seven men. Pistols were swinging on their hips in leather holsters. They had long guns, too, Winchesters, and a high-powered rifle.

"You ain't seen a wild man here, have you, boys?" Sheriff Bradley asked, gasping for breath.

"Nope, we ain't," Eif grunted back.

"Who saw a wild man?" I asked.

Sheriff Bradley leaned on a stump, still gasping. He was big in the middle and little on each end. He wore a broad leather belt around his stomach. His soft cheeks were as pink as peach petals.

"Plenty of people saw 'im along the highway," Sheriff grunted.

"He was carryin' a big white bone over his shoulder," said a lean, two-pistoled deputy.

"He made an awful racket," another one said.

"I heard a hellacious racket over on the other side of the mountain a while ago," I said.

"That was him," the Sheriff muttered. "Several men shot at him. Said they couldn't drap 'im. Said a bullet didn't faze 'im. A lot o' women-folks fainted in the backseats of the cars. They're in Greenwood now getting' treatment for shock at Doc Madden's office."

"He was naked as a picked chicken," said a heavy, Winchester-carrying deputy. "Said he beat his chest and squalled like a panther, then gnawed on a big bone he was a-carryin'."

"Didn't he come this way?" Sheriff Bradley asked.

"I ain't seen no man on this mountain but Burgis, there," Eif said as he leaned on his ax handle. "If he'd a-come this way, I'd been a-goin' yan way. You won't ever see me where there's a wild man. I just don't believe it!"

"Too many reliable people with good eyes seen 'im," Sheriff Bradley said. "They stopped their cars and shot at 'im. He came purt nigh down into the highway with that big bone. Guess he'd a-crossed the highway if Ugly Bird Skinner hadn't emptied his .38 special at 'im. Said he looked more like a varmint than a man."

"Do I look like a varmint, Sheriff?" Eif asked.

"Oh, no, Eif Stone," Sheriff Bradley groaned. "That wild man was as hairy as a goat. He could've picked you up and tore you into little pieces."

"Wild man," Eif laughed.

"Jist tellin' you boys," said the deputy with the rifle, "You'd better carry yer guns. He come this way."

"That's what I'm goin' to do," I said, shaking some. I was getting cold again since I'd stopped chopping. "I'll bet that fellow is living over there under one of the cliffs."

"I told the boys he was a-headin' this way," Sheriff Bradley said. "Livin' offen the people's cattle, sheep and hogs. We come this way when we heard choppin'. We thought you might've seen 'im."

"Nope, not us, Sheriff," Eif said. "Not unless I'm that wild man!"

"You'll never be the kind of man they said he was, Eif Stone," Sheriff Bradley said, then he led his posse up the mountain toward the cliffs.

"Stirred up, ain't they?" Eif whispered. "What about a feller without clothes and the same feller with clothes? Clothes can sure make a man."

We finished our day's work and went down to our shanty. We washed our beardy faces, ate our suppers and then we joined in a game of stud poker. Eif was happier than I'd ever seen him. Everybody was talking about the wild man. Eif told everybody he was the wild man. They told Eif to quit his kidding. Tobbie Bostick, our lumber salesman who was in Greenwood when the reports came to the Sheriff, said people in town were so scared they were afraid to go down the streets alone.

Next day we were back on the job. Eif and I had just got our lunch of cold beans, fried potatoes, and cornbread washed down with cold black coffee when Bossman Oliver Spriggs came up the hills with a newspaper. There was a headline on the front page about a wild man, and a picture of a man from the waist up carrying a bone over his shoulder.

"Let me see that picture, Boss," Eif said.

Bossman Oliver handed the paper to Eif.

"That picture doesn't look any more like a varmint than you, Eif," I said as I looked at the head and shoulders. "That's not your mouth and eyes. And you have more hair on your chest than this man has. It's not a good picture of you, Eif."

"First time I ever got my picture in the paper and they had to mess me up," Eif said, grinning. "Wonder how they could take a picture of me when I was a runnin' like a fox?"

"Don't be a fool, Eif," Bossman Oliver said. "Some artist sketched the picture for the newspaper when a man described him to the artist."

"I looked wilder than that without my clothes," Eif said, grinning. "See, Boss, the fellers in the shanty don't know this because I've never lost a-playin' strip poker."

"If I'd a-thought you'd acted a fool like this," Bossman Oliver gobbled like a turkey, "I'd never brought the paper up here. Eif, you're trying to make us think the wild man was you. But you'll never be the man people saw yesterday. He's loose on this mountain and I want all of you to wear your hardware from now on. If you can't capture 'im alive, plug 'im. Don't let 'im get away."

"I'd like to keep this paper, Boss," I said. "I'd like to show it to all the boys tonight so they'll know what he looks like."

"All right, Burgis, you're talking with some sense," he said.

He left the paper and went on about his duties of overseeing our work. Eif and I cut trees all day and went home to our shanty that night. All the talk after supper when we played stud poker and mumblepeg was about the wild man. When Eif and I went to bed we like to laughed our heads off.

Next day Bossman Oliver brought the paper up where we were working.

"Stop your sawin' boys, and look," he said, walking up. "That wild man turned up in Greenwood last night."

There was the same picture again with another headliner. The paper stated Mrs. Claradore Sizemore had gone out at daylight to feed her chickens and a man who looked like an animal jumped from a flower bed toward her. Said she screamed and ran toward the house, fell in at the door and fainted. Said her husband, Wordly Sizemore, jumped from bed when he heard her fall in a faint. Soon as she regained consciousness, she told him what had happened. He grabbed his shotgun but it was too late to apprehend the assailant.

"I really started something," Eif said proudly. "But I wasn't down there last night skeerin' Claradore and Wordly."

Bossman Oliver gave Eif a hard look and passed me the paper.

"You'd better stop loose talk before you're arrested for being off in the head," he warned Eif. "I don't want to lose a good man with an ax."

Bossman Oliver walked off toward the sawmill.

Saturday, Bossman Oliver Spriggs came with another paper. This time the wild man had been seen gathering eggs in a chicken house below Greenwood. The paper stated Icky Darlington had filled him full of buckshot as he made for the foothills. Said he jumped high and let out a wild scream when Icky shot, but that he held onto his eggs.

"Burgis, you bunk with me," Eif said. "You know I was home in bed."

We didn't get the Sunday paper but Bossman Oliver said there was another story about his doings. On Monday there was a short piece in the paper asking why the dangerous wild man had not been captured.

Tuesday's paper stated he had been seen at midnight on Main Street in Greenwood. Marshal Fly Butterfield had emptied his pistol at him, but yet, wounded, he had managed to escape.

"Poor marksmanship," Eif said, laughing loudly. "Greenwood needs a better marshal. But I wasn't there. I was in bed early after I helped Burgis cut the big beeches."

Wednesday, another woman who was out gathering eggs from a hayloft in the outskirts of Greenwood saw this wild man pilfering around the barn. She didn't faint but she screamed until all the people in the neighborhood heard her and came running. But the wild man ducked among the willows along Cedar Creek. Next day Silas MacMurray's boy, Hester, found his big barefoot track on the sand. He said the print was half as long as a sled runner and as broad as a crosstie.

A week passed and there wasn't anything in the paper about the wild man. Oliver didn't come to visit us. We wondered what had happened to him since the excitement was dying down.

"That wild man ought to stir again," Eif said. "This place is dead. No excitement now. Stud poker is still dull and mumblepeg is terrible."

Eif waited three weeks more until the trees were beginning to leaf.

"It's a good time to visit that road again before the timber gets too green," Eif told me.

Eif pulled off his clothes and boots and threw them in a pile beside a log. He got the bone from under the leaves, then he let out a hellacious wildcat scream and took off over the mountain. Eif made for the highway yelling as he leaped. I saw a car turn and speed back toward Greenwood. Then another car turned. One car stopped and I heard a pistol bark. I heard Eif yell as he started back up the mountain.

Eif didn't get back my way. So I hid his clothes under the leaves and started running toward the cliffs where the tall poplars grew. I saw men coming up the mountain. Sheriff Bradley was too fat to lead his armed deputies. He followed, shouting orders.

"Ketch 'im alive, boys," he panted. "We'll sell 'im to a circus for a fortune—enough to pay off Greenwood County's bonded indebtedness."

"Eif's gone," I thought. "They've got 'im headed up the gorge."

I saw Eif stand with both hands up. He didn't have the bone now, for the men closed in from all sides.

"Did you see 'im?" Eif yelled.

"See who?" Sheriff Bradley asked.

"That damned wild man," he panted. "He frailed me over the head with a big bone and took my clothes. I ain't runnin' from nobody. You know I'm not the man they been a-shootin' at in Greenwood."

"Then, where is he?" Sheriff Bradley asked as he waddled up the mountain pulling himself along by holding to the trees. "Where?"

"Don't ask me," Eif said. "I'd like to know myself. See if Burgis is safe."

"I'm safe, Eif," I yelled. "I dodged him."

"Hurry to the cliffs," Sheriff Bradley told his deputies. "Move on and stop 'im there! If you don't see 'im, scour every cliff!"

"Give me some clothes, fellers," Eif said. "I'm cold and I want to hide my nakedness!"

"I'd think you would," Sheriff Bradley said. "You're a woolier sight than that wild man is reported to be! You might even make a good wild man!"

Sheriff Bradley gave Eif one of the extra shirts he was wearing. One of the deputies had on an extra pair of pants. He took them off for Eif. Then, Sheriff Bradley and the six deputies hurried on to the cliffs.

I explained to Bossman Oliver what had happened to Eif and we took him off the mountain barefooted, in borrowed pants and shirt to where Doc Madden would treat him for shock.

Next day the *Greenwood Gazett* had Eif's picture on the front page with a long story about how the wild man had struck him over the head with a bone and escaped with his clothes. The paper stated that lumberjack Eif Stone would recover but had been badly mauled. It also stated that I, Burgis Raffitt, had escaped by hiding in a cliff.

"A man about has to wear clothes in this modern world," Eif said.

Eif was laid up two weeks which each day I took him a poultice of sweet milk and wild touch-me-nots and rubbed it over him to kill the poison he'd got from the vines on the slopes that touched most of his naked body when he ran through them.

All the lumberjacks laughed when they read the paper.

"I warned 'im," our Bossman Oliver Spriggs told the sawmill men and the lumberjacks. "Eif Stone was a smart alect with a lot of loose talk coming from his big trap. He wouldn't heed my advice. I warned all of you to carry your shooting hardware! Now you see who was right!"

Bossman Oliver didn't say anything more, our laughing would have drowned him out.

"Clothes Make The Man" was first published in *Story*, Vol. 33 (1960), pp. 131-138. It has been reprinted in *Modern Short Stories From Story Magazine* (New York, Grosset's Universal Library, 1960), pp. 131-138, and *Story Jubilee* (Garden City, New York, Doubleday, 1965) pp. 524-531. Woodbridge's *Jesse And Jane Stuart A Bibliography* lists four additional reprintings of the story, including Kenzo Soneda and Norio Shimamura, editors, *The Short Stories* (Tokyo, Aratake Shuppan, 1974), pp. 3-8. Stuart included this story in his unpublished manuscript, *These Are My Best—Twenty-five Short Stories Selected From Five Hundred Published Stories And MSS*—edited and typed January 1975, and his unpublished manuscript, *Twenty-five Tall Stories Selected From 461 Published Stories And Fifty Manuscripts*, circa 1975 (both from the Jesse Stuart Foundation Collection, Ashland, Kentucky).

The Cousins

Vaida laid her crutch beside the antique base rocker. She sat down and waited for them to come back. She knew they would be back as soon as the funeral service was over. She wondered if any of the distant cousins would follow the hearse that carried Alvie Parkinson to the cemetery. She would know in a little while, for the church was not far away. The funeral began promptly at two o'clock. She knew the service would be short. If they stayed only for the funeral, they would be back in an hour. If they followed the hearse to Pinecrest, that would take about another hour.

She had dusted and cleaned the living room. No one had offered to take her to Alvie Parkinson's funeral services. She had not cared to go anyway. Not the way the living room looked after all his first, second, third, and fourth cousins had come to pay their last respects to this deceased relative. It wouldn't have been so bad if they had cleaned the dirt from their shoes, she thought. For they had left little clumps of yellow dirt and little pockets of sand on the floors she had to sit down to scrub, polish, and wax. She was a good housekeeper—she knew that. She was a good housekeeper even if she wore a steel brace on a leg withered from birth and this leg could be used only by the aid of her crutch. She couldn't bend her leg, for the brace extended above the knee. That's why she had to sit down when she scrubbed, waxed, and polished a floor. But in the eight months she had been Alvie Parkinson's housekeeper, she had kept the big house clean. Mr. Parkinson had told her that.

During the first seven months and three weeks she had stayed with Mr. Parkinson, she had not heard of his cousins. Not one of them had come to visit him. Not until the day he had a stroke and the news got into the paper did anyone come. Then, a Mr. and Mrs. Burt Howerton came. They had asked her how Cousin Alvie was getting along. Vaida took them to his room, but Alvie didn't recognize them then. Mrs.

Howerton had brought along with her a pint jar of strawberry preserves for her cousin Alvie. He never knew anything about the jar of
preserves or her being there. For he was semiconscious then. The only
person he knew was Vaida. Half of the time he didn't know her. When
he didn't know her, and his eyes were half-closed, he would mumble
her name. He would tell her not to let anybody take him to the hospital. That was why she had protested when the local doctor, Dr. Harry
Evans, had suggested at first that he be sent to the hospital. Then, Dr.
Evans shrugged his shoulders and said he didn't have much of a chance
to live since he was ninety. He said his age was against him and it was
only a matter of time.

When this news was spread over Hampton, more cousins came.
Men and women in their sixties and seventies came and claimed to be
Alvie Parkinson's first cousins. Those in their forties and fifties claimed
to be his second cousins. Those in their thirties claimed to be his third
cousins. Many in their twenties claimed to be his fourth cousins. Vaida
knew that more than fifty of these cousins had come. Only two, Mr.
and Mrs. Howerton, had come before his death and had brought the
preserves. The others had come after his death. One of them, a Vernon
Seymoure, had made arrangements about his burial. Vaida couldn't
say anything. She was not related to Alvie Parkinson. She knew that.
She didn't claim to be.

She had known Alvie Parkinson all of her life. She was now forty-
six years old. But she hadn't known him very well. Not anybody had
known him very well. She remembered Mrs. Parkinson, too. She had
passed away about ten years ago. Alvie Parkinson had lived alone since
then. He had never had a housekeeper. He had done his own cooking.
Occasionally, he had eaten at the local restaurant. He had lived a se-
cluded life. Vaida had never thought much about him or how he had
lived until her father died. She had cared for her father in his old days,
the same as she had cared for Alvie Parkinson. Her father was an invalid many years, and, at his death, their property was sold to pay their
debts. When Vaida was left without a home, her first thought was to
go see Alvie Parkinson. For Alvie Parkinson and her father were about

the same age and she had cared for her father until the last. She knew that she could take care of Mr. Parkinson. She knew that she could, and by doing this she would have a home for herself as long as he lived. Alvie Parkinson had accepted her gladly.

It had taken her two months to get the house cleaned the way she wanted it. Alvie Parkinson liked the way she had put his home in order. The only thing he had disagreed with her about was the wasteful way he claimed she prepared food. When she had asked him to explain, he showed her what he meant. He had been watching her fry eggs. He suggested that when she broke an egg and poured it into the skillet she take her index finger and run around inside the eggshell and get more of the white of the egg and drop it also into the skillet. He said that his wife had always done this and that there wasn't any use of wasting this part of the egg. Then, she suggested to him that they boil the eggs and they could peel off the thin shell and get all there was in the egg. He thought this was a smart idea and from this time on, he thought of her as a thrifty person and never again questioned her.

As she sat facing the ancient Seth Thomas clock on the mantel, she thought of many things that had happened in the eight months she had lived there. It was now two-thirty and the clock kept ticking the time away in mournful tones. They were mournful tones to her. For she even wondered where she would go now? She didn't want to go to the County Home. That was the only place left that she could think of. Alvie Parkinson hadn't paid her anything to stay with him. She had expected nothing but a home, a bed, and her food. That was all she had asked. She knew that due to her crippled leg and her nearsightedness she couldn't have found another place to stay. People would look at her. That was enough. She knew they thought someone should be taking care of her.

Vaida knew she could take care of a house, though she had to work slowly. She knew that she could keep a house in tiptop shape. She knew she had done it for her father from the time she was sixteen, except the eight months she had been with Mr. Parkinson. She knew that it was easy enough if she worked twice as long as the average woman and that it wasn't too hard unless people like Alvie Parkinson's cousins came rushing in all of a sudden and forgot to clean their feet. That was bad on nice floors. That made a lot of extra work too. They would be back, she knew, and forget to clean their feet and mess the house again. She knew she didn't have any lease on the house and she would soon be leaving, but she wanted the house to be clean when she left. That would give her something to remember. Her mind would not be disturbed after she had gone.

She looked again at the Seth Thomas. It was fifteen 'til three. Just a few more minutes and all the cousins would be back. They would tramp over her floors. They would ask her questions. They would be ransacking everything. It worried her to think about them. She knew why they would be back. She had never asked Mr. Parkinson for anything except her food, a bed, a roof, and a fire to keep her warm. She had paid for these things, she knew, in her service to Mr. Parkinson. Not one of these cousins had ever come about and offered to do anything until now. And they were coming back for something else.

She remembered that it was on this very day, just one week ago, when she heard Mr. Parkinson fall on his upstairs bedroom floor. She had tried to get him to room downstairs but he wouldn't do it. He wouldn't change now, he had told her once, since he had lived in this room for sixty-five years. When she heard him fall, she sat down on the stairs and scooted up backwards in a hurry, carrying her crutch in her hand. She had managed, somehow, to get him upon the bed. Then she had phoned for Doctor Evans. Dr. Evans came and said he had had a stroke and wanted to send him to the hospital. It was then that Mr. Parkinson mumbled half-consciously for her not to let him be sent to the hospital.

Vaida wouldn't let him go to the hospital because he had begged her not to let anyone send him. Vaida waited on him like she had her invalid father. She knew she was just about as good as a nurse, since she had had so much practical experience. She remembered now with satisfaction how she had made Alvie Parkinson's last days as comfortable, she thought, as they could be made.

Then she heard many footsteps coming up the walk. She looked at the clock. It was ten minutes until three. They hadn't been gone an hour. She lifted her crutch from beside the rocker. She got up and walked to the window. There were at least thirty of them. They were not talking much to each other. For each cousin had seemed to her to be a world unto himself. Mr. and Mrs. Burt Howerton were in front. This was not all of them, she knew. There had been more in this house to pay respects to Cousin Alvie. That was, of course, after he had passed on. While she stood at the window another car pulled up, then, another, and, still a third one. She hadn't missed her guess. Not any of them had followed the hearse to Pinecrest on the outskirts of Hampton. Each cousin had returned. Though she could be fooled, it seemed to her that each cousin was trying to get to the house first.

Burt Howerton pounded the door hard with his knuckles. She opened the door, and he didn't bother to clean his feet. Mrs. Howerton didn't either. They came in as if they had already inherited the house. For Vaida noticed Mrs. Howerton, who had not yet spoken to her, start looking at the antique furniture, even the old Seth Thomas clock. But they hadn't more than come into the house until the small army of cousins, with hungry looks on their faces, surged in behind them. They did remove their hats, all but one, who claimed to be a fourth cousin. He kept his hat on. He was Mort Simpson. Vaida had known him all her life. This was the first time she had ever known that he was related to the deceased man who hadn't yet reached his final resting place.

"What do you know about Cousin Alvie's personal effects?" Burt Howerton asked Vaida gruffly.

"Not anything," she said.

"Where is his pocketbook?" Burt asked, while others stood silently and listened.

"I don't know," she said.

"You ought to know," Mrs. Howerton said.

"Why had I ought to know?" Vaida asked. "I don't know anything about his business."

"What did you come here for then?" Mrs. Howerton snapped.

"For a home," she answered quickly.

"You can tell that to the courts if anything around here is missing," Burt Howerton said.

"Just a minute, Burt Howerton," said a tall well-dressed man. "I am John Parkinson from Dartmouth. I am a first cousin to Alvie Parkinson and blood kin. You're not taking over everything around here. Remember," he said, as he pointed a trembling index finger under Burt's nose, "that others will have something to say around here. Others will share. This estate will not fall wholly into your hands!"

Then a quarrel started that made Vaida tremble. She made her way through the crowded room to the base rocker where she laid her crutch down beside it. Then she sat down. Everybody began to quarrel. Each person tried to tell how he was related to Alvie Parkinson. Two of the cousins started to strike at each other and John Parkinson got between them.

"Remember, about this time they are burying Cousin Alvie," John said. "Stay your blows until he is under the ground. It looks bad to be fighting now."

The men stood apart, but they looked fiercely at each other. Still the quarrel went on. Every person was a little separate world of his own in this house. Everybody had come for his-all first; if not his-all, he would be content with his part. They discussed the law. They discussed, after they had explained their kinship to the deceased man, how first, second, third, and fourth cousins would share the estate.

"Didn't Mr. Parkinson leave a will to anybody?" Vaida asked.

"That doesn't concern you," Mrs. Howerton told her.

"No, he didn't, Miss," John Parkinson spoke to Vaida with some respect. "I talked to his lawyer, Fred Smith, yesterday. He told me Cousin Alvie always talked about making a will and giving everything he possessed to his only living niece, a Mrs. David Newberry of Detroit. But he never made that will!"

"How did you know?" Burt Howerton asked.

"I got her yesterday on the phone," John Parkinson said. "She said she had never heard from him in her life, and she didn't know anything about his will being made to her."

She will be here, too, Vaida thought.

"You're certainly interested," Burt said to John.

"I certainly am," he replied. "I happen to know Cousin Alvie had his share of worldly goods!"

And he's not buried yet, Vaida thought, as she looked at the clock.

Vaida remembered Mr. Parkinson with sympathy. Thoughts raced through her mind about the quietness of the house when she had first come to live in the house. Now she thought about how he had told her to save more of the whites of the eggs. And for what? she thought. For this? She wondered, as she watched his cousins pointing accusing fingers at each other. She listened to them quarrel as she had never heard people quarrel before. She could not believe this if it were told to her. But she was listening with her own ears. There were curses in this house now, where only a few days ago, soft words were spoken and life had gone on quietly for the two of them.

After they had grown tired of quarreling among themselves about who shared Cousin Alvie's estate, they agreed to stop and to reason it out. John Parkinson took charge of the meeting. They sat in chairs, on the stairsteps, and on the floor while John presided. They agreed first to establish under oath their kinship to the deceased man. When they agreed to this, a tall man and his wife picked up their coats and hats and left the house. They slipped out quietly. They had never made known their names, nor had they done any quarreling.

Then they decided to let each one, according to the law and according to his closeness of kinship, share in the estate. Vaida sat among them and listened to all their proceedings and the agreements they made among themselves. On each point suggested, there was much argument. Everybody had to have his say. Everybody was excited. Many were mad. Everybody was a little world unto himself. And each little world wanted to guard carefully what might be his possessions. There were about fifty little worlds in this large living room.

After they had made these agreements, they agreed among themselves to look around and see what valuable possessions Alvie

Parkinson had left in the house.

"We must know what is here before we leave," Mrs. Howerton said, as she looked at Vaida suspiciously. "We are not sure about the pilfering that has already been done here."

"You don't mean to say I've ransacked this house?" Vaida asked.

"I mean the doors of this house will be closed before we leave here tonight," Mrs. Howerton said.

"But where will I go?" Vaida asked.

"That will be up to you," Mrs. Howerton replied.

"Now, where's the pocketbook, Miss?" Burt asked Vaida. "We're ready to look into some of Cousin Alvie's personal effects."

"I don't know about his pocketbook," she said. "I'll declare I don't know about it. I wasn't interested in his pocketbook."

"Come, come now," Burt spoke, as if she were hiding it someplace.

"Where's his old clothes?" John Parkinson asked.

"I put them in the upstairs clothespress," Vaida told him.

"Then I will get them," Burt said.

"Just a minute, Burt," Vernon Seymoure said. "I'll go with you."

When Burt went upstairs, he was followed by eight or ten others. They wanted to be sure he didn't get away with more than rightfully belonged to him. While they were gone upstairs, the others waited in silence until Burt came downstairs carrying the old clothes.

"The pocketbook is in his pocket," Burt said, looking at Vaida. "There'd better be money in it too. Cousin Alvie was never without money on his person."

When Burt took the pocketbook from his pants pocket, the cousins formed a circle around him. They watched him with eager eyes as he brought the big leather billfold out. When he opened it, they crowded closer so they could see its contents. They watched him bring out, one at a time, eleven one dollar bills. Then, everybody looked at each other with the mingled looks of surprise and disappointment written across his suspicious face.

"Let me look at his clothes," Mrs. Howerton said. "I know Cousin

Alvie always carried more money than that."

Mrs. Howerton got down on her knees inside the circle. She ran her hand into each pocket. Since Burt had brought Cousin Alvie's pants, underwear, shirt, and socks down together, clothes he had last worn before his stroke, Mrs. Howerton turned the socks wrong side out. Then she came to the soiled long white underwear. She stretched it out on the floor and patted it with her hand.

"Ah, here's something," she said.

Then she turned it wrong side out. There was a patch sewn on the inside. She ripped the patch off and everybody's face became alive with excitement. A small bundle of tens and twenties was packed securely where he had sat on it. She counted, while everybody watched, three hundred sixty dollars.

"I knew he had more than eleven dollars," Mrs. Howerton beamed.

"But you see I hadn't bothered his money," Vaida said.

Mrs. Howerton didn't answer Vaida.

"Where's his trunk?" Burt asked Vaida.

"You ought to know," Vaida said. "You're his cousin."

"Where's that trunk?" Burt asked Vaida again.

"I don't know," she said. "Find it for yourself!"

Then another hunt was on. Groups of five, six, and seven people went into each room. Vaida sat looking at the dirt on her clean floors and at Alvie Parkinson's clothes lying in the middle of the living room floor. He is under the ground, she thought. He is with Mrs. Parkinson. And I hope they both know what is going on here. Why didn't he make a will?

Vaida knew he must have some money for he had given thousands of dollars to charity. He very quietly had headed many of Hampton's Community Chest drives. And he had been the principal giver for the town of Hampton. He had given ground for two church houses, five schools, a playground, and a park. He had given sites for three different lodge halls. He had given Hampton its City Hall. But, after he had passed his eighty-fifth birthday, he hadn't headed the Community Chest drive, he hadn't given anything more to charity or the city. The mention of his name had almost disappeared from the papers. He had been forgotten until he was dying, then all of his cousins had come, for he didn't leave any children, brothers, or sisters.

While Vaida sat thinking about Mr. and Mrs. Parkinson, four cousins came downstairs with a trunk she had not seen before. It was a small trunk and it was roped securely by a once-white rope that had turned yellow with age. Just after they had set the ancient trunk in the middle of the living room floor, Burt Howerton came downstairs carrying an old leather suitcase.

"Now let's open these," Burt said, as he replaced his suitcase beside the trunk. "Call everybody in. We might have something here!"

All of the cousins returned before John Parkinson cut the rope around the trunk. All gathered close to see it opened. But the trunk was locked. Burt took the strong blade of his knife and jimmied the lock, rusted with age, until it let go. Again everybody crowded closer to see the trunk opened. They looked at each other with suspicious eyes. Then they looked at the trunk lid as Burt pulled it up and laid it back.

Vaida had never seen more disappointed looks on people's faces in her life when Burt started laying out little flat toilet paper rolls.

"The kind they use in hotels and public toilets," Jim Annis said.

"Maybe there's something down under it," Mrs. Howerton said. "Keep on goin', Burt!"

Burt Howerton laid out a tall stack of this paper in the center of the circle. He stacked it so high it fell over once. Then, he built another stack. Every eye was looking inside the trunk. When he got nearer the bottom of the trunk, he came onto stacks of small bars of soap. As he fetched them from the trunk he read the name of hotels from every large city in the South. Many hotels in large cities of the North were represented too. Everyone knew where Cousin Alvie had traveled. He had traveled extensively but that had been many years ago. However, souvenirs of his and Mrs. Parkinson's travels were in fair condition except for a musty odor. Burt went down to the bottom of the trunk and scooped up the last bars of soap with his big hands.

"This beats me," he said, looking at the empty trunk. "I know there's something somewhere around here."

Then he picked up the suitcase and unbuckled the straps. It was not locked. When he opened it the cousins were not as eager to look inside as they had been to see inside the trunk. The suitcase was filled with papers. Burt took each one out carefully. The first of these papers were old dress patterns. Then, came deeds for certain pieces of property. There were a few mortgages among the papers. He looked at each first, then gave it to Mrs. Howerton. She looked it over and passed it on to the other cousins.

"Here's something," Burt said, looking carefully at a scroll after he had untied a faded ribbon. "Looks like a will."

He unfolded the scroll and read. It was a will made by Nellie Hampton Parkinson and signed by her. Burt read the will aloud to all the cousins while they listened silently. The will was very simple and brief. She said if she died before her husband he was to receive everything she had. That was all there was to it. The will had been made twelve years ago, two years before her death, and had been signed by two witnesses who had since passed on.

"I'm glad it was that way," John Parkinson said.

"I am too," Vernon Seymoure agreed. "We'll search the place over. I'm sure Cousin Alvie didn't leave a will."

"If he had, Fred Smith would have drawn it up for him," John Parkinson said.

Then the cousins started over the house again. Not all of them. Mrs. Howerton was a little tired. She sat down in the large fireside chair directly across from Vaida. She looked at Vaida straight and hard while searching parties of four, five, six, or seven cousins took off for different rooms. Mrs. Vernon Seymoure, a much younger woman, stood in front of the fire.

"Woman, tell me," Mrs. Howerton said, "did cousin Alvie ever give you anything?"

"Not one penny," Vaida replied.

"Then why did you come here?" Mrs. Howerton questioned her

like a lawyer questions a witness.

"I didn't have a home," Vaida said. "Not after my father died. I didn't want to go to the County Home. That's why I came. This has been my home."

"But it won't be any longer," Mrs. Howerton said. "Not after we are through here. When we leave, you'll leave too, and we'll lock the door behind us."

"I had food to eat here, I had a bed to sleep on and a roof over me," Vaida told her. "That's all I asked. I paid in good measure for everything I got."

"How could you pay for everything you got?" Mrs. Howerton asked.

"I waited on my father before he passed on," she said. "Waited on him thirty years! It was no trouble to wait on Mr. Parkinson. I knew how, for I understood. I was as good to Mr. Parkinson as I was my own father. He was in the world alone and I was alone. I was happy here with him, for it was a home. His death has hurt me! I think of him now under the ground and all of you," Vaida screamed, "here ransacking Mr. Parkinson's house that I have cleaned, and he has been under the dirt not more than an hour!"

"And he never gave you anything to remember him by?" Mrs. Howerton chided Vaida. "Not after you worked for him? I'd think he'd treat you better than that!"

"The only thing he ever gave me," Vaida said thoughtfully, "was a picture of him and Mrs. Parkinson. It was a picture of them when they were first married. He said, 'Vaida, take this and keep it. Hold onto it as long as you live. It's my most prized possession.' And I took the picture. It's hanging in my room upstairs!"

"You won't get that picture," Mrs. Howerton said. "Not a picture of Cousin Alvie and Cousin Nellie. That will go to one of us, his closest kin!"

"I will keep it too," Vaida shouted. "He gave it to me!"

"That will go with his personal household effects," Mrs. Vernon Seymoure said.

"It will not," Vaida said. "I'll keep it as he told me to."

Then Vaida got up from the rocker, grabbed her crutch and made for the stairs. But Mrs. Howerton had two good legs and Vaida had only one. When Vaida sat down to scoot backwards up the stairs, Mrs. Howerton was almost to the head of the stairs. In a minute she came downstairs with the picture. Vaida wept when Mrs. Howerton held the picture up for Mrs. Vernon Seymoure to see. Here was the picture of a handsome young couple, taken perhaps seventy years ago. Alvin Parkinson was a handsome young man with a black mustache, and wearing a black bow tie. Nellie Hampton Parkinson was a pretty young woman with her black hair piled high on her head, a cameo pin beneath her swan-like throat, and wearing a dress with leg-o'-mutton sleeves.

"A handsome couple, weren't they?" Mrs. Vernon Seymoure said.

"But you never bothered to see him after he changed," Vaida wept. "He didn't look like that after she was gone and he lived here alone. You didn't come about," she sobbed. "What do you want with the picture that he gave me?"

Several of the cousins heard Vaida's screams and sobs. They returned to the living room without finding anything.

"That picture's mine," Vaida said. "That's all I have to remember him by. He told me to take it and keep it as long as I lived. It's mine!"

Then the cousins started looking at the picture. Billy Rister, who said he was a fourth cousin to Alvie Parkinson, happened to turn it over.

"What's this?" Billy Rister shouted. "I've found something important!"

Mrs. Howerton jumped up from the comfortable fireside chair. Mrs. Vernon Seymoure ran over and stood beside Billy. They looked on.

"It's the will," Billy shouted. "It's the will! Here's Cousin Alvie's will in his own handwriting."

There was a big commotion all over the house. Alvie Parkinson's cousins came running from all directions.

"It's to Vaida Montgomery," Billy said. "That's her sittin' over there on the stairsteps cryin'. Don't cry, Vaida," Billy shouted as he read the will to himself, "you've got everything."

"I never saw the writing on the picture," she said, her face brightening. "I didn't know it was there!"

"You knew it was there too," Mrs. Howerton told her, pointing her trembling finger accusingly. "I never did trust you from the time I laid my eyes on you!"

"I never heard of such a thing," Burt Howerton said as he came blustering into the living room. "Let me read that will!"

"Read it so we all can hear it," John Parkinson said.

"I, Alvin Parkinson, of Hampton, Greenwood County, being of full age and of sound mind and memory," Burt read so all could hear, "do make, publish, and declare this to be my last will and testament, hereby revoking all wills by me heretofore made."

"I direct that all my just debts and funeral expenses be paid out of my estate as soon as possible after the time of my decease."

"All the property, real and personal of every kind and description, wheresoever situate, which I may own or have the right to dispose of at any time of my decease, I give, bequeath and devise to Vaida Montgomery for the entirety of her life. And property remaining at her death I will, bequeath and devise to the Dartmouth Girls' Orphanage, Dartmouth."

"It's signed by Cousin Alvie and two witnesses," Burt spoke softly. "Can you beat this!"

"It's that little gold digger," Mrs. Howerton said, pointing her finger accusingly again at Vaida.

"You get out of my house," Vaida shouted. "Get out in a hurry! If you don't I'll call the Hampton police and have you thrown out!"

There was silence in the room as Mrs. Howerton got her coat.

"Don't you leave, Mr. Howerton," Vaida said. "Nor any of the rest of you!"

"I'll go too," Burt Howerton said.

"Not until you carry that trunk and suitcase back where you got them," she said. "You must clean up your mess and leave this house as you found it! If you don't I'll get warrants for all of you. I want all the money back too."

Vaida walked over by the aid of her crutch. She took the picture from Billy Rister and held it close while the small army of cousins started mumbling to each other while they put the house in order. Mrs. Howerton left the house, never looking back, but slamming the door behind her.

Vaida didn't call her back to help her cousins clean the house. A happy expression changed her face while she watched Mrs. Howerton from the window hurrying toward her car with her husband in close pursuit.

"The Cousins" was first published in *American Book Collector,* Vol. 9 (September 1958), pp. 25-29. It has never been reprinted.

*Jesse Stuart in his cornfield at his farm in W-Hollow,
Greenup County, Kentucky — circa 1942.*

Crabgrass

I was taking down a clothesline wire that had rusted and replacing it with one that wouldn't rust when I heard footsteps coming around the house. I turned back to look and there was Pa.

"Pa!" I said, tightening my grip on the hatchet-handle.

Pa laughed in his old familiar way. "What's the matter with you, Shan? Aren't you glad to see me? You act like you don't know me!"

"Sure, I know you," I told him as he came closer.

There he stood dressed in his brown suit, white shirt, and polka dot bow tie. But time was the same. The house, the backyard, the stream flowing under the house and surrounding hills covered with dogwood and redbud had not changed.

"I must be dreaming," I said.

"Wake up. Shan," he said. "Don't get old before your time! Wake up, boy, and let's laugh like we used to."

"But somehow I can't understand," I said. "Is that really you, Pa? Am I seeing and hearing you?"

"Sure you are, my boy," he replied with words quicker than the wind that rustled the dogwood leaves on the tree above us. "Don't let my little visit upset you. If I seem a little too happy remember it's the way I've always felt after I've been away on a visit and got back home to my valley."

Then he laughed again and slapped his long thin calloused hands on his sharp creased pant legs. "You ought to know your own father," he said, his voice louder than the murmur of summer wind in the dog-wood leaves.

Same old Pa, I thought. Can't be away anytime he doesn't worry about his home and valley. Tools can't be left out. Each tool must have a place. Each animal must have a home inside the barn away from the icy winds and winter snows. Every living thing must have a home. It must be fed regularly, too.

"Come to think about it," I spoke too quickly, "that ditch above the barn has filled up and the surface water has rotted the ends of the barn siding. And the barn roof sags and leaks—"

The smile left his red clean-shaven face but his blue eyes still looked searchingly at me.

"Where's the family?" he asked.

"At Blakesburg," I replied. "You should have met the car coming up the road!"

"The black one?" he asked.

"No, sand-colored," I corrected him. "It's been quite awhile since we had a black car."

"Oh, that's right," he said. "I should have known that."

He fidgeted around, putting his hands in his pockets and taking them out again. He took a step forward and then turned around. He was always as restless as an important high-spirited horse lined up for a race.

"Are you treating your Deanems all right?" he asked chuckling.

"Sure am," I said.

But that was Pa all right. He had always liked to tease.

"Say, Shan, what about old Dinah?"

"Dinah?" I said. "First time I've heard that mule mentioned in a long time. You remember she didn't live long after Old Dick died. We retired her on the green pasture. She died in three months. She grieved herself to death!"

"Oh, yes, I remember," he said. "I wondered if you'd remember!"

"Don't you remember her bones were picked clean by the scavengers before we found her," I asked him. "And don't you remember a forest fire got into our pasture, raced over the brown autumn grass and burned her bones!""

"But fire, Shan," he said, "you know how I fit fire and copperhead snakes with my little gooseneck hoe! Have you forgot that?"

I had neglected his land. I had not taken care of the farm like he had before he went away. He watched about forest fires, waterholes in the pastures, brush growing in fencerows and along the banks of the creek that flowed past his meadows. He inspected the roofs for leaks in all of his buildings before winter and cleaned the ditches.

He'd never let but one fire get on his fifty acres as long as he owned them. Lightning set that fire in three places but he soon reached these fires and put them out before each one got a head start.

"Watch fire while I'm away, Shan," he warned me. "You can't have me always to take the lead running to a fire with my little gooseneck hoe across my shoulder. I'm getting to be an old man you know! I can't run like a turkey, for my old ticker won't let me."

I nodded to him that I would.

"And something else I want to mention to you," he talked on, his face serious as he pointed his skinny index finger at me, "Have you watched the tires on the joltwagon wheels and when have you put axle grease in the hubs? Have you put the wagon wheels in water to soak the rims and spokes and tighten the tires?"

"Pa, what are you talking about?" I asked him. "We use the tractor and tractor wagon now."

Pa didn't answer me. Something was troubling him now. He wasn't as happy as he'd been when he first walked around the house. But it was like him to change his mood as suddenly as a wind can reverse itself and blow back the way it came. His mood had lined his red face with a serious expression.

"What's the matter?" I asked. "What's gone wrong now?"

"The Valley," he said. "My tracks have barely washed away from the fields and The Valley is neglected! Creek banks need scything' and the brush is crowdin' in. Son, you're too young to let the brush whip you."

"I know I am," I said apologetically.

Words spoken in his familiar voice always made me think. After each little visit he had ever taken, he came back finding fault when the little jobs had been neglected. This trip was no different from the rest. He had always been like this and would never change.

While there was silence between us, I thought of the time once when he told me that he'd dug up so much crabgrass from corn and tobacco with his little gooseneck hoe that when he departed from this life and was planted at Plum Grove, if we let that stuff grow over him he would grow restless in his grave. And, if there was a way he would get out of his grave.

He requested that I keep the crabgrass from his grave and that I use his little gooseneck hoe, as long as it lasted, to dig this grass up. I promised him that I would. And a promise to him, living or dead, was one I'd better keep. If any man could ever return from that silent homeland where Plum Grove men were laid, he would be that man.

"Well, I must be leavin' you, Shan," he said. "I want to get up on the hill and see the place—the barn and garden—oh, yes, I'm about to forget—what about my bull?"

"Which one?" I asked.

"You know—Old Boss, the last one and the best one," he replied instantly.

"Old Boss," I said. "Pa, what's between us?"

"Oh, maybe a little time," he said. "A little time—that's all. A little time can change everything. Let a man be gone—yes, even a little while and his wife and dog won't know him. A man and his bull are forgotten, and his place goes down. Shan, I tell you, you're lettin' this place go to hell."

I stood there beside him as stunned as when he first came around the corner of the house into the backyard in his Sunday clothes. I was glad to hear the sound of the car pull up in front of the house and slow down for the driveway.

"There they are," I sighed. "Pa, you wanted to see them. They're coming home now."

He didn't seem to hear what I was saying. He had something more on his mind to tell me before he went up on the hill.

"Shan, when have you been to Plum Grove?"

"Well, let me see," I said, putting my hand on my head as I tried to remember.

"I'll tell you," he interrupted me with words that came faster than a mad March wind. "Decoration Day—last May…"

"Well, that's…"

"Sure it's right," he interrupted. "That place is a wild hurricane of tall grass. I always saw to it that Old Alec cut the grass. My flesh and blood so neglectful, so full of broken promises…"

"But, Pa…"

"You promised me once," he went on, with his skinny index finger pointed at me.

"Oh, now I see," I said, but he was gone.

"Who were you apologizing to this time?" Deanems asked. She had come through the garage to the back of the house with Janet beside her.

When I looked quickly at Deanems and Janet, time was the present. Pa died in 1954. Deanem's hair was a dark brown then as an October whiteoak leaf. Now that brown was streaked with late October's frosted gray. Janet wasn't the pudgy little girl with the long pigtails and pink cheeks who came running to me for candy. She was tall as her mother now and she had her mother's eyes and hair. She was a sophomore at the University. Now she watched me carefully to see if my necktie was tied properly and if my cigar had a pleasant aroma. If time had reverted to the past, it now jumped back to the present.

"I was talking to Pa," I told Deanems. She gave me an understanding look. "He seems to think I've been neglecting things."

"Well, have you?" Deanems asked.

"Pa reminded me again of the things he told me to do before he went away. He accused me of being asleep when I was never more awake in my life."

"Daddy, are you sure Grandpa was here?" Janet asked.

"As sure as I live and breathe," I replied.

Deanems looked at me knowingly while Janet half-smiled as if she were a little amused by her aging father who wasn't fifty-four yet.

"It isn't hard to believe," Deanems said. "I knew your voice and the other voice sounded so familiar."

"If he wasn't here, then I'm the one who is dead." I said.

"Knowing your father as well as I did, I know he never came to see you without a reason," Deanems said softly. "Did he have one this time?"

"Do I have to answer that?" I asked.

"You could never break a promise with him," she said. "Have you broken one? Did you promise him something this time? Tell me, and maybe I can help you."

"Yes, if you can find Pa's little gooseneck hoe for me," I replied. "I put it away—but I've forgotten where."

Now she understood. But perhaps she had never doubted what I had told her.

"Crabgrass" was first published in August Derleth, editor, *Over The Edge: New Stories Of The Macabre* (Sauk City, Wis., Arkham House, 1964), pp. 135-141. It has never been reprinted.

Death Comes to Nicodemous

By-Jacks Tar rides down the path on a mule. He is ridin' bareback. His long legs dangle over the slab-sides of the mule. The August sun is high in the sky. It is twelve o'clock. The mule can step on the head of its shadow. The sun is hot enough to wilt the leaves and make them hang in wilted pods. The sun is hot enough to make the weeds smelly and to break the sweat from the mule's head, flanks, and ribs and run off in a little stream at the mule's navel and drip onto the dry-as-powder yellow sun-cracked Kentucky clay.

"Where air you goin', By-Jacks, ridin' that poor old workin' mule to death on this hot day?" Big Brownie asks. "Ain't you got no mercy on dumb brutes in sicha weather as this?"

"Goin'?" By-Jacks repeats. "Ain't no one been around to see you and broke the news about Nicodemous Pratt? He kicked the bucket at four o'clock this mornin'."

"The devil he did," says Big Brownie. He leans back on his scythe handle and wipes the sweat with his big fire-shovel hand from his cucumber-warty red face. He wipes a stream of sweat bigger than is drippin' from the mule's belly with his index finger and slings it onto the yellow-clay earth.

"I'll tell you," says By-Jacks, "our days air numbered same as the hairs on our head and when the Master rings the bell it's just like a dinner bell callin' a body home from the field to dinner. I've been out all over the neighborhood this mornin' tellin' the people about poor old Nicodemous, payin' my last respects to a good man and a good neighbor."

Big Brownie throws his scythe up in a sourwood bush by the road. The blade hooks over a wilted pod of leaves and hangs there swingin' in the air. He wipes the sweat from his warty red face again. He lifts his hat from his head and fans his face. His hair is wet with sweat and is stuck against his head in little wet piles. His big body wobbles down the rough-gutted yellow-clay road. By-Jacks rides the mule with his long legs danglin' in the blistery wind. They go down the road toward the house where Nicodemous lives.

"Nicodemous had somethin' like the flux," says By-Jacks. "He told me about it last April. He said he didn't think it was the poke greens that give it to him. Said he got the kivvers off'n the bed one night and the air of April chilled 'im and the next mornin' he got up with the flux."

The mule walks beside the old rail-fence where the blackberry briars grow in the fence corners and blue-bellied scorpions scale the fence rails and look for flies. The blacksnake entwines around the gray fence rail, and the greensnake twists like a gimlet around the green milkweed stems. A white cinder sun is in the sky above Nicodemous's shack.

"Hezzy," says Big Brownie, "sorry to hear about your pa. Sorry to hear about Nicodemous kickin' the bucket. But the hairs on your head is numbered and when the Master calls us we got to go. Nothin' we can do about it. Just like ringin' a dinner bell and callin' us home to our grub. Only Nicodemous has gone home to a bigger meal."

"You may be right," says Hezzy. "I hope you air, Big Brownie. Pap went to bed as usual last night. He just complained a little about the flux. Pap bought some yarb medicine from a Indian doctor in town last Saturday. He said it was bringin' 'im out of the kinks. Today Pap is a dead man."

"Hezzy," says By-Jacks, "when a man's time comes no doctor's medicine in the world ain't goin' to save him. Ain't I seen too much in my day and time? Your days air numbered. When the Master looks up your record on the time-book and sees it's time to ring the death bells fer you, you got to throw down your tools and go."

"When air youins goin' to bury Nicodemous?" Big Brownie asks.

"We're goin' to bury 'im this evenin' at four o'clock," says Hezzy. "We're goin' to haf to do it. It's too hot to keep milk from blinkin' when you put it in buckets and put 'em down in the well. Just can't bear to think of poor old Pap the way he's worked and all now dead in sucha hot weather."

"It's too bad," says By-Jacks, "but it's the Master's call fer 'im. His time ended and he jest had to go. The call might have come in cold weather. Might have come when a skift of snow was on the ground. It might have come in the plowin' season. It might have come in crop gatherin' time. Death don't have no season at all."

You can hear the hammers at the barn. You can hear the handsaws racin' through the black oak boards. You can see men standin' in the yard. Death has brought a holiday in the hills. Death came after Nicodemous in a surrey, maybe: Death came drivin' two black horses up the road past the old rock chimney where the roses bloom and where the red potato bugs eat potato vines in August and where Nicodemous's chickens wallow under the hollyhocks. Death saw all this and Death saw Nicodemous's log shack with holes between the cracks and the chinkin' and the daubin' gone from between the cracks where the wind was blowin' in. He knew where to find Nicodemous when the Master sent him. He knew where the house was. He reined his horses up beside the gate and threw the reins over the garden palin's. He got out of the surrey and knocked on the door for Nicodemous. "Wait just a minute until I put on my pants," says Nicodemous, "and I'll be ready."

"Don't have time to wait," says Death. "Get out of there and come on. The Master has sent me for you. The second is up."

Nicodemous rolls out of a good warm bed and goes. He goes down to the gate and climbs in the two-horse surrey with Death. Death pitches the reins from over the garden palin's, slaps the black horses on the rump with the reins, and drives away before daylight with Nicodemous. No one sees them drivin' down the road past the old stone chimney where the roses and the hollyhocks bloom. The big black horses chomp the steel bits and lift their forelegs high in the air. They paw the wind and their heads are high in the air. They charge against the reins but Death holds them and guides Nicodemous home to the Master.

"Is Green Eye takin' on any about Nicodemous's kickin' the bucket?" By-Jacks asks.

"Not a bit," says Hezzy. "'Pears like she don't care much about

Pap. Just a place to eat here and hang her duds where Ma used to hang hern. She don't seem to care if Pap lived or if Pap died. She did go up the holler and gather some wild cherry bark, slippery-elm bark, spicewood limbs, yaller root, boneset, and silkweed and biled 'em down to a gruel and give the tea to pap. It didn't stop the flux and give Pap a new set a bowels to bring back his old-time strength when he could lift the end of a saw-log and lift a barrel of sorghum 'lasses up and drink out'n the bunghole."

The hammers tap-tap-tap and the nails sink in the black oak boards at the barn. Chickens run over the yard and hunt for bumblebees and bugs. Men walk down the path from the barn. Women sit in the front room and talk.

"By-Jacks, since they are having the grave dug out on the pint," says Big Brownie, "we'd better shave Nicodemous and wash 'im fer burial."

"Okay," says By-Jacks. "I'm ready."

"Green Eye," says Big Brownie, "if it's all the same to you we'll lay Nicodemous out for burial. The men has his coffin done. Little Dink and the boys have about got his grave dug by this time."

"That's all right," says Green Eye. "I'll get you some towels, hot water, soap, razor, and the shavin' mug." Green Eye walks back into the kitchen. She moves with her big strong body swiftly as the wind in April. Her green eyes look you over sharply and hold you.

"They tell me," says Green Eye, "that Nicodemous used this razor all his life. His pap used it before him. Nicodemous told me that when he died he wanted to be shaved with it. Here's the hone. It might need a little honin'. Here's the towels, soap, brush, and mug." Green Eye walks back in the front room where the women are.

Sunlight falls through the window on the floor and flickers in little patches of yellow light on the poplar puncheon planks. By-Jacks and Big Brownie go back in the room where Nicodemous is sleepin' on the bed under a thin sheet. His unshaven gray beard stands up like bristly briars. They will not be too tough to cut when Big Brownie gets through honin' the razor. Then he shaves the hairs on his arm. "It'll cut his beard now," says Big Brownie.

By-Jacks pours hot water from the teakettle and makes a lather in the mug. He takes the brush and smears soap lather on Nicodemous's face. Big Brownie takes the razor and rip-rips through the beard. He cuts the beard like he cuts the ragweeds and horseweeds with a scythe. Rip-rip, and the big swathes of gray beard are scythed down the tough, wrinkled skin.

Marth Hailey fans her face with a wisp of spicewood leaves. Green Eye takes another wisp of leaves and shooes the flies and hits at them with the wisp of leaves. She shooes them out at the window. "Shoo shoo," she shouts; "get out at that dad-durned winder the way you come in—you nasty things!" The flies fly in little swarms out the window and light on the logs of the house. Soon as Green Eye leaves the window, the flies return. "Light up your pipe of the fragrant weed," says By-Jacks, "to kill this awful scent. I'll bet you that Nicodemous hasn't washed hisself since he started settin' terbacker last spring. Look at that water, won't you! But he's clean for burial. Green Eye, where is his burial suit?"

"Get his suit out'n the trunk," says Green Eye. "He's been married in it twice. Guess it's all right to bury him in."

Big Brownie gets Nicodemous's suit from the trunk—a black wrinkled suit—and he finds the white shirt and the big bow tie. He lifts up his legs and By-Jacks slips the pants upon his legs. Big Brownie lifts up the shoulders and By-Jacks puts his shirt around his shoulders, his arms through the sleeves. He pulls his suspenders over his shoulders and buttons the shirt. "Ain't the man he used to be," says Big Brownie. "Not nigh as heavy. Now he's skin and bones. Flux will get anybody if you let it run from April until August."

Big Brownie lifts up his shoulders again and By-Jacks puts the vest on him. He lifts up the shoulders again and By-Jacks puts his coat on him and buttons it down the front. "Just put socks on his feet," says Green Eye. "He won't need shoes now." She gives By-Jacks a pair of socks that she takes from the dresser drawer. By-Jacks lifts a foot and Big Brownie shoves the sock on his foot and straightens out the wrinkles at the toes.

"Ready for burial," says Big Brownie, as he puffs on his pipe.

"Let's get out of here," says By-Jacks. "Never was so hot in my life. Let's get out of here as soon as we can." They walk before the women in the next room and out at the front door.

"Air is fresh to breathe," says By-Jacks, "even if it is so hot it burns your nostrils." Big Brownie and By-Jacks suck on their pipes and blow wisps of thin smoke out to the hot wind.

"Got the coffin done," says Flem Harkreader. "Got a good one too. It'll last until the Judgment Day the way I spiked the oak boards together. Got a good bed in there fer Nicodemous's last sleep too—a better bed than he's ust to sleepin' on at home. I put quilt battin' in the bottom and on the sides of the coffin. I took a quilt and put over the battin' and a sheet and spread it over the quilt. It made it awfully pretty inside."

Winston Frazier and Ham Purcell carry the coffin to the house. Winston is in front and Ham is behind. They go in at the front door and they put the coffin on two chairs. Each end rests on a chair. Big Brownie and By-Jacks go back in the house. They carry Nicodemous from the back room and put him in the coffin and fold his hands across his chest and his face is white as milk. There are traces of the blue veins, those rivers of his life blood that now fail to flow, under the chalk-white skin.

"Take it easy, Green Eye," says Marth Hailey. "Just take it easy. He's gone to a better place than we air. I've known Nicodemous Pratt all my life. Never was a better man. Don't go back there and cry your eyes out." Green Eye goes out at the back door and toward the barn. "It's a funny funeral to me," says Big Brownie; "I ain't seen anybody shed a tear yet. Green Eye don't seem to be upset about it."

"She jest went out the back door to bawl her eyes out about Nicodemous," says By-Jacks. "Didn't you hear Marth Hailey to tell her to take it easy?"

"Not one of Nicodemous's seven boys has shed a tear," says Big Brownie. "It's a funny funeral to me. I've been to many a funeral but I never saw one like this before."

Six of Nicodemous's boys stand in the yard now: Ferris, Joe, Steave, Hemlock, Pert, and Hezzy. Silas is not here.

"Where is Silas?" Hezzy askes.

"Do you think I can run him down like a rabbit and know where he is all the time?" Pert asks.

"Can't you talk a little better and not so loud?" says Hezzy. "Don't you know Pap is dead?"

"Yes," says Pert, "at four o'clock this mornin' I could have told you that."

"Put two poles under the coffin," says Big Brownie. "By-Jacks and I will take the backend. We'll take the back pole. We air tall and stout and goin' up the pint yonder the weight will be on us. We'll be the wheel-oxen. Get two short men for the front pole. Get a big man to tail the coffin up the hill."

"Rabbit-Legs Seymour," says By-Jacks, "is the right man to tail that coffin. Big body way up there in the air on a long pair of legs. Right up there so he can put his weight agin it and push up that steep hill. Hammer Stout and Puss Skinner can take the front pole."

Turkey Blaine nails the lid down over Nicodemous's chalk-white face. He drives tenpenny nails into the boards and puts the draw-hammer in his hip pocket. He picks up the front end of the coffin. Charlie Hix picks up the backend. They lift it from the chairs and carry it out the front door. Their neck veins swell and their faces turn red as they lift the heavy box and the dead man in it. But only two men can carry the coffin through the narrow door out into the yard where the men can get their poles under it. The coffin doesn't have handles. "Hurry it up and get that pole under there, boys, before I drop my end of it," says Turkey.

Hammer and Puss run up to the front end of the coffin. Puss shoots the pole under and Hammer grabs the other side of it. The front end of the coffin now rests on a strong willow pole. By-Jacks puts the pole under, and Big Brownie takes the other end of the pole. Rabbit-Legs walks behind the coffin to tail it and shove goin' up the hill. "All set," says Rabbit-Legs. They move across the yard. All of Nicodemous's boys but Silas are behind their dead father's body. All of the women but Green Eye walk under the Kentucky sun and in the great waves of heat with Nicodemous to his last restin' place.

"Holler for Green Eye," says Marth Hailey. "Maybe she don't know we've started with Nicodemous to the grave."

"She ought to know to be here," says Weedy Starbuck. "Didn't she know when her own man's funeral was goin' to be? If she didn't know, who was supposed to tell her?"

"Reckon she's out cryin'," says Murt Hensley.

"Guess she's out cryin' with Silas," says Weedy.

Weedy Starbuck wheezes on her pipe. She wheezes a dry rattlin' wheeze like the wind blowin' against a corn shuck. The women are behind. The women get their breath hard in the hot sun. They move slowly up the hill as the wind moves through the wilted green clouds of leaves.

"God," says Rabbit-Legs, "this tailin' is a job. I'm shovin' the coffin and all the rest of you fellers. I just brace my feet and shove. How much fu'ther we got to go?"

"Up on top of this pint," says Big Brownie, "where Nicodemous's first wife, Lillie, was buried."

"We ain't halfway yet," says Puss. "We've got a good mile to go."

"Lord, but I'd like to wind a minute, and roll me a cig," says Hammer.

"Come on you fellers," says Big Brownie. "What's the matter with you? Can't you take it?" Big Brownie is getting' his breath hard. Sweat runs from the end of his nose and drips to the ground. He takes his index finger and slings off a streak of sweat. He flings it to the dry, parched earth.

"Where do you suppose Green Eye is?" By-Jacks asks.

"Didn't she come along?" Big Brownie asks.

"No, she didn't," says By-Jacks, "and Silas ain't here."

"Something strange about that," says Big Brownie.

"Yander they air," says Weedy Starbuck. "See 'em come from the brush!"

"Can you beat that," Murt Hensley whispers to Marth Hailey. "Out here in the bushes before Nicodemous's body is cold. Out here with her husband's boy by his first wife."

Green Eye runs out of the bushes ahead. She is cryin' and sobbin'. She flings her midnight-black hair to the slow-movin' wind. Silas waits back in the bushes. He doesn't know that Weedy has seen them. He doesn't know that the crowd goin' up the hill to the funeral saw them.

"How can I ever bear to see 'im laid in the cold clay?" says Green Eye as she comes sobbin' from the saw-briars and brush to the crowd of women on their way to the funeral. "Oh, Lord, how can I ever stand it?"

"The best thing fer you to do," says Weedy Starbuck, "is brush the leaves and dirt off your back and straighten up your hair a little and come on to the funeral."

Silas comes from the brush now. He pretends that he is wipin' tears from his eyes. "He's doin' more than the rest of the boys," says Murt Hensley. "He's at least pretendin' that he's sheddin' a few tears fer his pap." Green Eye walks with the women. They slowly climb up the path. They pull themselves up by weeds and sprouts and bushes. Sweat is breakin' out on their foreheads and runnin' off in little streams. Little white beads of sweat drop off to the dry earth.

"I'm just about gone," says Rabbit-Legs. "I'm about petered out. Nicodemous may have been skinny when he died but he gets fat by the time a body he'ps carry 'im to the top of this hill." Rabbit-Legs can't turn loose the backend of the coffin. He has to hold to it with both hands and shove with his weight against the coffin.

"We're the wheel-hosses," says Big Brownie. "By-Jacks and me's got the load."

"We'll soon be there," says Puss. "I can see the top of the hill. See it there through the bushes! See the light of the sky!"

"Looks good to me," says Hammer. "I tell you I feel like drappin' in my tracks. It's a job to carry a dead man in a oak-board coffin up one of these hills."

"Right this way," says Little Dink. "Right over here, boys. Set one end of the coffin on this stump and the other end on this rock."

The five men stumble through the wilted weeds and briars over to the stump and the rock. Puss and Hammer put their end on the stump and slip their pole from under the coffin. Big Brownie and By-Jacks and Rabbit-Legs put their end of the coffin on the rock. Rabbit-Legs falls on the wilted weeds. There isn't a dry thread among his clothes. "Lord, I'm petered out," says Rabbit-Legs. Big Brownie and By-Jacks take their pole from under the coffin. They sit down under the oak tree. They take off their hats and fan. Big Brownie wipes the sweat with his index finger from his forehead and slings it down to the wilted grass. Men stand around the grave with axes, picks, and spades.

"Here comes the funeral crowd," says Ike Blevins. "Hear 'em pant! That long hill's enough to make 'em pant. It'd kill the best mule in the country to have to carry a load up that hill."

"What about us men?" says Rabbit-Legs. Do you think we can stand more than mules?"

"Shet your trap, Rabbit-Legs," says Ike. "Can't you see the funeral crowd coming' right there? They'll hear what you air sayin'. Preacher Issiac McMeans is out there."

Green Eye walks with the women. Silas walks with his brothers. Green Eye's eyes are swollen as if she were weepin'. The women are wet with sweat. Weedy Starbuck knocks the ashes out of her pipe now. She gets her breath easier than the other women. "This hill wouldn't a-been anything fer me to a-clim' until I's seventy," says Weedy. "It was the influenza that got me down when I was seventy."

"A brother has come to this hilltop for his last long sleep," says Preacher Issiac McMeans. "He has left his fields of terbacker and corn and his lovin' wife and his boys. He's come here to sleep until Gabriel blows his trumpet on Resurrecton Morn. We'll get together and shake hands again in a new life and a new mornin'." Green Eye looks toward the other hill. She stands silently as a tree. Silas looks at the ground and roots his bare toe in a little pile of loose dirt.

"When did they jine the crowd?" whispers By-Jacks to Big Brownie. "Look at the leaves on the back of her dress." By-Jacks punches Big Brownie in the ribs.

"Dust to dust," says Brother Issiac McMeans. "We'll all have our last look at Brother Nicodemous—the last look until Resurrection Morn."

Turkey Blaine takes the draw-hammer from his hip pocket and pulls the tenpenny nails. He lifts the coffin lid and the people stream forward under the last sun that will shine down on Nicodemous's chalk-white face. "Poor old Nicodemous," says Weedy Starbuck. "Woe is man born of woman."

Green Eye looks at Nicodemous and then she looks at Silas. Silas looks down at his big bare toes. "Some might think he's ashamed because he didn't have no shoes to wear to his pap's funeral," whispers Murt Hensley to Marth Hailey, "but you know why he looks down at his big bare toe!"

They put the rope plow lines under the oak-board box and lower the coffin in the dry clay. Turkey nails down the lid. Brother Issiac crumbles dust into the grave. "Ashes to ashes and dust to dust," he says. Brother Issiac lifts his face to the heavens and prays that they'll meet again on Resurrection Morn under a new sun and on a new earth. Dink shovels the yellow dirt on the oak boards with a long-handled shovel.

"It's just a matter of years," says Big Brownie, "until no one will know that Nicodemous sleeps here—friend, and neighbor, and one of the best men to be born among and ever to live among these hills."

"Death Comes To Nicodemous" was first published in *Prairie Schooner,* Vol. 51 (1941), pp. 141-148. It has been reprinted in L.C. Wimberly, editor, *Prairie Schooner Caravan* (Lincoln, Nebraska, University of Nebraska Press, 1943), pp. 90-100. Stuart credited his friend from Greenup, Louie Stapf, with the idea for this short story. In Stuart's inscription to Stapf in Stapf's copy of *Prairie Schooner Caravan* he wrote, "W-Hollow – Dec. 24th, 1943. To Louis Stapf, my close personal friend who is able to pick up long lists of good names among these hills and is good enough to turn them over to me. Merry Christmas, happy new year. Jesse Stuart. Page 90 is the story you told me." (Stapf's copy of *Prairie Schooner Caravan* is a part of the private Stuart collection of David R. Palmore, Villa Hills, Kentucky.)

Jesse Hilton Stuart — circa 1958

First Journey to the Clan

"Sall, look for us back Sunday afternoon," Pa told Mom. "Pap will be glad to see us. But at his age two nights, a whole day, and parts of two days will be a long visit!"

This was a big trip for me. I was barefooted, wore knee pants and I was seven years old. I was going with my father Mick Powderjay to see Old Mick Powderjay who was his father and my grandfather. Grandpa Old Mick was eighty-two. My father, Young Mick, was thirty-one. And he was Grandpa's eleventh child by his first marriage. After Pa's mother's death all the Grandsons and Granddaughters called her First Grandmother. She had died before I was born. I heard my Pa talk a lot about his mother, how small she was and yet she had given birth to eleven husky sons and pretty daughters.

Then I had heard my father tell about her death and how he had cried when she was buried on Rove Creek, in a little country cemetery in an unmarked grave. Many times he had gone back there and tried to find her grave. I was too small to go with him. He went alone trying to find her grave and when he came home from each trip, he told Mom how he had searched but had never found.

After First Grandmother's death, Grandpa Old Mick married Ethel Spencer, a daughter from the Clan that had been an enemy to the Powderjays. Powderjays had killed Spencers and Spencers had killed Powderjays. I had heard Pa talk so much on winter evenings before our fire, how the Law of the Clans on the Big Sandy had been a death for a death sometimes two deaths for one. It was the old law an eye for an eye and a tooth for a tooth. But to this union, eight more children were born. Pa had always said he liked to go see his father, but he was afraid of his second wife. We grandchildren called her Second Grandma. Pa called her Old Ethel when he was away from her. He called her Ethel when he visited his father. Mom had told us this. I have never visited Grandpa Old Mick before.

But Mom had dressed me in the best clothes I had to go see my Grandpa Powderjay for the first time. She had cut the gray chambray cloth with skill and had made me a pair of pants which buttoned onto my shirt. I didn't wear cap or socks and shoes. I wore only two pieces of clothing, pants and shirt. Mom had put another change of clothes for me in a basket and a nightshirt to sleep in. Pa carried extra clothes for himself and me in the basket. Pa, with a basket on his arm and with me tagging at his heels, walked up the path that wound around the hillside from The Valley where we lived. We walked through a gap between two high hills and down a path into Tanyard Hollow.

"Shan, we'll be going down hill all the way now," Pa said.

We walked down to the Old Line Special railroad tracks. And now I followed Pa as he stepped from crosstie to crosstie, over the ragweed stubble between the crossties that had been shorn off by the cowcatchers on the Old Line Special engines. And on either side of me was a long line of rusty T-rails. I walked between two long lines of rusty T-rails. Once I got upon the T-rail to walk, but the morning April sun had heated the rail until it burned my feet. I jumped back off the rail onto the crossties again. When we reached the Riverton Railway Station, Pa pulled his watch from his vest pocket. This is where he wore it when he put on his dark blue serge suit with pegleg pants, his black shoes and hat and armbands to hold up his sleeves. He wore a white shirt and a black bowtie.

"You'd better watch that man of yourn," Marth Skinner, Uglybird Skinner's wife, once said to Mom. "He's the doddiest man I ever saw when he goes up Big Sandy to see his folks."

"I do watch him, Marth," Mom told her. "You never saw him go many times alone. Shan will tell me what his father does."

"We've got a twenty minutes wait before No. 8 arrives," Pa said.

When we walked into the Riverton Depot, Pa looked upon the wall at the depot clock. "My old turnip is right on time with the depot clock," he said proudly. "It's supposed to be right on the second."

Pa bought his railroad ticket. I didn't have to have one not even for half fare. After he purchased his ticket we walked out on the platform and waited for the train. I thought this would be the greatest trip of my lifetime. And it was. I would be going the fartherest from home I had ever been. I would be going forty miles, maybe fifty. And I would be going all the way by train. Now we stood looking down the tracks that were worn real bright by the wheels of many passing trains. We watched to see No. 8 come around the curve. And I was the first to see her and I hollered: "Pa there she comes!" She whistled that she was going to stop. Dark clouds of smoke were shooting up toward the blue April sky and a slim white cloud of steam lifted up when she whistled. She pulled into the station and stopped. Pa took me by the hand when we got on the passenger car.

"Now you sit over by the window where you can look out," he said to me.

I got over by the window and he sat in the seat by the aisle beside me. It was great to hear the engine whistle as we prepared to start. The train jerked a few times and we were on our way. I looked over to my left at the Ohio River. And here were broad bottoms of land where men were plowing with as many as three teams hitched to a plow on which one man drove all six horses that plowed three furrows. I had never seen this before. There were many houses along the track.

Then we slowed down and the engine whistled three times.

"Whistling to stop in Auckland," Pa said. "Look what a big depot they have here."

When the train pulled up and stopped, I looked from my window at a depot ten times as large as the one at Riverton. And there were people getting off the train going into the depot. I saw people standing there waiting for them. And they shook hands and some of the men and women hugged and kissed. And there were people coming onto the train to take the seats emptied by those that got off. All of this was wonderful to me. I had never seen anything like it.

"Now when we leave here, Shan, our next stop is Gate City," Pa said. "That's where we get off. From Auckland and Gate City is town all the way. And it is five miles from here to Gate City."

When No. 8 pulled away from the Auckland Station, I didn't see anything but houses and little yards. I didn't see how a family could live without a garden but there were no gardens behind these houses and there were little yards in front. When the train began to slow down and whistle, Pa stood up.

"We are pulling into Gate City," Pa said. He lifted his basket from the rack above our seat. "Follow me."

When he left the coach, I tagged at his heels down onto the Gate City Depot platform. Many people got off the train. Many I had seen get on at Auckland, just five miles away, got off here.

"Now, we've got an hour before we catch the Big Sandy Train," Pa said. "I want to go over here and buy Pap a present. I know what he wants. And I doubt he ever gets what he wants anymore."

I had heard Pa say many times that when his Pap married Ethel Spencer that she was young and he was the boss. Pa said he was the head of the house. But as the two grew older, Grandpa Old Mick grew old too fast. And this is when Ethel Spencer Powderjay became head of the house. Pa said she was mean to his Pap. And he said she was a dangerous woman and carried a pistol.

When we left the Gate City Railroad Depot, I followed Pa across the street. We came to a building where men staggered up and down the street in front. One man was asleep on the street with his face to the wall. But I followed Pa inside.

"You're not supposed to be in here," Pa said. "But I've not got anyplace to leave you while I come in, I can't leave you on the outside. I don't think the bartender will say anything."

Pa walked over to the bar. He sat upon a seat and ordered a beer while I stood beside the stool on which he sat.

"And I want a quart of Old Kentucky," he said. "It's your best licker ain't it?"

"Well, it's good," the bartender said. He wore a bowtie. And he had a long mustache. His white sleeves were held up by holders. He brought Pa a beer with foam on top. Then he went back and brought a bottle of Old Kentucky.

"It's my father's best kind of whiskey," Pa told the bartender.

"It's all right to have my son in here isn't it?"

"No, it really isn't," he told Pa. "A child shouldn't be in here. You are breaking the law by bringing him and I am breaking the law by letting you."

"We'll be out in a few minutes," Pa said.

Pa put his quart of Old Kentucky into his basket under the clothes. He finished his glass of beer.

"What a fine drink," Pa said as he left the stool.

He walked toward the door and I was behind him. We walked back across the street back to the station. And here Pa bought a coach ticket for the Big Sandy passenger train.

"It won't be long until you'll be seeing your Grandpa Old Mick Powderjay," Pa said. "And he's goin' to be proud and happy tonight when I give him his present. Now, Shan, when the Big Sandian rolls out of here at four p.m., I want you to hurry on the train with me so we can get a seat on the left hand side of the coach. I want you over near the window so you can see the Big Sandy River."

Pa walked out of the Station and up and down the platform waiting for the train.

"I want to see Pap," Pa said. "He's getting old. And he's liable to be killed by his wife's people. They don't like Pap. She never loved him. She knew he drawed a big pension. She could live easy on it. And when Pap leaves this world, she'll get his pension."

Pa walked up and down the platform talking like an addled man.

"We couldn't keep Pap from doing it," Pa said. "He married a woman right out of Powderjay's enemies. But an old man thought a young woman loved him. And he didn't use reason. She was a good looking woman…younger than my sisters Mary, Emma, Belle and Tillie!"

When the train pulled up, Pa rushed up and stood beside the coach with me close behind. When the last passenger came off, Pa and I were in front of all the others getting on. And there was a crowd of people getting on.

We were on the coach first and I got a seat by the window. Pa got the seat next to me. He held the basket on his lap. And I knew why. He was afraid the basket might fall down from the rack and break Grandpa Powderjay's present. Soon the coach had filled up and people were standing.

"This train always goes out of here loaded," Pa said. "It's the way people come down out of the mountains to the outside world. Shan, the Big Sandy and its two forks are over a hundred miles long. They're many people living up the Big Sandy and up its tributaries."

"What are tributaries, Pa?" I asked.

"Little rivers and streams that flow into the Big Sandy."

There were three whistles and the train slowly pulled away from the Gate City Station. We were on our way.

"After Hampton City, you'll see the Big Sandy River."

Hampton city was very close to Gate City. And beyond Hampton City I saw the Big Sandy River where maples and willows along the banks were green with leaves.

"Over there is West Virginia," Pa said. "Men from over on that side used to shoot at Kentuckians on this side. Often a battle got underway by men who didn't know or had never seen each other. Many got wounded but only a few got killed."

"It's a pretty river," I said.

The afternoon sun was shining on the water and it was a shining river in the sunlit glow. Willows and elms along its banks made shadows across the bright moving ribbon of flowing water.

"Pap used to say the Big Sandy earth was his flesh, the cliff stones were his bones and the Big Sandy River was his blood. He likes this country. He has fought for it. Went through the Civil War for the time Abe Lincoln called for 75,000 volunteers to carry on the war. Pap was one. And he was at Appomattox fighting under U.S. Grant when Lee surrendered. I've heard Pap talk about Meade, Hooker and Grant, generals he fought under. Yes, that Big Sandy River is Pap's blood."

I couldn't understand Pa's talk. The Big Sandy River in the sunlight looked like silver. Blood was red. The Big Sandy River wasn't red. Our Big Sandian passenger train stopped at Lookwood and a few people got off. A few got on.

"Next station will be Zachary," Pa said. "And we will soon be at Pap's. He doesn't live fur from the Zachary Station."

Now, up the Big Sandy River on my side, the over-hanging cliffs on Pa's side of the coach we rode into the sunset. And very soon the conductor came through our coach saying: "Zachary next stop. Zachary next stop!"

Pa and I were the only ones to get off at Zachary. And no one waited there to get on the train. Zachary had a store and a post office.

"This will be the last of your trip," Pa said. "We'll be there in a few minutes."

The setting sun was ahead of us. It was like a big red joltwagon wheel in the sky. And the rays from the setting sun made the Big Sandy River a silver ribbon bordered on either side by wind-quivering tender leaf green. I stepped on the crossties behind my father. We walked up on the tracks.

"See, up the there on the bank, Shan," Pa said. "That's where he lives! Up above the railroad and way above the river so he could look down on them. Pap is crippled up so bad he can't walk unless he uses two canes. But he manages to get out on his little porch to see the Big Sandy River. See, the Big Sandy River is his blood."

There was a little path from the railroad track up the bank.

"Grandpa can't walk up and down this path can he?" I asked Pa.

"No, but he's got some half-grown children who run up and down this path," Pa told me. "There's a wagon road that comes up the hill behind Pap's house. They can haul him out that way when he dies."

Now, I followed Pa up the little path. I would soon be seeing Grandpa, Old Mick Powderjay.

When we walked up to the shack, Grandpa was sitting on the porch watching the sunset.

"A-lookin for ye, Little Mickie," Grandpa said. "Your good wife Sall wrote and told me you'd be coming on the Big Sandian! I'm glad you got a wife who can write your letters! How are ye Mickie?"

"Just fine," Pa said.

"Who's the little man you got with ye?" he asked, looking at me.

"He's my oldest and only son," Pa said.

"Come over here and let me see you up close," Grandpa Powderjay said. He reached over with his cane. He caught the handle around my neck and pulled me over to him. He held me close with his big hands and looked up into my face.

"He's not got the Powderjay nose, eyes, and mouth, Little Mickie," Grandpa said.

Now, Second Grandma, who heard us talking, walked out. I didn't call her Second Grandma. When Pa spoke to her and called her Ethel, I called her Grandma and she liked me from the start. Then, four of Grandpa's children by Second Grandma Ethel came out. They were Pa's two half brothers and two half sisters. They were my half uncles and aunts.

"Bob and Erf," Pa said. "Arabella and Lucy. Where are the others?"

"They've jumped the broom," Grandpa Old Mick said. "As quick as one gets eighteen he or she marries. And these four are a year apart, from thirteen to seventeen! See, I don't run this place, Mickie. I just sit out on this porch when it's not too cold and look at my land, cliffs and my river! I just sit in the chair while time moves on, Mickie!"

"Yes, Mick, you do run this place," Grandma Ethel said. "Maybe, you don't think you do, but I know you do!"

"Pap, you just think you do," young Uncle Bob told Grandpa.

When he said these words he started to run. Grandpa tripped him with his cane. Then he came over with a larrup.

"If I was just a man again," Grandpa said. "Just back there in my young days of sixties and early seventies, I'd make ye youngins stand up and be counted. I'd run this place."

Pa held Grandpa's cane when he started to larrup Uncle Bob a second lick. When Uncle Bob got up he ran off the porch and around the house.

"I won't take back-sass, Mickie," Grandpa Old Mick said. "I never did take it until these youngins come along. First four married and gone were not so brazen! It's these younger four. They treat their father, Old Mick Powderjay with disrespect."

"It's not that bad Little Mick," Grandma Powderjay said.

"It is that bad, Ethel," he said. "You know it is that bad. Why lie about it. Mickie I want you and Shan to come to my room with me."

Grandpa Old Mick got up from his rocking chair. Supported by two canes he hobbled inside the shack and into his room. Pa opened the doors for him. I followed. I didn't know Grandpa Old Mick was so much bigger than my father. His neck was nearly as big as his head. His shoulders were almost too broad to go through the door. If he could have stood up straight his head would have touched the shack rafters that held up the upstairs floor. Grandpa Old Mick Powderjay had been a mighty man, just like Pa had always told us.

"In here are two beds," Grandpa said. "This one is mine and that one over in that corner is yourn and your boy Shan's. You don't mind sleeping together do you?"

"Not at all," Pa said.

"Ethel will call you when supper is ready," Grandpa Mick said. "I don't eat anything before I go to bed anymore."

"Would you drink something before you go to bed?"

"I've got nothing to drink," he said. "I used to ride the train down to Gate City and get my Old Kentucky!"

Pa looked under our clothes and took a quart of Old Kentucky from the basket.

"I thought you'd like it," Pa said. "I know you used to drink it."

"I'll say I did," he said.

"Now I can't get it," he told Pa. "Mickie, I sleep in here by myself. Ethel had to quit sleeping with me. She said I had nightmares. But I didn't have nightmares, Mickie! They come back. I'm telling you they come back. And to get rid of them I had to get up and light the lamp. They don't show up around my bed in the light. I see them in the dark."

"Who comes back?" Pa asked.

"The men I've killed," he said. "There was General Cooke's

waiter. When I treated my comrades with cigars he reached into the box and got a handful ahead of my comrades. I didn't take the time to shoot him. I hit him over the head with my rifle barrel. I was sentenced to be hanged by the wrists. Two hours up to the joist of an old house and four hours down. And I was heavy hanging up there, Mickie! Two hundred and forty pounds. See," he said showing me the white marks over the tops of his wrists, "my only scars from the war. The ropes cut my wrists. A general saved me. Made them cut the ropes. Said I was worth more to the army of fighting men than I was hanging to that joist. Well, that damned waiter haunts me more than any I've killed."

"Then old Ace Spencer, Ethel's uncle, who hunted me to kill me once," he said. "I hunted for him when I heard this and found him before he found me. I see him around my bed. There's old Rob Purdy of the Hatfield Clan. I was accused. I guess I must have done it. He's been coming around my bed…"

"Pap, it must be your imagination," Pa said.

"No, Mickie, I have to sleep with a lamp burning in my room all night," he said. "There are three Union soldiers that brother Marion and I were accused of killing after we stopped in the old Soldiers Home. We escaped the Home and they never found us. All old soldiers and all drinking. I don't exactly know what happened. I guess we did kill them. I see three men wearing the blue around by bed at night, Mickie. And there's about eight more. Little Mickie…even Old John Stump I had to shoot in the belly over my wife Ethel!"

"My goodness, Pap," Pa said. "This is real disturbing. I wonder if my boy Shan couldn't sleep in another room!"

"Not but six rooms in this shack, Little Mickie," Grandpa said. "And the only place your boy is safe is in this room. And give me that quart! I'll take a swig. You'll soon be going to supper. Ethel will have it ready. And I am not going to the table. I'll take a few swigs of Old Kentucky! I've not had a drink for a long time, Mickie!"

I had heard Pa tell how he had gone down to Gate City on a Big Sandy passenger train and how Grandpa had spent his pension money for whiskey to do him a month. Pa told how men would drink and fight on the train until they'd have to stop the train and put them off. And if someone on the train, after too much drink, hollered 'Hurrah for Jeff Davis' this started a war. Fighting didn't end until after men were stabbed and killed. At big family or church reunions when someone hollered 'Hurrah for Jeff Davis' men on either side ran where they had their teams and wagons hitched and took the breastyokes loose from the joltwagon tongues and fought with them. Grandpa Powderjay had waded in many a time with a breastyoke fighting to a finish. But he had killed men on 'his own side' when there was a fight.

There was a knock on Grandpa's room door.

"Supper is ready Little Mickie," Grandma Powderjay said.

Then, Pa got up from his chair. He left Grandpa Old Mick fondling the bottle of Old Kentucky. And just before Pa started for supper with me by his side, Grandpa got the stopper out of his quart. And he put the long bottleneck back under his mustache and the beard around his lips. He hid the bottleneck in his mouth.

"Gurggle, Gurggle. Gurggle. Gurggle."

"How good it is, Little Mickie" he said. "I'm glad you thought of me!"

"Go light on it, Pap," Pa said.

"I won't get too much," Grandpa said. "Maybe that crazy fourteen won't be around my bed tonight."

When we went inside the kitchen, Grandma and my two aunts and uncles were around the table. There were two places set for us. My young uncles and aunts called Pa, Brother Little Mickie and this seemed so strange. It was an awful mixup in Pa's family. Mom was right when she said it was a "mixup." Yes, it was a mixup. When we sat down we found a full table of grub and everybody reached and helped himself or herself. But Pa looked out after me. I was the smallest one at this table.

"Brother Mickie, I want you to try some of the fish," Uncle Robert said. "I caught them in the Big Sandy River today. Nice catfish. They're biting real good right now."

We had pork, fish, beans, cornbread, biscuits, turnip greens, jelly, sorghum molasses on the table. Grandma Ethel Powderjay had gone all out for us. Pa asked me what I wanted then he put it on my plate.

"I'm going to see my boy goes to school," Pa said.

Grandma Ethel smiled and Uncles Robert and Erf laughed out loud. My aunts looked at each other and smiled. We talked and laughed at the table, but I knew my father didn't trust his step-mother, Ethel Spencer Powderjay. I had heard him say too many times he wouldn't trust a Spencer as far as he could throw a bull by his tail. Pa was just being nice for he wanted to return to see his father. And he wanted me to see his father. Grandma Ethel wouldn't have invited us to come. She had sent word for my mother to stay away too. Now after supper Pa excused us from the table and we went back to our room with Grandpa.

"Pap, you're going heavy on that bottle," Pa said. "You've sunk it about a third!"

Grandpa was lying sprawled on the bed. He had got his pants and shoes off and he was in his blue shirt and long white drawers that encased his muscular knotty legs.

"Little Mickie, I see him!" Grandpa said. "Will you light the lamp? I see General Cooke's waiter! I could see the son-of-a-bitch the day I busted his head. He looks today like he did then. We were both young men, Little Mickie! And I see Old Ace Spencer…"

"Just a minute, Pap," Pa said. He took the globe off the lamp and struck a match and put the flame to the wick. When he put the globe back on the lamp there was a big mellow glow of light. "This ought to stop it, Pap!"

"Yes, they won't be seen in the light," he said. "They know if I get my old weak eyes on them, Mickie, I can still look a hole through them."

"Pa, I'm getting sleepy," I said. I didn't tell my father for Grandpa was lying on the bed across from our bed and he would hear me say that I was afraid of Grandpa Powderjay. After Pa lighted the lamp,

Grandpa Powderjay dozed off to sleep.

"I can't sleep with a light," I heard Pa say.

Then, he blew out the lamp and laid down in the bed beside me.

But in the night I was awakened when I heard Grandpa Old Mick Powderjay come out of his sleep shouting: "I see them Little Mickie! I see all fourteen! Get up in a hurry and light the lamp!"

Pa jumped up, struck a match, lifted the globe from the lamp and stuck the flame to the wick. He put the globe back on and there was a mellow light.

"They're gone, Little Mickie," Grandpa said. "Let the lamp burn until morning!"

Pa had said he couldn't sleep with a light burning in the room. He couldn't. He sat up the rest of the night. And I would go to sleep and wake again.

"In the morning don't mention we came here to stay two nights with Pap," Pa said. "We have to go back home in a hurry. We will leave in the morning. I can't stand this. I have to have my sleep. I can't get a night's rest here."

That morning when Grandpa awoke it was very early.

"Pap used to get us up at four in the morning," Pa said. "We were in the cornfield as soon as we were able to tell a hill of corn from the weeds. Pap spent five years in the army and he was in all the big battles. Pap has been a soldier all his life."

"If I could just get my hands on 'em Little Mickie," he said. "They wouldn't be around my bed at night. I don't know why they come back. What good can they do? Why are they after me now? I am a living man. They are spirits. They are ghosts of men. If I could get my hands on old General Cooke's waiter, I could choke that ghost!"

"Pap, I hate to see this happen to you," Pa said.

"Yes, Little Mickie, they've decided to come back and get me after I've got old," Grandpa said. "See they didn't dare to do this when I was a younger man."

Pa helped Grandpa dress and get ready for breakfast. He brought a washbowl of water, soap and towels to his room for him. Grandpa looked as big as a mountain and his face was covered with beard, his hair was a little long.

"Put Old Kentucky over there in the bottom dresser drawer," Grandpa said. "Ethel never looks in that drawer. Mickie, I'm so glad you brought it. But it takes a lighted lamp to keep the spirits away."

Just then Grandma Ethel knocked on Grandpa's door.

"Come to breakfast," she said.

Grandpa walked on his canes to the table. He sat at the head of the table. Pa sat near him and I sat by Pa. This was the way Grandma arranged our places. We had eggs, slab bacon, red-eye ham gravy, biscuits, jelly and sorghum.

"Today we have to be getting back," Pa said. "We have to leave all of you this morning. Got to take the morning train to Gate City."

"What did you come for?" Grandpa asked. "Did you come to get a hot coal of fire?"

"I wanted to visit all of you," Pa said. "And I wanted my oldest and only son to see his Grandpa Powderjay."

"Little Mickie, the Big Sandy earth won't be his flesh, rock cliffs here won't be his bones and the Big Sandy River won't be his blood," Grandpa said, looking at me. "You live in another world Little Mickie. He will never know the law of the Clan, the old law, an eye for an eye, a tooth for a tooth and two lives sometimes for one."

After breakfast, Pa put his basket on his arm. When he said goodby to Grandpa Old Mick, he cried. And Pa wiped his eyes. I said goodby to my Grandpa, Grandma, Aunts and Uncles and I followed Pa down the path to the railroad tracks. We walked down the tracks to Zachary where Pa flagged the train with his red bandanna handkerchief. He bought a ticket after we got on the train. At Gate City we got off one train onto the other. We made a quick connection. And now for a pleasant ride down to Riverton, looking at the big city of Auckland and the Ohio River most of the way and men on riding plows plowing the big bottoms. I had never had a trip like this one. It was the greatest trip I had ever had in my life. I had met my Grandpa Old Mick Powderjay. I had met my Second Grandmother. I would have a lot to tell Mom about after we had walked from Riverton to our home in The Valley. I wouldn't tell Mom how afraid I had been of Grandpa Old Mick Powderjay. I wouldn't tell her of how all the men he had killed had come back around his bed at night until he had to sleep with a light burning. I would let Pa tell her why we had come back home sooner than we had planned.

"First Journey To The Clan" was first published in *Rumors, Dreams & Digressions*, No. 4 (Spring 1976), pp. 3-6, 11-12. It has never been reprinted. Jesse Stuart included this story in his unpublished manuscript, *Twelve Reserve Stories To Back Up: These Are My Best*—selected in January 1974, typed in February 1974 (The Jesse Stuart Foundation Collection, Ashland, Kentucky). Readers who are familiar with Jesse Stuart and his work will recognize the autobiographical nature of this short story. As a matter of fact, certain episodes of this story have appeared in other works by Stuart such as his autobiography, *Beyond Dark Hills* and his biographical account, *God's Oddling: The Story Of Mick Stuart, My Father.*

Jesse Stuart in his tobacco barn at his farm in W-Hollow — circa 1964.

From the Mountains of Pike

This will do the trick, Sall," Pa said to Mom. "Look! See what I've got! This is the deed for the Sid Beverley property. All made ready to sign! I'll show Permintis Mullins something. He'll never outshine Mick Powderjay when it comes to tradin'!"

Pa held the clean unsigned deed for Mom to see. Mom was hooking a rug while she waited for us to return. She didn't look up when Pa held the deed for her to see. She kept on working on her rug.

"What's the matter, Sall?" Pa asked. "This is the deed for that property! Don't you want us to have it? Don't you want to see me buy it? Why don't you back me up like a good wife backs up her trading husband?"

Mom still didn't speak. She kept on hooking her rug while the night wind sang around our house. Wind flapped the loose shingles on the roof. Wind rattled our loose window sashes. We heard it moan through the barren branches of the apple trees in our front yard. Pa wouldn't have any kind of shade but apple trees. He said they were good shade trees and they bore fruit too. Mom couldn't understand this, since we had seven hundred eighteen acres of land in The Valley. We owned all of The Valley but two farms. Permintis Mullins owned seventy-three acres. Sid Beverley owned one hundred and sixty acres. But Sid Beverley had moved from The Valley back to Pike County in the high mountains. And Pa and Permintis had tried to buy him out and he wouldn't sell. Not then.

And what had caused all the excitement was a letter we got at The Valley post office in the four o'clock mail. I had gone to the store for groceries, and John Baylor, who runs our post office and store, gave me the letter. When I saw it was from Sid Beverley I knew the letter must be important. Important to Pa. I rode the horse home in a hurry. Pa was delighted when he read that Sid Beverley said he was ready to sell. Said he was happier back in the mountains where he was born and grew to manhood. Said something about going home to drink the water from the well of his youth and it tasted so good and things like that. How much fresher and better the air was. How much friendlier the people were. The smile left Pa's face when he read where Sid said he was writing Permintis Mullins and telling him too the farm was for sale. Said in the letter he was writing both at the same time. "I'm telling you that I'm writing Permintis," the letter said. "I'm telling Permintis I'm writing you. I know you don't get along too well. But both of you are my friends and I'm ready to sell my farm in The Valley."

When Pa read this he stood a minute and looked into the open fire. That's the place Pa looked when he was in a deep study. And when he looked into the fire he didn't speak to anybody. Then Pa shouted: "Adger, put the saddles on the horses in a hurry." I ran to the barn to saddle the horses. We had a car but in March our roads were impassable. We had to ride horseback when we traveled any distance. I didn't ask Pa any questions. I knew he'd hatched something. After I'd saddled the horses and run back to the house, I heard Mom say: "Don't do it, Mick."

But Pa and I ran back to the barn, led our saddled horses from the stalls. Pa climbed upon Moll's back like a young man. His foot in the stirrup and his other leg high up over Moll's back, he dropped into the saddle and we were off. I followed him. I knew something was in the wind. A big trade was on. He was off to beat Permintis Mullins.

"As fast as we can go to Blakesburg," he said. "Nine miles and an hour and a half to get there. We got to get there before the clerk's office closes. It closes at six. And we've got muddy traveling."

We made it all right. We had ten minutes to spare. But when we asked for the deed, it took more than ten minutes to make it. We were on the safe side now. Jack Willis, Greenwood County's clerk, belonged to Pa's party. Pa had ridden horseback everyday and part of the night for one week before the election to help elect Jack Willis.

"Sure, Mick," he said. "I'll favor you. You favored me. I'll never forget you. Got this office by forty-four votes and I think this work you did put me over. Yes, I'll make that deed."

Permintis Mullins rode his horse day and night for you too, I thought. But I didn't speak my thoughts. He belongs to the same party too. And I wondered if Jack Willis wouldn't tell Permintis the same thing if he'd come to have a deed made in the night. I wondered if Pa would think to ask if Permintis had been there before we arrived. Pa never left a stone unturned when he traded. This was one reason Permintis Mullins didn't like Pa. I'd heard Mom and Pa talk on winter evenings when they sat before the fire, how Sid Beverley, Permintis Mullins, and their wives and Pa and Mom had come from Pike County when they were young married couples. How they all worked with each other in the beginning. They were all traders. How they left Pike County where about everybody was a good trader and had all come to Greenwood County where there weren't many land, cattle, and horse traders. They'd heard great stories of the poor traders in this county and they came to get rich. And when Pa got ahead of Sid Beverley, Sid got sick at heart and went back to Pike County. I knew it wasn't the fresh air, the water from the family well he drank when he was a boy, and the friendliness of the people that called him back. It was Pa's doing so much better than he did. It was Pa's getting most of The Valley that hurt him. It was Pa's getting up at midnight and getting there first that beat Sid Beverley.

It was when Pa tried to buy Permintis Mullins' farm that Permintis turned on him. From that hour, Pa and Permintis never stood by one another again. And they never traded with each other. Viola Mullins, Permintis' wife, never came to see Mom again. Permintis' boys, Cief, Ottis, and Bill, never spoke to my brother Finn and me again. The big rift came between us when Pa got enough ahead by his trading to "buy Permintis out." Pa had insulted Permintis. And if anybody on earth knew the Mullinses we did. If anybody knew the Powderjays, the Mullinses did. They knew we had often carried "hardware" pieces. We knew they did too. They knew we had used them in Pike County before we left. We knew they carried them there and had used them too. We didn't want to get into it with each other. How many dead there would have been, would have been anybody's guess.

"Say, Jack," Pa whispered when Jack had finished making the deed, "I want to ask you something. Don't ever mention that I've asked you this. But I want a truthful answer right from the shoulder."

"You'll get it, Mick," Jack Willis told Pa. "I won't lie to you."

"Has Permintis Mullins been in here this afternoon?" Pa asked. "Have you made a deed for him for this Sid Beverley property?"

"He's not been here, Mick," Jack said.

"Thank you, Jack," Pa's face beamed with happiness. "I know you'd tell me the truth."

Then Pa pulled a big fat billfold from his hip pocket. He took enough bills from it to paper a small room. He started peeling off the ones with his big thumb to pay for the deed.

"I wouldn't take a penny for that deed, Mick," Jack said. "I know you've made the green lettuce in your day by trading. I know you got more lettuce than I'll ever have working in this office and getting myself elected every four years. But I wouldn't take a penny from you. It's a pleasure to serve you, Mick. It's a pleasure to have you for a friend. You're the greatest trader in Greenwood County. There's never been one as good and I don't think there ever will be."

Pa loved these words. His face turned redder than the cold March winds had ever made it. He looked at Jack Willis and smiled. Jack stood there looking at Pa, a large square-shouldered man, with a clean, folded, unsigned deed in his big stubby hand. Pa didn't insist that Jack take the money for the deed. With the other hand he slipped the big billfold into his hip pocket and buttoned the pocket and kept it there. That's where Pa kept his big money. He kept his "chicken feed" in a little pocketbook in his front pocket.

"Jack, you're a good man and a reliable friend," Pa said. "I appreciate this from the bottom of my heart. Appreciate it more than I have the words to tell you. My wife doesn't like the way I work all night when a trade is on. She can't understand it. But I have often told her if I go first, the one thing I want her and my sons to remember about me is I was a great trader. I want them to remember the grass didn't grow under my feet. That the early bird always got the worm and I was the early bird."

"You're that, Mick," Jack agreed as we left his office.

With the deed in his inside coat pocket, Pa went down the courthouse corridor laughing. His laughter echoed against the stone walls and returned to us, deafening our ears. When we got back to our horses, unhitched them from the posts, and were in the saddles again, Pa said: "See how men respect you, Son, when you do something in life. Boy, I'll make that Permintis Mullins live hard. He'll die when I get that Sid Beverley farm. His mouth has been watering for it ever since Sid went back to Pike. And I don't blame him," Pa shouted as we galloped our horses from Blakesburg. "Sweet meadows, timbered hills, good tobacco ground…who wouldn't want it?"

I didn't say anything. I rode along beside Pa.

"I want you boys to learn something from me while I'm alive and trading," Pa said. "You boys don't realize what a great trader I am. And you won't know it until after I'm gone."

"I've loved you for thirty years with all my heart," Pa said as he stood before Mom with the deed in his hand.

"Second to trading, Mick," she said. "I play second fiddle. It's your trading you think about. It's been your life since I've been married to you. All you do is trade and brag about it. Some of these times, somebody is goin' to be just a little smarter than you."

Then Pa laughed as I had never heard him laugh before. He put the deed in his inside coat pocket, pulled a cigar from his vest pocket, bit the end from it with his tobacco-stained teeth, wet the cigar with his tongue. Then he put it between his clean-shaven lips, pulled a match from his hatband, struck it on his thumbnail, and held the flame to the end of the long black cigar. He pulled enough smoke from the cigar into his mouth at one time to send a cloud of smoke to the ceiling. With the cigar in his mouth, he looked up at the smoke, put his thumbs behind his suspenders, pulled them out, and let them fly back and hit him while he laughed, smoked, and listened to Mom.

"You're too proud of yourself, Mick," Mom warned. She had

stopped hooking her rug now as she sat there watching Pa walk up and down the room. "You know Permintis Mullins is a dangerous man. You know he's a proud man. When you hurt his pride, you do something to him. He's liable to explode. You know the Mullinses back in Pike County, don't you?"

"And you know the Powderjays too, don't you?" Pa snapped. "You're married to one. We had pride back in Pike County too. And we got it now. That's why I own The Valley. I'll have Permintis Mullins hemmed. I'll own land all around old Permintis. And if he's got any pride left in his bones he'll come to me like a man. We'll set a price 'give or take.' And when he sets the price, I know he can't 'take it.' I'll get it all. What kind of pride do you call that, Sal?"

Pa laughed louder than he did before.

"We've been together thirty years, Mick," Mom said. "Even if you do stay on the road and trade, I want you to be with me a while longer. I just have a feeling something is goin' to happen to you. I don't know what. I do know Permintis Mullins!"

"Not anything is goin' to happen," Pa assured her.

Pa had stopped laughing now. He had taken his big thumbs from behind his suspenders. He didn't blow smoke at the ceiling. He held the cigar in his hand and looked at Mom. Mom didn't often talk to him like this. "We're goin' to have this farm before Permintis Mullins knows what's goin' on. I'm leaving here tonight. Adger is goin' with me. Finn is goin' with us to Auckland and bring the horses back. We're goin' to get that five o'clock train up Big Sandy. We're heading for Pike County tonight. Sid and Clara will be signing this deed for me at about noon tomorrow if the train's on time."

Mom looked at Pa and then she looked at me. Mom didn't know what to say.

"It's the early bird that gets the worm," Pa bragged. Then he started laughing again.

"I've heard you say that so much, Mick," Mom said. "But I'm afraid, Mick."

"Not anything to be afraid of," Pa boasted, as he walked toward the dresser and opened the drawer.

"No, Mick," Mom said, getting up from her chair. And then she smiled. "You don't need that. Not you. Anybody who can trade and make money like you, can protect himself with his big strong fist."

Pa closed the dresser drawer. He looked at Mom and smiled. Then he pulled her close to him with his big arms around her.

"Now you're talking like the little girl who used to love me," he told her. "That's the way I love to hear you talk. That puts the spirit in me. I'll have that farm now or I'll know the reason. Adger, get Finn out of bed. Have him dress and let's be on our way."

When I returned with Finn, Pa was still holding Mom in his big arms. He wasn't acting like the trader now. He was acting like a man in love when he held my beautiful mother in his arms. And I knew why Mom had bragged on him. She didn't want Pa to take his piece of hardware with him. She knew Pike County and she knew Pa. She knew Pa had as much spirit and pride as any man in Pike County. She knew if any man asked Pa to count to ten and then draw, Pa would do it. She knew there wasn't a Mullins of the name who could bluff my father.

Pa squeezed Mom tight and kissed her goodbye and we were off into the night. Finn and I rode old Ned double. Pa took the lead on Moll. It was past midnight. The moon was down. We rode through the mud and the night wind. We rode by starlight. It was four in the morning when we reached Auckland.

"Now, be careful goin' back," Pa advised Finn. "Don't go to sleep in the saddle. Don't get Moll's bridle rein tangled around you and let her drag you from Ned's saddle. Go home and get some sleep."

"Don't worry about me, Pa," Finn replied. "I'll get the horses home all right. I won't go to sleep in the saddle. I worry about you. Up all night and not any sleep. I've had some sleep."

"We'll get a little sleep on the train," Pa told him. "Business is business, you know, and when a deal is hot it's better to forget sleep. There'll be time enough for sleep when I have this deed signed. I'll sleep peacefully coming back on the train tonight. Be sure and meet us here with the horses."

"I won't forget," Finn said as he mounted old Ned.

We stood there in the starlight, not far from the depot, and watched Finn ride away. Then Pa turned toward the railroad station and I followed him. When Pa stood at the window getting our tickets, I just happened to look back and there sat Permintis Mullins. His eyes were about half-closed. He sat there dreaming like a lizard half asleep in the morning sun. I didn't say anything. Not to Pa. I'd let him see Permintis for himself. It made my heart skip a few beats to see him there.

"Here's your ticket," Pa said, looking up at about the same time.

When he saw Permintis Mullins, he froze like my Irish setter, Rusty, when he sees a bird. Pa didn't move a muscle. His big gray eyes narrowed down. When Permintis Mullins awoke from his half sleep with Pa's eyes on him, he jumped up from his seat. He muttered something we couldn't understand. I think he called Pa a bad name under his breath. He sat back down and looked at Pa. Neither one spoke. He knew what Pa was after. Pa knew what he was after. When Pa did move he walked outside the station and I followed.

"What do you know about that." It was hard for Pa to believe. "Do you reckon Jack Willis lied to me?"

"I'll bet he came later and went to Jack Willis' home and got Jack out of bed," I said. "That's how he got his deed. You know he's got one too."

"You reckon he has?" Pa looked strangely at me.

"Think I saw it in his inside coat pocket," I told him.

"Let's get our heads together and do some thinkin' before we get on the train." Pa wasn't laughing now. "Let's get on the same coach so we can watch 'im."

"But Pa, you don't want any trouble with 'im," I pleaded.

"We're not goin' to have any trouble," Pa assured me. "I just want to get close enough to watch him. Want to be close enough to feel any move he makes. Want one of us to keep an eye on him at all times."

"Suppose he's got a piece of hardware along?" I said.

"I'd a had my piece along if it hadn't been for your mother's soft-soapin' me right before I left," Pa explained. "Even a woman when she loves a man with all her heart is liable to get him hurt. Hurt by a dangerous character like that Permintis Mullins."

Permintis Mullins was a big Pike County mountaineer. He had a clean-shaven bony face. His handlebar moustache looked like a long black bow tie, tied under his nose with both ends of the tie sagging. He wore a big black umbrella hat. He was a big man but he wasn't built like Pa. He wasn't broad shouldered. He was tall. He had long arms and big hands. He was long legged and wore tight-fitting pants that bulged at the knees. Permintis had the eyes of an eagle. They were beady black eyes that pierced when they looked at you.

"When we get off this train at Bainville, let's make a run and get the first taxi," Pa suggested. "Take it all the way to Sid Beverley's. It's just three miles from the railroad station. I've been over that road many a time."

"You make the plans, Pa, and I'll follow 'em," I said.

"All we want to do is beat old Permintis there," Pa whispered.

When the train pulled up, we stood there waiting for Permintis. I happened to turn around and he was standing behind watching us. "Come on, Pa," I said.

And Pa followed me onto the coach. When we walked in and got a seat in the smoker, Permintis followed us. He sat on the other side of the aisle just a little behind us. When he sat down, I saw the deed in the inside pocket of his unbuttoned coat. Maybe it was my imagination, but I thought I saw the prints of a holster on his hip. I was sure he'd brought his hardware piece along.

When breakfast was called and Pa and I went to the diner, Permintis followed us. He sat about the middle of the diner. Pa and I got up in the front corner so we could talk.

"He's goin' to Sid Beverley's sure as the world," Pa said. "I wonder when he got that deed. We were the last ones in Jack Willis' office before he closed. After the way Jack talked to me, I don't believe he would get out of bed to make a deed for that scoundrel."

"But he voted for Jack too, Pa," I said. "He belongs to our party and he rode day and night last week of the election to help Jack Willis.

I understand he says he elected Jack. Said his work gave Jack the extra forty-four votes."

Pa couldn't believe it. He couldn't believe we were on the train eating breakfast in one end of the diner and down the midway sat Permintis Mullins. All of us heading for Sid Beverley's place on Wolfe Creek.

After breakfast we went back to our seats in the smoker. Strange, but Permintis finished his breakfast same time we did. When we sat down, Permintis had to walk past us. Pa scanned him carefully.

Just before noon, about the time we reached the border of Pike County, Pa got up to light a cigar and stretch his legs. Permintis got up too. He stood up and watched Pa, though he didn't speak. And everybody riding on this coach watched the strange actions of Pa and Permintis.

When the conductor called "Litchfield" Pa stood up again.

"Bainville's the next stop," Pa whispered. Then Pa walked out into the aisle while the train stopped. Permintis got up too. Pa walked in the opposite direction since he was a little shy of Permintis. Then we heard "all aboard" from outside. Pa walked back to our seat and sat down. He was so restless he couldn't wait. He didn't like Permintis Mullins' black eagle eyes trained on him all the time either. When Pa got seated the train was moving again.

"Where's Permintis, Pa?" I said, looking back.

"Men's room, maybe," Pa said, puffing on his cigar. Then, Pa looked back. "Do you reckon he got off this moving train?"

"There he goes, Pa," I shouted as I looked from the window. "He's running down the street."

"Let me off'n here," Pa screamed, jumping up.

"But the train is moving now, Pa," I said, holding him by the arm. "You can't get off. Not now."

"We're tricked," Pa shouted.

Everybody started looking at us and the conductor came running and grabbed Pa by the arm. "What's the matter with you?" he asked Pa. "Are you trying to commit suicide? You can't leave this train when it's moving like this."

"But that scoundrel," Pa screamed, shaking his head. "That Permintis Mullins! He's tricked me!"

"What fellow?" the conductor asked. "What did he do? Relieve you of your wallet or something?"

"Not that, Conductor," I said. "I'll explain it to you. He and my father are here to buy the same piece of land down in Greenwood County and it's owned by Sid Beverley on Wolfe Creek. The other fellow got off at Litchfield and is trying to beat us to Wolfe Creek. We're on this train and can't get off before Bainville. Which is closer to Wolfe Creek, Litchfield or Bainville?"

"Bainville, of course," the conductor said, smiling at Pa. "It's only three miles from Bainville to Sid Beverley's on Wolfe Creek. It's thirteen miles from Litchfield to Sid Beverley's. I know this country well. I live in Litchfield."

"Can we get a taxi in Bainville?" Pa asked.

"They'd laugh at you if you asked for a taxi there," said the conductor as he looked over his bright-rimmed glasses at Pa. "Bainville's not big enough to support a taxi."

"Can Permintis Mullins get one in Litchfield?" I asked.

"He can't get one there either," the conductor said.

Everybody on the coach had become interested in our problem. They listened when the conductor talked with us. There were whispers from one end of the coach to the other. And there was much laughter which Pa didn't like. His face got as red as a ripe sourwood leaf. The fire died in his cigar. Pa put it in his mouth and chewed the end. When the conductor left us to call the next station, Pa and I hurried to the end of the coach.

When the train stopped, we were the first to get off. "Taxi! Taxi!" Pa screamed. Somebody laughed at Pa. "Can I get somebody to drive me to Sid Beverley's on Wolfe Creek? I'm in a hurry." There wasn't any bidding. Not a single bid.

"Come, Adger," Pa shouted. "Not any time to lose. We've got to hoof it! We can beat him if we hurry! I know the way! Come on!"

We started off. I never saw Pa move like he was moving now. He threw the cigar down. I hoped, as we trotted along down the muddy road, somebody might come along with a wagon and pick us up. I wondered how Permintis was going to cover his thirteen miles if his road was muddy as this one. And I hoped it was.

"Now is the time to beat Permintis," Pa grunted with a half breath. "Pray for a ride and keep going. Let's strike while the iron's hot. Early bird…"

"He's got thirteen miles of the muddy road," I grunted. "We've got three…We can beat 'im…"

"But we lost time on that awful slow train," Pa stammered, for he was short of breath. "Permintis pulled a fast one."

After one mile on this muddy road, we stopped. We didn't talk, to save our breath. We doubled time on the second mile. We reached the mouth of Wolfe Creek. Then we crossed the bridge.

"Back to my homeland," Pa grunted. "Changed so I don't know it. Not my homeland any longer. The Valley…" And Pa stopped talking, saved his breath, and increased his speed.

When we turned the first big bend in the Wolfe Creek road, Pa stopped. "Yonder's where Sid lives," he moaned as he wiped streams of sweat from his face.

As we hurried the last quarter mile, our breath coming short and fast, we saw three men come from Sid's big log house. We stopped short when we saw them get in a car. They started driving toward us. To our surprise the car pulled up close beside Pa, who was spattered with mud, and stopped.

Permintis rolled the window down and stuck his head out. "Would you like to have this, old land-hawg?" Permintis shouted, holding up a paper for Pa to see. Then, he laughed slyly as he pulled his head inside and rolled the window up. The driver gunned the car.

Pa was stunned. We stood there in silence looking at each other and at the car as it moved slowly along, flinging two streaks of yellow clay into the bright March wind from the rear wheels.

"Wonder if he got that farm?" Pa said, breaking our silence as

Permintis' car crossed the Wolfe Creek bridge and was out of sight. "Let's go see what happened."

Sid Beverley, six feet five inches tall, and a big man for his height, opened the door when we walked onto his porch. His frosted crab-grass-colored hair was ruffled by the March wind. His blue eyes sparkled.

"Welcome home, Mick," Sid greeted Pa. "Welcome, Adger! Back to the land of your people. Come in! I've been waitin' for you all mornin'! Permintis told me you were on your way!"

We walked into the house, where Clara took Pa's hand. "How is Sallie, Mick?" Clara asked, but Pa didn't answer.

"I come to buy that farm from you, Sid," Pa said, turning to Sid.

"Well, the early bird always gets the worm, Mick," Sid told Pa. "You've traded enough to know that!"

"It beats all I ever heard tell of," Pa grunted as he wiped streams of perspiration from his read face with a blue bandanna. "Do you mean that Permintis outsmarted me?"

"Call it anything you like," Sid said calmly. "Permintis telegraphed the Sheriff of Pike County to meet the train at Litchfield with a car, a notary public, and a witness for a land deal."

"That scoundrel," Pa shouted as he shook his fist in the direction Permintis had gone.

I looked at my father as he stood there before Sid Beverley. The light that had always been in his eyes when he was about to make a good trade was gone. And then, I remembered how many times Mom had warned him that someday an earlier bird would get the worm.

"From The Mountains Of Pike" was first published in *The Georgia Review,* Vol. 7, No. 2 (Summer 1953), pp. 134-135. It has been reprinted in *The Georgia Review,* (Spring 1986), pp. 277-288, and Stanley W. Lindberg and Stephen Corey, editors, *Necessary Fictions—Selected Stories From The Georgia Review* (Athens, The University Of Georgia Press, 1986), pp. 277-288. (This story is incorrectly listed in Woodbridge's *Jesse And Jane Stuart A Bibliography* and the Jesse Stuart Foundation's *Short Story Finders Guide* as having first appeared in the June, 1938 edition of *American Mercury.*)

Jesse Stuart at the well in front of his home in W-Hollow — circa 1964.

The Guests in King Arthur's Court

The phone rang in the Jason Stringer Lodge at Greenwood State Park. My being behind the desk, a summer position I had obtained because my parents belonged to and voted for the Big Party—and our Governor had been elected and all positions from Park Manager down to Maid Service had changed hands. But, I'd not planned to keep the work I had a lifetime. I knew I couldn't do this anyway. One of these days in my State, a Governor of the Little Party would be elected and all the jobs from Park Manager down to Maid Service would change again. I'd planned to work only this summer, save my money and go to college. This was the reason I was behind the desk answering the telephone.

"Hello," I spoke softly when I picked up the receiver.

"This is Sarah Bostick," spoke a familiar voice.

"Oh, Miss Bostick," I said. "My teacher! It's so good to hear your voice. It doesn't change even over the telephone."

"But, to whom am I speaking?" she asked me. "I can't quite place your voice."

"Oh, oh, Miss Bostick," I said. I'm Clara Booth! You'll remember me."

"Remember you, Clara?" she spoke with her old familiar laughter. She'd always had a sense of humor. This was something about her besides her being a great teacher, that all of her students in Wonder High School loved. "You graduated this year. You know I'd remember you. I remember the students I taught for forty-five years. Well, I suppose many I wouldn't know that I taught in my beginning years if I were to see them today. And, I doubt if many would know me if they'd meet me on the street."

Now, she laughed loudly. Her meeting of the years, passing time she had accepted gracefully. She was one teacher who didn't mind growing old. She had taught, so she told us seniors in her English

Class—last one she'd ever teach at Wonder High School at sixty-nine—just before she reached seventy—because she liked to teach and so she would get more payment in her retirement check.

I knew Miss Bostick didn't make as much with her B.A. and her M.A. degrees, plus her forty hours on her Ph.D. in Education which she told us about—a degree she wanted but was never able to get, because she didn't make enough money and she couldn't spare the time. What a great and colorful English teacher was Sarah Bostick. I never knew whether she made enough money teaching in Wonder High School—a Kentucky high school—but I did know how much she made for she told us—and it wasn't as much as my father made driving a truck for Armaco Steel Mills.

"Miss Bostick what can I do for you?" I said.

"Maybe you can help me, Clara," she said, "you're my former student. All my former students help me—what I want Clara—and I think you've been at the Jason Stringer Lodge at Greenwood State Park long enough to know that if one, a citizen of our Commonwealth or if guests coming in from other states request a fire be made in the big fireplace in the Lodge—say one who is bringing guests—that this fire will be made!"

"Oh, yes, Miss Bostick," I said. "Sure, I know this. We've done this before—many times since I've been here."

"I know it's not really cold enough for a fire in the fireplace, but I'd like to bring my guests—and we'd like to sit before the fire with trays of food—watch the wonderful fire, sit, eat, talk—yes, reminisce—yes, about the past and what the future holds for us."

"Oh, yes, Miss Bostick, gladly will I do this," I said. "What time will you and your party arrive?"

"How long will it take you to get the fire in that large magnificent fireplace in the Jason Stringer Lodge?" she asked.

"Give us two hours," I said. "I'll get hold of Park Manager John Noakes right now. And we'll go to work. We have to carry in cordwood we've saved from Greenwood Park's fallen trees. But we can build that wonderful fire for you and your guests, Miss Bostick."

"All right, Clara, my party and I will be at Jason Stringer Lodge, Greenwood State Park, in two hours sharp," Miss Bostick said. "Now, I'll hang up the phone. You know me—when I tell you we'll be there at the certain time, we'll be there."

She hung up the phone.

Now, I left my position behind the front desk, a five hundred dollar a month position—while I doubted if my retired teacher, Miss Bostick, with all her years and experience and time spent, getting her education received as much as I did with my high school diploma and my political appointment. And, as I've told you, I got this because my father and mother were loyal to the Big Party which they voted for and supported with some of their money. They'd not given much to the Big Party. But what they'd given showed their hearts were right and got this appointment for me which put me in the real money. My parents had been more than paid for their Big Party donations.

When I left the phone, I just let it ring to help my wonderful teacher, Miss Bostick. I ran down the steps to the dining room. Here I found Mr. Noakes, our Greenwood State park Manager beside the cash register. He'd vowed—even promised our newly elected State Governor—accused of being hostile to school teachers—Governor Warfield Fox—that he'd make Greenwood State Park pay. Yes, he vowed he'd make a profit. If it didn't make a profit, I thought it might mean his position. And, Epfie Noakes, his good wife, who worked as a waitress, as a cook—yes, any place in the Jason Stringer Lodge—was the best worker I'd ever seen. She worked while her husband watched the cash register. She was out among the limited number of waitresses—that had been reduced—and even docked if ten minutes late, for economy reasons.

"Mr. Noakes," I said. "My former teacher—my wonderful teacher, Miss Bostick, is coming and she's bringing guests. I don't know how many. But she wants a fire built in the fireplace in the Jason Stringer Lodge Hall."

"Stop, stop," he said. "My heavens, I know her—a famous teacher in our Commonwealth. She will be bringing many guests here. Let's get that fire built."

He left the cash register, leaving it to the Head Waitress, Elmira Boyd, wife of a well-to-do business man in our Big Party. Her family had contributed to get the Governor Fox of our Big Party elected.

Mr. Noakes—and he wasn't really able for he'd had two heart attacks—short and stocky as he was—took off like a shot out of a gun. He went directly to his working wife. Both of them ran up the stairs. And I followed them. As young as I was I couldn't keep up with them. But I joined them in the Jason Stringer Lodge Hall.

"It's money if she comes in with a party," John Noakes, our Park Manager said. "Money we need here. Epfie, my good wife, muster in all the help you can to build that fire."

You should have seen the help mustered in to help build the fire. Anyone at Greenwood State Park knew that our Commonwealth Police, whose duties were to keep order around the place would not have been called in to build a fire in the huge fireplace in the Lodge Hall. Well, they were. They were chosen to carry in wood from the cordwood stacks outside the Lodge—wood sawed, stacked that the guests had so admired.

Waitresses were called in to help Mr. and Mrs. Noakes. And, I still away from my front desk and the phone, helped to build this fire for my teacher, Miss Sarah Bostick and her friends she was bringing to Jason Stringer Lodge at Greenwood State Park.

The State Police, Maintenance Workers, Room Service women, Mr. and Mrs. Noakes and I all helped carry in the wood and build this big fire. In two hours we had one of the finest fires going that was ever built in a Lodge Hall in any of our many State Parks in our Commonwealth. And we'd been a full two hours doing this.

Now, we awaited Miss Sarah Bostick and the many guests—perhaps, a busload she'd bring to our Jason Stringer Lodge, which would add cash to our cash register. And this would make Park Manager John Noakes and his hard-working wife Epfie very happy. He could hold onto his managerial position if he kept Greenwood State Park in the black. It was Little Party's Manager Haliburton Royster who put it in the red, first and only year it had been opened. It took parties, such as Miss Bostick would bring, organizations, clubs, high school and college class reunions coming to the Jason Stringer Lodge at Greenwood State Park to put us in the black so all of us could hold onto our jobs.

Now, with the fire built in the huge fireplace—a big roaring crackling fire from the dry wood, with Mr. and Mrs. Noakes standing in the lobby watching the fire in this palatial five million dollar Lodge, I was back behind the desk—back on the telephone. But, business was not good. I wasn't getting a phone call—not even a reservation.

When I looked toward the door, Miss Sarah Bostick entered— with that smile she always wore on her face—her lips always half-curved in smile—as if she were always ready to pop with laughter. Her big blue eyes, with a few wrinkles around them, were half smiling, too. She was wearing an old-fashioned, high neck dress, with a check in it, a patent-leather belt about everyone in her English classes— especially girls—could never forget it. She carried a little basket on her arm.

With her were two young girls, not quite as old as I—and there was a woman with her, whom I suspected of being another Kentucky teacher according to her wearing apparel. Her dress was old, outdated— actually a bit faded and frayed. It was the kind of dress my mother, wife of a truck driver for Armaco Steel, wore ten years ago.

Mr. and Mrs. Noakes didn't know my wonderful teacher Miss Bostick. But I watched him when Miss Bostick came bouncing over the floor toward him. When Miss Bostick, who was short and plump, walked she went in a hurry and seemed to bounce along.

But, Miss Bostick, recognized Mr. Noakes and there was a reason for this. His picture, but not his wife Epfie's pictures, had been in our *Greenwood County Gazette* so many times when he and Frazier Kinnard were both seeking this lush appointment from the State Park Commission after the Big Party swept over the Little Party in the Governor's race. But Governor Warfield Fox gave John Noakes his blessings. This caused Frazier Kinnard to leave the Big Party and join the Little Party.

"You're Mr. Noakes, the Greenwood State Park Manager," said Miss Bostick as she walked up to him. "I've recognized you by your fine picture—a real likeness of you in the *Greenwood County Gazette*. I'm Miss Sarah Bostick and this is my party!"

I thought Mr. Noakes, a man of few words, a businessman who looked over everything with an eye for money for Greenwood State Park would fall over. He did extend a trembling hand to meet her hand—the free one for she was carrying a basket with the other. He did take a step backward.

"Pleased—pleased to meet you Miss Bostick," he muttered in a low trembling voice. "This is my wife Epfie."

"It's nice to meet you too, Mrs. Noakes," Miss Bostick said. "Now let me introduce members of my party. This is Miss Ethel Bottomly, an English teacher retired from the Lantern County High School. We're classmates from college. And here is Miss Mamie Shrouse and Miss Deborah Lykins, two juniors she taught last year."

There were greetings between Mr. and Mrs. Noakes and Miss Bostick's three guests from Lantern County.

"Mr. Noakes, I want to thank you for being so courteous to build this good fire in this Jason Stringer Lodge," Miss Bostick said. "I know building this fire takes time and it takes wood. But I saw one built here last year and I never forgot it. It makes this Jason Stringer Lodge look like what I would have imagined that Great Palace looked like in early England where King Arthur met with his Knights at the Round Table. I've taught this story for forty-five years to my students in high school English Literature."

I thought Mr. Noakes might ask Miss Bostick what she had in her basket—but, his being a man of good manners he would not inquire. But knowing Epfie Noakes, whose manners were not as refined, she certainly might ask.

"Being a Kentucky school teacher for forty-five years, Mr. Noakes, as you know, we're not a wealthy profession—no matter if we do love our work and won't do anything else," Miss Bostick said. "So I've brought food for my guests. I couldn't afford the Park's from four to five dollar lunches. So, I brought this little basket with a few sandwiches and potato chips."

Mrs. Noakes turned and walked away. Her face was very red. But, Mr. Noakes stood facing Miss Bostick in silence. He was a well-mannered man with few words. And he had a reptilian face that was always serious. His thin reptilian lips, I'd never seen a curve into a smile.

"There is your fire over there," Mr. Noakes said. "Go over and sit before it. Eat the food you brought and enjoy yourselves."

"Thank you for this great fire and this privilege of sitting in this beautiful Jason Stringer Lodge Hall like King Arthur's Queen Guinevere, with my guests around me to partake of this beauty in our simple festivities," Miss Bostick said to departing John Noakes. "Kentucky teachers haven't made enough to buy food, clothes, shelter and books and have security after their teaching days are over."

Well, I knew Miss Sarah Bostick was telling the truth. 'The poor thing,' we girls used to speak of her in Wonder High School, when we'd see her return on a Monday morning wearing the same old frayed and faded dress she'd worn the week before.

While Miss Bostick and her party walked up and each took a plush seat before the flaming fire, there they began to take their sandwiches and potato chips from the basket. Epfie Noakes stopped in her tracks and began to look at me. Ten steps away Mr. Noakes stopped and looked back toward me. I pretended I wasn't seeing either of them.

I was the one when I got the phone call from my teacher Miss Bostick, who left my position behind the front desk and ran down the steps to the dining room where I found Mr. Noakes behind the cash register and told him excitedly the good news.

While the Noakes' stood staring at me in disgust, as if I had caused the trouble—yes, committed a sin. Now, what I did—since business was dull and I wasn't getting any calls for reservations, I just bowed out of the picture. I bent down behind the front desk where I would be slow to rise up again until Mr. and Mrs. Noakes moved on. My heart was with my teacher, Miss Bostick, over in front of the big fire, seated with her guests—where they were eating their sandwiches and potato chips like guests in King Arthur's Court.

"The Guests in King Arthur's Court" was first published in *Playgirl,* Vol. 1, No. 1 (January 1973), pp. 55-56, 62. It has never been reprinted. Stuart's picture is included in the editor's overview of the month's featured authors and poets and their literary contributions in this, the premier edition of *Playgirl* magazine. Interestingly, other Appalachian writers and poets made contributions to the first edition of *Playgirl* including Harriette Simpson Arnow, Lee Pennington, and Jane Stuart. Of "The Guests in King Arthur's Court," the editor writes: "In The area of education the often underpaid school teacher is recognized in a short story by a former educator, Jesse Stuart who is one of America's most versatile contemporary authors. Some of his most noted works include *Man With a Bull-Tongue Plow,* which was selected as one of the 1000 great Books of the World: and *Taps for Private Tussie,* which was selected as one of the Masterpieces of World Literature." "The Guests in King Arthur's Court" is clearly based on an incident at The Jesse Stuart Lodge at Greenbo State Park, near Greenup, Kentucky.

I Can Climb Higher Than You

When Finn and I saw Battle Cartee pass our house on his way to work, we started down the path to his shack to play with Sonnie and Ruth. Last year when we'd gone to play with them we didn't have to wait for Battle to leave for work. Battle wasn't their real father. He was dead and after he had died Nannie married again. When Nannie died she had left Ruth and Sonnie with Battle.

Their shack was just below ours and it was a lonely place. Nearly everybody in our neighborhood who had to pass this house at night claimed that he had seen or heard something. Erf Bascom had seen a big white dog walking along its roof top one night tearing off shingles with his teeth. Fidis Moore had seen a woman dressed in white jump from the upstairs window. Enic Pratt had heard chains rattle around this house one night. Everybody was afraid to rent this shack but Battle. He rented it and the garden for four dollars a month. Battle had to rent a cheap house since he worked for farmers for a small wage when he could find work. When he went away to work at daylight, Ruth and Sonnie were afraid to stay alone. They had heard people talk about the things they had seen and heard around this old log shack.

Finn and I weren't afraid of the house. We never thought about a dog on the roof tearing off shingles, a woman dressed in a white robe jumping from the upstairs window, and the rattling of chains. We had a good time playing with Ruth and Sonnie. The only person we were afraid of was Battle, and we'd never been afraid of him until after Nannie died.

We walked down the weed-lined path. The sun hadn't dried the morning dew from the deep hollow. We got ragweed seeds between our toes and the sand stuck to our dew-wet feet as we hurried to play with Sonnie and Ruth. And as soon as we came in sight of the shack where the red wasps and mud daubers built their nests under the roof-lap, Ruth and Sonnie ran to meet us. I thought Ruth was pretty wearing a pale blue dress with white flowers and a blue ribbon in her brown hair. I had always thought she was pretty. And she always smiled when she spoke to me.

"Look how fast I can run," Sonnie said as he came toward us with old worn-out shoes on his hands.

Sonnie couldn't walk with his legs. They dangled in the air above his head like two limp willow switches waving in the wind. Sonnie didn't look at the ground when he walked, though his head was close to it. He opened his eyes wide and looked up at us.

"Be careful, Sonnie," Ruth said. "You'll fall."

But Sonnie wasn't careful. He ran on his arms as fast as he could. He wanted to show us that he could do the things we could. And before he reached us, his legs went over the wrong way and he fell flat on his face. Weed stubble scratched his face until it bled. But he got up laughing and tried again. This time he walked toward us. The tiny trickle of blood that ran down his face and off at the end of his nose didn't make him cry.

"I told you, Sonnie, that you'd fall," Ruth scolded.

"But it didn't hurt," he said laughing as he reached the front gate and doubled his limp legs under him and sat on them. "A little scratch on my face can't hurt me."

Ruth, Sonnie, Finn and I played hide-and-seek in the brown broom sage that covered the slope of the worn-out mountain earth. We couldn't go into the thickets to hide for we were afraid of copperheads. We had to play on the broom sage slope or in the yard where Battle had cut the tall weeds with a scythe. Here, the stubble hurt our bare feet. And after we had played hide-and-seek until we were tired of that game, we fished for minnows in the creek. We bent straight pins and made hooks and tied them to little poles and baited our pinhooks with flies. Sonnie caught seven minnows, Ruth four, Finn five, and I caught two. We put them in a bucket of water and as soon as we were through fishing, Ruth felt sorry for the minnows and begged us to turn them back into the creek. We put them back in the deep hole under the willows where we'd caught them.

"Finn, we'd better be getting' back home," I said. "We musn't let Battle catch us here!"

"Don't go," Sonnie said. "Play with us some more. Battle just looks mean. He won't hurt you."

"Stay with us a while longer," Ruth said. "We'll play in our playhouse under the walnut tree."

Ruth wanted us to stay, too. I thought she was afraid to stay alone and wait for Battle. We'd never told Pa about what Battle had told us. He told us to stay away from his shack. If he ever caught us playing with Ruth and Sonnie again he would cut a long switch and whip our bare legs. I didn't know why he didn't want us to play with them. They didn't know either. We had always played together. We stayed with them all day many a time, and all we had to eat was cold cornbread. Ruth and Sonnie divided with Finn and me.

Our playhouse was at the edge of a rock cliff. It was a dry place when it rained. Sonnie said it had a better roof than the shack where they lived since they had to set buckets and pans under the leaks when it rained. When it rained on our cliff, white sluices of water ran over the cliff's edge. We watched the rain pour down from the sky. We liked to play under the cliff and that's the reason why we waited until we saw Battle.

"There comes Battle," Sonnie said.

"We'd better get goin'," Finn said as he ran from under the cliff. I took out after Finn for I was afraid of a man as big as Battle Cartee.

"You little hellions," Battle screamed at us. "I thought I told you to stay away from here!"

He pulled his knife from his pocket and ran upon the bluff to cut a hickory. And while he cut the hickory, Finn and I were running up the path as fast as our legs would take us. Sonnie and Ruth ran toward the shack.

"I'll give ye little devils the larrupin' I promised ye," Battle yelled as he ran off the bluff with the withe. But Finn and I were a hundred yards ahead of him running for home. We knew if we made it within sight of our shack, he'd be afraid to whip us.

Battle gained on us and I heard him getting his breath like a panting horse.

"Wind's too short to ketch ye atter I've worked all day," he grunted. Then he stopped. "But don't ever come near my place again."

Battle turned to go down the hollow while we slowly walked toward home.

"Will we ever go back down there?" Finn asked me as soon as he could get his breath to talk.

"Don't think so," I said.

But three days passed slowly while we waited. I wanted to see Ruth again. We waited until after we'd seen Battle pass our shack and then we hurried down the path to play with Ruth and Sonnie. Sonnie was out in the yard but Ruth wasn't with him this time. Sonnie came running on his hands to meet us. There was always a smile on his face and he always told us that he could do something we couldn't do.

"I can climb a tree you can't climb," he told Finn with his legs dangling in the air and his face barely above the ground.

Ruth hurried from the house and said, "Battle told you not to climb a tree!"

"Battle's not here," Sonnie said.

"But he will be here," she said. "And when he asks me if you climbed trees today, I'll tell 'im you did."

"Ah, shucks, Ruth," Sonnie grumbled. "I like to run, climb trees, fish and play hide-and-seek."

"Shan, you and Finn had better go home," Ruth said looking at the ground. "I'm afraid if Battle comes and you're here he'll hurt you!"

"Why does he have it in for us?" Finn asked.

"I'll tell you why," Sonnie said.

"Don't you tell, Sonnie," Ruth said.

"But I will tell," Sonnie said. "Battle wants to marry Ruth."

"Sonnie," she scolded.

"It's the truth," he said. "That's why he don't want you to play with her, Shan."

"Is that the truth?" I asked Ruth. "Are you going to marry Battle?"

"I'll haf to," she said.

"Why?" I asked.

"Mammie told Battle that she wanted me to marry him," she said.

"But she is dead," Finn said.

"Battle told me that she appeared to 'im when he's a-mowin' sprouts from Walker's pasture field last Monday," Ruth said.

"But you're too young to marry him," I said. "You're not fourteen. Battle's older than Pa."

"Battle told me that girls married at twelve," she said. "I guess it's all right for me to marry at fourteen."

"Everybody gets married," Sonnie said, "but not everybody can climb a tree like I can."

Sonnie ran toward a bushy-topped maple. And as soon as he reached it, he pulled his shoes from his hands.

"Sonnie, don't you climb that tree," Ruth screamed.

"I'll climb it too," he told her. "I'll show Finn that I can climb a tree he can't climb."

He climbed, pulling up branch by branch like a squirrel until he was high in the tree.

"How can you get down?" I asked him.

"I can get down easy as I got up," he said.

Sonnie sat high in the tree and looked down at us. I'd never seen him happier than he was now. He had climbed as big a tree as Finn could climb.

"I'll show you how to come down," Sonny said bravely and started swinging down from branch to branch with his withered legs dangling.

We stood watching him just as his tired hand lost its grip he started falling down, down among the branches—hitting this one and that one and screaming—and then to the ground as we ran to him. When we reached him, a bone from his arm was run into the ground.

"We'll haf to go get Battle," Ruth screamed.

"We'll haf to get a doctor," Finn said. "Battle's not a doctor. He can't set a broken bone.

"I'll go after 'im." I said. "I'll ride the horse to town in a hurry."

I hurried toward our barn while Finn and Ruth carried Sonnie toward the shack. I hurried to the barn, grabbed a bridle and saddle and ran to the pasture and bridled and saddled Fred. I rode 'im over the path to Greenwood and hurried to Dr. Madden's office. I told Dr. Madden about Sonnie who had to use his arms for legs because his legs weren't any good and how he'd broken one of his arms.

"Ride to the mouth of Ragwood Hollow," Dr. Madden said. "I'll drive my car that far. I can't drive a car into that hollow but I can ride in your saddle and you can ride behind me.

"All right," I said as I leaped into the saddle and galloped Fred from Greenwood to the mouth of Ragweed Hollow where Dr. Madden was already waiting. He got out of the car as I got off Fred's back. He leaped into the saddle and I climbed on behind him and we were off. Fred trotted us when he could find a place to trot. Most of the time he waded the creek. We had to go around cliffs where the path was narrow but we finally got there. I didn't go inside the house. I would have gone in if I had known Pa and Mom were there. But I didn't know it and I was afraid of Battle. I waited outside and I heard voices. I heard them talking loudly. I heard Dr. Madden quarreling with somebody.

"I can put this boy in a place where something can be done for his legs," Dr. Madden said. "And you can't keep me from doing it."

"But he's not going," Battle said. "And don't you ever darken this door again."

"I'll be back," Dr. Madden said.

Then Pa and Mom came from the house. Battle walked out on the little front porch with the roof that had fallen in. He stood there and called Dr. Madden bad names and shook his fist at him.

"How did Battle know Sonnie was hurt?" I asked Finn soon as he came out of the house.

"I told 'im," Finn said. "Ruth sent me to tell him. And as I passed home I told Mom. She hurried to the field and told Pa."

Pa called Dr. Madden to one side and was talking to him in whispers. I knew Pa was telling him that Battle was going to marry Ruth. And then I heard Dr. Madden tell Pa in whispers that were loud words so Battle could hear: "That's why he doesn't want me to take this boy to the hospital. He's afraid the Law'll get 'im for staying alone with that little girl."

Later when I rode behind Dr. Madden to the mouth of Ragweed Hollow so I could bring Fred back, he asked me questions about Ruth and Sonnie. He asked me how long I had played with them and if Battle had ever said anything to me. I told him Battle had tried to whip Finn and me because we played with them.

I was afraid to ride Fred back past where Battle lived. I was afraid he would shoot me so I rode Fred back around the ridge road, a much longer way home. I knew the paths and where the gaps were in the pasture fences.

When I got home, Mom wasn't there. I didn't know why there was so much excitement.

Next day, I could hardly wait to go with Mom and Pa and the four men and seven women, all our neighbors who had met at the house. When we reached the shack where Battle, Ruth and Sonnie lived, there was a crowd of men and women from town. Sheriff Whiteapple and Dr. Madden had brought an express up the hollow with a mattress and springs on it. We watched five men hold Battle when Sheriff Whiteapple handcuffed him. Battle called Sheriff Whiteapple and Dr. Madden bad names and when Sheriff Whiteapple took him down the path he was cursing us.

"Now, you'll go home with me," a kind, gentle woman from town said to Ruth. "I'll let you play with some girls about your own age. I'll get you some clothes and send you to school."

Ruth smiled when she talked to her. Her brown hair was pretty in the morning sunlight. Tears were in her eyes. I was glad Sheriff Whiteapple was taking Battle away. But I hated to see Sonnie and Ruth go. My eyes filled with tears as I watched them leave. We'd played with each other since we could remember.

"Good-by, Sonnie," Finn said as Dr. Madden and Pa carried him to the express.

"Good-by, Finn," Sonnie answered. "When I come back I'll run faster and climb higher than you can."

Ruth and I smiled at each other as she walked away with the woman from town. Finn and I watched them out of sight. Then we hurried up the hollow to catch up to Mom and Pa but I lagged behind Finn.

"I Can Climb Higher Than You" was first published in *Arizona Quarterly*, Vol. 15 (Summer 1959), pp. 121-127. It was reprinted in *Orient Literary*, Vol. 2, No. 3 (1964), pp. 25-29, and Albert Stewart, editor, *Deep Summer* (Morehead, Kentucky, Morehead State College Press, 1963), pp. 44-50. Woodbridge's *Jesse And Jane Stuart A Bibliography* lists one additional re-printing of the story.

Nine Bean Rows

When Miss Edna White walked into her clean, but small vegetable garden on that bright August day, with white clouds floating high above her palatial home, she carried with her a half-bushel basket. She was dressed, as she had always been, in frills and laces. She had been a teacher for forty-five years. Now, retired she lived with her very active ninety year old mother.

Miss Edna had had one marriage. At forty, she married a very handsome man, a fine dresser, who was twenty-four. They were happy for a number of years, as long as he was re-elected to a county public office. He was a man who couldn't take defeat. When he was defeated, he took to the bottle to help him drown his cares. But, Miss Edna and her mother were not in any way advocates of the bottle. So there was separation and divorce. Her handsome, well-dressed "Davie" had to take his belongings from the palatial home, inherited by Miss Edna, a showplace in Greenwood County, and go to a trailer he purchased in Greenwood. Neither Miss Edna or Davie ever married again.

"Davie couldn't be married to the bottle and to me," Miss Edna often said. "He had to choose one. Unfortunately, he chose the bottle. It was the bottle that took control of his life while he was still so young and handsome."

Now in retirement, Miss Edna, who all of her life was very active, raised a vegetable garden, also a yard which she landscaped herself, filled with varied flowers—her being a very fine painter could produce a yard with flora each season the envy of all her neighbors. She worked with retired teachers and for her political party. After retirement, she found more to do than she had ever done.

And, above all, not a teacher in the entire Greenwood County System had a keener sense of humor than Miss Edna. She would suddenly burst into laughter when friends around her were very serious. She walked into her garden, where there was not a weed in her bean rows, her cabbages, radishes, beets, cucumbers, corn, Irish potatoes, her sweet potatoes, okra, green peppers, red peppers (she always had red peppers for color) and lima beans vining up poles. Had she seen a weed in any row she would have pulled it. This was the way she kept her classroom. Not a piece of paper on the floor. If she visited a fellow teacher's classroom and there was a piece of paper on the floor she would pick it up.

On this August day, when she walked into her garden, she looked up at the white clouds floating high over her house and garden—clouds that made short morning shadows where her vegetables grew in her garden and long shadows on her spacious lawn where weeping willows, silver maples and cottonwoods grew.

"Nine bean rows have I here," she said with a smile, "but not a hive for a honeybee! Oh, what a poem, The Lake Isle of Innisfree and what a poet was William Butler Yeats. Had we been young together I could have fallen in love with that Irishman. Yes, nine bean rows have I here and they're loaded with white half-runner beans. I'll bet Mr. Yates never tasted white half-runner beans like this American woman has grown here. His Ireland couldn't have produced better ones."

Now, Miss Edna laughed with a cackle at her own words spoken aloud to the cool August morning wind blowing across her garden. She stood there, a short, plump, buxom woman, her large blue eyes surveying the nine bean rows in her garden. Wind moved her naturally wavy brown hair, still without a streak of gray.

"I'll bet my favorite poet never named his bean rows for people he knew as I have named mine for students. I have taught and remember so well," she said to the earless wind who couldn't catch the sound of her voice for making sounds of its own on this rare August morning which was the beginning of summer's declension—changing from July heat to early autumn cool—and to noisy nights of cidias singing and grasshoppers chirruping in meadow grasses on the warm days.

"My number one bean row is for Claris Townsend, who came from Beauty Ridge, walked eight miles each way to Maxwell High School when there were no school busses," she sighed. "She helped with the luncheon program for a free noon meal and finished high school. I helped get her a scholarship at State College and our woman's club sent her money. She wanted to be a teacher like I have been. She finished college, became a teacher and now she's principal of a large middle school. She did more than anyone in her class of forty-eight. She had the least chance but she did it. She has my number one bean row, which I've named for her. What a pretty row of productive white half-runners."

She took another step to look over row number two.

"Willie Anderson," she said, "was my favorite athlete at Maxwell High. Six feet six, center on our basketball team for four years...I remember how he used to come to me and brag 'Miss Edna come to the game tonight. We play Rosten. Come and watch me make twenty points.' Yes, Willie would brag all right, but the strange thing was he could back up everything he said. He'd make the twenty points plus a few extras. How I loved that big old handsome boy and I often thought if I had married young and had a family how I'd like to have had a son like Willie Anderson. He always came up in my English class with good grades, too! He was a good left-handed pitcher for our Maxwell High Bulldogs too. Ah, my Willie has to have a bean row in my garden."

"Row number three," she said taking another step. "Rollie Cremeans, he was my problem. I spent more time with him, gave him more attention than any five other pupils. Low grades and always full of mischief. Many times I kept him from getting expelled. I told Mr. Chadwick, my principal when we had him, that I would handle little Rollie. I always thought his size had something to do with his troublemaking. He wasn't over five feet tall and weighed about one hundred pounds. He was too small for football, basketball, baseball and too slow for track. So, he got noticed by giving us trouble. And the reason I have him as my third bean row he once said to me: 'Miss Edna, when I die, I believe, I'll turn into a snake,' when he said these words to me after my English class, I laughed loudly. 'And if I do turn into a snake, I want to turn into the meanest of all snakes. I'll want to bite the teacher I've loved the most. I wouldn't live up to my reputation unless I did!' When Rollie finished at Maxwell High School by the skin of the teeth, he went to Dayton, Ohio and got a job making refrigerators. That's the last I ever heard of him."

"Fourth bean row, I named Delmo Henderson for a young gentleman in my English class who will never be forgotten as a football player. Delmo, a square-shouldered, six foot, two hundred pounder couldn't get English but I helped him along with grades because I loved that sweet young gentlemen in my class who had the narrow mean black eyes that looked at me patiently and longingly from narrow slits. But he was a rough one on our football field. I always knew that boy had something. Today, he's the only one from Maxwell High School who heads a large electrical firm, which he built and is its president and he gets multi-million dollar contracts. Sure, I've named a bean row for unforgettable Delmo."

Taking a short step over to another row, Miss Edna eyed it from end to end.

"Outstanding, outstanding, she was Grace Van Husen was big, homely and never a boy in high school asked her for a date. A top student, a girl worth her weight in gold. First, after leaving Maxwell she became a nurse. She saved her money. She was admitted to a medical school and became a Pediatrician—one of the fine ones in Cincinnati, Ohio today. Yes, finally married and has two sons. I get a Christmas card from Grace each season. You bet she has number five bean row in my garden!"

Miss Edna now looked over her sixth bean row.

"Wonder why my favorite poet, William Butler Yates failed to name each of his nine bean rows in his garden on Lake Isle of Innsifree, for a friend or a fellow writer," Miss Edna asked the clean August wind that she was breathing and enjoying. "He could have had a lot of fun. My Thelma Trimble, the sweet pretty little girl who used to bring me bouquets of wild flowers she gathered from the slopes of hills and from the banks of the Tygart River—late summer, autumn and early spring flowers. She knew how I loved flowers. She's gone now! She went too soon. Unless members of her family, I remember her more than anyone. The typhoid fever got her. It's such tragedy when a young woman, pretty and smart like Thelma Trimble has to go at eighteen just when she finished high school and was blossoming like a spring flower into the April of her life. I certainly named one of my nine bean rows for her."

Slowly she took another step with her eyes on the seventh bean row.

"My Bert, that small wonderful redhead who made everybody laugh," she sighed. "He's gone too, and I wonder why he had to go. Who remembers him now? His parents are gone, too. I remember the crazy pictures he used to draw. What a sense of humor he had! He wanted to be a cartoonist and he would have been one if a bomb hadn't been dropped within six feet where he stood on a carrier out in the Pacific. Not one thing left of him but I have a bean row for him and as long as I live and have my memories he will never die!"

Now Miss Edna stood between her last two bean rows.

"Luster Gardner," she said. "He doesn't have to have my bean row named for him. A model pupil in his behavior, an A student who could throw a hard, fast baseball. He's pitched in three World Series before he was twenty-four years of age. He's to pitch tonight. Tomorrow morning I'll read my paper to see if Luster won! I follow him through each season. Wouldn't he laugh if he knew my eighth bean row was named for him?"

"And, number nine, Wendell Baylor, I never knew he'd be a minister when I watched him play football and tackle all over the field. I choose Wendell when I had many more to choose from—yes, a few thousands. There was young Jiggs, my two hundred forty pound clarinetist who played tackle for the Bulldogs. There was Ephriam Knucles who went on to be captain of the Pittsburgh Steelers. There was Martha Higgins who made the State Department of Education. There was Denver Symthe, now a top cardiologist in Cincinnati. But my favorite poet, William Butler Yates only had nine bean rows at his Lake Isle in Innisfree and this is all I'll have in my garden. Now I must pick my beans!"

Miss Edna walked over to a stool she kept in her garden, wearing her loose clothes was much much nicer than wearing close fitting ones should a male visitor come into her garden and find her stooped over.

She was short and plump and it was difficult for her to bend, not due to the years, but to the thickness of her body which she kept trim, plump, and attractive. She sat on her stool and moved it along to pick her beans. Now, she placed the stool at the beginning row, the Claris Townsend row. When she picked a row named for her former pupil she concentrated on her memories of that student to the end of the row. Now, as she used both hands picking beans she concentrated on Claris Townsend. She'd laugh when she thought of Claris, then she'd stop to wipe a tear.

When she came to the second row, the Willie Anderson row, her face brightened and she thought of the four winning seasons of basketball while Willie was the center. When she thought about how he used to come bragging to her and tell her how many points he was going to make that evening, she twittered like a bird. They never had a winning basketball season at Maxwell High before they had Willie and it was a long time after before they got one. Willie had gone on to a small college and played basketball. They had winning seasons with Willie.

She had scooted her stool along in the first Clairs Townsend bean row and she had come back in the Willie Anderson row. Now, she was ready to scoot her stool along the Rollie Cremeans row.

"Well, he did have to have a diploma from high school before he could apply for a job making refrigerators in Dayton, Ohio," she thought. "We helped prepare him for his future at Maxwell High School and I'm the one who did the most for him. I think little Rollie really loved me. But he liked the reputation of being meanest boy in school." Miss Edna laughed loudly as she thought of her little high school pupil who had a hard time making his grades. "But, Little Rollie's bean row is very productive one." She was pulling beans from the vines by the handsful. Her basket would soon be heaped.

"Wow," it struck her on the index finger.

"Little Rollie Cremeans is dead," she shouted jumping up, "I handled him in life and I can handle him in death for I am a well qualified school teacher, a good one if I must say so and I know what to do."

There were two small red dots of blood a quarter of an inch apart on her index finger, on her left hand. With her thumb and forefinger on her right hand she squeezed her finger above the bite, putting on all the pressure of her hand and fingers strength. She looked down to see the huge brown-and-golden copperhead, coiled like a rope around a windlass and as big as a lard can's lid.

"I have a hoe here, Little Rollie, but I won't kill you the second time," she said. "Not if this is eternity for you. I'll defeat you, Rollie. I know how to do it."

She left her basket of beans in the garden. Her face was moist from perspiration and she was wearing her old loose garden work clothes. She couldn't excite her ninety year mother, Aunt Willie, too much. But she trotted from the garden to the house. She entered holding her finger. "Mother," she said, "call Joe Prince with the ambulance."

"Oh, Edna," her aging mother sighed. "Did a copperhead bite you?"

"No, mother one of my former students from Maxwell High School, one of my first that I taught many years ago, Rollie Cremeans, bit me."

"Are you all right in the head, Edna?" her mother asked. "You are not dizzy or becoming delirious are you?"

"No mother, call Joe Prince."

She called Joe Prince.

"Joe said he was on his way and would be here in a jiffy," her mother said, her voice trembling and her body shaking.

"Now, call Bob and Ellen Prater," Miss Edna said. "This is Saturday and Bob won't be working today. He'll be home. Now don't get excited, Mother. Rollie Cremeans bit me! It's not going to make me sick!"

"You'll find out my Dear Daughter," her mother said as she hastened a phone call to Bob and Ellen Prater, their closest neighbors. Bob was Greenwood County's Farm Agent and Ellen was Home Economics teacher in Greenwood County High School.

"They're on their way," her mother sighed with relief.

The first there were Bob and Ellen Prater. Joe Prince pulled up in his ambulance behind their car.

"Where is the snake," Bob asked, as soon as he entered. "Did you kill it?"

"No I didn't." Miss Edna sighed. "It's in the third bean row about ten feet from the end of the row. You'll see the hoe standing up in the garden! But when you kill that snake it will be the second death of my former student, Rollie Cremeans I had in Maxwell High School years ago!"

"What?" Joe said, looking strangely at Miss Edna.

"He told me in school when he died he'd turn into a snake, and bite me, the finest teacher he ever had!"

"Ah, fiddlesticks," Joe said as he ran out the door toward the garden.

Just then Joe Prince walked in, tall, handsome, middle-aged and unmarried.

"Holding your finger aren't you?" he said.

"Yes, in a death grip," Miss Edna, said, then she laughed. "I can't go to the hospital like this in these dirty baggy clothes and I can't get them off for I can't let loose of my finger."

"We'll cut them off of you," Ellen Prater said. "We'll put a robe around you."

"Will you step outside Mr. Prince," Miss Edna asked him.

Joe Prince walked out into the yard where he watched Bob Prater swinging a hoe in the bean patch in Miss Edna's garden.

Ellen Prater cut Miss Edna's dress and slip from her body.

"Leave my bra and panties alone," Miss Edna told her.

Miss Edna's mother brought her robe. Ellen put her robe around her. Then she removed her garden shoes and put house slippers on her feet. She went to the door and said, "Mr. Prince we're ready."

Bob Prater arrived from the garden. "That was the biggest copperhead I ever killed. I don't believe it had moved. Coiled like a rope almost as big as the head of a fifty pound keg. I chopped him to pieces! Twenty pieces, maybe!"

"There goes my Little Rollie Cremeans," Miss Edna said, laughing loudly.

"Are you all right, Miss Edna?" Bob asked her.

"So far I am," she said.

She walked down to the ambulance but Joe Prince put her on a cot. Her ninety year old mother, Bob and Ellen Prater, sat beside her. And, Joe Prince with both sirens in full blast, went down curvy State Route Two, to Interstate 23 and here he made good time to Kingman Hospital in Auckland. With a copperhead bite, she was rushed to Intensive Care, still squeezing her finger with thumb and index finger to cut off the circulation of blood.

"I can't let my finger loose," she told her hospital doctor. "You'll have to pry my grip loose."

But they gave her anti-venom shots. Then, they pried the death grip of her thumb and finger loose from her bitten finger.

"How do you feel, Miss Edna,?" her doctor asked her. "Feel sick? nauseated?"

"No, not at all," she replied. "You see, I used to teach my class first aid, mostly boys and girls from farms if they got a poisonous snake bite what to do! I've gone through with all this before. Doctor, I retired from teaching after forty-five years. I could teach, Math, English, Home Economics and Health classes. I was a thorough teacher. But it was one of my students who bit me."

"What?" he exclaimed, stepping back from her bed and staring at her. "Are you all right?"

"Sure, I'm all right," she said. "This boy I taught prided himself as being the high school's bad boy because he couldn't get attention any other way. Rollie Cremeans was a poor student, too. He couldn't make good grades. I used psychology on him. I worked with him and helped him all I could -maybe the reason he finished high school by the skin of his teeth and got a good position working with his hands. But he told me once that when he died he wanted to turn into a meanest snake, which is a copperhead and bite the teacher he loved. I'm that teacher. I'm convinced Rollie is dead. I'll find out after I leave this hospital."

"Strange behavior," her doctor said. "It's hard to understand but I suppose we have people like that. In my profession we find a lot of strange things about people."

"We find out more things in my profession," Miss Edna said. "After all, teachers teach the doctors, too."

Miss Edna's hand swelled up to a black softness. Her arm swelled up to her elbow. Her doctor told her that what she did, holding the poison with her finger to keep it from getting into her blood stream had saved her life.

She was removed from Intensive Care after a night and day. Then she was removed to a hospital room for two more days. The width of the bite between the snake's fangs was measured on her finger and the bite was said to be by the largest snake ever to bite a patient brought to this hospital, and there had been many brought in with copperhead bites from spring until early autumn.

"And to think it never made me sick," Miss Edna boasted to her doctor.

When Joe Prince brought Miss Edna home, she had him stop the ambulance by the mailbox to get her afternoon *Auckland Observer*. She immediately opened the paper.

"My picture," she said with a laugh. "Woman Recovers from Copperhead Bite," she read the caption of the article. Before she left the ambulance she had read the article.

"In my forty-five years of teaching and as much good as I did for my pupils I never got as fine an article written about me as this one when I was bitten by a snake. But they had the caption all wrong. And more people would have read it if the caption had been 'Deceased High School Student Bites His Retired Teacher'."

She laughed loudly as he left the ambulance with the sounds of her laughter carried by the August wind, floating over her nine bean rows in her garden.

"Nine Bean Rows" was first published in *Saturday Evening Post,* Vol. 249, No. 4 (June 1977), pp. 26, 28-29, 120. It has never been reprinted. According to Stuart's sister, Glennis, during an interview with David R. Palmore in May of 2002, this story is based on an incident involving Stuart's long-time Greenup County friend, and fellow teacher, Ethel Bush.

Not Without Guns

It was in April. I was working on the hill. I was plowing corn ground. Erf Ealey come up the hill to me. I saw him climbing over the furrows. I stopped my mules and waited to see what Erf wanted. He come up the hill with his face all flushed red. He was getting his breath hard. I could tell Erf was skeered a little.

"What's wrong Erf?" I says.

"Plenty wrong," says Erf, "ain't you heard about it?"

"No," I says.

"Well the Short Branch boys and the Coal Branch boys have bunched together," he says, "and declared war on us Whetstone boys! Said they dared us to come to the Protracted Meeting tonight. Said we'd get our heads peeled with clubs. Said for us to quit taking the Short Branch and Coal Branch girls home. Said they's ending the whole thing."

"How did you find it out?" I says.

"Feel of the knots on my head," says Erf. "That's how I found it out! Ain't you heard about 'em waylaying me and beating me nearly to death?"

"No," I says.

"It's the news all over Whetstone today," says Erf. "They laid it on me last night. I took Susie Abrahams home. Her brother Dick Abrahams was one of the gang that laid the clubs to my head. If I hadn't tore loose and run to the brush I believe to my soul and God they'd a-killed me."

"You go around and round up all the boys," I says. "I've got to get this patch of corn ground plowed. If I don't Pap will raise hell. He says I've been doing too much sparking and too much churching here lately. Says I ain't been wide awake during the daytime since Brother Stokes started the Protracted Meeting at Short Branch. Pap told the truth too. I'm getting like an owl. I see better at night."

Erf went up Whetstone to round up the rest of the boys. I'll tell you the pump knots on his head were big as guinea eggs. I felt sorry for old Erf. "Let that gang try it tonight and they'll get the hot lead," I thought. "They won't be jumping on the least man on Whetstone. They'll be bucking up against some real men. I'm as good a man myself if I do say it as ever packed a pistol or wore a pair of pants."

I finished plowing Pap's patch of corn ground. I took the mules to water. Then I took them to the barn—unharnessed them. I put them in their stalls and fed them. I could hardly remember the right number of corn ears to feed each mule. I was thinking about the fight we would have with the Short Branch boys and the Coal Branch boys. When they come at us with their clubs we'd answer them with a load of hot lead.

I et my supper. Then I changed my clothes. I put old Hulda in her holster. I put on a coat to hide my holster. I was ready for church. "Boys go to church nowadays," says Pap, "to spark gals. They go to drink and fight. They don't go to hear what the preacher says. The world is on the road to hell and damnation."

"It may be Pap," I says. "I don't know. I just know I like to go to church. I go because they ain't no place else to go."

Pap looked hard at me. But I walked out'n the house and down the road. I'd meet the rest of the boys at the forks of the road. Then we'd turn to our left—climb the pint, go through a pine thicket on top of the ridge and then we'd turn over yan side the hill to Short Branch Church. The church was right on the divide between Short Branch and Duck Puddle and Duck Puddle flowed into Coal Branch. All the Coal Branch crowd had come up to Duck Puddle to get to the Short Branch Church. I guess that's what made them friendly with one another. We's on the other side of the big hill over on Whetstone and they hated us.

"Well," says Erf, "we are here. If this ain't enough to subdue 'em we can get reinforcements. Prince Taylor said he wasn't brewin' for trouble but said if it broke out tonight and they got too hot for us to send a boy back over the hill and let him know. Said he'd come with his autermatic shotgun with highpowered shells filled with chilled-buckshots. Said he used 'em for dogs among his sheep."

There was Lum Sperry, Butch Noell, Jack Todd, Ephriam Bates, Andrew Duncan, Rufus Powell, Bad-Eye Flannery, Steave Walker, Tom Brown, Estill Brooks, Erf Ealey and myself. "There's a dozen of us here," I says, "and they'll have at least three men to our one."

"That won't make any difference," says Butch, "we've got the difference between men on us. Every one of us is ready. We ain't taking no foolishness. We ain't thinking about fighting with clubs nor our fists either. We're going to take our girls home."

"Don't ever think they won't have more than clubs tonight," says Erf, "after the way they beat me up. They'll be prepared for us. They'll be ready and waiting. The club practice on my head was just bait to draw us all out tonight!"

"Well they've got us," says Lum.

"What can they do with us?" says Estill.

"Let's get going," says Bad-Eye Flannery. "Church will soon be started. We'll haf to go in late—all bunched together and have everybody watching this Whetstone crowd come in! I don't like to walk in a church house and have everybody to start staring at me and quit a-listening to what the preacher says."

Bad-Eye carried our whiskey. He had two one-gallon jugs with a strap buckled between the handles. He put the jugs over his shoulder to make them balance. Erf Ealey led the way up the path. We started over the hill to Short Branch Church. The moon was out. It was light enough to shoot a rabbit. The path wound up the hill like a snake. It was too steep for the path to go straight up the hill.

A rabbit jumped from a stool of briars. Bad-Eye jerked his pistol and aimed.

"Don't shoot," says Butch, "save your cartridges. We might need them tonight. That old rabbit's liable to have yougins anyway this time of year. You can't tell. Save the rabbits to shoot at next year."

Bad-Eye lowered his pistol. He put it back in the holster on his hip.

"I've always said," says Lum, "when a rabbit lives the season through here and dodges all the bullets shot at it, then the rabbit ought to be left alone until another hunting season comes around. It's only fair, boys, to the rabbit! If we hunt next year we've got to leave a few rabbits for seed."

"All right boys," says Bad-Eye, "hush your mouthing. I've put my pistol up. I don't intend to shoot at a rabbit. I's just limbering up—practicing on getting' my pistol out'n my holster."

We's getting' hot under the collars by the time we got to the pine woods on top the hill. Bad-Eye was sweating and panting with two gallons of licker swinging across his shoulder. "How about swigging a little from these jugs?" says Bad-Eye. "It'll kindly lighten my load a little."

"Suits me," I says. "I never was so thirsty."

Well we stood in the moonlight and passed the jug around. Every one of us took a big swig. Then we passed the jug around again. We took another big swig apiece. After each man took his swig he would go "aham" and spit on the ground. It was good whiskey. It was the real corn. It would put life in you. It would make you want to fight. It would make you take your part. It would make you wade right into a bunch of clubs. When you got this moonshine under your belt you didn't even fear the Devil himself.

"The jug's emptied," says Bad-Eye. "Now we must keep the other jug to nibble on while we are in church."

"Who's going to guard the jug," says Erf, "while the rest of us go into the church house?"

"I'll guard tonight," says Rufus Powell. "You guarded last night didn't you Bad-Eye?"

"Yes I did," says Bad-Eye.

We's feeling higher than the Whetstone pines above us. We felt the new life coming into our bodies. All of us had been plowing, or sprouting ground, or digging coal all day. But we wasn't tired now. We's rested and ready. We could see the white church house in the moonlight down in the shoulder of the hill below us. We could see the white strip of path winding around down the hill like a snake below us. We were on our way to the church. We could even hear them singing and hear the organ playing. We could see the bright lighted winders. They were brighter than the moonlight.

"Now boys," says Rufus, "when one of you feel the urge for a swig I'll have the gallon right out here by this black oak—right here next to the graveyard. Don't all of you come at a time. We might be indicted next Grand Jury for disturbing Public Worship."

"It's a damn shame," says Butch, "that we have to have a man to guard our licker at church. Of all the places on this earth you'd think your licker would be safe at church. But I've lost more licker at this church than any place in the world. Boys just come here and never go inside. They just run around the house like heathen and pilfer—hunting for licker. You haf to watch it here."

"Reminds me of crows," I says. "One will stand up in a tree above a shock of corn while the others get down and fill their bellies. The crow in the tree will caw-caw to the crows on the ground when he sees a man coming. Then they fly up and fly away. They work with one another—just exactly like we do. We have one of our crowd to watch our licker every night to keep a Short Branch man, or a Coal Branch man or a Duck Puddle man from stealing it."

"I've always said," says Steave Walker, "that they ain't any difference much between men and crows! They are all thieves and rascals. But they hang to their own gangs. They've got to do it in this world boys! Now look how Erf got beat up when he's by himself the other night! If we'd a-been with Erf it wouldn't a-happened. W'y I can shed tears every time I think of the pump knots on top his head! I run my hand over his head and it felt just like sweet-tater ridges!"

"Quiet boys," I says, "we're at church. Let's go in and act like men. Let's show Brother Stokes how nice the Whetstone men can act!"

"It's a go," says Butch. "We don't want a jail sentence for disturbing public worship nohow."

Brother Stokes was preaching when we went in. There was a big long seat in the back of the church. It was empty. We got this seat and we all sat together. Just across the aisle from us I saw the Coal Branch boys. They's on two big seats. They's off to themselves. In front of us was another long seat and it was filled with Short Branch boys. There was half of another long seat in front of us filled with Duck Puddle boys. I wondered why they weren't all together. But when it come to fighting us, I knew they'd soon be together. They didn't like the Whetstone boys. We had about the same love for them.

"This Protracted Meeting," says Brother Stokes, "is bound to be a success. Look at the young men from every creek and holler around here! Look at them won't you! They have come out here because they are interested in their souls! The older people all ought to be ashamed to let these young men come out and beat them! When so many young men come out, my Protracted Meetings are always a success. It shows that the people of the community are hungry for the Spirit. It shows that they crave the Spirit and they come."

We looked straight at Brother Stokes. We didn't make a lot of noise. Just one of us at the time slipped out to the jug Rufus was watching. After we got our swig we slipped back and let one of the other fellars go. We didn't make a lot of noise. We were quiet about it. I've seen men turn the seats over getting out. But that ain't in the blood of a Whetstone boy. We never acted like that around God's house of worship. We listened to Brother Stokes preach his sermon. We looked over the house too sorty until we found our girls. We didn't do a lot of neck-craning like the other boys. We behaved ourselves. Brother Stokes says: "I want to thank you boys for your good behavior tonight. I want you to come back until this Protracted Meeting is over. Maybe you will want to consecrate your lives to God." Brother Stokes dismissed us with a word of prayer. Just soon as he said the last word, we made for the door to get our girls.

Nine of us got Coal Branch and Duck Puddle girls. Three of our crowd got Short Branch girls. They would be separated from us. They would be going back the other way. They would be going toward Little Sandy River. Our crowd was divided. Butch, Rufus and Bad-Eye went back the Short Branch way. They were hanging onto the arms of awful purty girls. I didn't much blame them. Maybe they forgot all about the trouble we were going to haf to face.

I looked back as we started over the bank toward Duck Puddle. I saw a whole army of boys standing under the oaks in the Short Branch Churchyard. I thought they were brewing trouble.

Then I thought about the three Whetstone boys that went down Short Branch. They could beat them to death and the rest of us would be over on Coal Branch and Duck Puddle.

"Boys," I hollered to our gang going over on Duck Puddle and Coal Branch, "soon as you take your girls home, come back to the foot of this hill that leads up to the church house. Come here and wait until all nine of us can get together. Boys pass the word on to one another."

I took Susie Munn home. She said her Brother Jack Munn was hanging around the church house for something with a lot of other boys. Said they'd been getting together all day and plotting. Said she thought they were sore because our Whetstone boys had been going with the Coal Branch, Duck Puddle, and Short Branch girls.

I just let her go on and tell all she would. I wanted to get the lay of the land so if we had to fight we would know a little about their numbers and strength. If they were armed with clubs we had the advantage. If they carried the difference then we would be outnumbered three to one and we would haf to take cover and shoot from ambush. We'd haf to bushwhack.

The moonlight was so purty on the April fields. Susie was a purty little doll. But I couldn't love Susie an awful lot for thinking about what was to come in just a matter of hours. The plowed furrows looked good in the April moonlight on the Coal Branch hills.

The night was so purty. It was the purtiest time of the year. The apple orchards were white with bloom. There was the smell of wood smoke in the bright-blue night air. The Coal Branch farmers had burned their clearings and the smoke had settled down in the valley. The wind from the apple orchards was sweet to smell.

I took Susie to her door. I squeezed her right tight and kissed her a lot before I let her loose to go in the house. She didn't seem to be in a great hurry to get in the house.

"Oh if it wasn't for that infernal gang," I thought, "we could spark these purty girls in peace. Wait until that bunch comes to Whetstone and we'll be just as kind to them as they have been to us."

I hurried back down Coal Branch. It was nearly twelve o'clock. I didn't know how far the other boys had to take their girls. Some had to go a fur piece. Some had to go to the head of Duck Puddle. I spect it was every bit of three miles that I had to take Susie. I'd trot a little bit. I'd get to sweating. Then I'd walk until I got cool. I wasn't long getting back to the foot of the hill. Jack, Tom, Ephraim, Estill, Andrew, Steave and Erf were under the big oak tree at the fork of the roads waiting. They's smoking their pipes, cigars and cigarettes and talking to each other.

"Waitin' on you Oscar," says Jack—"all here but you and Lum! Where did you haf to take your girl nohow?"

"Must a-been to the head of Coal Branch," I says, "I've run nearly all the way back. I nearly walked Susie to death gettin' her there. I just thought you fellers would all be here waiting on me. I'm hot as a roasted tater."

"There comes old Lum," says Andrew—"bet he had some fur piece to take his girl!"

"You happy tooten," says Lum. "You said it boy! After we got to the head of Duck Puddle, Bertha says: 'nother hill to cross.' After we crossed that hill Bertha says: 'One more hill to cross.' But I found us another gallon of spirits. Boys our night ain't started yet—it's jest beginning—I've been thinking about poor old Butch, Rufus and Bad-Eye."

"You couldn't a-picked three from our crowd that would come nearer takin' care of themselves," says Erf. "All good shots. All tough as the devil wants them to be. Ain't afraid of hungry lions!"

"Just the same," says Ephriam, "we'd better kill what's in that jug and be on our way. We can't tell what has happened!"

We stood under the oak where the road forked. One road went up the hill to the Church and down Short Branch. The other road went up Duck Puddle and down Duck Puddle to Coal Branch.

We passed the jug around and each man took his swig in turn. That is one thing you can say for the Whetstone boys. They know how to drink out'n a jug. They ain't hoggish. Each man gets what' coming to him. Seems like he knows just how many swigs to take without counting them. He ain't stingy with his whiskey either. He divides with his friends.

After we killed the gallon we started up the hill. The sky was not as purty and bright as it had been. Little dark clouds had began to gather on the sky. The April air was so warm it felt like a little rain. We walked up the hill. We didn't talk. We were going toward the church house. We thought the gang would be there. They were there. They knowed we had to come this way. There wasn't another way for us to get back to Whetstone. It looked like an army of men. They were waiting for us in front of the church house.

"All right boys," we heard one say, "here they come. Get your clubs ready!"

"Hands on your guns, boys," I says.

They walked to meet us. Their clubs were the purtiest clubs you ever saw. They were peeled clubs. They were purty and white. They held them high in the air and marched toward us!

I held Hulda in the air. I shot twice!

"Who gives a damn for your guns," says one of their men. "We've got our guns too. If you start gun shootin' we'll wipe your little crowd out in two minutes."

One of their men pulled a gun and shot twice.

"To the woods, men," I says.

We broke for the woods. We tore out hard as we could go. It was a patch of oaks over across the road from the church house. They follered us to the fence and batted us across the behinds as we rolled over the fence. When we hit the ground on the other side of the fence, we hit the ground running for the patch of oaks. We fell on our bellies behind the trees. The big gang didn't follow us. They took cover in the churchyard. They couldn't find enough trees. They run to the graveyard and got behind the tombstones.

"Yaho," says Butch—"where are you boys?"

"Take cover," says Ephriam. "They are behind the churchyard trees. They are behind the tombstones. Get cover quick."

I don't know who shot first. I don't know how it all started. It was a gun battle. We turned our bodies straight out from the trees with our heads up close to them. We laid on our bellies and shot rapid fire at the white tombstones. We shot at the sight of their gun flashes in the churchyard. For every shot we fired they must have fired seven.

"Shoot low," I would hear them say. "Shoot low!"

Then we heard three guns barking on our right. It was Butch, Rufus and Bad-Eye. They had found a hiding place. They were firing from our right. We almost had to shoot over them. We could see the flashes of their guns. The bullets wheezed in the brush above us. They cut limbs from the trees. The limbs fell on us. If one of us had raised up we'd a-been a goner.

"I hate to shoot into a graveyard," says Erf, "but I haf to. Ma always told me it was a sin to step on a grave. I never do. I guess we won't wake the dead up. They won't know about their kin folks shooting over top of them and plowing the dirt with bullets above them."

"Shoot to bust them," says Ephriam. "Remember the pump knots on Erf's head. Remember a Whetstone boy can't come over here in peace. Pour the hot lead to 'em between the eyes!"

We could hear them holler. Then they would shoot. We'd hug the ground. The bullets would pass over us. I could remember the times when we'd go rabbit hunting and if we couldn't find a rabbit or quail to shoot at we'd stand off and shoot at each other. We'd get fur enough apart not to kill one another because it was in fun. We'd just sprinkle each other—make it smart—burn the hide a little bit. But I never was in a gun battle like this one.

The moon went under the clouds. We's still pounding away at one another. We'd wait until we saw the fire flash from their guns. We'd shoot at their fire. Our shooting wasn't fast as it had been. Our ammunition was getting slim.

"Go after reinforcements Erf," I says. "You know who to get. Crawl

over the bank on your belly. Walk low until you reach the top of the
hill. Wait until we sorty stop firing."

We eased up on firing. They took it as a token of truce. They eased
their firing. Erf slipped over the bank—twisted out around the hill.
Then he started to climb toward the top. They just fired a few times
when the lightening flashed. We could see a ditch we'd been shooting
over in the cow pasture. There was a big deep gulley. We could see
Butch, Rufus, and Bad-Eye in the ditch. They had stopped firing. Must
be they were out of ammunition too. They's just laying down and hug-
ging the bottom of the ditch.

"When we get chilled buckshot we'll run 'em from behind the
tombstones," says Ephriam. "That ain't over 125 yards over there.
Super shells with chilled buckshots'll send them screaming to the
woods."

It must have been two in the morning when our reinforcements
come. They crawled on their bellies up to the patch of woods. Erf was
in front. He led them to us. We's just shooting every now and then to
let each other know we's still there. We didn't know whether they'd
sent for reinforcements or not. We didn't care. We had the best position to shoot from. We's a little higher up on the hill. When the lightening flashed, we could see the tombstones.

"Seven new men," says Erf. "Five autermatics with shells used for
killing dogs that kill sheep. Two rifles—one a 30-30 Springfield. One
a muzzle-loader. Price Taylor, Chilly Bain, Pluck Reed, Wid Callihan,
Jake Henson, Mart Fields and Harlan Wurts."

"All right boys," says Price—"just where are they hiding?"

"Wait until I shoot," I says. "Then you watch their gun fire and get
their range."

I fired my pistol. There was a flash of fire from the graveyard. Fire
flashed from the trees in the churchyard. Our autermatics begin to
roar. Great streaks of fire jumped from the barrels like lightening. The
lightening flashed overhead. The rain started falling. I guess the rain
helped a lot of them. We heard them hollering when the chilled shot
begin to sprinkle the graveyards. We heard them take to the woods

above the church. When they got above the house we barely could sprinkle them. We poured the hot lead at that bunch of rascals. They'd been pouring it to us.

"Where are you Oscar?" hollered Butch. "Watch we're coming! Don't fire this way."

We stopped firing until Butch, Rufus, and Bad-Eye come running low and then fell on their bellies and scooted on the muddy ground in amongst us.

"Welcome home boys," says Jack.

"I lost a finger," says Bad-eye. "Rufus tied it up with his handkerchief. A bullet nipped it off clean as a whistle when we's taking cover. They had open field at us. We come up the road—we didn't know you's lined up already to fight."

"We've sent back and got reinforcements," I says. "Erf went back and got a few of the old hunters. We've run 'em through the woods!"

"Reckon anybody's been killed?" says Jack.

"Don't know," says Chilly—"if they have been they're close to the church house to have their funeral preached and close to a graveyard to bury them in. We ain't worrying about that. You boys will be safe in going back to church. I'll bet you two gallons against one. This would put the fear of Whetstone into that bunch!"

"The fun is all over," says Pluck Reed. "We'd better be on our way across the hill. Don't light your pipes or cigarettes yet. Someone may shoot at the light."

We walked up the path in single file. My leg felt a little stiff. I thought it was from laying down behind that tree so long. We walked through the rain—we were wet as possums. We had to hold to the sprouts to get up the slick path. The rain was still falling. We had to nearly feel our way. We took hands and held to one another. We finally reached the top of the hill. It wasn't raining so hard in the pine grove. We got under the pines—Chilly held his flashlight while we filled our pipes, lit our cigarettes and cigars.

"I've been scint on the leg with a bullet," I says. I looked down and blood was oozing from my leg.

"Let me see," says Chilly. He took the flashlight and looked at my leg.

"No more than a briar scratch," says Chilly. "Let it bleed, that will be good for it. This has been a lot of fun. Wait until you see a real battle. I was in a few not so long ago. You are just boys. Old Pluck and me's been there before! We put 'em on the run didn't we? It's hard to beat chilled buckshot for close range fightin'. Sawed-off shotguns are awful good for real close fightin'."

We stopped at Chilly's house when we got down on Whetstone. He give us a swig around. "Not much, boys," says Chilly, "but it's enough to keep you from takin' cold."

"Now boys," says Pluck, "before you all scatter out—you go back to church tonight. You don't know anything about all this shooting. You take your girls home just like nothing had ever happened. If they have you before the Grand Jury you don't haf to indict yourself. Remember it has been a dark night. You ain't seen no guns. You ain't disturbed no public worship. Be kind to Brother Stokes and help him all you can with the Protracted Meeting. Remember you won't have as many there tonight as you had last night. It's too wet to plow today and you fellars can get some rest. Remember you'll hear a lot of fellars bein' in bed sick with the rheumatics, with colds and the flu after this gun battle tonight. Just remember Oscar you all can go in peace now. They won't want to bunch on the Whetstone boys. It's all over. They've been weaned like suckling calves."

"Not Without Guns" was first published in *Esquire,* Vol. 12 (July 1939), pp. 38-39, 151-152. It has been reprinted in Charles Grayson, editor, *New Stories For Men* (Garden City, Garden City Publishing Co., 1941) pp. 497-508, and Arnold Gingrich, editor, *The Esquire Treasury* (New York, Simon And Schuster, 1953), pp. 342-350.

Jesse Stuart with his dog Sir Birchfield at his home in W-Hollow — circa 1953. (Photograph by Earl Palmer)

The Red Rats of Plum Fork

It's not been too long ago since it happened, but it was before we had heard of the guaranteed ways of getting rid of 'em. We didn't take any newspapers and we had to find our own way to destroy these rats which had come in such great numbers to our place. They multiplied so fast they'd about taken our place over. When I went to the henhouse to feed the chickens, rats came from the holes they'd gnawed through the floor. They'd look at me a full minute. I'd yell "shoo" at the rats and scare the chickens. The rats would walk across the floor while I kicked at 'em. They'd eat the corn I put in the feeder for the chickens. The chickens stood back and looked on with tiny glassy eyes from their little heads cocked sidewise.

We'd never seen anything like it. We lived the last house up on Plum Fork on the Tiber River. The Plum Fork jolt-wagon road came to our place and there it stopped. The semi-circled hills formed a barrier. And the giant cliffs walled us in until we didn't have to build a fence around our farm. All we had to do was build fences across the valley to make pastures for our cattle, horses and sheep. Then, we had plenty of limestone bottomland left to farm. And our land in this limestone valley produced more bushels of corn and tons of hay to the acre than any land in Greenwood County. We often had to leave corn in the fields. Pa said it was a good idea to leave some corn in the field to toll the rats away so our cattle, sheep and horses could have peace at feed times. But the rats came anyway.

The rats loved the warmth of the barn. That was before the first invaders' grandchildren started multiplying. And when this happened, they began to spread. They got under our floor. They got behind the rocks in the cellar under the house. They got in our smokehouse. They got into our granary. They gnawed holes through the weather-boarding on our house and climbed up the open space between the weather-boarding and the studding until they got into the garret.

Brother Finn and I slept upstairs. We'd lie awake and listen to a football game every night. We'd hear their fullback take off with a sweet potato Pa had stored in the garret to keep until spring. And as the fullback carried the ball we'd hear the squeaky shouts of the spectators.

After much rolling and falling on the garret floor, the game would end. Then, the spectators would get into a brawl over the game. And this would be too much. Finn would get out of bed and pound on the ceiling with a broom handle. He'd get back in bed and try to sleep and the brawl would start again. Then I'd get out of bed, my turn now, and I'd throw my shoes against the ceiling to break up the second brawl. It was this way every night.

One night a big brawl started. Finn pounded with the broom and I threw shoes. I don't know how many times Finn got out of bed and how many times I had to get up. Finally, Finn went downstairs and told Pa we couldn't sleep. Pa knew what it was. He and Mom and my sisters were disturbed downstairs by the rats climbing up and down inside the walls. Pa got his automatic pistol and came upstairs in his long flannel nightshirt.

"I can't help it if I do put a few holes through the roof," he said. "I'll break up that game they're a-playin' up there."

Pa emptied his pistol through the ceiling. He filled the chamber with cartridges and cut loose again after several of the rats must have felt the hot lead. And then he reloaded and shot again. Pa put so many holes through the roof that Finn and I could lay in bed and see the autumn stars in the big high blue sky above. It silenced the rats all right. But the next day, Pa, Finn and I worked all day fixing the roof.

We had nine cats. We had gray cats, yellow cats and brindle cats. Not a black one, because Pa was afraid of a black cat. He never wanted one to cross the path to the barn in front of him. If one ever did, he pulled off his hat, spit in it and mumbled some strange words. But the cats we had grew fat and lazy. And they couldn't multiply as fast as the rats.

But Pa did have a smart idea. He went to Blakesburg and brought home a rat terrier. Pa paid twenty-five dollars for Jerry. It was a little price to pay for getting rid of this world of rats. Jerry was everything

Tobbie Bostock told Pa he was. Pa hadn't more than turned Jerry loose until he went to work. He ran a rat under the henhouse. But we had concrete block footers laid under the henhouse and that was as far as Jerry could dig unless we tore down the henhouse and went under the foundation. Jerry ran rats up in the big barnlofts. We couldn't fork over tons of hay and get the rats. Jerry ran them under our floor. They had holes dug under the foundations.

When Pa saw a hole rats had gnawed through the weatherboarding, he took off that strip and replaced it with another. Then he'd have to paint that strip of weatherboarding white to match the rest of the house. It was a lot of work, but Pa did it. Then the rats got wise and dug under the foundations and gnawed through the studding and came up the walls to the garret. Jerry would run them to these holes and here he stopped and started digging. We'd have to fill up the holes and smooth the yard. Often he dug down in one of Mom's flowerbeds and this caused more trouble. He ran rats under the granary and behind the rocks in our cellar. We did manage to catch seventeen rats with him. That's when he caught a rat out in the open taking a morning walk and he picked him up on the ground. Once he found a nest of rats in their summer home, which was back under the bank of the little creek that flowed down through our barnlot. Jerry dug them out and killed them all. He was as much against the rats as we and the cats were. Jerry worked all the time, but there wasn't much he could do.

On days when it rained Pa took his pistol, Finn and I took our rifles, and we went to the barn. We turned the horses and cattle from the barns and we sat on mangers and feedboxes waiting for rats. We killed thirteen rats the first rainy day. Pa thought we might thin them down this way. But we learned rats were smarter than we thought. The next day it rained and we took our firearms to the barn, turned the cattle and horses out, but we didn't see a rat stick his head from a hole.

Pa even talked about selling our farm and moving away. Selling the most fertile farm in Greenwood County, Kentucky, a farm which produced over a hundred bushels of corn to the acre! Anything would grow on our limestone bottomland. We had more corn in bins, more livestock, hogs and sheep than any farmer in Greenwood County. We had money in the bank. Pa had stocks and bonds. He had invested in many places. But, Pa also had rats. Pa wondered if the rats had been sent to plague him for something he had done. He read where the plagues had been sent on the Egyptians. Pa had always been a church-going man. But he had never tithed. He thought the rats were a plague sent on him because he hadn't tithed. So he started tithing.

"I'd give a third of my earnings to the Lord," he told Mom, "if it would only stop this scourge of rats."

But his tithing didn't stop the rats. They kept coming, and multiplying. Once Pa prayed for a plague to strike the rats. That didn't happen. We kept old Jerry and he did what he could. Our cats multiplied to thirty-three. Pa said we should have had more cats. He thought the rats had carried away the young kittens while the mother cats and the toms were out looking for the rats. The rats killed our young chickens, climbed the cherry and apple trees and robbed our birds' nest of young birds.

"When I even think of a rat," Pa said one morning when we were feeding the horses, "I see something red!"

For the rats came out and ate with the horses after we'd put corn in their feed boxes. They ate with the cows and with the hogs. They were under the big hog pen. And they ate with every living thing on our farm except the cats, Jerry, and with us.

The night that Pa saw the most red was when sister Essie screamed in bed. Pa jumped up, turned on the light and a big old rat ran across the room. It had gotten into Essie's bed and had bitten her little toe. Mom got some medicine. The toe was bleeding and Essie was crying. Mom tied the toe up and Essie got in bed with Pa and Mom. She was afraid to go back to her own bed in case the rat would come back and bite her again. Pa laid his loaded pistol on a chair beside his bed. And the next night Pa brought a dozen cats, inside the house to protect us. Finn put a loaded rifle beside our bed.

"I don't know why we'd get this pestilence," Pa said. "I can't think of any reason why it was sent upon me!"

"We're rich farmers, Mick," Mom told him. "Maybe we've had this good land long enough. Five generations of your people have owned this land and prospered and handed something down from one generation to the other!"

"I've paid my debts and taxes!" Pa said. "I give a tenth to the Lord! If you think it just, I'll give more than a tenth to the Lord!"

"I think we'd better sell," Mom said. "Move away and let the rats have the place!"

"It breaks my heart to think of sellin'," Pa said. "I know every foot of ground on this farm. I know the trees and the great walls of white limestone cliffs. This farm is a part of me. I'd hoped to divide it and let my two boys carry on after I'm gone. My people never multiplied like these rats."

"People are laughing at us," Mom said. "It's funny to everybody. They know why you started tithing at Church, Mick. We're not fooling anybody. They know we have plenty. You know you loan corn to farms like banks loan money."

"But why not?" Pa said, his face getting red as a turkey's snout as he sat at the breakfast table and sipped coffee. "My rate of interest is not too high on my corn. I loan ten barrels to a farmer in autumn, and the next autumn I take back twelve!"

"And if you loan two barrels," Finn said, "you take back three. That's more than six percent. If you loan four barrels, you get back six the next autumn. That's something like thirty-three percent isn't it?"

"But corn's not like money," Pa argued. "You can write a check for money and you have to barrel corn. It's a lot of trouble to transact a loan."

"And we've got the rats," I said.

"Other people don't have them," Mom said. "I know this plague has been sent on us for a purpose."

"Rats know a good place when they see it," Finn said. "We feed 'em well. That's why they come here. What other farmer in Greenwood County feeds his rats as well as we do? I think rats talk like people. I think they go visiting other rats and tell them what a fine place we have here."

"Son, that's about right," Pa said. "Help me find a way to get rid of these boogers! All that stands between us and happiness are these awful pests."

"I'll help you all I can, Pa," I said.

"You'll never get rid of 'em until you give away everything we got," Mom said.

"I'm not givin' away any more," Pa said. "Givin' away a third now!"

"Old rats, I'm afraid of 'em," Essie said. "I'll never sleep in that room again!"

"It's a plague sent on us," Mom said as we left the breakfast table. "It might be something you did before I married you, Mick!"

"Women have funny thoughts sometimes," Pa said as we walked toward the barn.

That day we took two wagons down to the mouth of Plum Fork to haul cordwood Pa had bought from Billy-Buck Everyman. Billy-Buck cut sycamores and waterbirches that shaded his Tiber creek corn bottoms. Each year he cut cordwood for Pa's fireplaces and traded the wood to him for corn and hay. One year he traded wood for a fat hog.

Billy-Buck climbed on the wagon with Pa and me when we reached his house. Finn followed us across the bottom toward the stacks of wood.

"You got any rats, Billy-Buck?" Pa asked.

"Not that I know of," he answered Pa. "Why? What made you ask me that?"

"They're about to take over my place," Pa told him.

"You feed 'em well, Mick," Billy-Buck said.

Then Billy-Buck Everyman, a big man, with red beard all over his face, laughed until his stomach shook. He slapped his overall patched thighs with his ham-sized hands. His big fingers were like small sticks of stove-wood. His thumbs were sticks of wood, weathered by the seasons, that had been chopped off too short.

"Rats," Billy-Buck bellowed between spasms of laugher. "Rats! I don't have a rat and I don't have a cat! You got my rats, Mick. They went up Plum Fork to live with you! And you can have 'em, Mick! Warm 'em under your hearths with this wood I'm tradin' you for corn so I won't have to pay you corn interest!"

Pa's red face turned white as a frost-bitten pawpaw leaf as we rolled over the wagon trail across the bottom land that wasn't fertile as our limestone land. Pa wasn't laughing. It wasn't funny to Pa. It wasn't funny to me either.

"Know anyway to get rid of the pests?" Pa asked.

"Get you some cats and a dog!" Billy-Buck laughed harder than ever.

"I've got thirty-three cats and a dog," Pa said. "I've still got rats! They're all over my premises and they eat with my livestock and my fowls, they even eat my birds and my kittens."

The way Billy-Buck laughed he must have thought Pa was joking. All the time we loaded the wood, Billy-Buck laughed. And when we'd driven across the bottom and he got off the wagon at his own house, he was still laughing. He stood and watched us drive up Plum Fork and we heard him laughing when we got out of sight.

"I'll stop up here and see what Frog-Eye Scott says," Pa said. "Maybe he's got some rats. His land's a little better and he's got more corn to feed 'em. Maybe he can give a man a sensible answer."

When we reached Frog-Eye's house, we stopped. Pa gave me the lines and he got off the wagon. He just got through the paling gate when Frog-Eye stepped off the porch. He was a big heavy man, with a white moustache, clean red face and a pair of brown eyes too big for their sockets.

"Howdy, Mick."

"Howdy, Frog-Eye!"

"Something I can do fer ye, Mick?"

"Yep," Pa said, with a smile. "I want to know if you got any rats."

"No, I ain't Mick," he told Pa. "I heard you got all the rats. And that is one bit of goodness ye've done for me. You feed yer rats, Mick. They tell me ye let them eat with your chickens, livestock and hogs."

Pa turned and walked back through the gate and climbed onto the wagon.

"God almighty sent plagues more than two thousand years ago," Frog-Eye said, as he twirled his handle-bar moustache with his big soft hands. "Plagues are sent fer different things!"

"My hands are not as soft as milkweed stems in July," Pa said as I gave him the reins. "My hands are hard as the bark on tough-butted white-oaks."

We drove on and left Frog-Eye Scott standing in his yard in his clean-washed overalls and blue work shirt.

"I never liked Soda Rife too well," Pa said, "but I'm goin' to stop and see if he'll give me a civil answer when I ask him about these pests!"

Soda Rife, a man as small as Pa and whose hands were as calloused as Pa's, was chopping stovewood when he stopped. Pa got off the wagon and walked over and asked him if he was bothered with rats.

"Ain't got a rat, Mick," he said. He stuck his ax in the block. He was willing to talk with Pa about our trouble. "I think all my rats went up to your house because you feed them better. They didn't starve when they were here but a onery rat goes where he can better himself. He'll go where he can get a better handout. He likes something for nothing more than any varmit in this world."

"I must have everybody's rats," Pa said. "They're about to ruin us."

"They're tellin' this thing everyplace that it's a plague sent on you, Mick," Soda said. He got up close and looked Pa in the eye. "But I don't believe that. You're a good man and a good neighbor. You work hard and you save. You're free-hearted. Ye give to good causes. Give more to the Church than everybody else combined. You've got rats. That's all. Get rid of 'em!"

"But how?" Pa asked. "Tell me how and I won't charge ye any on the rent on the corn I've loaned you!"

"I know the answer, Mick," Soda said, almost getting close enough to whisper in Pa's ear. "I'll take ye up on that bargain. If it don't work, I'll pay you the corn interest this fall. Forty barrels principal. Eight barrels interest."

"It's a bargain," Pa said as Finn and I listened.

"Bonwock Bush's boy, Sach Bush, over on Little Frazier, has a ferret. Go over there and get that boy and his ferret. Put that ferret in the ratholes and stand back with clubs! Man, they'll run out of holes, pop up through the ground, scale the walls and the ferret will go right after 'em! Right up in yer garret!"

"That's wonderful," Pa said. "I believe Soda you've give me the answer to our future happiness! I must be on my way! Thanks. The deal is on!"

We trotted the team to the barn. Pa left Finn and me to unhitch the teams and unload the wood. He put a saddle on our sorrel mare, Kate, and a saddle on Bill. "Tell yer Ma, I've got the answer," he said. "I don't have time to tell 'er. I'll bring Sach Bush back in the empty saddle. Have clubs ready! Won't be gone two hours."

We did what Pa told us. We cut a half dozen nice clubs a little longer than baseball bats. And Pa and Sach came galloping up Plum Fork on the horses.

Pa climbed down from the saddle. "Boys, get yer clubs and get ready. This is going to be some fun!"

Sixteen-year-old Sach Bush was slower to get out of the saddle. In his hand he held a meal sack and something was squirming around inside.

"Boys, I ain't fed this ferret no meat," Sach said. "He craves blood."

"Fetch 'im here," Pa said. "Put 'im in this hole under the horses' manger. He'll get what he craves!"

Sach opened the sack, looked into it, reached down carefully and caught the long ferret by the nape of the neck. It was dirty-white, with pink eyes, little shoulders, short legs, and a big stomach. Its big stomach was back near its short hind legs.

"Where he can put that little head, he can go," Sach bragged as he put his head into the hole and the ferret was off. "He can work that stommick backward and forward if he gets in a tight squeeze and needs to. Afraid to put my hand on 'im he's so hungry fer blood. Get ready with yer clubs!"

A rat broke up through the ground in the middle of the stall and Pa cut down on him with his bat. It was a home run. Another jumped up and Pa got him. Two home runs for Pa! He grinned like a possum. Then, Finn got a three bagger on one. But the second strike he polished him off. I got one with three licks. Two rats got past Sach and made for the hayloft. He was a strikeout both times. He wasn't as eager to win the game as we were. Pa lost his smile when the two rats got away. Then something happened. He waited for more rats. They didn't come. Mom, Essie and Grace came to the barn to watch us rid the place of rats. Now everything had bogged down. Sach got down at the hole and called his ferret pet names. But the ferret wouldn't come out.

"He never acts like that," Sach said. "Something's wrong. Got a mattock?"

"Yes, we have," Pa said. "Go fetch it, Finn!"

When Finn brought the mattock, Sach started digging. He followed the rat hole across the stall leaving a big trench in our barn. Then, he got warm and Pa dug a spell. Finn dug and I dug. And we got back to Sach. Then Pa, Finn and I again. We dug across the barn stall and over into another stall.

"We're a-ruinin' my barn," Pa said.

"Can't help that," Sach said. "I've got to find my ferret."

Then Essie saw the ground move. She put her foot on the place, near where Sach was diggin. He lifted some dirt with the mattock and there was the ferret. He had killed three rats. One was behind him blocking the rathole and two were in front of him. He couldn't go either way. Sach lifted him up and said pet-words. And then he saw one of the ferret's eyes was gone and he had been bitten near the other eye.

"Never heard tell of rats a-fightin' a ferret before," Sach said. "They've about blinded my ferret. This is enough!"

"Got the rats hemmed," Pa said. "That's why they bit the ferret!"

"They're old residenters," Finn said. "This is their home and they're fightin' to keep it. And it looks like this place will be their home!"

Sach Bush charged Pa twenty-five dollars. And when Pa climbed in the saddle to take Sach home, he was a sad-looking man.

"Guess I'll collect the corn interest from Soda," Pa said sadly. "I didn't want it. Not if I could get rid of these rats! It's our last chance. I don't know what else to do."

Then, we went back to Pa's old idea. We got a few more cats. We got another rat terrier that we called Rags. We got more ammunition for pistol and rifles. And Pa bought fifty steel traps. We tried to keep down the multiplication.

One night Finn, Pa and I set steel traps at the mouth of every hole we could find. The next morning we had twenty-one rats in our traps.

"Boys, we've been doin' everything," Pa said. "I believe we can lick 'em with traps."

Pa was pleased. And we set the traps again. Morning after morning we looked at the traps. Occasionally we caught a half grown rat but never an old one.

"A rat is a smart thing," Pa admitted. "They know where all our traps are set!"

Then, Pa put meat rinds on the traps for bait.

"I'll feed 'em something and see how it works," he said.

He caught six rats the first night with fifty traps. And these were all we caught with bait.

It was a bright sunny November day. Pa told Finn and me to paint the roof of the big barn where he kept the livestock. Said the weather was right and now was the time to paint for there were a few rust-leaks in the tin. Paint it before snows laid on the roof and leaked on the hay. Finn and I had just opened a big can of bright-red roof paint. We had our ladders and brushes and were about ready to begin work.

"I hate this color," Finn said. "Bright-red is the color of October shoemake, sweetgum and sourwood leaves. When I see them falling I think of drops of blood. I think of the paint as bright red blood. I just don't like red. What is there about red that reminds one of blood and falling leaves and bad weather?"

Just then I heard the jaws of a trap under old Bill's manger. I heard a rat squeak and I ran up the hallway and looked over. There was a big rat in the trap. The steel jaws had barely caught him by the hind foot. I took the chain loose, carried rat and trap over to the paint can.

"I hate a rat too," Finn said. "I see red when I see one. Hold up the chain so he'll swing in the air! I'll paint 'im!"

"Why paint 'im?" I said. "Why waste paint on a rat?"

"Why not have a red rat?" Finn said. "Why not one of a different color?"

I held the chain while Finn painted the rat. Finn put a bright red coat of roofpaint on the rat.

"Now what are we goin' to do with 'im?" I said. "Kill 'im?"

"Oh, no," Finn said. "Turn 'im loose and let's have a red rat running around this barn!"

When I set the trap down and pressed the steel jaws with my foot the rat freed himself and dove into a hole under the manger. Then something happened we'll never forget. This red rat's kinfolks didn't know him. When he ran into his home, he scared his kinfolks! They started poppin' up in all directions. They even forgot the steel traps we had been setting for them. The jaws clicked all over the horsebarn. But we didn't have time to look about the traps. Finn climbed upon the manager and I jumped upon a five gallon can of barnroof paint to let the rats go by. I thought one might try to climb up and bite me! I never saw anything like it.

"A red rat," Pa screamed and dropped his ax on the woodblock.

I saw him take off toward the house screaming for Mom as the rats moved toward him, the red rat trying to keep up. It was a sight to see Pa running ahead of the rats.

"Oh, it'll work," Finn shouted. "Go to the traps and fetch me rats!"

I brought another big rat to Finn. The jaws of the trap held his hind leg. Finn put the red paint to him in a hurry.

"Turn 'im under the chicken house," Finn shouted.

I ran to the chicken house, set my foot on the steel jaws and freed him at the opening of a slick rat hole under the foundations. Talk about rats! They came from holes around the henhouse, up through the ground, leaped from the windows…from everywhere. They were on their way! They ran toward the cliffs but couldn't scale the steep lime-

stone cliffs! Then they turned the way the others had gone down Plum
Fork. And I ran back to get another rat for Finn to paint.

"Paint 'em red, paint 'em red," Finn shouted, shaking his tousled
blond hair. "Paint 'em red until this paint-smell leaves a-swimmin' in
my head!"

I carried more rats to Finn. Rats caught by one leg in the traps.
Those caught by both hind legs weren't any good. But the three-legged
red rats could keep close to the four-legged rats. They followed them
as they raced down Plum Fork between the cliff-walled valley. Finn
kept on painting them. We put one behind the rocks in the cellar. We
put one under the hay in each barn loft. One in each of the five corn
bins! One in the granary. Then we had to wait to take two to the house.
Jerry had run from the fleeing rats. First the terrier tried to kill them.
But they kept coming and were running over him. The cats started
work at first. Then, they knew something was wrong! When they saw
the swarms of fleeing rats, each swarm pursued by a red rat, the cats
took off with their long bushy tails riding on the wind! Many ran up
the apple trees for safety!

When we got to the house, Pa, Mom, Essie and Grace were standing on the porch watching the rats go by. Pa might have been praying.
I don't know. But I do know Finn hadn't spared the red paint on the
two rats we had in the traps. We put them in big slickworn holes under
the house and sprung the traps. And then we waited. We didn't have
long to wait. Rats came from under the house and from inside as they
made their get-away. When they ran across the porch Mom screamed
and jumped into the porch swing. Pa jumped up beside her. They held
to the porch chains as the swing rocked. Essie and Grace screamed as
they climbed up into the chairs. Behind this swarm of rats, two red rats
limped across the porch in hot pursuit.

"I told you, Mick, what was wrong," Mom said. "Now we can live
in peace and happiness!"

"Wonder what Soda, Frog-Eye and Billy-Buck are thinkin' now?
We've had their rats. Now they've got 'em back."

"They can have 'em," Essie laughed.

"Come on, Shan," Finn said with a grin. "We'd better get back on the job. We've got a lot of paintin' ahead of us on that barn roof."

"The Red Rats Of Plum Fork" was first published in Whit and Hallie Burnett, editors, *Story: The Magazine Of The Short Story In Book Form,* No. 3 (New York, A.A. Wyn, 1953.), pp 99-111. It has been reprinted in Whit and Hallie Brunett, editors, *Things With Claws* (New York, Ballantine Books, 1961), pp. 84-96, and Robert B. Downs, editor, *The Bear Went Over The Mountain— Tall Tales Of American Animals* (New York, MacMillan, 1964), pp. 45-56. Stuart included this story in his unpublished manuscript, *These Are My Best – Twenty-five Short Stories Selected From Five Hundred Published Stories And MSS*—edited and typed January 1975, and his unpublished manuscript, *Twenty-five Tall Stories Selected From 461 Published Stories And Fifty Manuscripts,* circa 1975 (both from the Jesse Stuart Foundation Collection, Ashland, Kentucky). In the editor's preface of the 1953 edition of *Story,* where "The Red Rats Of Plum Fork" first appeared, Stuart explains the background of this story. "About the *Red Rats* story, this is not an allegorical thing. Some reader might think so, with all this investigation of 'reds' and so on. It is not this sort of thing at all...not symbolical of anything. It's a story that happened. Last summer Deane and I went to visit our friends in Greenup County, over in the Tygart River country. They play old-time music, banjo, Spanish and steel guitars, and they have many old ballads there. This is one of the last homes that has the genuine old-time music. So, between playing and singing, we got to talking. And the men at this home are the two fellows that painted the rat with red barn paint, put him in a hole, and the other rats took off. The whole story is almost the same as they told it to me. They got rid of their rats. I laughed until I cried when they told this story. To them, rats have been a serious business. But when I laughed, they started laughing, too. So it was one of those good evenings and the right way to get a story. Get them where they happened. So, the story, 'The Red Rats of Plum Fork' (really not Plum Fork, but I changed all names to be safe as I always do nowadays), came from the Greenup County people and the Greenup County, Kentucky earth. And, another thing, it shows some of the Kentucky mountain or hill people's ingenuity. They'll fool and fiddle around until they find some unusual way."

Seth Winters

"It's good to see you Seth," I said, reaching my hand to greet him.

"It's fine to see you, too, Mate," Seth said, clasping my hand.

It was hard to believe Seth Winters stood before me, that he was on leave, maybe an emergency leave. But I wouldn't mention that to him. I didn't think he wanted to talk about all that had happened since he'd been away. I would wait for him to mention the trouble that had come to him while he was away.

"You sure look fine, Seth," I said. "You've got a good tan. Looks like you've been where there's plenty of sun!"

"I have," he said, smiling, "and there's plenty of heat too!"

"And I wish that I could wear what you are wearing," I said as I looked at the different service bars, studded with many stars, pinned across his chest.

"I've been through a lot to get 'em," he said. "But I've found a lot of people here at home don't know what they mean. One of these stars means that my cruiser was sunk and that I was in water for ten hours! I could go on and tell you what each means, but there's no use."

I didn't tell Seth that I hadn't paid any attention to service bars studded with stars and service medals until after I'd gone into the Navy myself. But I was ashamed to talk. Here was Seth with a wife and baby at home and another on the way when the Japs bombed Pearl Harbor, and he enlisted. And I'd waited until I was ready to be called in the draft before I enlisted. That was why he'd seen foreign service and the reason why I'd never seen the ocean yet; but my time was coming soon as I returned from "boot leave."

"Where're you going now?" Seth asked me.

"Just walking about the old home town," I said. "Just walking around to see a few old friends."

"Would you care to take a walk with me?" he said.

"I'll be glad to," I said.

"I've got to have somebody to talk to," he said.

We walked down Main Street together. And tiny boys from the grade school up to the high school seniors spoke friendly to Seth and even stopped to look at him. I could tell by the way they spoke to him and looked so admiringly at him that he was a hero to them. They spoke to me but not like they did to Seth. And fathers and mothers and old men and women spoke so kindly to Seth and stopped us on the street and shook hands with us. I could tell it was Seth they wanted to see. There'd been a lot in the newspapers about him. And I remember how proud, Betty, his wife, was when he won the Purple Heart. And I knew when people spoke to him what they were thinking. They were thinking the same as I was and they were silent about it as I had been.

I walked with Seth to the end of Main Street and then we started down the highway toward Lantern High School. Between the highway and the schoolhouse was the athletic field where Seth and I played many games of football together. Only a few small boys played on the athletic field now. We looked toward the school and our old playground in silence. And when we reached the lane that led to the high school, I thought Seth would walk up and look the place over, but he didn't.

"If I could've only got back three weeks sooner," Seth said.

"Yes, if you only could," I said.

"But things happen suddenly," Seth said. "And there's not anything anybody can do about 'em!"

The April sun was high in the blue sky above us. And a light, cool April wind rustled the thin-leafed fingers of the willows along the creek whose wind-blue murmuring waters mirrored the loose, floating sails of white clouds in the April sky. I wanted to ask Seth if he'd remembered the days when we'd pin-hooked minnows from this stream but I didn't because his face was sober and I knew he didn't want me to keep reminding him of bygone boyhood days. And I couldn't mention it to him, for it would remind him of days when Betty fished with us and Seth would bait her pinhook with a fly and she'd flip a minnow from the deep shaded hole beneath the willows. The creek had not changed any; the willows were here still only they'd grown much taller.

And the schoolhouse, with its big playground, was up on the little slope above the creek.

"You're the only one I would ask to come here with me today," Seth said. "I think you'll understand."

"Yes," I said.

Now I knew where we were going and I didn't want to go. But I would go with Seth. I'd do anything I could for him. I'd help him in any way I could. But to visit a cemetery always made me feel sad, and that's why I never went to one. But I'd do it for Seth. I felt toward him like all the boys, girls, mothers, fathers, and the old people in Lantern. Though I too was in the Navy, Seth was not only my shipmate but he was a hero to me.

When we walked through the cemetery gate, I glanced at Seth to see if the expression on his face had changed. And it had. He had a determined expression that he used to wear when we were in a tough game of football and he blocked for me to carry the ball. And I wondered if this was the same determined expression that was on his face when he went into the battle at sea. But I knew it was.

"Do you know where they buried her?" he asked me.

"No, I don't," I said.

"We'll find out," he said.

The cemetery sloped gently from the low ground near the creek toward the heavy-timbered hill. Tall threads of tender April grass were rustled by the April wind. And as I looked at the wind-blown grass I was reminded of my Latin class when I studied Caesar. When he spoke of his Tenth Legion a thought always popped in my mind and it was this: Since Caesar and his Tenth Legion are dead and dust after these many centuries, they are now legions of the grass.

"She should be buried on this high slope," Seth said. "There should be a fresh mound of dirt."

"Yes," I said.

We couldn't see over the burial ground until we'd climbed near the timberline.

"There it is," Seth said, pointing down the hill toward the creek.

"There it is down in that low ground."

Then we walked down the slope toward the newly made grave.

"First of our people that's buried here," Seth said, "and I guess they wanted to start our plot someplace. But I wouldn't 've had Betty laid there!"

When we reached the spot, I wondered if Seth would shed tears. But he didn't. I could tell that he was deeply moved. I could tell that he was hurt. If he hadn't 've felt so deeply he'd 've been to the cemetery before now. He'd been in Lantern almost a week before he visited her grave. Seth had always thought things through in school, and I knew he would think them out now. He stood in silence over the freshly heaped mound of earth. I stood in silence with him and I was deeply moved, for I'd played with Betty and Seth from the time I could remember. And since we had played together, since we were classmates in twelve grades of school and since I was the best man at his wedding, I thought these were the reasons he'd asked me to come with him. Of all the places I didn't want to go when I was home on "boot leave" was the cemetery.

"Shan," Seth said thoughtfully, "I'm going to have Betty lifted!"

"Why?" I asked.

"For two reasons," he said. "I don't want her buried in low ground. I hate to think water is near her grave. And I want to see her again!"

I stood in silence. I knew Seth had made up his mind what he wanted and he would have just that if it could be had. He'd always been that way. I've heard him say when he was nine or ten years old that he would marry Betty someday. And he did. And now he wanted to see her again, and he would see her.

"You'll think I'm crazy, Shan," Seth said. "But I'm not crazy. I know what I'm doing. And I know what it will take to satisfy me before I leave for my ship. I know people have to die. I've seen them die. I'm not disturbed like a lot of people by death. I've just been so long away from Betty and to come back and not find her is not right. I've been with her and loved her all my life! And I just have to see her!"

I knew if she had been my wife I would not have moved her. I would have let her rest where she was. But this was none of my business. Seth had planned to do this five minutes after he'd seen her grave. He had his mind made up to change things.

"Do you know who I'll have to see about getting permission to have her lifted?" Seth asked.

"The Lantern County Health Department, I think," I said.

"Since everybody's been wanting to do something for me at home," Seth said, "all I want is just permission to have her lifted and moved up on the knoll. And I just want you here with me when it's done!"

"I'd rather not be here," I said. "Seth, I'll do anything for you, but I hate to be here when this is done."

"Don't worry if you'll think I'll carry on," Seth said. "I won't do that. There won't be any scene. Not anybody will know what I'm doing. I'll have this done quietly. I'll not tell 'em I want to see her. I'll just tell 'em I want her lifted. And when she's lifted, I'm going to ask to have a look at her."

"When will you want me?" I asked.

"Tomorrow afternoon," he said. "I'll get permission tonight and have everything ready by 2:00 P.M. tomorrow."

After we left the cemetery and I'd gone home, Mom and Dad asked me what had come over me. I think they thought I was dreading to leave home and go back after my first leave was over. And they tried to encourage me by telling me what a hero Seth Winters was. But I was thinking about Seth Winters. I was thinking about the things that had happened to him and how he had his ideas about things. I thought about his love for Betty. It was a deep, silent love. And I thought he was doing a crazy thing until I put myself in his place. He hadn't seen Betty for two years. And he hadn't seen his second son until he was walking and talking. And though at first I thought Seth's idea was crazy, I thought if this had happened to me, I would do the same thing.

On the afternoon of the following day, I slipped away from the house quietly. I hurried to Shady Grove Cemetery. There was no one on the ground but the sexton, Bill Tooley; his helpers, Ronald Martin, Alf Skinner, Lus Stamper; and the county health agent, George Pratt.

Seth was with them, directing the whole affair. They had the casket removed from the grave. They had refilled the empty grave, had sodded it, and had dug a new grave on the knoll.

"We've been workin' here since dawn," Seth said. "We've lifted Betty from this swamp and we're ready to take her up on the knoll. Join in and help us carry her."

It all seemed like a dream to me. I couldn't realize that we were carrying Betty Winters across the legions of the grass to a new grave, one high above the water mark. But we carried her to the new grave. And here was the new grave smoothly sloped within, with a vault at the bottom and the heavy box to hold the coffin placed in the vault.

"You know, sir," Seth said to George Pratt, the county health agent, "I wasn't here when Betty was buried and I'm not sure that she's in this casket. I'd like to have it opened to be sure!"

"But I'm sure it's your wife," George Pratt said. "I was at the funeral. I saw 'er with my own eyes!"

"But I want to be sure, sir," Seth said almost pleadingly.

"Mr. Pratt, caskets have been opened here before," Bill Tooley said.

"And I want to see my wife again," Seth said. "I never got to see her. I just want to see Betty again."

"But we don't have a screwdriver to open the lid," Bill Tooley said.

I knew he thought Seth would probably take on a lot when he saw her. I could have told him Seth wouldn't. I knew that was the reason he didn't want her casket opened.

"I can take the screws out with my knife blade," Bill Tooley said.

"All right then, if you want her coffin opened," George Pratt said.

Seth watched the sexton remove the screws from the lid. And when he raised the lid, Seth stepped closer to the coffin and looked down silently, grimly...All of us stood back while he looked on, all but the sexton. Bill Tooley stood beside Seth.

"She's Betty, all right," Seth spoke without emotion. "She looks just as natural as if she's at home in bed asleep. Gee, how I've wanted to see you, Betty. It's worth my trip just to come to see you. I couldn't have gone back without seeing you!"

Then Seth dropped a white percoon blossom inside the coffin, though its white petals were a little wilted where he'd held the wild flower in his warm hand.

"Here, Betty," he said. "You always loved percoon in April."

We stood silent; and I was moved to tears. Each man wiped tears from his eyes, but not Seth.

"Thank you, sirs," Seth said. "This was kind of you to do this for me! I would like to go now. Will you see that the grave is finished neatly?"

"Don't worry, my boy," Bill Tooley said. "I'll see all is finished before we leave."

I walked away with Seth. Neither of us spoke as we walked toward Lantern, facing the church spires and housetops outlined against a blue bank of peaceful April sky.

"Seth Winters" was first published in Edward Seaver, editor, *Cross Section, 1945* (New York, L.B. Fischer, 1945), pp. 246-253. It has never been reprinted.

Jesse Hilton Stuart — circa 1967

Sour Grapes

I don't know how I got into the world. I just remember being there. The first time I remember being in the world was when I tried to follow Ma out'n the cliff. She went out first and shoved me back. She closed the gate that kept me shut in the cliff. I cried and cried after Ma. She was the only person I ever saw then. All the light I ever saw came in at the mouth of the cliff.

I remember every piece of furniture we had in the cliff. We had a flat-topped stove. It had a pipe that run up straight, then elbowed and went out along the top of the cliff to the outside. We had a big flat rock inside the cliff for a table. Ma spread a white cloth over it. We had a bed-tick made of coffee sacs and filled with oak leaves. We slept on this together. I slept in Ma's arms then. We had two quilts that Ma worked for and carried home. We had a few pots and pans, and some dishes. Ma had a big washtub, a wash-kettle and a washboard. The washboard was bright and pretty with little ridges across it.

In the summertime I didn't wear any clothes. I had to stay in the cliff. I went naked. In wintertime I wore a pair of pants and a shirt. The cliff was long. I used to go and go before I'd come to the end of it. There was dry sand on the bottom for my feet and some dry piles of oak leaves. At the door of the cliff Ma hung a quilt during the wintertime to keep out the wind. In the summertime Ma just kept a high gate fastened to keep me inside. Mister Seagraves used to keep his cattle in this cliff before Ma brought me here. Ma worked for Mister Seagraves now. He let us have the cliff.

I remember how Ma used to leave me. She would leave bread on the white cloth spread over the rock. She would leave a pitcher of water for me to drink. She would fasten the gate. She would twist a wire on the outside so I couldn't reach over and untwist it. I couldn't open the gate and get out. I had to stay in the cliff. It was the only place I'd ever been. I could tell you every piece of rock in the cliff from the gate in the front, back to where the water dripped down. I could show you every pile of leaves. I could tell you about every dish we had and pot and pan.

Ma used to come up the hill to the cliff. She would be nearly out'n breath. She would have a big sack of clothes across her back. She had brought them to the cliff to wash. Ma would wash them in the cliff. Snow would be on the ground outside. Ma was a big woman. She had big arms. She would come down with her weight on a dirty pair of overalls. The suds would fly. She'd rub and rub. Then she'd twist and twist the pair of overalls and the water would come out by squirts. When she'd wash the sack of clothes she'd hang them to dry on a grapevine across the cliff.

Before I went to bed Ma would take me in her arms and sing to me. The last I'd remember were the pretty words Ma'd sing. I'd wake up in the morning and Ma'd have breakfast. We'd eat again and Ma would leave. She'd be gone all day. I'd stay in the cliff. It was good and warm. The wind couldn't get to me. I'd sometimes go up to the door and pull the quilt to one side and look at the snow on the high hills. It was a white world. I could see the trees that stood dark and without leaves, in the snow. The winter would pass. Summer would come again. The trees would get green. The cattle would eat green grass in front of the cliff. I would like to watch the cattle eat. I would watch them from the cliff. I'd hear the birds sing. I'd watch the butterflies fly from one blossom to another. They were pretty things.

I don't know how old I was. I don't know how big I was. I'd never seen anybody but Ma. I know she was big. But Ma let me get out'n the cliff. She watched me. She stayed close to me. I remember the grass was green. I remember the feel of the wind against my naked body. I remember the warmth of the sun. It was spring. The birds were singing. The grass was growing. The cattle were picking the grass with their mouths. It was a big room. I couldn't run to the end of it. Ma was at my heels all the time. But I jumped around like a young calf in spring. I tried to catch the birds. I nearly caught a butterfly on a purple blossom. After I ran around over the pasture on the steep hillside below the cliff, Ma took me back and put me behind the gate. She fastened me up.

Ma would let me go out now. She took me to a patch of berries. I picked them from the ground. Ma told me the names of things. She called them strawberries. They tasted good and sweet. I saw flowers in bloom on the hill. I saw honeybees. Ma told me about them. Ma told me everything. But Ma stayed right beside me. After we picked the strawberries and ate them and Ma brought an apron load to the house, Ma fastened me in the cliff again. We once heard a voice. It was a strange voice. Ma took me by the hand and run with me through the woods.

Ma would take me out from the cliff. She would tell me the names of trees, flowers, birds and plants. I would see the rabbits. I would watch dogs run the rabbits. I would hear them bark. I would want to run after the dogs. Ma wouldn't let me. She would hold me. Life was different. It was big. I didn't want to go back and be fastened up in the cliff. I got tired of the cliff. I hated it. I wanted to get out. I wanted to stay out. I wanted to run after the snakes. Ma wouldn't let me. She told me the snake would bite me. I would die. I didn't know what she meant when she said I would die. She told me the black snake would hurt me. The black snake was the color of Ma's face.

But I didn't look like Ma. I warn't the color of Ma. My hair was another color. I warn't the color of the black snake. I was the color of the blowing viper. When I pointed to my face and to Ma's face and to Ma's hair, she grabbed my hand and run through the woods to the cliff with me.

I had been over the fields about the cliff now. I just hated to stay in the cliff. Ma went away to work. I climbed over the gate. I run over the hill to the strawberry patch. I was eating berries. I heard voices. I crawled on my belly thru the weeds and I saw something I had never seen before. I saw a man plowing. I saw two boys with hoes. They warn't the color of Ma. I laid in the weeds and watched them. Their dog started barking. He came toward me. He was growling and kicking up the dirt. I jumped up and started to run. The man plowing saw me. The boys saw me. The boys run after me hollering, with their hoes up in the air. They was trying to hit me. I didn't have on any clothes. I could outrun them. The man said: "What do you know about that! A wild youngin!" I outrun them to the thickets of green brush and green briars. I run back to the cliff.

One day Mister Seagraves came to cliff. I'd heard Ma say that name. She had said it to me. He come on the outside and hollered to Ma. Ma went out. She says to me: "Adger, you stay in here. I won't be out but just a minute." I slipped up to the gate and listened.

"Mollie," says Mister Seagraves, "Adger has been slipping out. You can't hide him any longer. You are going to haf to send that boy to school. You are going to haf to do something about it. Lake Sperry and his two boys saw him down at the cornfield yesterday morning and it's going around here there's a wild youngin loose in the woods. People are scouring the rocks and woods for this wild youngin."

"I know, Mister Seagraves," says Ma, "but he can't go to school here. What will I do? What will Mister Zeb do? Oh, I can't do it, Mister Seagraves."

"You will have to do something now," says Mister Seagraves. "I'll see Zeb about it. I'm going to town Saturday. I'll put Zeb wise."

I saw Mister Seagraves. He was a big man. He was the color of the man I saw plowing. He wore clothes like this man. He had a big stick in his hand that helped him climb the hill. He had a big bag of salt on his shoulder. He spread the salt on the rocks. The cattle come up and licked the salt with their long tongues. Ma came back in the cliff.

Ma didn't go to school with me. Mister Seagraves sent me with his boy. I was afraid of the other boys. When I got to school all the children looked at me. They just kept looking at me. I was afraid of them. Ma had put clothes on me. I wore a white waist and a little pair of pants that buttoned to the waist. The teacher asked me my name. I says: "Adger." The children laughed. She says: "Is that all the name you got?" I says: "Yes." The children looked at one another and laughed. I saw things they called books. There was pictures in the books. I had seen things that looked like the pictures. There was little black things in the book. The boys and girls would look at these and say words I couldn't understand. We were two kinds of people. None was the color of Ma. A lot wore clothes like Ma. I'd never seen girls before.

When we went out of the house the boys gathered around me. I wanted to run. I didn't run until one of the boys started to bark like a dog. Then I run like a rabbit. The boys took after me. The boys were all barking. I started for the cliff. I didn't get to the cliff. They were getting too close to me. I climbed up a tree. The boys tried to climb up and get me. Many of them stayed under the tree and barked. When they tried and tried and couldn't climb up to get me, they started throwing rocks at me. Just one rock hit me. It hit me on the side of the head. The blood run down and made my white shirt red. The teacher come out and made the boys leave the tree.

She tried to get me to come down. She tried to find a boy who would climb up to get me. She couldn't find a boy who could climb the tree. I was afraid to come down. The teacher took the boys back to the schoolhouse. She went with them. I heard her ring a bell. I could look from the top of the tree. I saw the boys in one line, the girls in another. They marched into the schoolhouse. When they went in the house I came down out'n the tree. I ran hard as I could go back to the cliff to Ma.

Ma washed my head where I'd been hit with a rock. Ma cried when she took my white waist off. It was red with blood. I was glad to get my clothes off. I went out in the pasture field and laid down in the sun. I watched the cows come back and lick the rocks where Mister Seagraves put the salt. Ma says: "Adger, you won't haf to go no more to that school. You can stay here with me." I didn't know what school was. Just a lot of boys and girls in a house. The teacher was big like Ma but she warn't like Ma. The boys and girls warn't the color of Ma neither.

One day when I was dragging in poles of wood for Ma, the teacher and a big man come up the hill to the cliff. I saw Ma go out to them. The man was bigger than Mister Seagraves. He was getting his breath hard after he climbed up the hill. He was fat like Ma. He was the color of Mister Seagraves. The big man says to Ma: "I am the Superintendent of Schools in this county. I've come here to investigate. I've heard there was a wild boy loose out here. Then Miss Harkreader reported that a boy enrolled in school and wouldn't tell his name and the boys ran him away with rocks."

"He was hit with a rock," says Ma. "Yes sir, he was hit with a rock."

Ma was shaking like a leaf. Ma's eyes got big. I stooped down behind a bunch of blackberry briars. I watched them. I listened to them. I laid my two poles of wood down beside me.

"Is he your boy?" says the big man.

"No, he ain't my boy," says Ma.

Ma began to cry.

"The boy is white," says the teacher. "If you could see him—He just acts funny. He don't know how to play with children. He don't know what a book is. He is afraid. He acts like a wild boy."

"No wonder," says the Superintendent, "living in a rock cliff. I've come here to investigate this situation. He's in the school law, isn't he?"

"Yes," says the teacher, "he must be. He didn't know his age. I asked him. He didn't know what I was talking about. He just stood and looked at me. No one had ever seen him before. No one knew where he lived. I found out where he lived from Mister Seagraves' boy, Erf. He said he heard his Pa tell his Ma that they lived in the cliff."

"What are you doing with this boy then," says the Superintendent to Ma, "if he's not your boy?"

"Oh, don't ask me that, Mister," says Ma.

Ma cried harder and harder.

"I'll see the boy goes to school," says the Superintendent. "I'll stop the rock throwing if I have to put this situation in the hands of the County Judge. Where is this boy? I'd like to see him."

"I don't know," says Ma.

"Yes you do," says the Superintendent. "I want to have a look at him."

When the Superintendent said this I jumped up and run from behind the briars. I left my poles of wood there. I took off across the pasture field.

"There he goes," says the teacher.

"He looks white to me," says the Superintendent, "but he is wild as a quail. He's got red hair. He must be sent to school."

"I won't be responsible," says the teacher. "I'm afraid I can't handle the school the way the children act when he's there. You'll have to get another teacher."

I hid behind another bunch of blackberry briars in the pasture. I saw them come back down the hill. I heard them talking. The Superintendent was smoking his pipe. He was walking with a cane.

He says: "If that's not a white boy I'm fooling. He's white as I am. She's kidnapped that boy. We'll further this investigation. I'll put it in the hands of the Sheriff when I get back to town. That boy is big enough to be ten years old. Running wild without a stitch of clothes on."

They went out of sight. I heard them talking and talking but I couldn't understand what they were saying. I run back up the hill and found Ma laying on the bed of leaves in the cliff. She was crying and crying. I told Ma what I heard them say about the Sheriff. Ma got up and says to me: "Now you stay here until I come back. I won't be gone long."

Ma went over the hill toward Mister Seagraves' house. I waited in the cliff for her to come back. Night had come when Ma got back. Ma got my white waist and put it on me. She made me put my pants on. I didn't want to wear them. Mister Seagraves came up to the cliff.

"Where is the stove, Mollie?" he says.

"It's right over there," says Ma. "I'll take it, and my dishes, pots and pans, but I'll leave the bed tick. I'll take the quilts."

Ma took one side of the stove, Mister Seagraves the other. They carried it over the hill. Mister Seagraves had a wagon waiting. They lifted the stove on the wagon. Then they come up the hill to get the rest of the things.

"You're stout as a man, Mollie," says Mister Seagraves. "I've never lifted with a stouter person in my life."

Ma and Mister Seagraves got the rest of the things. I carried the stove pipes down to the wagon. We got in the wagon. Mister Seagraves set up front and drove the horses. Me and Ma rode back with the furniture. Ma held me in her arms most of the way. I remember the stars in the sky. I remember the moon in the sky. I remember the grinding of the wagon wheels on the gravel and the horses splashing water in the creeks.

I heard Mister Seagraves say: "I'm just doing this for old Zeb. He didn't have no business getting into this mess. He's a friend of mine. We were boys together."

Then he says: "Get-up!" to the horses. He slapped them with the lines. The horses trotted on and on through the night with the wagon. I don't remember all of the trip nor the way we went. I slept with my head on Ma's lap. I just remember waking up in front of a pretty little white house. It warn't daylight yet. Ma and Mister Seagraves lifted the stove from the wagonbed and carried it into the house. I carried the pipes in the house. Ma and Mister Seagraves carried the rest of the things. Mister Seagraves left his lantern with Ma.

"I thank you so much, Mister Seagraves," says Ma as he got up in the wagon and drove away before all the morning stars had left the sky. Ma set up the stove. She fixed us a bed. We laid down for a little sleep. I couldn't sleep. The place was so strange. It warn't nary a bit like the rock cliff. There warn't no leaves on the floor. No water was dripping from the roof.

That day a man came to the house. He smoked a pipe like the Superintendent smoked and like Mister Seagraves smoked. He wore a black hat. He walked in the house. He just stood a long time and looked at me. I wanted to run. But I couldn't get out'n the house. Then he looked at Ma.

"Well, Mister Zeb," says Ma.

Ma looked at Mister Zeb.

"I see you've got here all right," says Mister Zeb. "Now you can start to work for the Missus today. She's expecting you up to the house this morning. This boy must go to school. You can't leave him here in the house."

"I know, Mister Zeb," says Ma, "but he tried that going to school out on Shelf's Run. The boys run him like he was a possum. They treed him. Then they threw rocks at him. Look at that place on the side of his head."

"I know about it," says Mister Zeb. "Charlie Seagraves told me the whole story. We'll try him in the other school. The one down here on the creek. You have a home here, Mollie. You can help my wife. You are far away from Shelf's Run now. Let the Sheriff go back there. You are in another county now. He will not find anything but the empty cliff."

Mister Zeb took his hat off. He fanned in the house. It was a little warm. I saw Mister Zeb's hair. It was red, too. It was like my hair. It warn't a bit like Ma's hair. Then Mister Zeb put his hat back on. He puffed on his pipe.

"Now you get up to the house, Mollie," says Mister Zeb, "and help the Missus. I told her I'd get her a woman to do the work the other day. She doesn't know you. You don't know me either."

"No, I don't, Mister Zeb," says Ma. "I don't know you. I've just come for work. I've come to live here."

"I'll get you a bed in here," says Mister Zeb. "I think we've got a old bedstead up in the garret you can have. I'll have it brought down to the house. I'll give you enough money so you can buy a few little things you need. I'll take this boy down and let Slim's boy take him to school. He can go with Slim's boy, Jeff, down to the school by the creek."

I wore my white waist and my pants buttoned to them. I went with Mister Zeb. I saw Ma go up the hill to the big brick house. It was bigger than our rock cliff. There was a lot of big trees in the yard. I saw the flowers in bloom upon the hill around Mister Zeb's big house. We walked down the road until we come to a little plank house by the road. I saw a boy coming out'n the house with his books in his hand.

"Jeff," says Mister Zeb, "take this boy to school with you this morning."

"He can't go to school with me," says Jeff, "he's going to the wrong school!"

"No, he's not," says Mister Zeb. "You do as I say, young man."

Jeff was the color of Ma. He was one of Ma's people. He was the color of a black snake.

"Take care of 'im, too," says Mister Zeb as he puffed his pipe and walked away. He stopped in the road and looked at us as we walked away together. We walked beside a barbwire fence. Then we turned to our right and walked out a road until we crossed the creek. Jeff wouldn't talk to me. He just looked at me. He was like the boys I'd met before. Only Jeff was the color of Ma. He wouldn't walk close to me.

We walked up the bank to the schoolhouse. I saw a lot of boys and girls. They were all Ma's people. They were all the color of Ma. When I went up in the yard the children begin to laugh. They jumped up and down and laughed and looked at my hair. The teacher came out. He looked at me. The children began to laugh. He tried to stop them. They wouldn't stop.

"You've come to the wrong school," the teacher says to me. He was a man bigger than Mister Zeb. He was the color of Ma. He was as big as Ma. "You belong at the white folks school down in town. What is your name?"

"Adger," I says.

"Adger, who?" he says.

"Adger," I says.

"No name," he says. "Where did you get him, Jeff?"

"Mister Zeb sent him down here with me," says Jeff. "I didn't want to bring him in. Mister Zeb told me to bring him and take care of him. I don't know nothing about him, Mister Porter. I've just brought him because Mister Zeb said for me to."

The children looked at one another. They started laughing. I was afraid. I was ready to run. Two big boys looked at me. They acted like dogs wanting to get to a rabbit. The big teacher walked back in the house. The children gathered around me and laughed.

"Get 'im, Slick," says Jeff. "He ain't our kind. He don't belong here nohow!"

"What do you say, Big Charlie?" says Slick to the other big boy that snarled his lips at me. "Let's get 'im."

"Pretty red hair," says Big Charlie, "where did you get it?"

I run down the road hard as I could go. I could nearly catch a rabbit before I left the cliff. I could outrun these boys. They was all after me. Big Charlie and Slick was close to me. I kept away from them. All the boys and girls was after me. Rocks whizzed past my head. I went out the road and turned the corner by Jeff's house and took up the road. I looked back. I heard the school bell. They started back across the creek to the school on the bank.

"Don't ever come back here, Red-Head," says Big Charlie.

"It won't be any good for you if you do," says Slick. "We'll get you the next time."

I went up the road. I went back to the little white shack. I went in and laid down on the bed and waited for Ma to come from Mister Zeb's house. I waited all day in the house. I didn't get out and hunt the butterflies. I was afraid. I was afraid of people. Mister Zeb was good to me. I warn't afraid of Mister Zeb.

"Why didn't you stay at school, child?" says Ma.

"They run me away," I says to Ma.

"Where was the teacher?" says Ma.

"He went in the house," I says, "and Big Charlie and Slick run me away. All of the children run after me. They throwed rocks at me. I outrun them. I came back to the house."

"No place in the world for you," says Ma. "Neither school will have you. I'll tell Mister Zeb about it. But you won't go to school no more. You will stay right here with me."

I didn't go to school anymore. I started to work for Mister Zeb. I pushed the lawnmower and cut grass in the yard. I fed Mister Zeb's hogs. I learned to milk the cows. I learned to harness Mister Zeb's horses and drive them over the farm. I learned how to take them to town. When Big Charlie and Slick run along and tried to get upon my wagon I used the rawhide on them. I would crack the rawhide in their faces and lap it around their shoulders. They would run away cursing and screaming and I'd slap the horses with the lines and get away before they could hit me with a rock. I couldn't drive thru town where Ma's people lived. They would holler at me and curse me. Then they would take after my wagon. They would holler something about my red hair and asked me how I liked my first day of school and when I was coming back.

Mister Zeb would come back from his office. He would be standing out watching me work lots of times when I didn't see him. He would be smoking his pipe. He would say to me: "I wish Young Zeb was as good to work as you. I'd give anything on earth. You don't mind to work. Here is some extra money for you. Buy yourself some clothes. Don't let Mollie know I give it to you. This is for you." Then Mister Zeb would go away.

Young Mister Zeb didn't work, he went to school. He was the only child Mister Zeb had. He would get in the big automobile and get Missus Zenophine in the front seat with him. Mister Zeb would set in the back seat and smoke his pipe. They would go off every Sunday afternoon and drive around. Young Mister Zeb wore good clothes. I wanted to dress like him. But I couldn't. I didn't know how. He looked so much like Mister Zeb. He was the size of Mister Zeb. He had red hair too. It seemed like a lot of us had red hair.

I didn't know how to drive a car. I did know how to drive a team. Mister Zeb showed me how. He showed me how to plow. It was easy for me. I could do it just as easy. I would plow while Ma worked in Mister Zeb's house for Missus Zenophine. Ma would come to the shack and get my dinner. We would eat together and then we would go back to our work. I didn't want to ever go back to the rock cliff. I didn't want to ever leave Mister Zeb. Ma didn't want to leave her job working for Missus Zenophine. We liked it fine here. Ma was happy but she was always afraid of Missus Zenophine. I was always afraid of Young Mister Zeb. He got so he didn't like me. I'd never done anything to him. I washed his car. I done everything he told me to do. But he would look hard at me. He would look at my hair. Then he would look meaner at me.

I worked for Mister Zeb five years. He never quarreled at me. I got to be as big as Mister Zeb. I was a lot stouter than Mister Zeb. I was as stout as Mister Zeb and Young Mister Zeb put together. I was stouter than Ma was. I got me a long suit of clothes. I tried to dress like Young Mister Zeb. When I put my first long suit on I went down through town where Ma's people lived. I saw Big Charlie. He come walking over to me. He says: "You think you're something on a stick, don't you? Well, you know who you are? Red-headed—ha! Well, I'm going to color that hair for you right now!"

Before Big Charlie had time to change the color of my hair, I had him knocked cold on the ground. I hit him under the chin with my fist. I run as hard as I could go after I saw what I'd done to Big Charlie. I thought I'd killed him. I run back home. There weren't no place for me to go but just walk around. Mister Zeb's people wouldn't have me nor Ma's people wouldn't have me. I was afraid of them. Just two people I warn't afraid of. That was Ma and Mister Zeb.

When I went back to town again I met Slick. He saw me and he came over where I was walking down the railroad tracks. He run out to me and looked at me. He stopped in the railroad tracks. He just stood there. His lips pulled apart like a dog's. He showed his teeth.

"You whipped Big Charlie," he says, "but it ain't no sign you can whip old Slick. I aim to get you right. I'm going to tear you apart with my hands! You got purty red hair and a mighty purty suit you got on there. Where did you get that?"

He made at me. I grabbed a cinder. I held it in my hand. I hit Slick between the eyes with the cinder. It cut a long gash. The blood squirted. Slick fell down on the tracks. I pulled him off the tracks. He was bleeding. I run back to the shack hard as I could go. I never told Ma or Mister Zeb about it. I thought Mister Zeb would be mad. If I'd killed Slick nobody would know who done it. I never told. Slick got all right but he had a scar between his eyes. He never bothered me again. When he saw me he went the other way. Big Charlie did too.

Ma got her new clothes. She looked good in her new clothes. She put them on one Sunday afternoon. She dressed up the best I ever saw Ma dressed.

Ma says to me: "Let's go to church, Adger. There's a prayer meeting down to the church today. I ain't been to church in so long. You dress up in your new suit and let's go to church."

I put on my new suit. I dressed up too. Just Ma and me living in the little white shack down below Mister Zeb's big brick. We had a pretty little shack. Hollyhocks bloomed around the door. Birds built nests in the elm trees around the shack. Bees and butterflies lit on the hollyhock blossoms. I was so happy with Ma. I didn't care if she was another color. I warn't ashamed of Ma. I went to church with her.

I saw Big Charlie at church. I saw Slick there. He looked hard at me. Everybody looked at me coming in with Ma. They looked at my red hair. The women and men and children were all the color of Ma. I was among her kind of people. The women looked at me and whispered. The preacher got up to preach. He was a big man. He was bigger than Ma.

He says: "My text will be children: 'The fathers have eaten sour grapes and their children's teeth are set on edge.' Now this sermon will hit hard, Sister Mollie. But we are all just like children and when the shoe fits one of us we got to wear it."

Ma says to me: "Come, Adger."

She took me by the hand. We got up and left the church. Ma cried all the way back to the house. We didn't go around the road. We cut across the field by the railroad tracks. We crossed the creek on the big elm tree that had blowed down by the swimming hole. Ma didn't want anybody to see her crying. I was glad to get out'n the church. I didn't feel at home there. I would rather be with people like Mister Zeb. Ma always wanted to get back to her people. But they didn't want Ma. They didn't like Ma. They didn't like me. I didn't like them.

The day after we went to church I looked at myself in the looking glass. I looked at my jaws. I looked at my eyes. I looked at my hair. I says to Ma: "You know I look a lot like Young Mister Zeb. I am bigger than he is now is all. I am a stouter man than he is."

Ma didn't say anything. I put on my old work clothes and went to the barn. Young Mister Zeb was at the barn where he kept the automobile. He says to me: "Adger, the car is muddy. Clean it up!" He looked hard at me when he said this. He gritted his teeth. I just stood there. I thought a whole lot. I didn't move.

"Hear me, Adger," says Young Mister Zeb. "Clean up that car!"

I didn't move.

Young Mister Zeb went in the barn. He came out with a rawhide whip that I used on the horses. He hit me around the legs. I didn't move. He hit me again. I didn't move. He hit me again and again and again and I didn't move.

The blood run down my legs.

"Can you feel it?" he says.

"Not as hard as a weak kitten like you can use a whip," I says. "I could break you in two. But I won't. You look too much like me!"

Then he whipped me harder. He started crying. He threw down the whip. He run to the house. I looked at my legs. My pants legs stuck to my legs. The blood had wet them. It had soaked through. It was dripping off. I started to the house. Mister Zeb was away at the office. I saw Missus Zenophine running down to the shack. She run to the door. She went in. I saw Ma come out.

"Get out'n here, you old wench you," says Missus Zenophine to Ma. "I understand it all now. You get out of here! You old bitch you! You good for nothing wench! Get that bastard and get out of here! Go before I get a sheriff up here! Leave everything in this house. I want to burn it."

Ma run out'n the house. I went with her. We left the shack. I looked back at it when we got to the turn of the road. I saw the hollyhocks in bloom there. I saw the wagon under the elms. I saw the big horses in the barn lot. I saw Young Mister Zeb have Missus Zenophine by the arm. He was helping her up the hill to the big brick. She was crying. Ma was crying. I didn't have Ma by the arm. We didn't have a big house to go to. I didn't know where we'd go. I felt like helping Ma but she didn't need help no more than I did. The blood was still running down my legs where Young Mister Zeb whipped me with the rawhide. I didn't have a change of clothes to put on. We took Missus Zenophine at her word and got out while times was good. Me and Ma could a whipped Missus Zenophine and Young Mister Zeb. But we didn't fight them.

Ma and me started down the road. I never asked her any questions. I just went with her. She was the best friend I had. If it warn't for Ma I didn't know what I would have done. But she stuck to me. I would stick to her. I was ashamed of her people. They were ashamed of me. I didn't like them. They didn't like me. Mister Zeb's people wouldn't have nothing to do with me. Mister Zeb was good to me. He was good to Ma.

"Well," says Ma, "there's not but one thing for us to do. We must go back to the cliff. Have you got any money with you?"

"I got half a dollar," I says, "that Mister Zeb gave me yesterday."

"Give it to me," says Ma, "and I'll go in the store and buy us some cheese and bread. It'll take us all day and all night to reach the cliff. I know a way to go through the hills. I went that way many years ago."

Ma got the bread and cheese. We started on our way.

It was daylight the next morning when we reached the cliff. We found our old bed of leaves in the cliff. Ma says to me: "Adger, I'm sick. It's a fluttering. I feel hot. I want water. Go tell Mister Seagraves."

I went down and told Mister Seagraves. He came to the cliff. He looked at Ma. He says: "She's bad off. She's got the fever, I believe. I'll go back to the house. I'll get help. I'll let Zeb know about this." He went away. No one came back. Ma got worse. She made loud noises. Night came. It was dark on the outside. Ma laid on the leaves. I laid down beside her. I must have gone to sleep. After a while I didn't hear any more noises.

Next morning when I got up, I tried to get Ma up. She was still. She wouldn't speak. She warn't getting her breath. Ma was dead. I was scared. Just me in the cliff with Ma and she was dead. I cried and cried. I remember when Ma told me what it was to be dead. I didn't know then. Now Ma had come back here and was dead. Ma was run off from the shack. She'd walked all day and all night. She was sick a day and night. Now she was dead.

Missus Seagraves come up the hill to the cliff. It was the first time she'd ever been here. She looked at Ma. She says: "Poor Mollie. She's dead. She was a good worker." Then she says to me: "Adger, Mister Seagraves will attend to this. You stay here until we get a coffin." Missus Seagraves went away. Ma used to work for Missus Seagraves. She went down over the bank to the house.

That night Mister Seagraves, Mister Sperry and two other men I didn't know come up the hill. They were carrying a coffin. It warn't one made of planks. It was a pretty coffin with bright handles. It was soft lined, prettier than any bed Ma had ever slept in. They brought it up and set it down in front of the cliff. Mister Sperry was carrying a lantern and Mister Seagraves was carrying a lantern.

"Take Adger and go back down at the foot of the hill and get the tools," says Mister Seagraves to one of the strange men.

I went with him down to the foot of the hill to get the picks, mattocks and shovels. When we got back to the cliff Mister Seagraves and Mister Sperry had Ma in the coffin. Four men carried the coffin. Mister Seagraves and Mister Sperry walked in front and led the way with lanterns. I followed them and carried the tools. We come to a high spot on the hill above the cliff. The ground was loamy and soft. Mister Seagraves and Mister Sperry come to a stop.

"This is the place," says Mister Seagraves.

They hung their lanterns up on trees under the green leaves where the bugs made noises up among the leaves. They started digging. They didn't talk much. I helped them dig. By midnight when the moon was getting over on the far side of the hill, we had the grave dug. It was a deep hole scooped out in the mountain loam for Ma. There warn't another grave near. Not one of Ma's people had ever lived here. Not one of them had ever been buried among these hills. They let Ma's coffin down with rope plowlines. They shoveled in the dirt. I cried and before they had the last dirt shoveled over her, I run out through the woods the way we had come with the coffin. I found the cliff. I slept there that night.

The next morning I found a piece of dry bread and some cheese Ma and me had brought to the cliff. I ate the dry bread and the cheese.

I left the cliff. I didn't know where I was going. I walked all day. I just walked and walked. When it got dark I thought about sleeping in a haystack. I couldn't find one. I hated to sleep in the weeds. I was afraid of snakes. I was afraid to crawl in a barn loft and sleep. If the farmer found me the next morning he was liable to do something to me. I walked to a river. There was a covered wooden bridge across it. There was a loft in this covered bridge. I heard the birds up in the loft. I saw a hole where a man could go through. There was notches cut on the post leading up to the hole. I climbed up in the loft. It was dark. I couldn't see. I just went to sleep. I didn't know more until morning.

I was so hungry. I couldn't think about Ma. I had to think about something to eat. I climbed down the notched pole. I run down the road by the river. I took out'n a field and found a watermelon patch. I found ripe sugar melons too.

I says to myself: "Right here is where I stay."

I would slip melons up in the loft. I would pull green corn down in the bottoms and take it back on the hill and roast it. Then I would carry it up in the loft of the covered bridge. I lived in the loft two weeks. One night I heard two men walk across the bridge down under me. I heard one say: "Too bad about Zeb killing himself."

"What made him do it, do you reckon?" says the other man.

"I heard," says the first voice, "that he got hitched up with some old wench and had a child by her. Brought them right in under his wife's nose for five years. His wife found it out. She had a nervous breakdown. She sued Zeb for a divorce. Said this wench had a bastard baby by him. A right good scrapper. Cleaned up the town!"

"You don't say," says the second voice as they passed over the end of the bridge and walked down the road by the river.

I climbed down out'n the bridge. I followed the river to the town. It was daylight when I got there. I slipped out on the hill above Mister Zeb's house. The graveyard where his Pa and Ma are buried is right above his house. I thought they would bury him there. I slipped through the woods above the graveyard. I watched the men dig his grave.

In the afternoon the hill was covered with people. They hauled

Mister Zeb up in a big automobile. I saw Young Mister Zeb down by the grave. I saw Missus Zenophine. I stayed up on the hill and watched. I heard the preacher. I just had to think about the way we buried Ma. I didn't have to wonder where the coffin come from. It was a good coffin. I just wondered if Mister Zeb's own coffin was as good as Ma's.

But we buried Ma at night. It was dark. But Ma was dark too. She was the color of the black snake. They buried Mister Zeb in the daytime. He was light like the day. We buried Ma in the dark woods by lantern light. The bugs made drowsy noises up among the dark green leaves when we buried Ma.

After they buried Mister Zeb and had all left the hill, I slipped down by his grave. I did know where it was. I could come back to it. But I couldn't go back to Ma's grave. I couldn't find it. I looked at the flowers heaped on Mister Zeb's grave. I was glad. Big wreaths of flowers covered the fresh dirt. I pulled a flower from one of the wreaths. I would keep it. There was something that I couldn't say. It was just in me. I ran across the road, took the path across the fallen tree by the swimming hole the way Ma and me had come from church.

I run to the railroad tracks. I waited for a freight train.

"Sour Grapes" was first published in *New Anvil*, Vol. 1, No. 3 (August-September 1939), pp. 15-24. It has been reprinted in Jack Conroy and Curt Johnson, editors, *Writers In Revolt* (New York, Laurence Hill and Co., 1973), pp. 162-178.

Jesse Stuart in his W-Hollow home with his grandsons
Erik (left) and Conrad (center) Juergensmeyer — circa 1973.

Sunday Morning on Sulphur Creek

This happened when my father used to mine coal and we lived in sight of the Sulphur Creek Mine in a one-room log shack on the mountain top. From our front yard we could see the dark cavernous mouth of the coal mine on the jagged slope of the mountain that faced our shack. We could see the long coal-tipple and the small mountains of blue slate dumps. The deep Sulphur Creek Valley was between our shack and the coal mine. There was a coal-wagon road that circled from the mountain top where we lived, around the head of Sulphur Creek Valley, sloping gently down to the coal mine. Since the railway company could not build a branch line from this mine to the trunk line, five trucks hauled the coal over this winding road to the mountain top, through a gap and down the other side, for a distance of twelve miles, to the valley where there was a railroad. And on this winding road that led from our house to the coal mine, Tom Leffard, one of the truck drivers, lived. He lived in a shack that fronted on the winding road but was held up on the lower side by log stilts fifteen feet high.

My father had never liked Tom Leffard, and I knew the reason. He told my mother and me late one afternoon when he had come home from work, that Tom Leffard whipped his cow when she wouldn't stand still for him to milk her. When he plowed his garden he cursed and beat his horse. My father told us the cat was afraid of him. He said Tom Leffard was mean to people he could bully and cruel to domestic animals that looked to their master for love and kindness. He told us the truck drivers knew how he killed wild game for the love of killing, game which he left lay where he had shot it down—how he would laugh with joy when he shot a rabbit which he wouldn't eat.

"But I like Mr. Leffard." I said.

"Why do you like 'im?" Pa asked, turning to me.

"He promised me a puppy when his dog has pups." I said. "That's why I like him."

"That's a good enough reason for you to like him," my father said. "But I know he's a mean man. I've seen him beat his poor old skinny cow and horse until I felt like beating him. I don't want trouble with him. He boasts about his shooting wild animals. He called it his favorite sport. I've never shot a rabbit or a squirrel for fun. The few I've killed we've eaten."

"The time will come when somebody will call his bluff," my father continued. His face flushed as red as a turkey gobbler's snout. "Leffard is a mean man. Anybody that's not kind to animals is mean."

I didn't try to prove to my father Mr. Leffard wasn't mean because he had promised me a pup. My father's temper rose up like steam from the spout of a boiling teakettle of water on a red hot stove when he mentioned Tom Leffard's name. But I couldn't feel toward our neighbor like my father did. I'd never seen him whip his cow. I'd only heard about it. I'd heard my father do most of the talking too. I thought—but I didn't say it to Pa—one reason Pa talked about Mr. Leffard was over our chickens once getting into his garden and he shot two of them, cooked and ate them and told Pa about it later. He'd never warned us before to keep our chickens away. We never let our chickens get near his shack again.

It was on Saturday afternoon that Pa had talked so about Mr. Leffard. And the next morning, Sunday morning, was the time I was to go after my puppy. Mr. Leffard told me that the four boy puppies had been spoken for and that I would have to take the girl puppy, the only one he had left. That didn't matter to me, girl puppy or boy puppy as long as I was getting a puppy. And it didn't matter to my father and mother. They approved of my bringing a girl puppy home same as a boy puppy. My father had already helped me make a little house for her. And on that Saturday night, after my father had talked so about Mr. Leffard, I went to bed and dreamed about going down to get my puppy and Mr. Leffard came out of the shack with a big rawhide whip he had used on his horse when he plowed his garden and took after me. I dreamed I ran up the road and the whip cracked like thunder at my heels and just as I looked back and Mr. Leffard was about to catch me, I let out one scream after another. Then I felt somebody's hand on my shoulder, shaking me and saying, "Wake up, Shan!"

It was my father standing over me, and Mom had got up and lit the kerosene lamp.

"You were a-havin' a nightmare, son," my father said. "What was after you, a bear, a wolf or something?"

"Not anything," I said, rubbing my eyes.

"Now, go back to bed and go to sleep," my father said very gently.

My father was kind to animals. And now he had quit hunting wild animals. He said they had a hard time living through the cold winters when food was so scarce for them.

I pulled the quilt back up around me and went back to bed.

That Sunday morning we were up at six, which was early on his day of rest from digging and loading coal at the Black Diamond Mine. I ate breakfast when it wasn't good daylight. I wanted to hurry down to Mr. Leffards's then, but my father wouldn't let me go this early. It was another hour before daylight came to our mountaintop home and he would let me go.

The late October wind was brisk that morning as I ran down the winding road where the loaded coal trucks had left ruts. I jumped over these ruts and my brogan shoes wetting against the bright red, yellow and gray leaves that had been shaken down from the treetops by October winds. I ran all the way down to Mr. Leffard's shack to get my puppy. I knocked on the door. I pounded on it and Mr. Leffard came to the door.

"I've come for my puppy," I said before I said "good morning" to Mr. Leffard.

"You've not got any puppy here," he said with words as cold as the morning October wind that had just been hitting me in the face.

I couldn't speak to Mr. Leffard. Not just then. I didn't know what had happened to me. This man who was larger than father, with eyes as blue as a robin's eggshell, and as cold as ice, stared at me, and I couldn't speak. Black beard covered his face and since his lips were wide apart and he had a front tooth missing I could see his tongue behind the discolored teeth in his mouth. Before I could speak, while

I stood there looking at him and he was looking at me, I thought I heard a puppy some place.

"What—what happened to my puppy?" I finally stammered.

"It died," he said.

"What caused it to die?" I asked.

"Don't ask so many questions and you'll make a wise old man," he grumbled.

"Did you bury the puppy?" I asked.

"Yep, it's buried all right," he said, with a smile showing all his ugly teeth.

"Did you give away all the boy puppies?"

"They're all gone," he said. "I gave them all away. All but the little bitch pup and she's dead. Now you'd better get going for a lot of cold air is coming through this door into my house."

Mr. Leffard closed the door in my face. I stood as silent as one of the blue slate dumps at the end of the tipple of the Black Diamond Mine. I didn't know what to do. The brisk October winds whistled in the apple trees' barren branches around Tom Leffard's shack. They whipped the cold apple tree branches like my father had said Tom Leffard whipped his cow and horse. It wasn't the woo-woo-sound of the wind among the apple trees that I heard again. Mr. Leffard had gone back in the shack, maybe, back to bed or to his breakfast. I didn't know. I heard a faint cry that sounded like a puppy to me. I heard it down below the shack. I walked toward the sound. Mr. Leffard couldn't see me. All of his shack but the upper wall was on the stilts. I went down the steep slope holding to the stilts. When I got down under the shack, I could hear the puppy plainer than ever. The mother dog was fastened by a chain to one of the stilts under the shack. She stood outside the large box that was without bedding which was her home. Her tail was tucked between her legs and her big brown eyes looked sad as she walked the length of her chain, back and forth. She looked toward the outdoor privy and whined.

Then I walked down the little winding path, where steps had been dug into the mountain and stone steps put in these little dug-out places.

I walked down these steps until I reached the toilet. There was not any mistake about it now. I heard a puppy whine in the toilet. I went inside and I couldn't find the puppy. I heard it crying down deep somewhere. Even if it were a toilet and a man like Tom Leffard had used it, I put my ear over the seat and I heard a puppy below. I couldn't believe it! I thought about what my father had said about Mr. Leffard and how I couldn't believe him when he told my mother and me how mean the man was to domestic animals and how he shot wild game in the woods and left it lay just for the fun of killing. It was hard for me to believe anybody could be so hard-hearted and so cruel! But the puppy was down there. I spoke to her and she tried to answer.

How can I get her out? I thought. What can I do? What will I do? Could I put a plank down to her and she could climb up the plank? Would the plank be too steep? I wondered. When the puppy cried, I cried too. I wondered how long she had been down there for her little whines and puppy-yelps seemed very weak. I knew she was cold too. I was crying and hating Tom Leffard when I heard somebody's steps coming. It's Tom Leffard, and what will he do to me. I thought as I ran out fast as my legs would carry me. And I almost ran into Kitty Leffard. Tom's wife, a small, skinny, stooped woman. I don't know who was scared the most. She ran back up the steps and I ran under the shack pulling up by stilts as I hurried toward the road.

I'd reached the road all right when Tom Leffard come from the front door. Mrs. Leffard had reached the back door of their shack in a hurry. I heard her tell her husband I had just come from the toilet.

"You little devil," Tom Leffard shouted to me. "What are you a-doin', you onery little scoundrel, trespassing on my property?"

"Don't you do anything more to my pup," I shouted. "I'll tell my father if you do! I'll tell everybody! I know where she is!"

If Tom Leffard had his horse whip in his hand I never knew because I didn't look back. I don't know how far he followed me. I was running faster than I'd ever run in my life. When I reached our mountaintop shack I opened the door and fell inside.

"What's the matter, Shan?" my father asked.

"He's out of breath," my mother said.

"Did old Tom Leffard run you?" my father asked. "What happened? Where's the pup?"

"Down in the privy vault," I sighed. My breath was short.

"Down where?" he asked.

"In a privy vault," I repeated.

"I told you, Sall, about that man," my father said.

He went to the clothes press and got his coat.

"Be careful, Mick," Mom said. "Anybody that would do that would do anything."

"I said he was cruel but I didn't know he was that cruel," my father said. His face colored as red as the October shoe-make leaves that had rained down when I walked down the truck road to Tom Leffard's shack. "I've always told you he was a mean man. "We'll get that pup out of that vault and we'll get it out in a hurry!"

"Take it easy, Mick," my mother pleaded.

"But it'll die, Mom," I said. "They're using that place and my pup is down there, I know she's down there. I put my ear over the seat and I heard her crying. She's begging to get out. Her mother is chained to a stilt that helps to hold their shack up. She can hear her puppy crying. She is walking the length of her chain back and forth and trying to talk to her."

"That makes my blood boil," my father said.

"Don't get in a fight with him, Mick," my mother pleaded. "Ask him the right way to let you take the puppy out. Then, if he won't listen to reason, let's invite your fellow coal miners to help us. Try to get him to listen to reason. He might be glad to listen before this is over."

"If I just had a rawhide whip," my father said. "I'd whip it out with him. I'd fight him with a whip. But I don't have one in this house and never had one and I'd never used one. But I could use one on him like he's used it on his horse and cow."

"But let's go back down there in a hurry," I said. "They might kill my puppy! They might think I'll tell you about her and put her to death so no one else will ever know."

"I'll go down there," my father said. "You stay here, Sall! You go round up three or four other men in a hurry, Shan."

"All right," I said. "But hurry down there! I'll hurry and get the men."

My father opened the door and was off down the road toward Tom Leffard's shack. I kicked the dead leaves under my brogan shoes as I ran to the closest shack, where Hester Crump lived. I told Hester, a coal miner, and told him my father had already gone to Tom Leffard's place.

"I'd better hurry," Hester said. "Your Pa and Tom don't get along very well together."

Hester was a powerful man with big hands and broad shoulders and a face like my father's face. But my father's face turned red when Tom Leffard's name was mentioned. Hester Crump walked away like a big clumsy turkey-globber. I ran on to Will Thombs's shack. Will Thombs was a truck driver and when I told him at his breakfast table what Tom had done to the puppy he said: "I know Tom is a cruel man the way he has whipped his poor skinny horse and kicked his cow every time he has milked her, but I didn't know he was that brutal. I'll go over there right now." He got up from the table. "There might be trouble between him and your Pa. I'd better hurry."

I ran down under the mountain to Jack Byrnes's shack. I told Mr. Byrnes what had happened as fast as I could. He was milking his cow. I stayed longer because he asked so many questions. When I answered his questions he quit milking his cow. He hurried toward his shack, with a milk bucket in his hand. "Anybody that would do that," he talked to himself as the milk sloshed from the bucket, "is a mean man." Then, I hurried down to Royster's shack, which wasn't a hundred yards from where Jack Byrnes lived. Dave and his brother George, who lived with him, were both coal miners. When I told him the story, he told me to hurry on to see about my puppy, that they could both be there. I thought six men were enough. Then I ran as fast as when I left Tom Leffard's place. This time I ran toward Leffard's place and not away.

"If I had a shell fer my gun I'd shoot ye, Mick Powderjay," Tom Leffard shouted at my father, just as I got there. "It's none of your business what I do with a bitch-pup that belongs to me. People put pups in a sack, weight it with rocks and throw them in the river when they want to get rid of 'em, don't they?"

"You promised that pup to my boy," my father shouted back. "You don't have to kill her by slow torture down in your human filth. Why kill anything that can't fight back. Don't you move, Tom! Let that water get cold!"

My father was standing on the steep bank holding a stilt with one hand; with the other he was holding a rock. Below him on a stone step Tom Leffard stood with a bucket of hot water. The steam was rising from the bucket to the cold October wind. Tom was looking up at my father and he was afraid to move.

"I just got here in time," my father said to Tom Leffard. "You heated that water since my boy was here to scald that pup down in that awful place. You won't do it now. My son's pup is coming out of there."

Just then Hester Crump waddled down the road. He saw my father with a rock and Tom with a bucket of water with the steam rising from it.

"I didn't think you could be that low, Tom," Hester said. "I've always known how mean you were to your horse and cow. I know how you kill wild game for the love of killing. But I didn't know a man could be this low."

"I'll get rid of that bitch-pup the way I please," he said. "It's my pup and I'll kill it the way I please."

"She's not yours either," I said. "And I want her out of there."

I couldn't keep from crying.

"We'll get it out for you, Shan," Hester said.

"I say we'll get her out," Will Thombs said as he came walking up the path from the road below.

"If I had shells for my gun you wouldn't," Tom Leffard said in a louder voice.

"I'd stand by my window and let ye have both barrels!"

"You would stand behind a window," my father said.

"I told ye not to do that, Tom," Mrs. Leffard said.

She stood on their high porch and looked down.

"But when I gave the other pups away that bitch-pup started whining and I couldn't sleep," Tom answered her. "You know that. I put her in a place so I could go back to bed and sleep."

"I couldn't do a thing like that and sleep," Jack Byrnes said as he walked up the path. "That went through my blood when young Shan told me. The milk in my milk bucket looked red instead of white!"

Then George and Dave Royster walked up.

"What are you doin' bringin' in all the neighbors?" Tom Leffard asked.

"Goin' to get that puppy out of there," my father said. He walked toward Tom Leffard. "Don't you start anything either, Tom!"

"You're not goin' to touch my property," Tom said.

"That's what you think," Hester Crump said. He came down the slope holding to the stilts.

"I'd kill every last one of you if I had shells for my gun," Tom Leffard threatened. "And you little devil," he raised his voice and turned to me. "I'd like to use my rawhide on you just once. You wouldn't be out a-stirrin' up bushels of trouble over a little bitch mongrel pup! When I got through you'd never want to stir up trouble again."

"Don't talk to my boy like that!" my father walked closer to Tom. "You ever touch him with a rawhide just once. You won't be whippin' your poor animals that can't help themselves. I'll help my son!"

"I want my puppy out of there," I said. "I hear her cyin' to get out! Her cries are weaker than they were an hour ago!"

The men were all looking at Tom and he was looking at them as they moved closer. Not one of them noticed the mother dog as she walked back and forth the length of her chain. She whined and the puppy answered her.

"Don't move, Tom," my father said. "Drop your bucket of water. It must be cold by now!"

"If it was hot I'd throw it in your face," he said.

"Let's get that puppy out," I said.

"Leave that bitch-pup alone," Tom warned. "I'm a-tellin' all of you to get off my property!"

"All right, boys, go after the pup," Will Thombs said.

My father walked toward the outdoor toilet. He was trembling like a leaf in the wind. Maybe this was because he could hear the puppy whining in the vault below. Maybe he was stirred as the wind stirred the October leaves when he saw my puppy's mother walk the length of her short chain like a fox in a cage when she talked to her puppy. My father could always get riled when he saw a man mistreat an animal. Now he was riled as I'd never seen him riled before.

"Let's tear down this place," he shouted.

"Don't you do it, Mick," he said in a high voice.

"Quiet, Tom," Will said.

"Let me put my two-hundred-and-eighty pounds behind it," Hester said. "Maybe I can shove it over!"

"The posts might be set in the ground," Dave Royster said.

"That won't matter," Hester said. "I can shove the posts out!"

Powerful Hester Crump put his broad shoulders against the building, braced his feet and began to shove.

"I saw it give," George Royster said.

"Be careful, Hester, you don't go with it," Jack Byrnes said.

Then Hester gave another mighty heave as Tom Leffard looked on. The toilet leaned over when the upper posts rooted from the ground. Hester shoved again and it toppled over the steep hill, end over end. Only the seat was left open to the wind of October.

"This thing too," Hester said. He lifted it up, threw it aside and exposed the vault.

There was my puppy down there for everybody to see. She was almost swimming down in this vault. She was shivering, crying and begging not to die. Maybe it was good that Tom Leffard stood in his tracks. Maybe it was better he looked at the ground and didn't say another word. I never saw redder faces than those of the men who gathered around the vault and looked down. They looked down at my puppy while I cried.

"It's seven or eight feet down there," Dave Royster said.

"But how'll we get that pup out," George Royster asked.

"Let me go down and get her," I said.

"What will we put around her when we get her out?" my father said.

"There's an old sack under the shack," Jack Byrnes said.

"Let's work faster," Dave Royster said. "That little thing can't last much longer down there."

"I'll tell you how we'll do it," Hester said. "I'll hold Mick by the legs and he can hold Shan by the legs and we'll make a human chain and go down and get that puppy!"

"That's a good idea," Jack Byrnes said. "That's about the only way!"

"All right, take me by the legs and hold tight," I said to my father.

Hester showed me where to lie down by the vault. Then, my father tightened his hands around my bird-legs just above my ankles. Then Hester took Pa's bird-legs just above the ankles with his big hands. Hester, big and powerful, scooted us forward until I went over the wall.

"Hold to me, Pa," I said. "It's not pleasant here."

"Hold on to me, Hester," my father said.

Then Tom Leffard laughed a wild laugh.

When I reached the puppy, I grabbed it with both hands.

"Ready," I said. "Take me up!"

"Help me boys," Hester said as he started drawing us up from the vault. "Now, go easy, men!"

"Hold to me, Hester," my father said. "Don't let your grip weaken."

"Hold to me, Pa," I said. "I've got my puppy!"

She had stopped whining when I touched her with my warm hands.

Then, I pulled the poor shivering, wet little thing up against me. I didn't care. I had my puppy. And when we came to the top, I don't know when any puppy had more friends.

"That poor shiverin' thing," Bill Thombs said.

George Royster came with Tom's bucket of water. It was just milk warm now. George washed the puppy and he washed me too. My father gave me his red bandanna to dry my puppy. And Hester used his bandanna to dry me. I took my puppy to her mother to feed before I took her home. The mother cried to her and she cried to her mother.

"What are you a-goin' to do about my privy," Tom asked.

"That's your worry," Bill Thombs said.

"I'll report you to the Law," Tom threatened us.

"I think the Law will want to know what you've done," my

father said.

"All the miners and the truck drivers will know about this, too," Dave Royster said.

"We're not through here, boys," Hester said.

Big Hester walked up and grabbed Tom around the waist. He lifted him up and started to the vault with Tom.

"I'll give you some of yer own medicine," Hester said.

"Oh, no, don't do that, Hester," Jack Byrnes said. "Two wrongs won't make a right! We've had enough trouble here."

"Don't do it, don't do it," Mrs. Lefford screamed from the high porch.

Then Hester put Tom Leffard back on the ground.

I hated to take my puppy away from her mother. But I picked her up and wrapped her in the dry sack. Her mother looked up at me with her big brown and sad eyes. I held the sack in my arms as I followed my father and our friendly neighbors up the steep bank where the cool October winds whistled in the barren apple tree branches. My little puppy was shivering in the sack in my arms and she tried to talk to me like she had talked to her mother.

"Sunday Morning On Sulphur Creek" was first published in *Kansas Quarterly,* Vol.4, No.3 (Summer, 1972). It has never been reprinted. Stuart included this story in his unpublished manuscript, *Twelve Reserve Stories To Back Up: These Are My Best*—selected in January 1974, typed in February 1974 (Jesse Stuart Foundation Collection, Ashland, Ky). According to Stuart, this short story is based on an incident that his sister Mary told to him that had happened when she was married to Leonard Darby and living in a coalmine camp in Winding Gulf, WV. The little boy in the story was her son, Gene Darby. "Mary came home to visit our parents about 1934 or 1935. She told this very cruel story at our home to a family who loved both domestic and wild life. This was an unforgettable story to all of us... This story that Mary told us stirred me deeply. I took down notes. I had never been to Winding Gulf to visit Mary and Leonard. I was never there in my life. So, I moved the story. I made it a 'Shan story'—that is the narrator of the story happens to be the writer... In the 1930's, I wrote this story. I didn't send it out to a magazine until many years later. I kept it over the years..." (This information is from an unpublished manuscript of Stuart's account of the writing of this story in the Jesse Stuart Foundation Collection, Ashland, Kentucky, *Sunday Morning On Sulphur Creek.)*

Two Sides of the Fence

There was only a barbed wire fence, with sound locust posts eight feet apart with six strands of barbwire tightly stretched and stapled to the posts that separated my Great-Grandpa Billy Weston's farm from the Uncle Ray Pennix farm. This fence was more than two miles long. And this high ridge between the farms was called Backbone Ridge. I don't know when or how it got its name. Great-Grandpa, now in his eighty-fifth year, said it was called Backbone Ridge when his father, my Great-Great-Grandpa, another Billy Weston, bought this farm over a century ago. Names just don't change in my country. And farms stay in families even if the hills are steep and the valleys narrow. Even if it is hard to make a living on them.

I say names don't change. There was my Great-Great-Grandpa Billy Weston, there is Great-Grandpa Billy Weston, his son Billy, my Grandpa, dead and planted under a cedar in the Western graveyard. He was gored to death by a bull, believe it or not. Then, there was my father, Billy Weston, who was brought back from Vimy Ridge in World War II in a wooden overcoat and planted near his father under the shade of the same cedar. I was too young to remember my father. And I don't remember when my Great-Grandmother Cynthia Weston died. This was long before I was born.

I do know, my father has really been my Great-Grandpa Weston. I am the last male heir of the Westons and my name is Billy. And this is why Great-Grandpa took such a-likin' to me and why Mom went to live with him. Mom is as kind to him and treats him like he is her own grandfather. And this is why Great-Grandpa has deeded me this farm and everything he has when he leaves this world. He insists that I marry. But I'm fifteen, turning sixteen, now. And I do drive my mother's car for I have sure hands and good judgment. I want to live. I hope to marry if I can find a girl who will marry me and this land and be content to live here. When she marries me she'll be marrying Great-Grandpa's two thousand acres, too.

I mentioned about the good wire fence, strong enough to hold cattle between Great-Grandpa's farm and the Uncle Ray Pennix farm. There has to be a strong fence, always kept up until cattle, mules, and sheep can't get from one farm to the other. There is more than this fence that separates the two farms and the Pennix and the Weston families. I could say a broad river, a deep canyon, a gulf or a really high mountain...higher than a ridge separate the farms and the families that have owned them nearly a century and a half. For the Westons settled one valley and the Pennixes settled the other. It has been said that they came to this land when there wasn't a stick of timber a-miss. This means not a tree had been cut with an ax. I don't know exactly how early they settled this land.

I think our families back then were dependent on one another and there was friendliness and neighborliness between them. I think they helped one another at house raisings, corn-shuckings, apple-peelings and they danced together to the same fiddle tunes on the early puncheon floors. And I think they might have gone to the same groves when a wandering preacher came through and held revivals. When churches were established they might have gone to the same church. But they don't do it now. They haven't done it for more than a hundred years. Over on the other side of the ridge, Pennix Valley, is what we call Pennix Land. On this side of the Ridge is Weston Valley and it is Weston Land. Our Valleys have gone by these names in Greenwood County longer than any of the living or recent departed dead can remember.

And what divided us into two families and two worlds with never a marriage between our families, and I'll say the Pennixes have had and still have some good looking women, but the War Between the States, or the Civil War, divided us. The Westons became Methodists and the Pennixes became Baptists. And the Pennixes joined the Big Party and we Westons are in the Little

Party. My ancestors went away to fight for Northern Blue while the Pennixes went away to fight for Southern Gray. And more from here went away to fight for Southern Gray than went away to fight for Northern Blue. We were all Southerners but the Westons were against slavery and they were for the Union. And this was the way here our political parties were formed and they are still this way with the Pennixes and Westons.

Now on the other side of the Ridge in Pennix Land, Uncle Ray Pennix is the same age of Great-Grandpa Billy Weston. And his Great-Grandson and his mother stay with him. The situation is exactly like our situation. His Great-Grandson Ray Pennix, is nearly sixteen, same age as I. He lost his father in World War II in Germany and Ray was too young to remember him. His father, like mine, was brought home in a wooden overcoat planted in the Pennix Graveyard over in Pennix Valley…a place I've never been and am not about to go. And his Grandfather and Grandmother are dead and planted there. So is his Great-Grandmother. And Ray Pennix is the last male descendent of the Pennixes. Uncle Ray, so I have heard, is going to deed him all his twenty-five hundred acres with the promise he marries in hopes he'll beget some sons to carry on the Pennix name.

And here is the strange thing. Uncle Ray Pennix, Ray's Great-Grandfather and Billy Weston, my Great-Grandfather are bedfast with the same incurable disease. Each one has to die and a big National Election, Presidential Election, is coming on and Dwight D. Eisenhower is our man. He's our man because he's on our "ticket." And we belong to the Little Party. I know I do, because I was born that way. Adlai Stevenson is the Big Party's man for the second time trying to get "our man Ike."

One day in August when I went in from checking our cattle in the pasture, Mom had Great-Grandpa sitting up in bed with pillows propped up behind his back. He had once weighed two-hundred pounds that he carried on a muscular six-foot-four frame. Now, he was down to about one-hundred-sixty and his once ruddy-complexioned, weather-tanned face was almost as white as the sheet spread over him.

"Son, I have a big ideer," he said to me. He always called me Son. And his old eyes sparkled and his pale face came to light. "I know I have to go. I have to leave this farm and our Weston Valley. I may not get to the polls' to vote 'the ticket.' But I'll get to vote just the same. I want you to get me an absentee ballot so I can vote 'er straight. I don't believe I'll make November. I'll fix that Old Fox on the other side of the Ridge. Old Ray Pennix hasn't got gumption enough to think of this. And I hear he won't be around by November either. We've been a-killin' one another's votes…well, say about sixty-four years in County, State and National elections. This time, I think my vote will count. I'll be one up on the Old Fox in these sixty-four years."

A smile spread over Great-Grandpa's face. Knowing he had to die in a matter of weeks, maybe he could live two more months, maybe until after the election. But he was happy to think he would slip one by on Uncle Ray Pennix. As he said he'd be a vote up on him.

"Great-Grandpa, can you vote an absentee ballot like this? Don't you have to be out of the county or the state? Don't you have to be traveling?"

"Son, where do you think I'm goin'," he said. "Before the election I might be on my way on a very long journey and I won't be comin' back. I've been a-layin in this bed and thinkin' a lot…and you know how I hate a bed. I'll be seeing your Great-Grandmother Cynthia. I allus called her Cinth. I'll be seeing my own dead father who wore the Blue for the Union and my own dead Mother. I'll be seeing the four sons and two daughters I lost. And I'll be seeing some of my ancestors, I hope, who came here when there wasn't a stick of timber a-miss'…when this land was as God had made it. Of course, there were Injuns still around. And they fit 'em and that's how we got Weston Valley. I'll find out when I see all of them."

"Do you reckon you'll see all of them?" I asked.

"Maybe not all, for there could have been some strays amongst us, like in all families," he said.

Mom heard us talking and she came from the kitchen.

"Don't tire your Great-Grandpa too much," Mom told me.

"He's a Weston, Rilda, let him talk," Grandpa said. "We're havin' some man-talk and spiritual talk. Son has to carry on the name. He's got to help carry on the Party and work at the polls like I have always done until that blasted cancer struck me last spring! Strange how it struck Old Ray last spring, too. I really felt sorry for the Old Pup. He's been a good fighter on his side. But I never could stand him."

When Mom drove our car to Greenwood and we met Ray's mother, Beth, driving Uncle Ray and young Ray from Greenwood, Great-Grandpa would raise his hand in a way like he was speaking. And I think Great-Grandpa and Uncle Ray had spoken down through the years when they had met. Each might have said to the other 'it is a fair day' or 'it is a foul day' but three months before an election, County, State or National, neither spoke to the other. I had been in the car with Great-Grandpa and Mom when Great-Grandpa raised his hand, but he always looked straight ahead.

"In your long journey Great-Grandpa, if you meet any of the Pennixes, what are you going to do?" I asked him. "You know they may not have any more strays than the Westons and you're liable to run onto a lot of 'em there!"

"They can stay in their valley there and we'll be in our valley just like we have done here," he replied. "Son, don't you think this hasn't crossed my mind too while I have been in this bed. The only thing that troubles me will messages from this earth get through. If I vote absentee ballot and I go before the November election, don't you think I won't be watching for a man of our party to join us and bring the news of the election if it's our man Ike or if it's old Ray's Adlai."

Mom left Great-Grandpa's room and when she went through the door I saw her shake her head. See, Mom wasn't a Weston. She was a Crawford who had married into the Westons. And she had often told me if one who married a Weston didn't belong to the Little Party he or she had better change it to have peace. But Mom already belonged to the Little Party before she married my father. And this made the Twain as One. The Church didn't matter as much as the Party was something more than a Party. The two parties were two Worlds separated over a hundred years ago. Two Worlds with that broad river, that gulf, that sea, that tall mountain between them. Here Backbone Ridge and a strong barbed-wire fence separated the Weston World and the Pennix World.

"Son, something else, I want you to do besides get an absentee ballot for me," Great-Grandpa said. "I want you to write a letter to that young Ray and set a time to meet with him on Backbone Ridge and go over that fence with him. See there's not a staple out of a post. See each wire at each post is fastened tight. I can't leave my world happy not knowing that it is a good fence. One that will hold their livestock on their side and our livestock on our side."

"Great-Grandpa, who will I see to get the absentee ballot?" I asked.

"See young Frank Menach," he told me. "He's a young Warhorse in the Little Party. Son, in years to come, when I am a goner, take our Little Party counselin' from him. He will guide you straight. He knows only one way, his way, our way, and he'll give our enemies hell right down to the wire. And you can trust him and tell him why you want it. He won't norrate the news so that Old Pup on the other side of the ridge will get my secret. Explain how after sixty-four years I want to get one up on him!"

I followed my helpless, bedfast Great-Grandfather's advice. I wrote the letter to Ray and set the morning of August 21st to meet Ray at the Big Oak, which was a line tree in the Ridge fence. I told him at eight in the morning and to bring his wire stretchers, hatchet, ax, staples and maybe some nails to renail the braces in the fence. I told him I would bring the same. We actually had never used each other's tools when we'd gone over this fence before. Now that I was driving my Mom's car, I could have driven down the road in Weston Valley to a place where Weston Branch joined Pennix Branch and the two branches flowed off joyfully together in one stream to the Tiber River. And here the two roads joined and were as one to the Tiber River road. I could have driven up the Pennix Valley road and told Ray to meet me on the Ridge long before the letter would reach him. The letter had to go to Greenwood and back. But the Pennix Valley was forbidden land as far as a Weston was concerned. And in Weston Valley we'd never seen a Pennix. Our Valley was forbidden land as far as the Pennixes were concerned.

Now, the second thing I did that very afternoon after I'd talked to Great-Grandpa, I asked Mom for the car and told her what I wanted with it. That I wanted to go see Frank Menach and get an absentee ballot for Great-Grandpa. Mom had tears in her eyes when she said, "Yes, Billy, but do be careful. You're all I've got. You're all the Westons have got left. You have to carry on."

My mother was really a Weston, too. When she married my father the Twain were really One. Death had parted them, but still the Twain were as One.

My journey to Greenwood was about twenty-three miles. When I got to Greenwood, I went straight to Frank Menach's office...not a Office Holder's office or a lawyer's office in the Greenwood County Courthouse...but it was a railroad office. Frank Menach was some kind of a railroad official who had an office and traveled a lot for the company. But when I went I was lucky to find him in. He was just locking his door and getting ready to go some place in a company car. I told him what I wanted.

"Wonderful," he said. "Now keep this a secret. He will not only get an absentee ballot but I will come out personally with it and vote him before he goes on the long journey. Say, this is smart! This is wonderful! Did your Great-Grandpa think of this?"

"Yes, he did," I said.

"And he's real bad off, isn't he?"

"I don't think he'll live until the November election."

"We'd better get this in a hurry," Frank said. "It will be a vote saved. And our Little Party in Greenwood County needs every vote. We're out-numbered three to two. Your old Great-Grandpa has been a Warhorse in the Little Party. He stands for something. He stands hitched. I hope he can be one up on Old Ray Pennix. That Old Pup! Gee, this is smart. This is wonderful. You go home and tell your Great-Grandpa, Old Uncle Billy Weston, that his young friend Frank Menach will be right out there with the absentee ballot tomorrow evening. See, I want to see the condition of your Great-Grandpa too. We can't afford to lose his vote. We want to make it count. We may not carry the county but we're goin' to try to do it this November! And we might even carry this State."

Well, I drove back home very happy. I called Mom in to Great-Grandpa's bedside and I told both of them just what had happened.

"I'll vote that absentee ballot just to be on the safe side," Great-Grandpa said. "But what if I don't die before the election? I will not have gone on my long journey and I wonder if my vote will count."

Mom and I couldn't answer Great-Grandpa's question. I had heard her say she didn't think he would be here later than early October when frost hit the leaves and they began to turn and fall. Well, leaves on many of the shoemakes, maples and poplars turned in September and the winds blew them helter skelter through the air and to the ground. There was silence.

"But I shouldn't worry," Great-Grandpa said. "I'll go happy if I get to cast my vote before and it's counted. If I can be one up on Old Ray…one up in sixty-four years. I will go on my long journey a happy man to join my kin. They've all gone younger than I have. I've lived without regrets. Just so I can for one time outfox that Old Fox on the other side of the Ridge."

Frank Menach was as good as his word. He was what Great-Grandpa had said he was. He was right at our house with an absentee ballot.

Big, blustery, cleancut, well-dressed forty years old Frank Menach walked into Great-Grandpa's room.

"How're you Uncle Billy?" he said with a big smile.

"Pretty poorly, as you can see," Great-Grandpa said. "And a-getting' weaker and feebler every day. I just wonder how Old Ray Pennix is!"

"We're not worrin' about him," Frank said. "We know he's against us! And we know we're against him. What we want here is to take no chances. We want your vote. See, I handle all the absentee votes for our party. I know I will see that it counts if you have gone on your long journey. And if you've not quite gone, I think we can hide you until you go and make your vote count."

Great-Grandpa laughed at Frank's joke. Mom laughed and so did I.

"So, I've got it all fixed up here," Frank said. "All you have to do is vote. Do it today. Don't put it off."

"But this is August 15th and the election is not until November," Great-Grandpa said.

"Don't worry about this," Frank said. "Put your John Henry down same as you've done for sixty-four years!"

"It's a straight vote, only one cross for my ticket, the Little Party," he said. "You know, Frank, I won't change it on my deathbed. Just keep this quiet, Frank!"

"Don't you worry," Frank said. "I never talk on a thing like this. I just act. I am not one to be outfoxed. I have your vote here and it will count."

After Great-Grandpa had voted absentee, Frank told him some things that pleased him that the Little Party planned to carry Greenwood County and the State.

"We've got it in the bag," Frank said.

Then, Frank shook his pale old withered hand and said:

"Goodbye, Uncle Billy. But just one thing. I want to be a pallbearer at your funeral."

"I want you to be," Great-Grandpa told him.

"When Frank Menach walked out of the room, Mom and I followed him outside.

"He won't be here in November," Frank said. "He'll do well to make September. He's been a powerful man even in his old age. I've never seen a man go down so. Remember, I'll see that his vote counts. And be sure to keep this quiet. Don't let the news get to the other side of the Ridge."

Ray got my letter and he had his tools and was waiting for me at the big oak when I arrived with mine. He greeted me with a smile and I greeted him with a smile. I wish he could have been closer for I went to Maxwell High School with him…rode the same bus, but he was a Pennix and I was a Weston and we were Two Young Worlds. I had to climb over the fence for the wires were nailed to the posts on the Pennix side. The fence was really in top condition. The wires were rusted by weather but strong and durable. We had so little to do. There had been a good fence between these farms as long as there has been barbed wires, staples and locusts posts. There was never one time when Pennix livestock got over on Weston land.

Ray and I never mentioned our Great-Grandfathers. We never mentioned the Big or Little Parties. We never mentioned our Ike or their Adlai. We talked about Maxwell High School and girls. But Ray acted like he knew something he'd like to tell me but he couldn't for I was a Weston and he was a Pennix. I knew he was holding something from me. He was gay and happy and full of himself. He acted this way all the time we went over the fence. And when we parted at noon he smiled and I smiled, but we didn't ask one another to come for a visit.

When I went back home I said to Great-Grandpa: "That fence is good. Wild foxes either have to dig under or jump over."

"That's good news, Son," he said. "I want it that way before I leave here."

And Grandpa didn't have long to wait. He went on his long journey on September 19th. He went in his sleep. And when we buried him, Frank Menach was a pallbearer to help carry him from the Methodist Church to the hearse and then to his last resting place beside our Weston kin—only he was laid beside Great-Grandmother Cynthia…his Cinth he'd gone to meet—under the shadow of the big cedar. This was the biggest funeral ever in Weston Valley. Frank Menach must have passed the word around for people of the Little Party, our party, to come. Mom and I didn't know one out of twenty at his funeral. But there wasn't a Pennix at Great-Grandpa's funeral.

On October second there was another death on the other side of the Ridge. Uncle Ray Pennix had died. There was not a Weston there. We only heard about what a big funeral it was. We heard the Baptist Church, larger than our Methodist Church, couldn't hold the people. His big farm had gone to Ray, the last Pennix. Great-Grandpa's farm had gone to me, the last Weston.

But Mom, Frank Menach and I held the secret. We knew that Great-Grandpa's vote would be counted. And that he was up on his old rival and foe, Uncle Ray Pennix. This time old Ray Pennix's vote wouldn't subtract Great-Grandpa's.

It wasn't until after the November election had come and gone and our Ike didn't carry Greenwood County, but he did carry the State and was elected President of the United States, people in the Big Party norrated the news that Uncle Ray Pennix, who didn't think he would make it until the November election and who knew he was going on a long journey had voted the absentee ballot thinking he would be one up on my Great-Grandpa. And now we turned the word loose, rather Frank Menach did, that Great-Grandpa Weston had voted the absentee ballot in August for he, too, was aware his long journey might come before the November election and their straight votes had cancelled each other's just as it had been for sixty-four years. Neither was a vote up on the other. And neither had ever missed one election, County, State or National, since he was twenty-one, which was sixty-four years ago.

People now go, friends, relatives and from the Big Party to the Pennix Graveyard in Pennix Valley and see the headstone:

Ray Watson Pennix
Born Apr. 22nd 1871
Died Oct. 2nd 1956
Age 85 yrs. 5 mos. 10 days

The people who visit the grave know he voted for Adlai Stevenson.

While in our Weston Graveyard in Weston Valley, our kinfolk, friends, from the Little Party, came to see Great-Grandpa's headstone:

William Adger Weston
Born Apr. 22nd 1871
Died Sept. 19th 1956
Age 85 yrs. 4 mos. 28 days.

People who read his name and dates on his headstone know he voted for Dwight D. Eisenhower.

"Two Sides Of The Fence" was included in Stuart's unpublished manuscript, *Twelve Reserve Stories To Back Up: These Are My Best*—selected in January 1974, typed in February 1974 (Jesse Stuart Foundation Collection, Ashland, Kentucky). There is no record in Woodbridge's *Jesse And Jane Stuart: A Bibliography* or the Jesse Stuart Foundation's *Short Story Finders Guide* of "Two Sides Of The Fence" having ever been published.

Uncle Sam Married an Angel

I believe everybody in Greenwood County knows Uncle Sam Bradley. He's the greatest bricklayer in Greenwood County. And I hate to say this, for Grandpa Pate Bradley is an old-time stonemason and bricklayer. Grandpa Pate can go out and find what he calls the right kind of stone that will split. He can split and hew stone like men score and hew trees for railroad crossties. He can build a fine house out of rocks from the fields and cliffs on the bluffs to be found in this rocky county. This is why I hate to say that Uncle Sam is a better brickmason than Grandpa Pate. Another reason, and I hate to say this, is that Grandpa Pate trained Uncle Sam; my father, who is Dee Bradley; and his twin brother, Uncle Fee. People are always getting my father and Uncle Fee mixed up because they look so much alike. And then there is Uncle Cal who is a bricklayer, too.

Grandpa Pate, my father, and my uncles are all bricklayers because Grandpa Pate trained his sons to work in brick and stone. Another thing Grandpa Pate can do with his big hands is play the fiddle, banjo, and guitar. My Pa can play just about any stringed instrument, and he can make a fiddle cry. Uncle Fee and Uncle Cal play fiddles, banjos, and guitars, too. But Uncle Sam is the best of the lot. Hear him play the fiddle once and you never want to hear Grandpa Pate, my Pa, Uncle Fee, or Uncle Cal play a fiddle again. Uncle Sam can make a fiddle talk or cry. And he can sing and make love with his guitar, his mandolin which he calls a "tater-bug," or his dulcimer.

One would never think a man as big as Uncle Sam Bradley, with big bricklaying hands, arms as big as fence posts and a neck like a bull…well, not much neck at all…too short really for a shirt collar, could play a fiddle and other stringed instruments like he can. This is where he fools everybody. Just to see him chew tobacco and spit his amber spittle into the mortar and then trowel that mortar between the bricks is really something! I know because Pa let me work with Uncle

Sam. See, I have two brothers to help Pa. Uncle Fee has two sons to help him. Uncle Cal has four sons—two help him and two help Grandpa Pate. All of us cousins and brothers are learning to be bricklayers. It is said around here the Bradleys are bricklaying, fiddle-playing, and dancing fools. Everybody talks about us like this. Now my elders look the part of being stone and brickmasons, all are big husky men. They all chew terbacker, smoke black cigars, and take their likker straight from the jug or bottle without a chaser. They drink moonshine from the jar or jug and they drink store-bought whiskey from the bottle. It is said a flask is too small for a Bradley, but Uncle Sam has never been without a flask in late years and I will tell you why later on in this story.

But, maybe I'd better tell about Grandpa before I go on with this story. He had four sons, Sam, Dee, Fee, and Cal, by my first grandma. Then he left her for a younger wife, and really I don't know how many young'uns he has by her, six or seven, I think. They're younger than my cousins and me. They're all boys among the Bradleys. No girls. I said the Bradleys were like bulls and they are. They're the breed of bulls that will jump the high fences to get over to the cows. People around here talk that way about us. We really don't have a very good name except we're good musicians and we're good brickmasons and stonemasons. Grandpa Pate's taking himself a young wife and leaving Grandma really threw a monkey wrench into our family. There's a lot of disagreements and hard feelings anymore. Grandpa Pate and his sons don't take big jobs together like building high schools and public buildings. Each one now goes for himself.

Because Uncle Sam never got married until late in life, Pa loaned me to him to learn the trade. And Uncle Sam is so hard to get along with! Pa told me if I could work for him, stay with him, that I would one day be the most talented bricklayer of the Bradleys. Pa said his brother Sam had more talent than any of the Bradleys. It's even hard for Pa to admit the truth, too. Well, I'll say this—Uncle Sam pays me more to stay with him than my brothers get from Pa and my cousins get from Uncle Fee, Uncle Cal, and Grandpa Pate. And this is because Uncle Sam gets more work than he can do.

Now, Grandpa Pate used to say this of his son, Uncle Sam, that he had sowed more wild oats than all of the Bradleys put together. I'll say, then, Uncle Sam sure sowed a lot of wild oats. According to Grandpa Pate, Pa, and my uncles Fee and Cal, there just was never anything wrong with Uncle Sam when it came to women. They all say that Uncle Sam is the bull among them that leaped over more fences, some of them high ones, too, getting to cows than any bulls among the Bradleys and that they were all bulls. Everybody else in the neighborhood said the same thing. They missed some work among the God-fearin' people because they were afraid for a Bradley to work around their homes, especially if they had wives and daughters.

But then a big thing happened to Uncle Sam. People just couldn't believe it. I know I couldn't believe it. Uncle Sam began to date, at fifty, a woman who was fifty. Miss Esther Manfree was her name. She was a small dainty woman who was organist at the Baptist Church. She was very religious. She owned a fine home, which she had inherited from her mother and father. She was an only child. How Uncle Sam ever got to know her and why she ever dated him surprised everybody, and most of all the Bradleys.

"I'll tell you, Bob," he said to me, "I've had the other side of life a half century. Now, I'm goin' to change my ways and settle down. When I marry, I've allus said I'd marry a Lady. I'm really sparking a Lady now. No foolishness with her. She's really an Angel."

Well, Uncle Sam had an old model car, a Willys-Knight, that he had for years. It was as long as two fence rails. And when Uncle Sam used to drive me around to see the houses, schoolhouses, flues, and chimneys that he had built, he called them his children. And he often referred to them as living monuments. When he drove around to see his living-monument children, he dressed in his best suit—peg-legged pants and double-breasted coat with broad lapels—and a flashy necktie with a big stickpin. He even wore a diamond ring. When he did this he didn't chew tobacco, carry a bottle, or a jug, but he smoked long expensive ten-inch dollar cigars. He had his gold-tipped flask which he carried on the inside of his coat in a pocket he had made in it for this purpose. And as he drove along he often sipped from his flask. When I rode with him, he wasn't the same man I worked for laying bricks. He had the best reputation of laying bricks and mortaring them in a straight perfect wall or cylinder of any bricklayer in the county. He was an expert working with bricks. Don't you think I didn't have to work to keep bricks and mortar to him! But I did it.

"You know, Bob," he said to me as we were building a chimney for Judge Ephriam Sowards, "Esther won't put up with drinking. She won't have it in the house. Of course, I have had my flask on me when I dated her. But she didn't know. See, she's a Lady and I know it. And I've never pulled her up close yet. But I will get to that and when I do she might feel my flask on my inside coat pocket. She's so pretty, Bob, and so dainty that I feel like I'm going with an angel from Heaven. When I take her to the Baptist Church, believe me, Bob, I'm real proud of her. And when she plays the church organ, a lot of my past comes back to me. Bob, I nearly wilt."

"I'll tell you, Bob," Pa said one day when I went home from working with Uncle Sam, "it's talked everywhere in Blakesburg that your Uncle Sam is going to marry Miss Esther Manfree. Really, I don't believe it will work. You know how your Uncle Sam has lived. Now to tie himself to a little woman like her. Your Uncle Sam is not just an ordinary bull; he's a bull's bull. He's all bull. Miss Esther, as she is called, won't weigh more than a hundred ten pounds. She goes dressed in fancy clothes and hats and always wears white gloves. It takes a woman for my brother Sam. Brother Sam is, I believe, taking his eggs to a bad market. I tried to talk with him. I brought up this subject and planned to talk with him as I have talked to you. He told me to shut my damned mouth, that he was going with an angel, an angel from Heaven. Well," Pa said with a sigh, "she's taken him to church. Not a Bradley of the name goes to church but Sam. And I believe people everywhere think Sam has changed and that is why he's getting all this work to do. I can't believe men aren't afraid of him around their wives and daughters anymore."

When Uncle Sam told me he was engaged to Miss Esther and that in two more weeks she would be my aunt I just stood there with bricks in my arms. We were working on the wall of a house. I didn't have to windlass the bricks and mortar up to him. I carried the bricks on my arm. Uncle Sam stopped using his trowel but he did spit a sluice of ambeer into the mortar on the board.

"Yes, Esther is a Lady," he said. "I could have looked the world over and never found another one like her."

There were some questions I wanted to ask Uncle Sam. But I thought if I let him do the talking he would tell me all I wanted to know.

"Yes, I put the old flask away," he said. "I won't have a bachelor's room at Blakesburg Hotel much longer. Of course, I can go back and have my drink after my date with Miss Esther. She's not going to be Miss Esther Manfree long. She's going to be Mrs. Sam Bradley, and don't you think for one minute I won't walk on the wind when our marriage knot is tied in the First Baptist Church in Blakesburg. That's where it will take place. I've got to the place where I can get next to her on the sofa and hold her a little closer so I left my flask in my hotel room. I was afraid she would touch it!"

"But what about…"

"I know what you're goin' to say, Bob," he said. "That is a problem. She's already told me there wouldn't be a spittoon in her parlor. And cigar smoke runs her crazy. But I figure I can do these things on my job. See, I'm a contractor and I have no boss and I can do as I please on the jobs. But when I go home to her, Bob, I'm going to Heaven to be with an Angel. And to live with an Angel, I'll have to do as my Angel says."

Well everything was done right. I suppose everything was done right. I wouldn't know. Miss Esther's picture was in the *Greenwood County News*. And there was a story about her forthcoming marriage to Mr. Samuel Bradley. Invitations were sent out to Uncle Sam's friends and to her friends. There was never a Bradley, so Pa said, married in a big church wedding. Not a picture of a woman who married a Bradley was ever in the *Greenwood County News*. Invitations to a marriage of one of our Bradleys had never been sent out.

"Brother Sam is getting the Bradley name up in the world," Pa said. "Maybe Sam is marryin' an angel. Miss Esther Manfree looks like a little dainty angel. I mean the way I think an angel would look. Of course, I've never seen an angel."

On the Sunday afternoon when Uncle Sam and Miss Esther were married, there were more people there than got invitations. All the Baptists, mothers and fathers, must have come and brought their families. I believe all the Bradleys were there. And this was the first time for some of us ever to be in a church. Well, men came who had danced when Uncle Sam fiddled for the Fourth of July and Labor Day celebrations. And people came where Uncle Sam had built them living monuments. People stood in the back of the church and in the aisles. And I never saw Uncle Sam look better. He even had a flower in his lapel. I didn't know what kind it was for I'd not seen one like it grow around here. I learned later it was a white carnation. Miss Esther carried an arm bouquet of autumn flowers.

There was some soft music and then a ceremony, one like it I have never seen before. Then, Reverend Leonard Rennington quoted the scripture and joined them together as man and wife. And we got to see Uncle Sam kiss the bride. And when he kissed her, maybe it was a thought I shouldn't have had, I didn't think of the other lips his lips had kissed, but I thought about all the jugs, jars, bottles, and gold-tipped flasks that he had put to his lips. I thought about all the cigars his lips had held and all the tobacco spittle that had passed between his lips and mixed in the mortar. I thought about how Uncle Sam laughed and said there was more ambeer in the mortar of his living monuments than any other man's and he'd bet his life on that. He also said his ambeer in his mortar gave his walls better color and held the bricks together better. And now we saw his lips meet his little angel's lips. When Pa saw this he had to turn his head. He almost laughed aloud in the church. But he held his laughter and I am glad he did. Pa has the Bradley laugh which is hoarse and loud like a blowing winter wind or a mules's hee-haw, hee-haw.

Some friends, including Uncle Sam's brothers and nephews and his pa, Grandpa Pate, tried to get close but they couldn't even get near. People from the church rushed up to them. Miss Esther, now Mrs. Sam Bradley, had been organist in this First Baptist Church a long time. I heard someone say she played the organ here when she was a girl. But Uncle Sam and Aunt Esther were taken to a side door to get away from the crowd of well-wishers. I even heard some elderly man say, "She will soon have Sam a saved man in our church!" But that elderly man didn't know Uncle Sam as well as I knew him. I wasn't so sure that Uncle Sam would change that much and that fast. I knew he had quit wearing his flask in the built-in pocket of his Sunday suit.

When I got out of the First Baptist, I saw Uncle Sam closing his car door after his bride got in. And then he went around to the other side of "her," his old make car as long as two fence rails, and they left the church parking lot.

"Sam looks like a Philadelphia lawyer the way he's dressed," Pa said.

"No work for me for ten days," I said. "Uncle Sam and Aunt Esther are off on a honeymoon."

I wondered what Uncle Sam would do for a smoke, a chew, and a drink. But that was none of my business. If any man could manage he could.

After the tenth day Uncle Sam had parked "her" in the spacious yard of Mrs. Esther Bradley's old home. But I knew Uncle Sam would not be leaving "her" out when autumn would soon be coming on and then winter. Well the first job we did was build a nice brick garage for "her" at the edge of the lawn. When we worked this close to the house, Uncle Sam took his chew and when he saw Aunt Ester coming toward the garage he spit the chew over the bank. And he had his gold-tipped flask hidden in a pile of bricks which he went to every so often. He stood behind the brick pile and pretended to be counting bricks when he nipped. Nipped is what he called little drinks. And after the days were gone when we worked on this garage, Aunt Esther and Uncle Sam, dressed in their best, took a ride or went to church or some church socials. I didn't know where they went. I didn't ask. I know she wore her pretty hats and white gloves. A little woman, she sat up there on the front seat of "her," beside Uncle Sam whose shoulders were as broad as a corncrib door. As so many people said "that couple sure is a funny sight."

Down below the finest home in Greenwood County where they lived, there was another home, which was deserted. This old house was owned by Uncle Cal who told his sons and nephews they could use it but to be careful and not burn it down and always to put out the fires when they left the house. My brothers and cousins, plus a few of our friends, went there and built fires at night. And we had tables and chairs, and we played cards for fun and sometimes we played poker. We never had any women around this house. But we had our drinks and we relaxed and had a good time. Sometimes we met on weekday nights. Always we met here on Saturday nights and usually stayed up all night and sometimes over into Sundays. We took our sandwiches and made coffee. We had plenty to eat and drink.

Early one Sunday morning somebody knocked on our door. I went to the door and opened it slightly for I thought we might have been reported and it might be the law, Sheriff Elwood Smith and one or two of his deputies. But there stood Uncle Sam. And when I saw him standing there I shouted to all his nephews, "It's Uncle Sam! Come in, Uncle Sam!" I said.

"Boys, I wonder if you've got a drink around here someplace," he said. "I'm just dying for a drink!"

"We've got plenty, Uncle Sam," Cousin Pate, Uncle Fee's boy, said.

"Yes, did you bring your flask?" I asked. "If it's empty and you brought it, we'll fill it for you."

"See, boys, I've just not been able to get away by myself and get myself something to drink," he said. "Every time I go someplace in 'her' with my wife I can't buy from the store, the bootleggers, or the moonshiners. My wife is a smart woman. She'd ketch on pretty quick. Boys, I've chewed more Sen-Sen since I've been married than I chewed all the rest of my life. I'm even out of Sen-Sen. Got any of that stuff?"

"No, we don't use it here, Uncle Sam," I said. "You know Sen-Sen never was used by the Bradleys. If we ever wanted to get the smell off our breath, we always just chewed a little sassafras bark."

Uncle Sam joined us in his wild Bradley laughter. Then he swigged from our bottle, again, again, and again, while Cousin Pate filled his flask.

"Are you driving Aunt Esther to church this morning?" I asked.

"Yes, Bob, I am," he said. "You know she's back playing the church organ. They missed her so when we were on our honeymoon."

"Well, Uncle Sam, four long swigs are enough," Cousin Rile, Uncle Cal's boy, said. "You can't drive 'her' if you get too much."

Now Uncle Sam wanted a cigar. I gave him a handful.

"I'll have to hide 'em," he said. "What about chewing tobacco?"

Only two of my cousins, Bill, Uncle Fee's boy, and Rodge, Uncle Cal's boy, had chewing tobacco with them. Cousin Rodge gave him a paper sack of Honest John Scrap tobacco. Uncle Sam tore into the sack and put half of it behind his clean-shaven jaw. It made a lump on his jaw as big as a goose egg.

"Damn, boys, I feel better," Uncle Sam said. "I might have taken four long swigs too fast. I've got to hurry and get back and dress for church."

He left our house which was different from the house where he lived.

"Poor old Uncle Sam," Cousin Pate said, shaking his head sadly, "how much longer can he live with an angel?"

We played another game of cards and started out to our cars to go home. I guess I saw it first. I saw a car, a long car, too, standing on its end in the creek that flowed in front of Uncle Sam and Aunt Esther's big home. We didn't take time to get in our cars and drive up. We went running. When we got there Uncle Sam and Aunt Esther were in the car. We opened the doors and got them out.

"Sam what happened?" Aunt Esther asked. "You've always had such good powerful hands."

"Angel, I made a mistake and got 'her' in the wrong gear," he said. "I never did that in my life before!"

Uncle Sam and I built the garage with the doors opening the opposite to the highway and the stream. Aunt Esther wanted it built this way. There was a little road leading out from the garage to a little bridge over the stream and onto the highway. At the end of the garage toward the stream was a solid brick wall. When Uncle Sam put "her" in gear, he shot it in reverse, gave it the gas, had torn out the whole wall, backed into the stream, and the car was standing almost straight up.

"I must get to church," Aunt Esther said. "But I believe I'm so nervous I can't play the organ."

"Angel, we must get 'her' out of the ditch," Uncle Sam said. "Bob, will you go home and get your Pa and his big truck and some log chains and see if we can pull 'her' out?"

"Yes, Uncle Sam, I'll go," I said. "I'll drive in a hurry and fetch him."

And away I went to my car while my brother and cousins stayed with Aunt Esther and Uncle Sam. Of course they and Uncle Sam were figuring ways to fasten the chains on this big car Uncle Sam had always loved so much. When I told Pa about what had happened, I didn't tell him we'd given Uncle Sam four swigs from a bottle.

"Strange about Sam," Pa said. "He was always such a careful driver. Your Uncle Sam has good hands!"

When we got back my brother and cousins and Uncle Sam had it all figured out. Aunt Esther had gone back into the house. And when we hooked the chains onto the bumper and then onto the truck, Pa got into the truck and gave a pull and off came the bumper. I thought Uncle Sam was going to cry.

"The only way in the world to get that car out of there is to go to Blakesburg and get John Hampton's big wrecker. This car has to be lifted from that ditch."

So, I went to Blakesburg and got John Hampton to come with his wrecker. He didn't want to come. He was ready for church, but he came, for Uncle Sam and Aunt Esther went to the same church. And when he came, he knew how to fasten the chains and do the job. He lifted "her" and set her in the road.

"Without a front bumper," Uncle Sam sighed. "No church until she is fixed."

"I'll take your car to the garage and fix it, Sam," John Hampton said.

"Uncle Sam, I'll come and get you and take you to Powderjay's to build the chimneys tomorrow. And I'll bring you back home tomorrow afternoon.

"Your car will be repaired and will be here waiting for you," John Hampton said.

Uncle Sam went back into the house to be with his wife and we departed for our house down the road where we got in our cars and drove home.

While we built the four living monuments for the Powderjay home, Uncle Sam was at his best. The car he loved was fixed and he and his angel went to church on Sundays and other places through the week. They attended Bible Society meetings. They went where Aunt Esther wanted to go. But while Uncle Sam and I worked on these chimneys, fireplaces, and hearths, he chewed his terbacker and made what he called a gold-tinted mortar. And he smoked his cigars and he swigged when he wanted. Only a few times did I have problems with Uncle Sam. There were a lot of wasp nests up under the eaves of the Shan Powderjay home. I tried to keep these torn out before we got a chimney built up near the roof. About a dozen wasps flew from under the eaves out of the first nest we missed and stung Uncle Sam who was up on a scaffold. They got tangled in the hair on his chest which was like a doormat and they stung him some more. He came down the ladder in a hurry.

"Fetch me a drink," he said. "I'm almost sick."

After Uncle Sam swigged twice he said he felt better.

"But no more swigging, Uncle Sam," I said. "If you had more I'd be afraid for you to get back on that ladder and stand up there on the scaffold."

This happened one more time before we finished the job. Wasps got tangled in the hair on his chest, since on warm days he worked stripped to the waist, and this time they gave him a powerful stinging. Uncle Sam swigged four times before the pain eased. It was so close to quitting time we went home. But with the chimneys up, back walls in the fireplaces, and grates in, hearths as smooth and pretty as only Uncle Sam could make them, mortar trawled between the bricks and tooled as only Uncle Sam could do it, the Powderjays were happy people. Shan and his wife, Diane, invited Uncle Sam, Aunt Esther, and me to come over and they would celebrate this occasion with music.

The Powderjays had a piano and an organ. Mrs. Bradley was to play the organ which was nearest the fireplace in the big living room where they laid the first fire. Diane was to play the piano and Uncle Sam was to play the fiddle. Uncle Sam was to lead. And I was to play his guitar to second. Well, I'll never forget how Uncle Sam and Aunt Esther dressed for this occasion to celebrate four more of his living monuments, his children.

But before the celebration started, Aunt Esther asked Mrs. Powderjay if she would stop all the clocks from running in her home. She had eight large clocks. She said she couldn't bear to hear clocks ticking time away. Mrs. Powderjay looked strange but she did as her guest ordered. And then Aunt Esther turned to Shan Powderjay who was enjoying a cigar in his own home and asked him if he would put his cigar away until the program was over and they had gone. He threw his cigar in the fireplace on the wood.

With the clocks stopped and the cigar in the fireplace, Uncle Sam struck a match to the kindling and the flames leaped.

"No blowouts over the back walls in these fireplaces," Uncle Sam said. "Watch that chimney draw. One of our four living monuments, Angel. Four of our children."

Uncle Sam picked up his fiddle. "It has to be hymns," Uncle Sam said, "but 'Over the Waves' first!"

Uncle Sam was making his fiddle cry. Mrs. Powderjay and Aunt Esther joined on piano and organ. And I strummed the guitar. But we hadn't got through "Over the Waves" when it happened. A downdraft blew ashes and smoke all over the large living room. But Aunt Esther caught most of the ashes in her hair and all over her clothes. Everybody started coughing and Shan Powderjay ran for the door. He opened it to let the smoke out and fresh air in. Aunt Esther couldn't get the ashes from her hair or clothes. Mrs. Powderjay hooked up the sweeper and drew the ashes from her clothes and hair. But this ended the party.

"I'll check that blasted back wall," Uncle Sam said. "I don't know what went wrong."

So Uncle Sam, a very sad man, Aunt Esther, a very unhappy woman, and I left the Powderjay home. And Mrs. Powderjay, I suppose, started all her clocks running and Shan Powderjay, I suppose, lit another cigar. I got in my car and went home. Uncle Sam had never told me that Aunt Esther wouldn't let a clock tick in her house and that he had to put his shirtsleeve down over his arm to soften the tick of his watch so she couldn't hear it.

"When your Aunt Esther dies there won't be enough people go to that home to lay her out for burial," Pa said. "And there won't be ten people go to her funeral. She is so cranky. You know she has said she will be hauled to the cemetery in a hearse but she won't be embalmed and she wants women of her church to dress her for burial. And Brother Sam is sure to go along with all her wishes."

All the Bradleys wondered how long Uncle Sam could please Aunt Esther. But they didn't have long to wait. Aunt Esther dropped dead just as she was ready to go to church one Sunday morning. And her friends, women from her church, did lay her out for burial as she had requested. They dressed her in the dress she had requested, even put white gloves on her hands. With her hair pulled up on her head the way she always wore it with silver combs and pins in her silver hair, she looked like an angel in her coffin.

And I'll say Pa and everybody else who said or even thought she wouldn't have ten people at her funeral, which was preached at First Baptist, were wrong. The house couldn't hold the people. They stood on the outside. And when Louie Stell hauled her thirteen miles in the hearse, people followed her in their cars. They went with her to her resting place with her parents. That was the longest line of cars ever to follow a hearse in Greenwood County. Louie Stell said he believed there was a line of cars for five miles behind him. I never saw anything like it. I drove "her" for Uncle Sam while Pa sat beside him in the rear seat. People along the way stood in silence and some with bowed heads as we passed.

"I married an Angel," Uncle Sam wept. "I'm all broken up. I'm finished. I don't know what I'll do now. Not when she goes under the ground."

Now all of us Bradleys wonder if Uncle Sam was not right. We never had one like her in our family. We just about have to believe Uncle Sam had been married to an Angel.

"Uncle Sam Married An Angel" was first published in *Ball State University Forum,* Vol. 13, No. 3 (Summer, 1972), pp. 3-11. It has never been reprinted. Stuart included this story in his unpublished manuscript, *These Are My Best— —Twenty-five Short Stories Selected From Five Hundred Published Stories And MSS*—edited and typed January 1975 (Jesse Stuart Foundation Collection, Ashland, Kentucky).

A Witness for Noonie Paw

Do not think I'd not been tipped off about what was going on in Noonie Paw Sturgill's three hundred acre pasture field—a rolling land, all could be cut over by tractor and blade—and about as pretty a pasture field as we have in Greenwood County. Noonie Paw Sturgill had the largest dairy herd in Greenwood County. He had fifty cows.

Beginning early October, just before the hunting season opened up on rabbits, Noonie Paw's big pasture field sounded like a battleground. Automatic shotguns were firing all over the pasture and truck lights and high-powered flashlights had their bright rays criss-crossing in all directions—even sometimes they pointed up toward the clear blue, starry October sky.

Well, being Game Warden of Greenwood County, wearing a pretty gray uniform with double rows of brass buttons up the coat front, stripes of black up and down the outsides of my pant legs and around my coat sleeves near the cuff, I had a leather shoulder strap that held my shotgun in a holster on my side. I also carried another concealed short gun in a holster in my right armpit under my coat. Anyone in this Commonwealth knows a Game Warden can't go too carefully armed and be too careful when he has to do his duty to arrest law violators and game poachers when they hunt out of season even if they are hunting on their own property, as Noonie Paw Sturgill and his two sons Gilfrod—called Gil—and Riley—called Rile—were doing now.

I have learned how to cope with law violators. I drove my truck with a bulletproof windshield and cab up to his large pasture gate. Noonie Paw had a chain through his gate and around the post and padlock in the chain. I knew he had to stop, unfasten the gate, and here is where I had him and his sons. I backed my truck back into the shadows and switched off my lights. I sat there watching lights play over the pasture field. And I never heard so much shooting in my life. I heard his truck running and stopping. I would catch these law viola-tors with their slaughtered wildlife—the poor rabbits out in the wild-ness of night, trying to share clover with the cows.

But let me tell you about Old Noonie Paw. He's not any small man. He's built like a tough-butted white oak, big hands—like small fire shovels—big feet, big arms and legs—shoulders as broad as a cornbin door—and a short bull neck which holds his small pear-shaped head, with the little end of the pear turned up, on his shoulders. Old Noonie Paw when he began his dairy used his wife, two sons, and three daughters to milk his cows. His hands were too big to milk a cow. Even his fingers were larger than the cows' teats. Later he mod-ernized his dairy and got mechanical milkers. See, I know a lot about this man.

Now, let me tell you about myself. I'm just about the same size and build as old Noonie Paw Sturgill. Only I look different, being an officer who has to uphold law and order. I'm so big I have to have uniforms made. But I think I have a much nicer name than Old Noonie Paw Sturgill. My name is Leadford Bowling. I don't have any middle name. Never needed one. Two names I've learned are enough. I'm called Lead Bowling—Lead, short for Leadford. I was named for my mother's people.

Now, Old Noonie Paw Sturgill knows me as well as I know him. I know he and his boys are gunmen—guns they use for law violations, such as hunting out of season. They're gun-happy people.

I must have waited forty-five minutes before the flashing lights quit criss-crossing up toward that pretty, cold, starry October sky—and the guns were silenced. I saw the lights of Noonie Paw's truck that he rode in over his vast holdings of land—and especially this pasture field. He was so big and heavy he didn't walk very well. But one thing he could do and loved to do was hunt and kill. He loved his guns better than any one of his five brothers. I watched the truck rolling up to the gate. And Old Noonie Paw, the one I hoped would get out, got out to unlock and open the gate. I let him take a big ring of keys from his pocket, get the right key and put it in the lock. I let him turn the key. For he could have kept that lock locked and stayed on the other side and I couldn't have got through to him. I'm so big I can't run very well either. Yet, I'm smart, don't leave any of the little things undone. When he'd half-opened the gate, I stepped out into the road.

"Noonie Paw, consider yourself under arrest," I said.

"Oh, it's my old friend Lead," Noonie Paw said. Then, he gave a wild laugh as loud and rustling as a sleeping wind awakening and taking off in a big blow among dry sedgegrass, sawbriars, and hickory sprouts. "Old Lead has caught us red-handed, boys."

Then, Rile and Gil, strapping big two-hundred pounders about nineteen and twenty-one, got out of the truck with smiles all over their faces like they thought poaching at night, out of hunting season, was very funny.

"Yes, Lead's got us, Pa," said Rile.

"No foul play around here," I said. "Law is Law. Order is Order. We can't have one without the other! Now I want to see the evidence in the back of this truck!"

"Just have a look, Lead," Noonie Paw said.

"Some pile of rabbits," I said. "How many?"

"Sixty," Rile said. "I counted them!"

"You know I could confiscate these rabbits," I said.

"But, Lead, we've always understood one another," Noonie Paw said with a poking-stick toothy grin. "I mean we respect one another. Don't you think it better I keep these rabbits?"

"What will you do with them?" I asked.

"I'm not going to waste them," Noonie Paw said. "These rabbits are fat and for a very good reason. I'm going to dress them tonight and put them in the freezer. We like wild rabbit meat! And, Lead, if you'd take these from me, we have more guns than you, but we're old friends. We'll let you take the rabbits. Only, it won't be wise for you to do it. Remember we Sturgills are law-abiding citizens!"

"You've just broken a law," I said. "Now, you say you're a law-abidin' man!"

"Well, we are law-abidin' people," Rile Sturgill interrupted before his father could speak. And there was a scowl over his face. It came like a dark cloud blocks out the sun and makes the earth a shadow. "If you want to know why we killed the rabbits—"

"Just a minute, Son, this affair is for your Pa," Noonie Paw said. "You know this is an older-man's business. We killed the rabbits because they're sucking our cows!"

Now my laughter went up like the sudden awakening of sleeping wind tearing through the sedge, brairs, and sprouts. Mine was a wild rustling laughter, too! Higher than the sound of a rising wind.

"I've heard a lot of things," I said. I could hardly speak for laughing. "But I've never heard of a thing like this—never—never—never—funniest thing I ever heard."

And I laughed as wild as a soaring mad wind again. But, Noonie Paw, Rile and Gil Sturgill stood there, silently with serious faces, staring at me with their little mean black eyes that reminded me of dark winter possum grapes in deep sockets, surrounded by narrow slits. I knew they meant what they said. They believed it.

"Did you see this happen?" I asked.

"No, but when we brought our cows in each afternoon the ends of their teats were wet," Old Noonie Paw said. "And the cows went down in milk, too. We got sixty fat rabbits in this truck—fat on clover from our pasture and milk from our cows."

"I'm not bothering your rabbits," I said with laughter, for I couldn't keep from laughing. Wild rabbits milking cows! "But I'm taking out warrants for all three of you hunting out of season. And for hypnotizing those rabbits by carlights and ten-celled powerful flashlights fastened to the barrels of your shotguns. You know killing rabbits this way is illegal in this Commonwealth!"

"Just anyway to kill them, legal or illegal," Noonie Paw said. "Let me stand trial first! I took my boys with me to do this! If I'm convicted then my sons will pay the same fines I do!"

"You want to go to trial on this?" I asked him.

"I certainly do and I want a jury trial," Noonie Paw said.

"You'll get it," I said. "You're going to be the laughingstock of Greenwood County."

"Maybe, I'll be," Noonie Paw said. "But something had to be done about these damned rabbits. I'll bet there are a thousand more in our dairy herd's good pasture and they're not just there for clover."

This ended our meeting at Old Noonie Paw's pasture gate. I left him and his sons there, got in my truck and drove away laughing.

"I hope that jury will be all farmers!" I thought. Then I laughed loudly again.

Then I knew I'd invite several people to this trial which would be tried in the Lower Court, County Judge Larry Tardy's Court, with a jury of six farmers. I hoped to get these, for Deputy Sheriff Denzil Quillen was a special friend of mine. I'd like for him to go out and find a jury of six men. Saturday morning would be a great time to have this trial when people from all over Greenwood County came to Greenwood to buy and sell. And the old farmers sit on the courthouse yard in seats prepared for them, where each brought his piece of wood—pine, oak, and poplar—and tried to whittle the longest shavings. Sheriff Rodney (Rod) Ratterman and his six deputies were friends of mine. They belonged to the Little Party. So did County Judge Tardy.

Now Prosecuting Attorney Seymore Dails belonged to the Big Party. He'd prosecute in this case. Well, Noonie Paw Sturgill and his sons belonged to the Little Party. And we couldn't keep politics out of a trial here. But one thing I knew, Old Noonie Paw and his sons Rile and Gil were goners. Even if they did belong to my Little Party, I wanted them prosecuted to the fullest, convicted, and fined. They were law violators! They'd broken two laws, killing wild game out of season and killing it the way they did.

When I went home and told my wife Betsy what had happened and why it happened she laughed until she cried.

Next morning I went to see Judge Larry Tardy and I got two indictments for Old Noonie Paw Sturgill. When I told Judge Larry Tardy about what Noonie Paw told me about rabbits milking his cows he

laughed as I had laughed, and his secretary Lucille Tardy (his wife—
we keep offices in the family here) laughed as loudly and as long as
her husband.

I don't know whether our High Sheriff or one of his deputies served
the subpoenas on Noonie Paw Sturgill to appear in court on the next
Saturday morning October fourteenth. But, I do know I was getting
my way. As I've told you, when it comes to these trials and getting law
violators convicted, I'm not foolish.

On Saturday morning at ten o'clock, so many people—all with
smiles on their faces—had gathered in Judge Tardy's office. There
wasn't standing room.

"We'll move this trial upstairs to the Higher Courtroom where we'll
have more room," Judge Tardy said.

For outside the County Judge's Office door was Deputy Sheriff
Denzil Quillen with seven men, prospective jurymen. They were whit-
tling farmers who had come to Greenwood for a day of rest and recre-
ation. But why not make five dollars for an hour or so on this funny
trial?

Now, all of us, almost a multitude of people, followed Judge Larry
Tardy up to the big Circuit Courtroom which occupied all the third
floor of the Greenwood County Courthouse, except the small office of
His Honor Judge Odder Timmons who was Circuit Judge of Greenwood and Lantern Counties. Then, there were two small consulting
offices where attorneys took their clients. But when we got into this
big auditorium it was two thirds filled and more were coming. Why
not come? I'd talked about this trial far and near—when I told the
people they laughed and said they'd be there. Where could or would
they find better free entertainment?

After Judge Tardy called for order, pounding with a gavel from the
high seat where Circuit Judge Odder Timmons sat in the High Court,
everyone got very still. When Judge Tardy read the indictments, two
charges against Noonie Paw Sturgill, six of the seven men were sworn
under oath and placed on the jury. Then, I was called to the stand and
asked to tell my story of what had happened. I told my story just as

I've already told you. When I mentioned what Noonie Paw had told me about the wild rabbits milking his cows, a roar of laughter came up from the visitors. I looked around and all the men on the jury were smiling. I knew I had Old Noonie Paw. He couldn't say I'd not warned him that he'd be the laughingstock of Greenwood County—that this trial would go beyond our county, maybe our Commonwealth and all over the Nation.

When Old Noonie Paw Sturgill was called to the stand he told the same story he had told me. But there was so much laughter Judge Tardy had to pound with his gavel for order in the courtroom.

"Ladies and Gentlemen, this is a trial and not a farce," he said. "If you don't get quiet, I'll dismiss this trial and we'll try it over."

These were country people. They were farmers, wives of farmers, and children of farmers. They knew about rabbits and they knew about cows. Judge Tardy got the people quiet and the trial went on.

There was not any cross-examination of me or Noonie Paw. When Noonie Paw left the witness stand he turned to Judge Larry Tardy.

"Your Honor," he said, "since we didn't see the rabbits in the act, but know they milked our cows, would it be permissible to put a material witness on the stand?"

Then Judge Tardy turned to Prosecuting Attorney Seymore Dails:

"Your Honor, I see no reason why we can't put his material witness on the stand. I have no objections."

Even Seymore Dails could not hide his laughter. He was always a serious minded poker-faced man at trials when he was prosecuting, but now his face was covered with a smile. During our testimonies on the stand I saw him put his hand over his mouth and press hard several times to hold his laughter.

"Who is this material witness?" Judge Tardy asked.

"Your Honor, he is Frank Menach!"

Now a sigh went up from all the people gathered to hear the trial. Frank Menach, immaculately dressed, dark suit, white shirt, bow tie and dark-rimmed spectacles, took the stand. Frank Menach was well known all over Greenwood County. He was the Little

Party's political chairman.

Judge Tardy swore him to tell the truth and nothing but the truth. Frank held up his hand and said, "I do."

"Mr. Menach, you are one of the best known men in Greenwood County," Judge Tardy said. "You're not a farmer. You began as a timer and now you're a foreman, hold one of the best positions with one of the big railway companies of this country. You live in Fontaine, most wealthy suburb of Auckland, Kentucky, which is in Greenwood County. In what way are you a 'material witness' in this trial?"

"Yes, I am all you have said," said Mr. Menach. "But, I've not always been as successful, Judge Tardy, as you have said I am now. I'm one of eight children and I used to hire out to farmers as a young farmhand for my keep and fifty cents a day. This was in Matson County in our Commonwealth. This was in the Blue Grass Country and we used to have thousands of rabbits. Farmers used to invite hunters to come and kill them. Dairy herds were milked by the rabbits. I've often seen them do it!"

A hush fell over those I had invited to the trial. Then I looked over at the jurymen who were farmers I knew and had asked Deputy Sheriff Denzil Quillen to select. I'd passed them on the courthouse square, sitting in seats placed there for their convenience trying to whittle the longest shaving—Lonnie King, Thadeus Chaffins, Roy Van Bibber, Woodrow Wilson Creech, J. Elmer Miller, and Tom Mullins—all farmers. Smiles had gone from their faces.

"Now, to tell you frankly, I was visiting the home of Noonie Paw Sturgill on another little matter when his sons, Gil and Rile, brought the herd into the dairy barn. Noonie Paw said to me: 'Frank, my cows are going down in milk. When we put the milkers on them we find the tip of each cow's teats are wet.' 'Have you got any wild rabbits in your pasture?' I asked him. 'Hundreds,' he replied quickly. 'Get 'em out of there,' I told him. As a young itinerant farm worker I saw rabbits with my own eyes milking cows. Gentlemen, this is why I was asked to appear as a 'material witness'."

"Mr. Dails, do you have anything to say to this material witness?"

Judge Larry Tardy asked.

"I've plenty," he said. "Your Honor, this witness is politically motivated! He's a rich man, living in a big fine home, drives the largest and most powerful car made in America. He's not lived on a farm for thirty years! What does he know about rabbits and cows? Does he know a wild rabbit and a cow apart?"

"Your Honor Judge Tardy, may I answer that," Frank Menach said. "I know more about cows and rabbits than this county prosecutor knows about law. I know and remember what my eyes have seen!"

"This is the most ridiculous trial that I have ever witnessed tried in your Honor Larry Tardy's Greenwood County's Lower Court. It is too ridiculous even for me to prosecute. Mr. Noonie Paw Sturgill has already confessed to his law violations as charged in these two indictments. I'm ready for these jurors, these six sensible farmers who own farms, have cows and wild rabbits in their pastures."

"All right, jurors, will you return to the Jury Room and render a decision."

The jurors got up and walked out. While they were gone, people talked about rabbits and cows.

"I never heard anything as silly."

"How did this ever get into Court?"

"Why didn't they throw this out of Court!"

"A rabbit milking a cow?"

Then, there was a loud laughter to follow.

But everyone stayed on waiting for the decision. Not a man, woman, or child left the courtroom.

Very quickly the jury returned and walked up and stood down below the high seat where his Honor Judge Larry Tardy sat. Judge Tardy pounded with his gavel for quiet in the courtroom.

"Have you reached a decision?" His Honor Judge Tardy asked.

"We have, your Honor," Woodrow Wilson Creech said. "And I've been selected by other members of the jury to announce our decision to you. We find the defendant, Noonie Paw Sturgill, not guilty!"

It was like the hometown high school football team winning a football game by kicking a football through the center of the uprights with two seconds to play, winning the game nine to eight. Wild jubilation broke loose among the spectators. I don't know how I felt. I never felt worse in my life as all the jurors came up and were shaking hands with Noonie Paw Sturgill and his sons, Rile and Gil, and His Honor County Judge Larry Tardy and the rest were lined up in a long line to shake hands with Frank Menach.

"A Witness For Noonie Paw" was first published in *Appalachian Journal*, Vol. 3, No. 1 (Autumn 1975), pp. 80-86. It has never been reprinted. Stuart included this story in his unpublished manuscript, *Twenty-five Tall Stories Selected From 461 Published Stories And Fifty Manuscripts*, circa 1975 (Jesse Stuart Foundation Collection, Ashland, Kentucky). The story was based on a news article that had been sent to Stuart by Nashville free-lance writer, William Boozer. Boozer had clipped the article from the October 29, 1972 edition of the Memphis *Commercial Appeal.* The article related a factual court case in which the defendant claimed he wasn't milking his neighbor's cows; rather, rabbits were suckling the cows. In a subsequent letter that Stuart wrote to Boozer on January 20, 1973, Stuart noted, "This morning I got the clipping about the rabbits and the cows. It interests me very much. I heard that once here, never believed it—in fact we thought the man was a mental. Everyone laughed. Now, after this man, owner of a dairy herd, comes up with the same thing, I'm not so sure this couldn't happen. I don't think there's any difference in a Mississippi rabbit and a Kentucky rabbit. I think they both would like sweet milk." In a follow-up letter to Boozer, Stuart wrote, "...The title of the 'rabbit' story is 'A Witness for Noonie Paw Sturgill.' *Appalachian Journal*, a very nice magazine, published twice a year and try-ing to become a quarterly, I suppose, will publish it.... You should see how I made a story of this incident you sent me." (This account is published in William Boozer, editor, "Jesse Stuart to William Boozer: A Decade of Se-lected Letters, 1968-1978," *Register of the Kentucky Historical Society*, Vol. 80, No. 1 [Winter, 1982], pp. 1-64.)

A Woman of Stature

When I went to the door, there she stood. She looked up at me and smiled. She waited for me to speak. I knew she didn't think I'd know her. It had been a long time since I had seen this unusual woman.

"Anna, you didn't think I'd know you," I said. "Come in!"

"No, not after 24 years," she said. "Mr. Stringer, how did you know me? What characteristics have carried over most prominently?"

"You're about the same size you were in Maxwell High School," I said. "And you haven't grown an inch taller!"

"My height," she said. "I remember you commented on it once or twice in my high school days!"

"And for a very good reason," I told her.

Anna Long McKnab seated herself in a wingback fireside chair in our living room. The back of this chair was a little higher than the average chair. And Anna's head didn't come up to the back of the chair.

"I've had to see you again," she said.

"Well, how are you getting along teaching?" I asked her.

"This is one reason why I've come," she replied. "I have come to tell you I won't be teaching this year!"

"You mean you have quit teaching?"

"No, I'll be the principal of Floyd Elementary School in Beston County," she said. "We have eleven elementary schools in Beston County. Eight of the elementary principals are men, and three now are women. This may not mean too much in a way. But it means a lot to me. I'm elated over this promotion."

"I am too," I said. "I congratulate you. But I'm not surprised that you got this!"

"That's just it," she said.

"This is why I am here to tell you. I thought you would be glad to know. You and my teacher Ethel Bostick used to say so many kind, encouraging words to me!"

"We should have said kind and encouraging things to you," I said.

"Anybody who would do what you did to get an education should never be forgotten by teachers and principal. You are the most unusual girl I have ever taught in high school. I wonder how many girls in America, in the years you went to high school, did what you did. And I wonder if there is a young girl in America today who will work the way you did to obtain a high school and college education."

How well I remembered when I was 25 and superintendent of Greenwood County schools, the youngest county superintendent in Kentucky then or before or since, a man came walking into my office on a Friday morning with a young girl beside him and a lantern with a smoked globe on the other side.

"Mr. Stringer, I'm Ceif Long," he introduced himself. "This is my daughter Anna. I have brought her to take the common school examination. I understand it begins today. That is what Mr. Rodney had posted on the bulletin board in the Beauty Ridge School."

"I'm glad to meet you, Mr. Long," I said. "I am glad to meet your daughter Anna. This is quite correct about the common school examinations." I looked at my watch. "It's nine-thirty now. The exams begin in 30 minutes at the Blakesburg City High School building. Do you know where the high school building is?"

"No, we don't," Mr. Long said. "We don't know Blakesburg very well."

"Come over to the window," I told them. "See that spire over there about two blocks from here? That's Blakesburg City High School. Go over and register now!"

"How much will it cost?" Mr. Long asked me.

"Two dollars," I said. "And you pay over there."

When he opened his pocketbook and took out the two dollars, I could see he only had one dollar left.

Now Mr. Long and his daughter Anna left my office. He was carrying his lantern. This was unusual, to see a man in Blakesburg on a Friday morning carrying a lantern.

Pupils from the 82 one- and two-room schools in those days took a common examination before they were permitted to enter high school. This was long before consolidation and a promotion from one year to the other from first grade to twelfth. The old one- and two-room rural schools, where in the one-room school one teacher taught all grades from first to eighth and in the two-room school one teacher taught the first four grades and the second teacher taught the fifth, sixth, seventh, and eighth grades, couldn't offer a promotion system that would permit pupils to enter high school without an examination first.

When I had first attended the rural one-room school, it had been five months long. Before I left the one-room school to take the common school examination, one more month had been added, making the rural school six months now. And when I became Greenwood County School Superintendent, the length of time was still six months. I was working to get seven months, then eight, then nine months and consolidation. We had to give this common school examination just after the rural schools ended. Rural school began in mid July at the time when crops were laid by and youth were not needed to help their parents on their small hilly farms. Now with six months, schools were out in January. This was the month we gave this examination. And now the days were short, and the nights were long. Hence, Mr. Long had come into my office with his lantern.

After I had conducted some details, telling my secretary Monnie Rister, an elderly woman, how to handle them, I walked over to the Blakesburg High School, where the examination was in progress. From 82 one- and two-room schools in Greenwood County, there were approximately 40 pupils who had come to take this examination. Since the Blakesburg City Schools and Greenwood County Schools were separate school districts, we had rented two rooms in the Blakesburg City High School to use for this examination. We had too many pupils for one room and not enough for two. We employed two county teachers to give this examination. When I went over to see what progress was being made, there was an examiner in each room, and outside by the door sat Mr. Long in a chair with his lantern. Inside was his daughter Anna on the front row.

After being with the examiners for an hour, checking progress, answering questions from examiners and pupils, I returned to my office where I had work waiting for me. I had all the work of the 82 schools, plus one high school, and I didn't have an assistant. I had only a secretary. Just before the close of the day, I walked back over to the Blakesburg City School to see about the examination. When I arrived, they had finished for the day. They would resume tomorrow. Now youth were going home. This was when there were only a few miles, four, I believe, of hard-surfaced road in Greenwood County. There were dirt roads which would be frozen over in this cold January weather, and people who owned cars could drive them, for they wouldn't bog down over a frozen road. Many of the pupils who had come from the rural areas rode away in old cars, driven by a father or some older brother or person; many rode horseback; some came in buggies. But when Ceif Long and his daughter Anna, who could stand under her father's arm—and he was an average-sized man—left the high school building, they were walking.

"Are you walking home tonight, Mr. Long?" I asked him.

"Yes, we are," he replied.

"Now, I'm new as superintendent here, and I'm from about the center of this county. I don't know exactly the location of Beauty Ridge School," I said.

"It's in the western part of the county," he said.

"How many miles?" I asked him.

"I don't rightly know, for I've had no way to measure," he said. "But it is a right smart piece down there. And we have to get back. We couldn't stay over here in Blakesburg even if I had the money to pay expenses."

"I'll let you have the money," I interrupted him quickly. I knew he only had a dollar in his pocketbook. "And I'll help you get rooms here."

279 · **New Harvest**

"Mr. Stinger, we have to get back, for my wife is an invalid," he said.

"But you will be late," I said.

"Yes, but just so my wife knows we'll be coming tonight, everything will be all right," he said.

I watched Mr. Long and his short blondish daughter, Anna, walk toward the railroad tracks. Then I went back over to my office.

"Miss Rister, have you ever visited the Beauty Ridge Rural School?" I asked her. "Do you know how far Beauty Ridge is from here?"

"I've never visited the school," she said, "but I remember Mr. Ruggles, your predecessor, always dreaded going there to visit the school. He said it was the one farthest away from Blakesburg and the most inaccessible one. It's 26 miles from this office to the Beauty Ridge School."

"Don't tell me it's that far," I said. "Mr. Long and his daughter Anna, who were in this office, went walking back that way. Well, they walked toward the railroad tracks. I presumed they were going to walk part way on the tracks."

"They can go all the way to Farlington on the tracks," she said. "Then they have a mountain to climb. And they have a ridge line road to walk over."

"I just don't see how they walk it," I said. "Anna Long isn't five feet tall."

In those days so many people walked. I was young and single, and my position didn't pay well. So I walked five miles to my father's home, where I stayed. And next morning I walked five miles back to my office. I didn't own a car, and I couldn't drive one. My mother often walked eight miles one way to church and eight miles home. She had to walk sixteen miles each Sunday if she went to church and came back. And she never missed a Sunday. But walking twenty-six miles from Beauty Ridge to Blakesburg and then walking back I could hardly believe. No wonder Mr. Long carried a lantern.

Just before ten Saturday morning I went to Blakesburg High

School to see the pupils and examiners before the last day of examinations began. And when I walked over, feeling very good after my five-mile walk, Ceif Long and his daughter Anna came up the walk to the door. He was carrying his lantern, and the globe was smoked black. It was smoked the way a globe smokes when there is wind that disturbs the flame.

"Well, Mr. Long and Miss Long, I see you've made it back," I said. "Do you live very far away from the Beauty Ridge School?"

"Bout half a mile on t' other side," he replied.

"Well, you have had some walk," I said.

"Yes, a right good walk," he said. "But my girl Anna wants to go to high school. And I aim to see she goes if she passes these examinations. A body can't give his child anything better than a eddication. It's something no one can steal or take away."

"Are you going back tonight?" I said.

"Yes, and we won't have to rush," he said. "We'll take our time."

Anna now went inside to begin her tests.

"And we get through here at about two this afternoon," he said. "This will give us more time."

"Mr. Long, how tall is Anna?" I asked.

"Four feet ten in her stocking feet," he replied. "Same height as her mother exactly."

When I left, Mr. Long was sitting in a chair in the corridor in front of the schoolroom door where his daughter was taking the examination. I did a little simple arithmetic. Twenty-six miles one way, and their coming and going yesterday made 52 miles. Then, today they'd do 52 more miles. This would make 104 miles for a fourteen-year-old girl to walk in two days. Besides, she would have taken when she finished today examinations on eleven subjects. These examinations, with questions made out by the State Department of Education, were not easy. Several of the teachers, including the one at Beauty Ridge who had taught Anna, would have difficulty passing this examination. When we graded, examiners and I, these papers, I wanted to watch carefully to see if Anna Long passed. I wanted all of the pupils to pass. But I certainly hoped Anna passed. Any fourteen-year-old girl who would almost do the impossible, I wanted to see her achieve her goal. Pass this examination and enter Maxwell High School.

By Tuesday of the following week we had graded the papers. We graded with figures. Anna Long had made an average of 86. An average of 75 was passing. And the pupil couldn't make below 60 on any subject. If he or she did, this was failure. Several pupils had made higher than Anna. And there were several below her average. She had made about a B average.

From county superintendent I went to be principal of Maxwell High School when Anna was a sophomore. She was one of the first pupils I singled out with whom to have a conversation. I wanted to ask her about herself. I wanted to know how far she walked and how she was getting along in school and at home.

"Mr. Stringer, I walked four miles each way, and I ride the school bus eight miles each way," she said. "I have to do the housework at home and cook for my mother and father before I leave and after I come home."

"Does it give you enough time to study?" I asked.

"Yes, I keep a book in the kitchen when I'm getting supper," she said. "And I have learned to study on the school bus with noise all around me."

"I've not checked upon your grades yet," I said.

"Well, I can tell you," she said. "There are 25 in my class, and I am about twelfth from the top and from the bottom. I stay in the middle all the time."

"It's very good for your circumstances," I said. "We have some in the class who have all the time they need to study. They don't have any responsibilities. And some of these are below in scholastics."

"I've not told you, Mr. Stringer, but I work in the cafeteria for my noon lunch," she said. "Several girls wanted to help, but Miss Ethel Bostick saw to it that I got one of the places. She has been wonderful to me."

This was when the cafeteria in Maxwell High School was not operated by the school. This was before a state-school-operated cafeteria. This was before hot free lunches for pupils who couldn't afford them. Anna Long would have been one qualified for these. Her father, who couldn't read and write, was a farmer on Beauty Ridge with a horse, cow, and two hogs, and he raised corn and tobacco. Beauty Ridge was a most difficult area. In Greenwood County all farming was hard, but here on Beauty Ridge it was harder.

"If anything comes up for you, let me know," I said. "I will help you all I can."

From the time she was a sophomore until she graduated, we taught her at Maxwell High School. She was an average student, but she was the most ambitious student in her class. To get a high school education was one of her dreams. To get a college education was her big dream.

"Mr. Stringer, I can manage the high school education," she said. "What I don't know about is going to college. I want to talk to you about it."

"When do you want to go?" I asked her.

"As soon as I graduate from high school," she said. "I know what I want. I want to be a teacher like Miss Bostick."

"What about your mother?" I asked her.

"Daddy's sister, Aunt Grace, has lost her husband, and they don't have any children, and she will come and take care of Mother while I'm away," she said.

Ethel Bostick and I helped arrange for Anna Long to go to Morehead College. I knew President Reece personally. I wrote him a letter, explaining about Anna Long. I told the story about how far she walked in two days to take the common school examinations. In this day and time college scholarships were scarce. And the valedictorians and salutatorians were always in line for first and second scholarships. Anna graduated twelfth down from the top of her class. After I explained how she was an only child, with an invalid mother who hadn't walked since her only child Anna was born, President Reece gave her a two hundred-dollar scholarship. And

Ethel Bostick, who belonged to the Blakesburg Woman's Club, gave Anna Long a hundred-dollar scholarship. Three hundred in scholarships then was a great help. And Anna had a job in the cafeteria. She could manage on this amount plus what she worked at Morehead College. Each year and summer her scholarships were renewed. Each year and summer her average was a little over B. In three years and three summers, when she was 21, she had finished college. Fred Mannard, Superintendent of Greenwood County Schools, gave her her first teaching position. Her old teacher of Beauty Ridge School had retired. And she taught her own rural school.

In the meantime Anna married Les McKnab, who was a graduate of Maxwell High School. Before he was off to World War II, she had given birth to a son, Ceif Edwards McKnab. During the war when men and women were away in service, there was a cry for school-teachers. Anna's Aunt Grace now took care of her mother and was babysitter for her son. Two years Anna had taught this way. Then she lost her husband at the Battle of the Bulge. She continued to teach until her son was six in the Greenwood County Schools. She continued to teach, first college graduate ever to teach there, her home school in Beauty Ridge.

She wrote me that she was offered a better position with better pay in Beston County School System, which was in the richest county in all East Kentucky due to its heavy concentration of industries there. I told her to take the position. Ethel Bostick, to whom she had written for advice, told her the same thing. Now she moved away from Greenwood County Schools to an apartment in Auckland and to better pay. Her son Ceif Edwards was old enough for her to take to Floyd Elementary School, where she began as sixth grade teacher.

First she lost her mother, she wrote and told me about this. A year later she lost her father. She wrote and told me he had grieved himself to death in one year for her invalid mother. She told me her Aunt Grace had gone to live with a brother. And she told me she had sold the farm to her Uncle Fred.

Later I got an invitation to come to Morehead State University to her graduation. She was getting her master's degree. Morehead College had been elevated to university academic status. I couldn't go to her graduation for some reason I have now forgotten, but I believe I was making a high school commencement speech on the same evening. And now she had come in person to tell me about her promotion to principal of Floyd Elementary School.

"Mr. Stringer, what ever happened to Marjorie and Rabbie Funston, valedictorian and salutatorian of my Maxwell High School graduation class?" she asked me. "Sister and brother, and they were really smart."

"He operates a filling station," I said. "Marjorie is a housewife." Her husband, another of your classmates, Hugh Silster, drives a gasoline truck for Auckland Oil Company."

"What happened to Ernest Hinnton?" she asked.

"Now you know Ernest didn't go to college," I said. "He was in the bottom of the class. He's inherited his father's farm, where he farms today."

"Twenty-five graduated in my class," she said. "I've been too busy to keep up with them. I know World War II got most of the boys. Were any lost in World War II?"

"Yes, Jimmy Potters and Rufus Hale," I said. "I saw their names mentioned in the paper as missing. And Denver McCall, remember him?"

"Oh, yes," she replied. "I remember him well. He's the only boy in my class ever to ask me for a date."

"He's in the Veterans Hospital," I said. "I understand he will never be well. I can't go through the class and tell you about everyone. But I do remember two more of your classmates. No, three of them. Worldly and Major Hunt work for the State Highway Department. Frank Bill Simpson works for the Tennessee Gas Company."

"Am I the only one in my class to finish college?"

"I believe you are," I said.

"Helen Boswell moved away from here. I don't know what she did. But I remember she had planned to go to college. But World War

II interrupted so many young people's lives. I was in the war myself. I went with my students. So I don't know where and what happened to many of them. But I think you are the only graduate. And, of course, I am doubly sure you are the only one who has a master's degree and now heads a school system. I'm really proud of you! It's something when the student in a high school class of 25, who has had the poorest chance and never was the top student, but yet accomplishes more than any classmate."

She looked at me and smiled.

"And I know a record you held for a fourteen-year-old girl," I said.

"I know what you're going to say."

"Walked 104 miles in two days and took examination on eleven subjects and passed," I said. "And only four feet and ten inches tall. How did you do it?"

"I don't know," she said. I lived out there on Beauty Ridge, and I saw the people. They were my people. But I wanted to do more than they had ever done. I was hungry for something. I wanted to amount to something. I wanted to be somebody."

"You're somebody now," I said. "What about Ceif Edwards, your son?"

"He's a senior at Morehead University."

"Is he doing all right?"

"Yes, he is."

"Is he going to be a teacher like his mother?"

"No, Mr. Stringer, he's taking pre-med," she said. "He's going to be a doctor. Now, I just wanted to come by and tell you about my last promotion. It's the highest achievement, in my great respect for education and teaching, I have ever attained. Where is Miss Ethel Bostick?"

"Very near retirement," I said. "But she lives in the same beautiful home. Remember it?"

"Yes, I do," she said. "I'm going there to thank her. Thank you for all you have meant in my life. Thank you for being so kind and helpful in a time of need."

Time had dimmed her but little. She was more attractive now with age than she had ever been in her life. I watched her walk down our front walk with a bed of mixed and multicolored flowers on either side. She walked down to her car. When she drove away, I was standing in our door watching this unusual woman, who waved to me, and I waved to her. Here was one of the most remarkable young women I had ever taught among approximately 10,000 high school pupils.

"A Woman Of Stature" was first published in *Appalachia*, Vol. 7, No. 2 (October-November 1973), *pp. 35-40*. It has never been reprinted. The editors of *Appalachia* introduced the story by noting that the story is based on the life, in Mr. Stuart's own words, "of one of my unforgettable students." In a signed inscription of a copy of the periodical belonging to Lou Ashworth, his editor at McGraw-Hill, Stuart wrote: "Dear Lou: This couldn't happen in the U.S. we live in today. But did happen in the past and women like this have been and still are a pillar in our vast educational system—Jesse. 12/27/73." (Ashworth's copy of *Appalachia* is a part of the private Stuart collection of David R. Palmore, Villa Hills, Kentucky.)

A Chronological List of Jesse Stuart's Books

1. Harvest of Youth, 1930.
2. Man with a Bull-Tongue Plow, 1934.
3. Head o' W-Hollow, 1936.
4. Beyond Dark Hills: A Personal Story, 1938.
5. Tim, a Story, 1939.
6. Trees of Heaven, 1940.
7. Men of the Mountains, 1941.
8. Taps for Private Tussie, 1943.
9. Album of Destiny, 1944.
10. Mongrel Mettle: The Autobiography of a Dog, 1944.
11. Foretaste of Glory, 1946.
12. Tales from the Plum Grove Hills, 1946.
13. The Thread That Runs So True, 1949.
14. Clearing in the Sky and Other Stories, 1950.
15. Hie to the Hunters, 1950.
16. Kentucky is My Land, 1952.
17. The Beatinest Boy, 1953.
18. The Good Spirit of Laurel Ridge, 1953.
19. A Penny's Worth of Character, 1954.
20. Red Mule, 1955.
21. The Year of My Rebirth, 1956.
22. Plowshare in Heaven: Stories, 1958.
23. God's Oddling: The Story of Mick Stuart, My Father, 1960.
24. Strength from the Hills: The Story of Mick Stuart, My Father, 1968. (abridgement of God's Oddling)
25. Huey, the Engineer, 1960.
26. The Rightful Owner, 1960.
27. Andy Finds a Way, 1961.
28. Hold April: New Poems, 1962.
29. A Jesse Stuart Reader: Stories and poems selected and introduced by Jesse Stuart, 1963.

30. Save Every Lamb, 1964.
31. Daughter of the Legend, 1965.
32. A Jesse Stuart Harvest, 1965.
33. My Land Has a Voice, 1966.
34. A Ride with Huey the Engineer, 1966.
35. Mr. Gallion's School, 1967.
36. Rebels with a Cause, 1967.
37. Stories by Jesse Stuart, 1968.
38. Come Gentle Spring, 1969.
39. Old Ben, 1970.
40. Seven by Jesse, 1970.
41. To Teach, To Love, 1970.
42. Autumn Lovesong, 1971.
43. Come Back to the Farm, 1971.
44. Come to My Tomorrowland, 1971.
45. Dawn of Remembered Spring, 1972.
46. Tennessee Hill Folk, 1972.
47. The Land Beyond the River, 1973.
48. 32 Votes Before Breakfast: Politics at the grass roots, as seen in short stories by Jesse Stuart, 1974.
49. My World, 1975.
50. Up the Hollow from Lynchburg, 1975.
51. The World of Jesse Stuart: Selected Poems, 1975.
52. The Only Place We Live, 1976.
53. The Seasons of Jesse Stuart: An Autobiography in Poetry, 1907-1976, 1976.
54. Honest Confession of a Literary Sin, 1977.
55. Dandelion on the Acropolis: A Journal of Greece, 1978.
56. The Kingdom Within: A Spiritual Autobiography, 1979.
57. Lost Sandstones and Lonely Skies and Other Essays, 1979.
58. If I Were Seventeen Again and Other Essays, 1980.
59. Land of the Honey-Colored Wind: Jesse Stuart's Kentucky, 1981.
60. The Best-Loved Short Stories of Jesse Stuart, 1982.
61. Songs of a Mountain Plowman, 1986.
62. Cradle of the Copperheads, 1988.
63. New Harvest, 2003.